THAT NEXT moment

A Moments of Us Novel

Stefanie K. Steck

ISBN: 979-8-9866169-2-6 (Paperback)

Cover design and illustrations by Erika Plum

Edited by Cindy Ray Hale
Proofread by Allie Samberts

To my girls;

Pyper and Hadley.

Be strong; just like Ophelia. Don't let

anything stand in your way.

The Moments of Us Series is highly inspired by songs –
specifically songs by Thomas Rhett.

Clay and Ophelia's story was inspired by:
The Hill and *Grave*

They are worth a listen, trust me!

Prologue

-Clay-

Then—Ten Years Ago

"You can't be serious." Ophelia spun away from me, her hair flying as her body's movement matched her tone. "We agreed. . ."

"No," I countered. "We never actually agreed." I pointed at her, my finger aiming like a bullet, trying to prove my point. "We've talked about it numerous times, but we've never set anything final."

Ophelia leaned her head back and looked up to the sky, a long sigh coming from her. Hunching her shoulders, she quickly shook her head.

"New York. . ." she stammered.

"Was just an option. There are fashion companies in Seattle, boutiques you could work for—possibly even start your own—"

"Clayton," Ophelia spat, her Southern drawl coming out every time she said my full name. "I have an offer in New York City to work for Harold Martin, one of the biggest names out there. You even helped me send my application! If I give this up to go work at some boutique, that would literally be killing me."

I furrowed my brow and glared down at her. I towered over her. Being six-foot-two, I was always considered for a sports team—even though numbers were my thing. To Ophelia, being a little over five feet, I was a giant, especially now as my anger rose and I took a step toward her. I simply felt taller.

"And asking me to go work for some bank instead of a law firm would be humiliating to me." I pointed at my chest. "I have an offer at Jackson and Rye—a very prestigious law firm in Seattle. If I don't take this—Ophelia, it would be the end of my career as an accountant. I would never be able to succeed in anything ever again."

My eyes burned, searing into her as she pursed her lips, her body building so much tension that it could have been cut with a knife. I was *not* going to give up something I had worked so hard for just because we hadn't actually reached an agreement.

That's all it was anyway, right—an agreement?

"That's a little dramatic, don't you think?" She pinched her brow and raised her arms, only to slap them down against her thighs. "The woman always has to give up her dream for her man."

The way she said "man" hit me the wrong way. The fire in my throat rose, and before I could stop myself, I snapped.

"Yes, Ophelia, yes. Your dreams can happen anywhere. You can buy a sewing machine and make clothes anywhere, but for me, an offer like this only comes once in a lifetime, and I will not be giving it up to sit behind a counter at a bank counting bills for the rich. I will never grow from that. Come with me to Seattle or. . ." I scuffed and took a step back, taking a deep breath, my mind reeling. How could she not support me here, how was I the one who was expected to pack up and leave everything? "Or we're. . ." I tried to finish.

Ophelia held up a hand, stopping me from saying anything else. Her bottom lip began to quiver. Her plump, soft lip that I had kissed so many times, that I had run my thumb against over and over, was quivering. At any other time, my reaction would be to wrap her in my arms, calm her nerves, and take away all her tears, but tonight. . .

Tonight, I wasn't going to give in.

She blinked, and a tear dropped onto her cheek. "So." Her voice shook. "I take it we're not getting married then?"

I inhaled and stood up straight. I licked my lips and shoved my hands in my pockets. Looking into her deep eyes, I could see the tears puddling up before they fell. I loved Ophelia, but I needed a stable life with a stable career, and she obviously didn't want to be in it.

It was hard to believe that just days ago, I proposed, promising her a life that she deserved, willing to give her anything and to put my life on hold so she could become the great person she was supposed to be. But the job offer at Jackson and Rye: simple account data entry with the possibility of promotion from within. Full Benefits. A 401k. A company car. A life of luxury. She expected me to turn that down for a dingy New York apartment.

For the life of me, I couldn't figure out why she didn't want to come with me.

I shrugged. "I guess not," I finally muttered.

The tears flowed freely after I spoke. Ophelia's breath was shaking, and she nodded, her body tense as she turned her back and walked away.

I watched her as she took my heart with her, as her body grew smaller and smaller with each step she took.

Chapter One

-Clay-

Now

My alarm clock rang at 5:00 a.m. like always. The memory of a dream that always seemed to haunt me pulled me from my sleep. I reached over Rebecca's body to grab my cell phone, silencing the annoying tone. Rebecca moved against me, reminding me that she was still very much naked under my sheets. I kissed her shoulder and ran my hand down her bare arm, feeling her shudder under my palm.

"Go back to sleep," I whispered.

She didn't need to be told twice. Giving me a slight hum, she nestled back into the pillow and was asleep almost instantly.

I left the bed and rubbed the back of my neck, still forcing my body to wake up. I dug into my shoulders and tried to remove the knot that sat in my muscles, one that no matter how hard I tried, I could never get rid of. It was there forever, and unfortunately, I had learned to live with it.

With one final glance at Rebecca, I stood and began to get myself ready for work. Shower, cologne, suit, tie, wing-tipped shoes—dressed to the nines as always. I had to look my best for Jackson and Rye. After years of working my way up the ladder, starting at the lowest level of data entry, I was now the lead accountant manager for a team of accountants and their clients. I oversaw every spreadsheet, every check, and every deposit that entered my department. It paid very well and gave me more than the life I ever expected. And damn, I was good at it.

I took my time lingering in my modern kitchen, pressing my coffee in my French press. The day's current newspaper sat on the counter, and my steel travel mug waited to be filled. I poured the coffee, stuck the paper under my arms, and grabbed my briefcase and keys. Taking one final look into the bedroom where Rebecca still slept, I snuck out the door, knowing full well she would make herself at home before she left.

My Tesla, which I promptly named Tessa, was waiting for me, fully charged in the underground parking. The screen lit up as the car hummed awake. I would never get used to the quiet that an electric car provided—something a gas-powered car couldn't compete with. Security. That's what this car offered.

My life was full of security.

Just the way I needed it.

Jackson and Rye took up the 33rd and 34th floors of a 40-story building in the heart of Seattle. The closer to the top the better, right? The elevator was packed every morning, people grabbing their coffee mugs and briefcases as the small cube got more and more crowded. I always stood near the back, taking pride in knowing I was one of the last to exit. When I left the elevator, there were only a few souls remaining. Every time I took a step into Jackson and Rye's office, I knew I was near the top of the building. That, to me, was power.

"Good morning, Mr. Nolan." Jasmine, the receptionist, smiled as she said my name, no doubt thinking of the one night we'd had together when she first started.

I winked at her and turned to the left, heading straight to my office, shutting the glass door behind me before relieving the tension in my shoulders. Setting my coffee and paper down on my large, wooden desk, I reached behind and rubbed my neck again. I needed to go see someone about this. A nice massage was in the cards, I could tell.

Rolling my neck in circles, I pulled my chair and sat, my computer waiting for me and a stack of papers in the file that no doubt my assistant had put in there. Ignoring the documents for a moment, I turned the computer on, notifications hitting instantly.

The title of the email was the first thing I noticed. Normally, the subject gave some insight into what I would see, but all this said was *Atten: Clayton Nolan team lead, URGENT.*

Urgent. I had seen that before in numerous emails, but never with my name attached to it. This urgent was specifically for me. I opened the email and read the single line message in the body. *Report to Mr. Jackson's office promptly at 9 a.m.: urgent matter to discuss.*

I have only met Carl Jackson once in my ten years here. He was the top of the top. My jaw dropped, and my back straightened. The small clock on my computer told me it was 8:52 a.m. I stood, buttoned my suit coat, and left my office. The thrill of thinking about what was coming caused my heart to beat faster.

Another promotion perhaps? Head of the entire accounting department?

It didn't even hit me that my team, the seventeen people I oversaw, weren't at their desks. Each one sat empty.

"I'm sorry, can you repeat that?" I asked, stunned as if Mr. Jackson didn't just tell me what he told me.

"You've been fired, Mr. Nolan. As have the members of your team," he said again, leaning back into his huge leather chair, his eyes fixated on me. "We've been informed of the embezzlement coming directly from your team. We have all the evidence we need to take you to court, and if you don't leave the building immediately, security will escort you out."

"Embezzlement?" I repeated, trying not to choke on my words.

My mind was reeling. Embezzlement? Embezzlement!? My neck began to ache.

"I can assure you, Mr. Jackson, I have had nothing to do with this."

Mr. Jackson closed his eyes and let out a long, exasperated sigh. "I have more than enough proof to know you did indeed have something to do with this." He sat forward, grabbing a large manila folder with a red sticker on the front, holding it in the air as if to taunt me with it. "You may want to find yourself a decent lawyer. Ours will be contacting you."

Blink, Clay. Remember to blink.

"You're excused, Mr. Nolan. Please collect your things and leave the premises at once. Jasmine has termination papers you need to sign."

"Termination?" I slumped in my chair. The word termination was so much worse than fired.

Mr. Jackson's head motioned toward his office door, the manila folder slapping his desk as he set it down. "Good day."

The rest of the morning was a blur. I emptied my desk and grabbed my belongings from the shelf. I signed the paperwork Jasmine had waiting for me, that same smile—no, smirk—on her face. This paperwork was on her desk when I walked in. She already knew.

I rode the empty elevator down in silence.

I left the building into the chill of the Seattle air.

I started Tessa.

I drove back to my apartment.

I left everything in my car and fell on my leather couch, the large flat-screen TV staring at me as if it too was taunting me, just like that damn manila folder.

I looked at my watch. It was barely past ten.

Rebecca was long gone.

The security was long gone.

Everything was long gone.

I got a lawyer; we went to trial. My name was on every news station out there. Of course, I lost the case—settled, actually, to avoid going to prison. I plead guilty, even though I had absolutely nothing to do with it. No one from my team came forward. They all let me fall. A huge black mark now sat on my record. Getting a job in the future would be out of the question.

I was able to pay Jackson and Rye with my savings and was able to live for a few months on what I had left. Until I had nothing.

I sold every piece of furniture I owned.

I sold my apartment.

I had to give everything to them.

I had one single suitcase and my Tesla key.

I lost everything.

My money.

My home.

Everything was gone.

And now, here I was, six months later; knocking softly on Milo's front door. I knew I could count on Milo. I had nowhere else to go. When I called him weeks before, he told me I'd always have a home with him. Milo answered the door, a look of shock on his face that instantly turned to remorse. He opened the door wider and let me walk past him. His apartment was somewhat of a mess. Random empty boxes stood in a corner as he prepared for his move and upcoming marriage. Holly was excited to see me, even showing me some of her favorite books that we could read together. Even her sweet "Uncle Clay!" and her warm hug didn't pull me from the fog that I had created over the past six months.

"Welcome home, man." Milo hit my back and passed me as I stood in the living room, taking in my new "home."

At least I had him.

Chapter Two

-Ophelia-

"My... own... boutique?"

I repeated the words over and over, trying to get them through my head. My last show in Portland had been a huge success—and *that* was an understatement—and one of my new clients wanted to open a boutique specifically for my brand. An entire store front filled with *Ophelia Fuller*'s line.

Casual day wear, business attire, elegant dresses—dare I say wedding gowns?

"Yes." JoAnn Harmon smiled across the table; her eyes wide with excitement. "Our boutique on Broadway completely sold out of your lines faster than we could stock the shelves. We want to open your shop on 5th Avenue."

I was stunned. I'd worked my way up the fashion world so I could someday be right where I was sitting now. It was a dream to have my own storefront. I never expected it to happen, especially on 5th Avenue.

"Ophelia? What do you say?" JoAnn asked.

"Um. . ." I stammered. *Form words, Ophelia, actual words! You can do it.*

"It, of course, won't be done right away. It will take a few months to get the location just right, and then we will need to hire a designer to set up the shop. You'll have to provide the designs, and the clothes will have to be made. But, Ophelia, we want this to happen if you do." JoAnn kept talking, spouting off details I couldn't even keep track of.

Then a detail of my own popped into my head. My best friend, Madeline, was getting married in August, and I obviously needed to be there for that. I was the maid of honor, after all.

"What does the timeline look like?" I asked, interrupting JoAnn as she kept talking about the color scheme she saw in her head.

JoAnn furrowed her brow and shuffled a few papers around on the desk in front of her. "If all goes according to plan and the paperwork and logistics go without a hitch, I'd say about ten to twelve months."

I nodded. "That's manageable." Very, very manageable, actually.

"Is that a yes?" JoAnn leaned forward.

I took a deep breath. "I won't be in New York for the summer. Is that an issue? My best friend is getting married."

"Are you designing the wedding gown?" JoAnn lit up, her chin tilting up, making her smile seem wider than it really was.

"Yes, custom. I need to be there from start to finish. I'm leaving in a few days for Portland—"

"Oh!" JoAnn shouted, as if a light bulb went off. "That's perfect. I have a social media guru who would love to travel with you and record the process of the dress. It would be great publicity for your boutique."

I mean, *yes,* but the dress was supposed to be secretive. Madeline's fiancé, Milo, didn't know I was custom-making the gown. He just thought I was going to be helping her with the picking and alterations of the dress. Perhaps, there wouldn't be a problem if Milo was blocked from my social media feed?

"Yes, that should be okay, but let me check with the bride first, since she will have to be on some of the posts, and I know she doesn't want her fiancé to see the dress."

JoAnn nodded. "I'm sure we can manage that. This is the perfect thing to get your boutique off the ground, and with this kind of presence on social media, we may be able to jump the timeline." She shuffled more papers. They seemed to be appearing out of thin air. "When's the wedding?"

"End of August."

JoAnn smiled. Then with a sigh, her eyes met mine. She was excited. Something sparked, and she was rolling with it.

"I can make that happen." She nodded, determination in her voice.

"Three months?" I choked. "You think we would be able to secure a spot and open a boutique—complete with the clothing—in three months?"

JoAnn narrowed her eyes and nodded, at least pretending to consider my words. She waved her long fingers in the air and finally said, "Six months. November, just in time for the holidays. You can design a winter line, right?"

"Well yes but—"

My head was beginning to spin. I was still on cloud nine hearing that I was getting my own boutique and that they wanted to document my wedding gown adventure with Madeline, but now I had to finish a winter line up, manufacture it, and have the storefront ready in six months.

"I don't know if I can have it ready in six months," I admitted.

JoAnn heaved a sigh and tilted her head at me. "I'll provide a team."

"To design?" I stumbled.

JoAnn shook her head. "Oh no, to manufacture. You provide the designs, and we will make them."

"I'm very picky about the quality of my work." I held out a palm, stopping her from thinking she could whip out my designs in no time.

"Ophelia, we will be selling them on 5th Ave. I assure you the quality will be the same—if not better—than your previous lines. All we would need is the designs. You could pick the fabrics from Portland, and then we will produce them in time for the shop to open. You'll be in Portland designing the perfect wedding gown, and when you return, we will have a grand opening party. Ophelia Fuller on 5th Ave." JoAnn's face lit up as she seemed to watch her vision unfold.

On paper it sounded nice, I'll give her that. During my summer in Portland, I would have someone following me around to document the making of Madeline's dress. I would give them designs and pick the fabrics and watch my dream come to fruition. This could work. This could work really well.

I narrowed my eyes and looked at JoAnn, whose smile was still so wide I could make out a hint of green spinach in between her teeth. That's what you notice when your best friend is a dental hygienist. *Damnit Madeline, always mentioning teeth.*

"What do you say?" JoAnn asked, standing tall from her seat and stretching out her hand across the table.

I stood and repositioned my blouse. Taking a deep breath, I grasped her hand. "Let's open a boutique."

One thing I loved about New York, especially living in Manhattan, was the fact I didn't have a car. I lived not far from my office and had to walk across Central Park to get home. I was never worried about the walk, even in the dark. Being a Black woman in the heart of Manhattan, I had had my fair share of scary encounters, but that only added to my tough skin. New York was where I belonged, and it was always where I would stay.

I made it home in record time, suddenly wishing I had a dog or cat—hell, even a *goldfish*—to tell my good news to. It still felt so surreal. I was getting my *own* storefront. On 5th Ave! I couldn't wait to tell Madeline, but I felt like this was news to tell in person. She would want to celebrate with me. I knew we would go out for a drink and spend the night envisioning what the boutique was going to look like.

I made myself a quick salad and grabbed my glass of wine, making my way over to my design table that sat perfectly in the bay window that overlooked the city. Clicking on the lamp and turning on some music, I smiled. If any stress was hanging on me during the day, it would instantly be lifted as soon as I sat on this chair with The Avett Brothers serenading me. This was my happy place. I took a seat on the tall chair, the half-finished design attached to the angled desk staring back at me.

It showed a woman looking off to the side, her long hair braided and gently sitting on her shoulder. The wedding gown fit her like a glove. Lace flowers dancing over the bodice and flowing sleeves. The V-neck dipped down into the bust, with flowers trailing to buttons that cascaded down the back of the skirt. The fabric on the sleeves and the dress would be lace, almost see-through, but elegant just the same.

I picked up my pencil and leaned down to the photo, adding some more flowers to the skirt. I wasn't sure if this was going to be Madeline's dress, but the moment she asked me to design a gown for her, ideas poured from my mind. I had stacks of drawings for her to choose from, all neatly placed in a portfolio that I would carry with me on the plane. To me, these drawings were gold and had to be protected.

My mind went right back to the boutique. As much as it would be amazing to have styles for all seasons in the boutique, I wanted to design gowns. Elegant wedding gowns and pieces that could be worn to galas, only enhancing the woman's beauty. I didn't know if it was the pure fact that I was hyper-focused on Madeline's dress, but I could feel a new passion lighting inside of me.

Ophelia Fuller, wedding gown designer.

"That would be the ultimate dream," I said aloud to no one.

The small ding from my phone brought me back to reality. I placed my pencil down and reached for my wine, taking a sip before unlocking my screen.

JoAnn: I drew up paperwork and hired Carter to go to Portland with you. Photographer and Instagram extraordinaire.

Carter. Photographer *and* Instagram extraordinaire.

Ophelia: He sounds great. When do you need the paperwork signed?

JoAnn: Just before you leave. We need to get started right away. Booking a hotel for Carter. Where are you staying?

Ophelia: With my friend, but there are a lot of great places to stay in Portland. Carter will have a blast.

JoAnn: I'm sure he will. Talk tomorrow, Ophelia.

I closed the text thread. Instantly needing a friend, I pulled up Madeline's number.

Ophelia: I have some amazing news to share. You free to FaceTime tomorrow?

Madeline's response was instant.

Madeline: Of course! After work?? Say 6 my time??

Ophelia: You got it. Can't wait to tell you this! Milo CANNOT be around when I do. Ok?

Madeline: Now I'm intrigued.

Ophelia: I'll leave you hanging. It has to do with your dress

Chapter Three

-Clay-

"Daddy!" Holly's voice rang in my ears as I heard her run through the apartment. I tried my hardest to keep my eyes closed. Going on two months of sleeping on Milo's couch had its cons. Holly not being aware of me every morning was one of them. Or maybe she was aware and was just trying to wake me up. Either way, I didn't like it.

"When is Mommy coming!? I don't have the books Maddy gave me!" Holly screamed as she ran past the couch, her feet thumping louder than I ever remember.

"Madeline got you a Kindle for the flight, and keep your voice down. Uncle Clay is still sleeping." Milo tried to keep his voice to a whisper, urging Holly to do the same. I heard her suck in some air.

"Oh, I forgot," she whispered. *How could she forget? It's been two months.* "Do you remember where I put my Kindle?"

"No idea, but your mom is going to be here in about ten minutes, so you better find it. You have a plane to catch." I heard Milo hit a few buttons in the kitchen, and then a gurgle of the coffee maker began. Thank the *Lord* Milo knew I needed coffee.

The last two months had been incredibly hard, not what I was used to in my life. Milo had agreed that I could stay as long as I needed, but his two-bedroom apartment forced me to stay on the couch. During the summer, before the wedding, Holly was traveling to Scotland and Ireland with her mom and stepdad, and Milo's days were full of wedding planning. He was going to move into Madeline's house at the end of the summer once Holly got back from her trip. What were my plans then? Couldn't tell ya. Absolutely no idea as to what I was going to do.

I currently had five hundred dollars to my name, maybe less. It had been a while since I had actually checked my bank account. My Tesla was the only thing of value in my life, and I refused to sell it. Milo had let me live here rent-free while I tried to pull myself together, but I had a feeling I wouldn't be able to get back on my feet as fast as they were hoping. As fast as *I* was hoping.

I groaned and rolled over on the couch, facing the back cushion. I tugged the thin blanket over my head and closed my eyes tight. Maybe if I ignored the world, nothing would matter.

"When is Uncle Clay going to wake up?" Holly's sweet voice was muffled under the blanket, but it pulled at my heart all the same.

"Not sure, sweetie. Just get ready. Okay?"

There was a light knock on the door and a loud gasp from Holly.

"That can't be Mommy!"

"Most likely is. Go get your bags."

Staying under the blanket, not wanting to see or talk to Hannah, I heard Milo open the door.

"Hey!" I heard Hannah, her voice unusually loud for how early it was. *What time was it anyway?* "Is Holly ready? Donald has the car going, and her brothers are very impatient to see their sister."

Hannah had lightened up since their custody agreement ended. Holly had lived with Milo during the school year and with Hannah during the summer and some holidays. Even though it was a rocky beginning for both of them, Milo and Hannah were able to form a solid friendship, making their trade-offs easy.

"Almost. She can't find her Kindle." Milo's voice was still quiet. Poor man thought I was still asleep.

"Oh." Hannah's voice dropped to match his. "Is Clay still here?"

Of course I'm still here. Where else would I go?

"When is he going to find his own place?" Hannah's whisper was *not* a whisper.

"He's just going through a tough time. He knows we're moving into the house after the wedding, so. . ." Milo paused.

I opened my eyes, the light coming through the blanket as best it could. I had the summer to get my life back together, but in all honesty, I could see myself living in my Tesla before that happened.

"He's lucky to have you but—"

"I know, I know. Just give him more time. Let me go check on Holly."

I exhaled, trying to remain silent, turning to lay on my back once again, keeping the blanket over my head. I could lower the blanket, be a decent human being and say hello, hug Holly goodbye. The desire to keep myself burrowed away was stronger. I would be able to talk to Holly over FaceTime during her trip, and I'd see Hannah again, eventually. Until then, I would just pretend I wasn't here.

"Got it!" Holly's scream filled the room.

"Holly, be quiet. Uncle Clay—" Hannah began.

"I know he's sleeping. He's always sleeping," Holly grumbled.

I was not.

I closed my eyes again.

Then again, maybe I was.

"Donald is in the car, sweetie. Your brothers, too. Are you sure you have everything you need?" Hannah spoke softly.

Holly must have nodded because Milo spoke next. "I'm sure she's forgotten something. We tried to pack as best we could. If you need any more books for her Kindle, just shoot me an email, and I'll see what I can do."

"How many books is she going to read?" Hannah asked.

I had never seen a nine-year-old read as much as Holly did. She would devour books faster than a kid eating all their Halloween candy. I guess she had Madeline to thank for that. Madeline was the bookworm, teaching her soon-to-be stepdaughter a thing or two about literature.

"You'd be surprised. I hope you have fun. Call me every night and bring me back some souvenirs."

"You got it." Hannah's voice had a smile to it. "We'll see you at the wedding?"

"You two haven't RSVP'd yet, so we don't know if we need to add your cards to the seating chart." I could hear the sarcasm in Milo's voice.

"Donald and I will be there, and the boys will be staying with my mom. I have the RSVP right here. We'll see you soon. I hope Clay is okay."

I rolled my eyes.

"He will be. Bye, Holly. Have a wonderful time, and I'll see you soon."

"Bye, Daddy."

The door closed, and finally, it was just Milo and me in the apartment.

"You can stop pretending to be asleep now," Milo said, his voice louder than before, no longer caring that I was "sleeping."

I flopped the blanket down on my lap and glared at the white popcorn ceiling. "Her Kindle was in the bathroom. She had it charging in there for some reason," I mumbled. "Did she have the charger?"

"You could have told us that when she was running around looking for it, and yeah, I stuffed it in her bag as they were leaving."

I sat up and pulled my legs to the side of the couch, piling my blanket into a ball and setting it in the seat next to me. "And miss her running around in a frenzy? No way."

"You did miss it."

"I heard it," I grumbled.

Milo raised his eyebrow at me and went into the kitchen, pulling the coffee pot off the hot plate. He already had two mugs on the counter, filling them both. I stood and stretched, walked over to the kitchen peninsula, and took a seat on the bar stool. He scooted a mug toward me, lifting his to take a drink.

"Any fun plans for the day?" Milo asked, his voice still heavy from swallowing his coffee.

I shook my head. "Nope. Same as always, I guess."

"Ah, staying in and watching TV." Milo was teasing me, but in the tease, there was a hint of truth.

"When does Holly get home?" I asked, diverting the subject.

"A few days before the wedding. She needs to be there for the rehearsal dinner."

I looked at the counter and saw the small card that Hannah must have given Milo. *2 guests, chicken,* was written in Hannah's neat writing. I narrowed my eyes on the card. To me, it was weird that Milo had invited his ex-wife and her new husband to the wedding. A part of me thought it was for Holly's benefit, but Madeline had told me that she wanted them there. There was no tension between the two, despite the conflict they had gone through.

"I still can't believe how close you and Hannah are. I'm just shocked it doesn't bother Madeline anymore," I mumbled as I could hear a key slide in the lock.

"What doesn't bother me?" The door opened all the way, and Madeline appeared in the kitchen. Milo wrapped his arm around her waist and pulled her close to kiss her temple.

"Just my relationship with Hannah," Milo repeated, giving me a side eye. "I think Clay thinks you need to be jealous."

"Not jealous. It's weird." I looked at the granite counter and brought my mug to my lips.

"Why have tension and hatred when we can have an easy relationship? There's no reason to hate an ex. I saw them as I was coming up. I got to give Holly a huge hug goodbye, and she told me she would buy me a magnet." She narrowed her eyes and looked up at Milo.

Magnets seemed to be an inside joke between the two of them, one that I never understood.

"I came to say bye to Holly and steal some coffee before I head to the office." Madeline pulled away from Milo and turned to the cupboard.

"Don't you have a coffee maker?" I grumbled. It's not that I didn't love Madeline, I just didn't really care for the happiness she always brought with her. I'd rather curl up on the couch again and play a video game with Milo. Or sleep.

"I do," she said over her shoulder, "but I'm out of creamer, and I knew Milo would have some."

I rolled my eyes and took a long drink from my black coffee.

"Oh, come on, Clay." Madeline's voice rang in my ears. I looked up and locked eye contact. She definitely caught my eye roll. She didn't say anything else. She just held my gaze. She was already holding a Hydro-Flask that Milo kept here for her, steam coming from the top, and she placed the lid on. Sighing, she turned and gave Milo a quick kiss. "See you tonight?"

"Mm-hmm." Milo hummed, watching as she turned to leave the apartment. Once the door was closed, he tilted his head and glared at me. "Thanks."

"What?"

"Clay—"

"Milo—" I snapped back. I had a feeling I was in for an intervention.

"What are you doing?"

I shrugged. *That's a good question.*

I heaved a sigh, deciding the best form of action here would be to completely ignore his question. I had no idea what I was doing. I was spiraling. I should have been back on my feet by now, but the further into the future I went, the darker the days got. I knew my time was almost up, mooching off Milo, but I also had this feeling that I wasn't going to be able to get another job, not with Jackson and Rye hanging over my head. Sadly, my plan of action was probably going to be moving in with my parents.

Joy.

I met Milo's eyes once again. "I don't know," I finally mumbled.

Chapter Four

-Ophelia-

Carter was persistent. The man who sat across from me seemed to be in his late thirties, had dark bushy hair and a black rubber wedding band on his finger, and he did not seem happy to have been assigned to this project. Not only did he want my personal Instagram login on his phone, but he wanted to create one for the new store front, which didn't even have a name yet. He was a tiny bit controlling, and dare I say, overwhelming? He micromanaged at best, and I could see him getting more and more frustrated with me as the meeting went on. Not only did I refuse to give him access to my Instagram account, but I made sure my rules and guidelines were set.

By the end of the day, he knew who was boss. At least, I think he did.

He left the meeting grumpier than when he arrived. I sat in my chair, arms folded, staring at the door where Carter exited.

"So, this is going to be fun having him follow me around." I looked at JoAnn, who had her nose buried in the paperwork. "He understands the importance of keeping the dress top secret, doesn't he?"

I still hadn't told Madeline about this little adventure. We had a standing FaceTime date tonight. All the details would be shared with her then, and I didn't know if I was going to get excitement or fear from her. She had already texted me several times trying to get information out of me, but I told her she needed to wait, reiterating that Milo couldn't be around.

JoAnn looked up at me through her eyelashes. "He's very good at his job, Ophelia. He'll stay in the background, take photos and post to Instagram. That's all."

I nodded, feeling my hoop earrings hitting my cheeks.

"Now, the paperwork is pretty straight forward." She began to seep into legal terms and issues, so many terms flashing through my mind. It was hard to believe that just yesterday I had agreed to, this; and now, here I was signing the paperwork already.

Every single time she pointed to a page, mentioning me and my accountant, my mind couldn't help but flip to a memory—one I tried to ignore as best I could.

"The numbers speak for themselves," Clay said, looking at the budget I wrote up on our move to New York. "We won't be able to live in Manhattan for a while, so we should look in Brooklyn. . ."

"Brooklyn is just as expensive, babe. Trust me, living in Manhattan is right where we need to be." I wrapped my arms around his neck, kissing just below his ear. "Plus, I'll have you to help me with all my finances." We had lived together for two years since graduating college, two blissful years of being with Clay, day in and day out, and I knew this feeling would stick, no matter what city we lived in.

Clay scoffed. "Yeah, it's a good thing I like numbers." He laughed and turned to kiss my lips.

"Ophelia?" JoAnn's voice snapped me back to the paperwork in front of me.

I narrowed my eyes and tried to focus. I hadn't thought about that particular moment in a long time. My arms around Clay's shoulders, a sweet kiss on the lips. I pursed my lips and tried to remember what he felt like, but alas, after so many years, the feeling had faded.

And that fact didn't bother me. Or I told myself it didn't bother me.

"Yes, sorry, I just got distracted by the numbers. They aren't my strong suit." I leaned forward, drawing my attention back to the paperwork.

JoAnn laughed. "Well, that's why we have accountants. All I need you to focus on is the fashion."

I sat up a little straighter. "Now that, I can do."

8:00 p.m. arrived faster than usual, the sun still shining over the city as I sat at my desk, the glass of wine untouched as the music gently played in the background. My phone pinged, and Madeline's contact showed on my phone. Lifting it up, I answered, placing it up on the desk so I could keep drawing.

"Hey, Maddy!" I answered, not even looking at the phone.

"Hey." Milo's voice forced my head up. My heart jumped. He needed to be *gone*. "Don't worry, Madeline is currently covered in raw chicken, but she told me I *had* to start the call before you forgot."

"I wasn't going to forget, but you need to be gone," I said bluntly, my Southern drawl turning "gone" into a longer word than it needed to be.

Milo shook his head. "Don't worry. I need to go pick up—" His voice stumbled. "I'll be leaving really soon."

"He really is, Phe!" Madeline called. "I just need to wash my hands. Milo, you can put the phone down to go get Clay. Dinner will be done soon."

Clay?

I shook my head. "Yes, Milo. Take your time. I need complete privacy."

Milo waved goodbye and then set the phone down. I could still see the kitchen. He must have propped the phone up on something. Madeline had her auburn hair up in a messy bun, still wearing her scrubs from work. Milo came over and gave her a quick kiss on the cheek as she washed her hands. I grinned at them, still in awe that they finally found one another, and returned to the drawing on my desk.

This wedding dress was riskier to show Madeline. The deep neck went down to the waistline, and the bust was almost completely see-through. This was not the one I wanted Madeline to wear, but it was still fun to design.

"Okay, okay, I'm here, and my hands are dry, and Milo is gone." Madeline picked up the phone and turned. "I heard the door lock, I promise."

"I need to see the house." I pointed my pencil at the phone.

Madeline narrowed her eyes and flipped the screen, showing me an empty kitchen and even emptier living room before she flipped it back to her.

"Okay good. This is about the dress."

Madeline gasped. "You can still design it, right? I haven't even gone shopping yet. Even Milo was kind of freaking out about it."

"Oh, I'm still designing it, but it just got a whole lot more excitin'," *Excitin'*. . . there was that Southern drawl again. I honestly tried to hide it where I could, but talking with Madeline, it came out more often than not. "Do I have some news for you."

I began to tell Madeline everything and watching her expression was the best part. Her eyebrows were raised, and her jaw would drop. During my show in Portland, the one that landed me JoAnn, Madeline left before she saw the finale of the show to go get Milo. I was never bothered by this. I knew how important Milo was to her. Plus, I knew I was going to get her in that dress. That dress wasn't in any stores. Even though it made a hit at the show, it was always meant for Maddy.

"I signed the paperwork for it this morning. It's officially happening!" I exclaimed. "You'll need to come out for the grand opening."

"Well, duh." Madeline smiled. "I wouldn't miss that even if I was dying, but Milo could have been here for that. Well, except for the dress part." Her eyes lulled to the side, her lips pursing and head tilting.

"Well, yeah, I haven't gotten to your dress yet. JoAnn wants to use the dress as a promotion for the store. She hired a photographer to capture all the elements of the design and post it on the stores and my Instagram feed so that it gets people excited."

"Phe!" Madeline shouted. "Phe! That's going to be amazing, plus such good publicity for you!"

"Maddy, the dress with *you in it* will get photographed and posted *before* the wedding," I emphasized.

She nodded. "I won't have to be in the photos, will I?" Her voice dropped.

I shrugged. "Well, I need to make it to fit you. You are my framework. So. . .yes?" I trailed off.

Madeline furrowed her brow and nodded. "Milo needs to be blocked from *all* photos."

"Carter, the guru who I can just see is going to be so fun to work with, is aware of how sensitive this is. I shouldn't have even agreed to this before talking to you."

"No, Phe. I love it. It's going to allow me to look back at the making of my dress. We just need to make sure Milo doesn't see anything. But really, this guy needs to make me look like a princess."

"Who's going to make you look like a princess?" I heard the front door, and Madeline's eyes looked up. Milo's voice was faint as he walked back into the house.

"He was *not* gone long enough," I grumbled.

Madeline laughed. "Oh, trust me. He was gone the right amount. We've been on the phone for forty minutes. My lips are sealed. Hey, when's your flight?"

"Thursday. You're picking me up, right?"

"Of course. I'm leaving work a bit early to get you, then we'll talk about all things wedding. You'll get to meet Jamie!" Madeline beamed.

I smiled back at her. Knowing Jamie was the Portland version of me, I was excited to finally meet the other member of the wedding party.

"I can't wait. I better get going, I need to gather all these drawings into my portfolio so you can see them all."

"What drawings?" Milo appeared in the frame.

"For my store." I smiled, hoping he could see through my lie.

He nodded and left the frame. "I can tell him about that part, right?" she whispered.

"Please do. We need to celebrate!"

"Hell yeah. Have a good night, Phe. I'll see you in a few days!"

"I'll see you soon. Love you, Maddy."

She blew me a kiss, and then the FaceTime ended, my screen turning black. I laughed, even though no one heard, and placed my phone on the table beside my desk. I looked at the sketch in front of me before shifting my gaze to the city lights from my bay window. The Empire State building rose off in the distance, and the glow from the World Trade Tower and Central Park lit up as the last few people walked through. This view would always knock me off my feet. One day, I could see myself settling into a Brownstone, still nestled into the city, but for now, this was my home.

"We won't be able to live in Manhattan for a while. We should look in Brooklyn. . ."

Clay had been wrong. I was where I was meant to be. My dreams were coming true, and they wouldn't have happened if I didn't live in this beautiful city.

Chapter Five

-Clay-

"**W**as that Ophelia on the phone?" I asked, a slight hint of hesitation in my voice.

"Yup." Madeline smiled, stabbing her chicken taco salad with her fork, the hard-shell cracking underneath it.

Now that Holly was gone, Milo spent the majority of his time here with Madeline, and his apartment was all mine. He even told me I could sleep in his bed. A bed. It had been months since I last slept in an actual bed, so of course that's where I rested last night. When Milo came and pulled me from the apartment moments ago, I had no choice but to slip on my shoes and follow him out to his truck, sliding my fingers against my black Tesla as we passed it.

She sat untouched and undriven since I had moved back to Portland. Having no insurance and not a dime to register the plates would do that to a car.

"She's coming out for the wedding, right?" I asked again, looking down at my own salad.

Madeline nodded. "Yeah, she's flying out on Thursday, actually. That reminds me." She turned to look at Milo. "She's using the guest room."

Just then, a low grumble came from behind me. I turned and looked at the giant husky on his bed, watching our every move. He licked his nose and shifted his head between his paws but stayed firm on his bed all the same. I cracked a piece of my shell and tossed it in his direction. He was able to just use his tongue to lick it up, not moving his face at all. I chuckled at him and turned my attention back to the conversation.

"Well, that will be interesting," Milo mumbled. "I have a feeling she won't want me here because of *confidential wedding stuff*?"

"Well," Madeline kissed his cheek, and I instantly looked away, down to my food. "Yeah. Lots of confidential stuff that you can't see until the wedding day. So, maybe we have a few nights and then back at your place with Clay?"

"Wait," I interrupted. "She's flying out this Thursday? The wedding isn't until August."

Madeline nodded. "Yes, Clay, this Thursday. She's my maid of honor. Did you think being the best man you wouldn't see her?" She chuckled. "She'll be here all summer."

I'd expected to interact with Ophelia during the wedding planning, but I hadn't thought it would take three months. I'd hoped to talk to her during the wedding rehearsal and maybe ask for a dance at the wedding. Other than that, I'd stay out of her hair. I knew I messed things up when she moved to New York, and if I were being honest with myself, I regretted each and every day since she walked out of my life. Seeing where she was now, looking her up on Instagram every now and then, I knew I didn't fit in her life, especially where I was currently sitting.

Ophelia deserved the world, and I was *definitely* not the world.

"So. . ." I mumbled. "Can we make Holly's room up so I can sleep on her bed?" I asked sheepishly.

Milo chuckled. "Yeah, I'm sure we can do that."

I nodded and slouched back to the table, stabbing my salad.

"You're going to be okay with Ophelia here, right?" Madeline asked, her eyes stinging like daggers.

"Yes, of course, we're all adults." I nodded, not even believing myself.

The moment that Ophelia would be back in my life I'd be a dead man.

I slowly trudged back into the apartment alone. Milo had given me his truck and house key and told me to enjoy the solitude. Honestly, that was exactly the opposite of what I wanted.

I had gotten used to Holly running around and asking me questions about Seattle, having me read random stories to her at night and just simply having life in the apartment. I had lived alone for so long in Seattle that coming here felt weird at first, but I was able to squeeze myself right in. Sure, I was mooching off Milo, and most likely overstaying my welcome, but the bigger part of me told me I wasn't. That Milo would take me anytime, no matter what.

I grabbed a beer from the fridge and went to sit on the couch. I had worn down the cushions a bit since sleeping on it. It was a lot softer than I remember it being. Popping open the can, I made a mental note to myself to buy him and Madeline a replacement once I was rich again.

Again.

Yeah, right. That will most likely never happen.

Since the settlement, finding a job had been the hardest task. The one place that was willing to hire me on the spot was Home Depot. I grabbed that orange apron and ran out the door. Nothing against those who work there. It's honest work, but going from finance to retail, that's just something my brain wouldn't be able to wrap around.

I needed to figure out how to get back to where I was. How to climb that ladder and rid myself of this horrible black mark that was placed there after my settlement trial.

However, no matter how I looked at it, there was only one way to do things.

From the ground up.

I needed a plan. The last time I had a plan was in college, and we all saw how that ended up. Jobless, depressed, homeless, and sipping beer from my best friend's fridge.

I only had a few months to get myself together enough to find my own place once Milo's lease was up and he moved in with Madeline. A few months to find a job, get car insurance, find an apartment and be the best man to my best friend on his wedding day.

And see and talk to Ophelia on a daily basis.

Well. . . shit.

How in the world was I supposed to try to fix my life with her around? I took a sip of my beer and let my thoughts get the better of me.

You could give her the silent treatment. You could tell Madeline that you would only talk to her during the rehearsal and the wedding, nothing more. You could tell her you still love her and letting her go was the biggest mistake of your entire life.

I let out a loud groan, filling the empty apartment. I truly was a dead man.

Chapter Six

-Ophelia-

I watched as Portland, Oregon came closer and closer from my window seat. I may not have been born here, but Portland was home. The city sparkled as the plane descended, and I could feel the butterflies rising in my stomach—that was until I looked in the cabin and saw Carter a few seats ahead of me.

How that man managed to get on the same flight as me rattled my bones. I told JoAnn that I wanted a few days with Madeline before we began designing her dress and pulling all the loose strings together, but Carter was certain he needed to be there for everything. He wanted to follow me around and take photos, uploading everything to the new account, which already had over one thousand followers. After arguing, he finally agreed to sit this night out. Madeline was here for me, and he would take a taxi to the hotel. I had his contact information. I would be in touch with him when I needed him.

The plane finally landed, and I instantly took my phone from airplane mode.

Ophelia: Landed!

Madeline: I'm here! Jamie and I are at baggage claim!

Ophelia: What's for dinner? I'm starving.

I grabbed my carry on and tucked my phone in the side pocket. I watched as Carter stood and began to step down the small aisle. I followed suit, a few people behind him, knowing he was most likely going to be waiting for me once we were off the jetway. My phone buzzed in my bag, rattling my shoulder, as I took each step off the plane and finally into the warm air of the Portland airport.

Carter, as expected, waited for me. I guess that was kind of nice. Maybe he wasn't too bad.

"I already called myself an Uber, Miss Fuller. I plan on sticking to the hotel tonight, but you'll call me in the morning, right?" Carter didn't even look up from his phone as we made our way toward the baggage claim. *Oh, maybe not.*

"I will. Thanks, Carter. Have a good night at the hotel. Where are you staying again?"

"Woodlark."

Ah, fancy.

And with that, he was gone. He disappeared into the crowd as I made my way to the baggage claim. Soon, I saw Madeline's auburn hair bounce up and down, a smile on her face as she radiated joy. Next to Madeline stood Jamie, her wavy strawberry blonde hair dancing as she shook her head at Madeline.

Madeline couldn't contain herself anymore. As soon as I got closer, she ran and wrapped her arms around my neck.

"Phe!" she screamed in my ear. "You're here! You're here! And for the entire summer!"

"I'm here," I repeated. "But won't be for long if you keep squeezing me." I chuckled, yanking myself away from Madeline's grip.

"I told her to keep her cool. She was basically dancing in the car. I couldn't tell you how many red lights we ran," Jamie said, her voice sweet and soft as she approached. "I'm Jamie, by the way. I'm really excited to finally meet you. I mean, I know we've met over FaceTime, but in person is totally different." Jamie stuck out her hand for me to shake, but instead, I pulled her in for a hug.

"I've heard so many great things about you, Jamie." I held her at arm's length and took her in. She was naturally beautiful with a hint of spunk. My mind instantly went to what color dress she would be wearing at the wedding. "I'm making our dresses too, right?"

"Of course," Madeline answered.

"You're making my dress?" Jamie asked with a smile. "Maddy, please tell me I'm not wearing teal or yellow."

"You know Milo and I don't have certain colors." Madeline turned her back to us and went to the baggage carousel. "Same bag as always, Phe?"

I nodded to her question. "What's for dinner, Maddy?"

She turned back to the luggage and leaned forward once she found my bag to pull it off the carousel. "We can go out, or we can order in. You must be tired after traveling. Milo is working tonight, so he will be out late and then he's just going to his place."

"A night in actually sounds relaxing. We can order Chinese and drink wine. Just like college."

"Except there will be a giant husky in the way. I doubt you had one in college." Jamie laughed.

"Yeah, but he's a good boy. We love Niko," Madeline sang.

"Miss Fuller!"

I spun as I heard my name. Carter came rushing through the crowd again, his bag in his hand and phone to his ear. I rolled my eyes and watched as he got closer and closer to me.

"JoAnn would like you to check in with her as soon as you get to your hotel. I mean, your friend's house." Carter looked at Madeline. "She's been trying to reach you."

"Hi." Madeline smiled at Carter. "I'm Madeline. Are you the man who's going to be photographing everything?"

Carter took Madeline's hand and shook it lightly, remaining silent.

"Maddy, this is Carter, the social media guru and photographer extraordinaire that JoAnn hired." I waved to Carter, assuring him that I would check in as soon as I was able. Tomorrow.

"Nice to meet you, Carter." Madeline smiled as she released his hand, pulling it away sheepishly as he looked up and nodded at her, a faint smile spreading across his lips.

"Nice to meet you. Miss Fuller, we'll talk tomorrow." He nodded again, as if that was the only motion that man knew, and turned to catch his Uber.

Shaking my head, I turned back to the girls. "Well, shall we?"

I sent JoAnn a quick text, letting her know I arrived safely, and after a quick phone call with her going over another fine detail that was added to the plan, I joined Jamie and Madeline in the kitchen. We had ordered Chinese, and the wine bottles were already opened and on the counter, the three glasses waiting to be filled.

"So, what's on the agenda for the next few months?" I asked, grabbing a bottle of white to fill my glass.

"Wedding prep pretty much. I really want to talk to you about the bachelor/bachelorette party." Madeline grabbed the same bottle I had set down to pour into her glass.

Jamie grabbed the only bottle of red and filled her glass with only a sip, twirling it around in the bottom of the cup. "You mean *parties*."

"Nope, party. There's just the six of us, so we figured it would be better if we all did something one night, but we're leaving it up to the best man and"—Madeline glanced up at me—"the maid of honor to plan it." She formed a small grin. I sucked in through my teeth, knowing that was me, before returning her grin. Although my grin wasn't cute like Madeline's. It was cheesy and forced. I knew what was going on through her head.

"Whew." Jamie blew a breath of air. "I'm off the hook."

"Oh, no. I have things for you to do. Trust me." Madeline began to spout off a list of things to Jamie, but my mind went straight to this party she wanted me to plan.

Me and the best man to plan.

Meaning. . . Clay.

Clay was the best man, and I was the maid of honor.

I hadn't seen Clay since that night he broke my heart. Sure, he entered my mind every now and then, but I had never intended on seeing him ever again. I knew when Milo and Madeline got engaged that I was going to have to see him, that it was inevitable, but I wasn't planning on spending more than a few hours in his company.

My head started to race. Planning a party with Clay. Would Madeline hate me if I refused?

"Can we go back to this party thing?" I interrupted. Madeline and Jamie both looked at me. Jamie had her glass of wine to her lips. She had poured more than the small sip, and her eyes were wide. "I'm planning it?"

"Well," Madeline smiled. "Yeah, wouldn't that be fun? Or will it be too much with the dress?"

"No, no I can definitely plan it, but can't Jamie help me? There really should be two parties."

"Did you not just hear all the things she has me doing? I mean I get it, Maddy is busy, but holy hell. I thought this was going to be a small wedding," Jamie muttered.

"Table dressings, table layout, and invitations isn't that long of list," Madeline mumbled. "I'm not being a bride-zilla, am I?"

Jamie chuckled. "Oh, no. My sister was way worse."

"Okay, but the party," I said, placing my hands on the island to balance myself. "You want me and Clay to plan it together?"

Madeline pursed her lips.

"Maddy," I continued, "I can't."

"Phe." Madeline gently placed her glass on the counter and looked me in the eyes. "Clay has been going through a really hard time, and I honestly think this will be good for him. Get him off Milo's couch and back into the real world."

Real world?

"What do you mean?" I asked.

"I thought you knew. It was national news." Madeline heaved a sigh. "Phe, Clay lost his job. He lost his house, his savings. Everything. The only thing he has left is his Tesla which he hasn't been able to drive because he lost his car insurance. He's been living on Milo's couch for the past couple months, and he can't seem to get another job."

National news? Clay had made national news, and I missed it? My social media feeds mainly followed other influencers, other fashion icons. Any news I got came from a quick scroll through my Google home screen, and I would have remembered seeing Clay's name. I furrowed my brow. "What happened?"

"Some big lawsuit regarding his accounting team. They were embezzling from the firm, and since Clay oversaw them, he was to blame. He had to pay a settlement, so they didn't send him to prison for the rest of his life."

"So he's just. . ." My voice trailed off. I didn't even know what to say. Clay had his life together last I knew. He had a fancy apartment in Seattle, one that he valued more than anything. He seemed to have become a material person, all about the number in his bank account, but now he was living on Milo's couch?

Madeline nodded. She could tell that I couldn't piece together what was happening. "Yeah, he's not in a good place. He needs encouragement to get out and find a job and his own place before he ends up living in his Tesla. This party would be the best thing to get him out of the house and *living* again."

I took a deep breath and looked at Jamie. Her eyebrows were pinched, and she slowly sipped her wine.

"Does he know we're planning a party together?"

Madeline shook her head. "Not yet. I need to talk to him, or Milo does. I'll text him and tell him to talk to Clay tonight. We're thinking about the weekend before the wedding, before Holly gets home."

I picked up my glass and drank the wine gone, feeling the sweet chill fall down my throat, Clay's brown eyes in my mind the entire time. Once the glass was empty, I set it down and grabbed the bottle again, refilling to the brim. "Alright then. I guess I am planning a party with Clay and making three dresses, all the while being followed by a photographer."

"It's too much, isn't it?" Madeline asked softly.

"Not at all. I have three months to space this all out. I'm fine, as long as Clay's fine. . ." I sighed, seeing Clay's smile in the back of my mind. The smile that I always loved, the one that made me feel like the only one in the world. "I'm fine."

Chapter Seven

-Clay-

I missed my Tesla. I couldn't think that enough. Milo let me borrow his truck, his massive, loud truck, to go visit my parents once a month, and unfortunately today was the day where I had to pretend to be excited about having dinner.

My parents, Paul and Elizabeth Nolan, had met in college, got married directly after, and then built their lives around me. I was an only child, but not by choice. My mom had a few miscarriages before finally having me, and from what she says, it was a rough pregnancy. After I was born healthy and happy, they decided I was it and stopped trying to have a big family. I didn't mind being the only kid, but when it came to family dinner or holidays, it was up to me to build the family into something bigger and they always made sure I knew that. They were ready for grandkids.

My mom was secretly hoping Rebecca was my forever since she was the girl I had kept around long enough to tell them about. None of my past "girlfriends" even knew my parents' names; Rebecca came close to meeting them, but all in all, she wasn't it. No one ever was.

Now, here I was, going to their house in Milo's truck, wearing blue jeans and a gray hoodie, my five o'clock shadow showing through, with the potential to stay for the week, with no girl to introduce and no new information to give them on the job or. . . life. . . front. Normally, I would try to dress better, more normal, for these dinners, but tonight, I simply didn't care.

I opened the door and was greeted by Grim, the massively fat black cat my mother adored. He meowed and rubbed his body against my legs. I bent over and pet his back, having him arch up.

"Hey, Grim. Bud, you've gotten fatter."

"Oh, he has not. He's lost weight." My mom appeared from the kitchen, rubbing her hands dry with a towel. "How was the trip here?" she asked, pulling me into a hug.

I squeezed her back, still enjoying being held by mom. "It was fine, loud."

"Loud? Where's your Tesla?" She walked toward the front window and took a look at Milo's blue Chevy in her driveway, "Did Milo drive you? He can join us for dinner?"

"Nah, he's at home. My Tesla's insurance expired so. . ." I shrugged.

She pinched her brow and tilted her head. I knew my mother, and she was disappointed. "Are you still living with Milo?"

"Yeah, Mom. That hasn't changed." I walked past her into the kitchen. I needed to do something to get my mind off her upcoming questions. I reached for the cabinet and pulled out three plates and cups. "What's for dinner?"

"The lasagna is cooking and should be done really soon." She came up behind me and put the towel back on the oven handle. "Have you tried looking for a job, Clayton?"

"Yes, Mom, but that embezzlement charge that shows up on background checks doesn't help," I grumbled. I had been over this with her. She knew what had happened and how there was absolutely no way out of it. "Home Depot was the only place—"

"Home Depot?" My dad's booming voice came into the room. His hair had turned gray since hitting his sixties, and his glasses had seemed to get bigger. My dad was freshly retired and still in the "honeymoon phase" of his retirement. He seemed to enjoy being able to make things with his hands again, turning the garage into his workshop. "You could get me a discount on wood."

I pinched the brim of my nose. "I'm not working at Home Depot, Dad."

"Why not?" my mom asked, grabbing the plates I had pulled down and making her way to the table. "It would be a way to get out of Milo's house." After setting the final plate down, she stood straight and looked back at me. "You're always welcome back here, you know."

"Mom, I'm thirty-five. It's bad enough I sleep on my best friend's couch. I'd rather sleep in my car than move back home," I said a little too harshly. I knew they meant well. They wanted to see me succeed again, but if I was going to get my life back together, it didn't involve living with my parents. "I have a few months before Milo gets married and moves out. I'll figure it out."

"You need to figure it out sooner or later. If you need money for a down payment on something, or if you want to put the Tesla on our car insurance, we can work something out." My dad came up and placed his hand on my mom's shoulder. The look that was in both of their eyes, the expression on their faces, this was some sort of intervention.

As much as I tried to force it down, my mind snapped.

"What is this?" I asked. "I came for dinner, not the third degree."

"Clayton," my dad argued back. "We want to help you. We want you to soar again."

"Yeah, well, that's not possible. Jackson and Rye screwed me over, or my team did. I had nothing to do with it, but it shows, and therefore, companies don't trust me." I walked to the table and picked up my plate. I had no intention of staying here for dinner if this was the conversation. "Home Depot would hire me on the spot for minimum wage, but that won't cover a place in the city. Either way, no matter how you look at it, I'll be homeless in a few months. Nothing is going the way it should, and this is all just a pile of shit." I swung open the cabinet and gently—even though I wanted to chuck it—placed the plate back on top of the others. "I love you guys, and I'll see you in a few weeks."

I heard them sigh and begin to talk as I left, shutting the door with a bang.

Milo was sitting on the peninsula when I walked through the door, a slice of pizza in his hand with a book laid out in front of him. If anyone had their life together, it was Milo. Decent job, no debt, an amazing fiancée, and sweet little girl. He had all the things. A pang of jealousy hit the moment I saw him, one that I forced down with all my might. There was no need to be jealous of my best friend, especially after he had helped me so much. I tossed his keys on the counter and walked closer to him.

"That was a quick dinner," he mumbled.

"I didn't stay." I slid the pizza box over and saw a few slices left. "Can I?"

Milo nodded. "Yeah, it's not thin crust." Milo paused, and I met his eyes. His eyebrows were pinched, and he was following my every move. I knew exactly what he was thinking about, but before I could say anything, he spoke. "Everything okay?"

"Nope," I mumbled, shoving the slice into my mouth, looking away from him.

"Do you wanna talk about it?"

"Nope." I shook my head. Short and sweet.

"You sure?"

"Will you stop? I already had my parents asking me questions. I don't need it from you either." I shot him a look, snapping on him and instantly regretting it. I dropped the pizza slice and placed my hands on the counter. Milo's hands went up as if to surrender.

"Okay, I'm sorry. I just didn't expect you back until late, and you hate thick crusts on pizza." He leaned back into the chair and crossed his arms over his chest.

I shot him a glare.

His eyebrows raised, and he shuffled in his seat. "Let me guess, they asked about finding a job or an apartment?"

I took another bite of pizza and looked at him through my eyelashes. "To them I'm just a failure. They offered for me to move in with them."

"You know you can stay here as long as you need—"

"But what happens when you move?" I interrupted him. "They're right in the grand scheme of things. I can't be here forever, and I doubt you and Madeline want me living with you."

Milo didn't answer that last bit. He just looked at me, his eyebrows raised and pinched in the middle, his eyes where heavy.

"I just need to figure my shit out. How? No clue."

Milo sighed and stood from the chair, grabbing his book and closing it. "Madeline and I wouldn't mind you staying with us. Again, you can be here as long as you need. I even thought about talking to my landlord to see if you could take over the lease when I move out." He made his way back to his bookshelf, putting the book back in its place before taking a seat on the couch.

"Yeah, but how would I pay for rent?" I grabbed another slice of pizza and went to join him on the couch.

"Well, I would keep paying for you. My expenses aren't going to change just because I'm married."

Shocked, I looked over at him. "I can't let you do that."

"It wouldn't be forever, and it would at least keep you out of your parents' house. Madeline and I have talked about it, actually. We want to help you as best we can."

I heaved a sigh. "I couldn't accept that."

Well, I could, but I wouldn't.

Home Depot didn't sound too bad now.

"Anyway." Milo sighed, telling me he was changing the subject. "Ophelia got into town last night."

My heart skipped a beat, and I did my best to hide it. "Oh, yeah?" I asked, trying to remind myself to sound as normal as possible. "She's staying with Maddy, right?"

Milo nodded. "And there's something else."

"What?" I glared at him.

"Well, she is the maid of honor—"

"I'm aware."

"—and we would like you and Phe to plan a bachelor party. . . thing." Milo waved his hand in front of him, trying to draw the words out his mouth, except they weren't coming.

"A bachelor party *thing*?" I repeated.

He nodded, his teeth clenching. "Yeah, with everyone. Elliot, Jamie, me, and Maddy. Nothing too big. I think Madeline has a few people she'd like to invite. Maddy already texted me, telling me Ophelia was on board."

"She's. On. Board?" I asked, each word coming out with care. "What does that mean exactly?"

"Well. . ." Milo shifted in his seat, reaching up for the remote control on the coffee table. "It means that you and Ophelia are going to be seeing each other a lot more than you originally planned."

I nodded, my eyes wide as I turned to the TV. *You and Ophelia are going to be seeing each other a lot more than you originally planned.*

Oh shit. . .

"She can't know," I blurted out.

"Can't know what?" Milo asked, raising his brow and turning toward me.

"She can't know that I lost my job. She can't know that I don't have any money, and she definitely can't know I've been *living* here." My heart began to race. There was no way on God's green earth that I was going to let Ophelia Fuller know I was a failure.

"Just tell her I'm staying here for the wedding, to plan the party, and that I'm working remotely from here for the summer—"

"Clay. . ."

"Nope." I stopped and looked at Milo, interjecting his comment before he even had time to say it, "Please, she can't know."

Milo's brow was pinched together as his eyes began to fill with concern. "Okay," he said simply. "I'll, uh. . . I'll text Madeline to let her know to not let anything slip."

I nodded once and looked at the now cold pizza slice in my hand. "Thanks, man."

Chapter Eight

-Ophelia-

"This one." Madeline jumped at the drawings I placed on the table. She didn't even hesitate when she saw *the* one. "This one, this one. *This one!*"

"Okay, okay. I get it. This is the one." I placed my fingertips on the drawing Madeline picked and slid the others out of the way. "This one is actually my favorite." It was the same design I was playing with right after getting the news of my own boutique, the one I knew was for Madeline: Bohemian style with the lace and fabric that would flow from her arms and waist gracefully. I loved it in every way, and I was thrilled that Madeline had chosen it.

Click, click, click.

I glanced over my shoulder and saw Carter already snapping photos. I rolled my eyes ever so slightly and focused back on Madeline.

"Can you two move?" Carter's voice made both of us turn. "I want to get the drawing."

He came up between us and began clicking away at his camera, getting closer to the paper than I think I had ever been. It's all in the details, I guess.

Madeline watched him closely as he took photos from all angles. I could see the sparkle in her eye fade as she looked at Carter, taking the photos of the drawings, placing the others on top of the one she picked, and then finally setting it up like it was a masterpiece.

"Is this going to be all the time?" Madeline whispered.

Carter lowered his camera and shot up, his eyes hyper-focused on Madeline. "Yes." Carter glared at her before stepping away, letting us get back to the drawing.

"Okay, so." I pulled her back to me. "The skirt is double layered, chiffon on the bottom and lace covering it. I was thinking of a light floral design, a few buttons running down the skirt." *Click.* "The back of the dress dips down to a V at the waistline. Are you okay with a bare back?" I looked over at Madeline, who was still studying the design.

She tilted her head. "I'm sure I can manage that for a night. I just love the sleeves." She traced her fingers down the billowing sleeves.

"Those would be lace as well, more bohemian than anything. The front will have a corset. It won't be see-through. I promise."

"Oh, thank goodness. Holly is the flower girl, and I don't want to give her a show."

I laughed and shook my head. Madeline was an average woman. Average build, average chest, average height, and I also knew her well enough to know that she wouldn't want to show off anything. "V-neck as well, to match the back, but the lace covers a thicker material, enough to hold you in so you don't need to worry about a bra or falling out."

Madeline furrowed her eyebrows. "Maybe the back shouldn't dip so low."

"I can totally change that. Now, color." I turned to pull my swatches of fabrics, pulling out the chiffon and lace. "If you want white, I can do that, but I was picturing this in ivory."

"Ivory," Madeline said, matter-of-factly. She came up and held the fabrics in her hands.

Click. Click. Carter walked closer to us to get a detailed photo of the fabrics. I did my best to ignore him.

"The bust"—I turned again, leaving the swatches in Madeline's hand—"will be made from this material. See? Thicker, more durable?" I shrugged my shoulders. "Cotton and polyester."

"I adore you and I am in *love* with this design, but," Madeline clenched her teeth. "I don't need to know all the fabric details. I trust you. This is the one."

Madeline flung her arms around my neck, the swatches she was holding hitting me in the back. I wrapped my arms around her, taking in all her excitement. Nothing could possibly ruin this moment between us. Now all we had to do was start putting it all together.

Click.

I shook my head ever so slightly on Madeline's shoulder and pulled away from her grasp. "At least that hug will be documented forever."

"Are we done here?" Carter asked, lowering his camera and fiddling with the bag on his shoulder. "I'll go upload these and post them on Instagram."

"Perfect. Thank you, Carter. Just let me help with the caption and do not, I repeat, *do not* tag Madeline." I turned quickly to look over at him.

"Yes, please don't." Madeline mimicked my turn, sudden fear in her eyes. "I can't have Milo seeing any of this. He thinks we went looking for dresses today, not picking my custom design." She touched the drawing away, and her lips tugged in a sweet smile. "I want to surprise him."

"Oh, he will be surprised, trust me." I began to stack all the other designs carefully and place them into my portfolio. Who knows? One day, these may be on mannequins in my own store. The thought of my store crept into my brain. I should text JoAnn and tell her how things were going, ask about the location search.

JoAnn went from being a purchasing client to pretty much being my number one investor. She was deep in the hunt for a location and trying to do her best to let me enjoy my time in Portland. I was sure that Carter was texting her details. Why wouldn't he? The store would be hers, after all, just carrying all my designs, all my work. I knew I would have to be in the store from time to time, and of course do all the work, but JoAnn was the brains behind the business. As I placed the designs neatly in the portfolio, I began to wonder if she would allow my boutique to be wedding dress only and continue to carry my other designs in her other stores.

"What is going through that head of yours?" Madeline asked, bumping her hip into mine.

I sighed, still in awe that my best friend could tell my brain was buzzing, even without sharing a single word. "JoAnn. I was just wondering if she would consider only selling wedding gowns at the boutique. I have a lot of designs here and they could be *the one* for other brides, you know?"

"They are all stunning, Phe." Madeline smiled. "JoAnn's not the deciding factor, is she? It's your store."

"Well, it will be all my designs, but JoAnn is funding it and basically starting everything from the ground up. So, she does have a say." I snapped my portfolio, slinging it over my shoulder. "I need to get in touch with her, talk to her about my ideas."

Madeline wrapped her arm around my shoulders, pulling me into the pocket of her arm. "She'd be an idiot to turn you down." She smiled, her voice full of hope. "Now, when can we see those photos Carter took? I want to see how magical it all looks."

The email from JoAnn shot through me like lightning. They had found the perfect location. Already? So fast? And she wanted designs. She wanted them faster than I had anticipated. I took a deep breath through my nose and exhaled through rounded lips, my eyes closed.

"Uh oh." I heard Madeline come into the kitchen, plopping grocery bags on the counter. "Calming breathing?"

I shook my head. "Nah, just preparing myself for so much work."

"The store?"

"JoAnn found a location already, and she wants designs faster than I thought. I just hope she keeps the timeline the same. She said before the holidays." I closed my laptop and stood to help Madeline unload the groceries.

She had a bottle of white and red wine, a case of beer, a Dr. Pepper for herself, and all the ingredients she needed to make dinner.

"What are you making?" I asked, looking at the random spices and ingredients on the table.

"My mom has this delicious pasta sauce, and since Milo and Clay are coming over for dinner. . . I thought I'd make stuffed pasta with the homemade touch. It's kinda our thing." She smiled, ignoring the look I was giving her. I loved her, but sometimes she kept little tidbits to herself, like the fact *Clay was coming for dinner.*

"Oh, well." I coughed, pushing down all my annoyance. "When will they be here?" I grabbed the bottle of red wine.

It's not too early to open this, is it?

"Um. . ." She turned her head, her auburn hair flipping in the air. "Thirty minutes."

"Mm," I hummed.

I'm an adult. I can be cordial.

"Oh, and. . ." Madeline's voice trailed off. "Milo messaged me. Clay doesn't want you to know about anything that happened with his job or the fact that he's living with Milo, so can you play it off like I've told you absolutely nothing?" Pinching her eyebrows, she clenched her teeth.

I furrowed my brow. "Why doesn't he want me to know?"

She shrugged. "I'm not sure. Milo was very vague. He just said that Clay wants you to think he's working remotely and that all is hunky dory. If I had to guess, he may be trying to impress you."

I laughed, tilting my chin back and letting the single laugh fill the room. *"Impress me?* Why would Clay Nolan be trying to impress me?"

Madeline slumped, her hands on the counter and her eyes fixed on mine. "Phe, he's not over you. He's never *been* over you."

"Don't be ridiculous," I grumbled, reaching in the drawer for the bottle opener.

"I'm not."

"We're changing the subject, Maddy." I snapped as I poured the red liquid into my glass.

She pursed her lips and raised her brow. "Okay. Just remember—"

"Yeah, yeah." I grabbed my glass and headed toward the living room, passing Niko as he slept on his bed. "I won't say a thing."

Thirty minutes and one-and-a-half glasses of wine later, Milo walked in the door, Clay closely following him. Milo went straight to the kitchen, wrapping Madeline in his arms, kissing her temple, but Clay? He stood in the doorway, wearing gray slacks and a light green, button-down shirt that was tucked in, showing a very shiny belt around his toned waist. His dark hair was longer than I remembered it ever being, neatly brushed and just hanging over his ears, a few strands falling in his face. His brown eyes were simple, full of worry and dread, but even through the emotions, they still captured me. His body may have changed, turning that boy from college to the man that stood before me, but his eyes were the same, and I found myself still in love with them.

"Hey, Ophelia."

His voice hit like a ton of bricks. Still deep, still smooth, still able to turn my knees into Jell-O. If I tried to stand right now, I would only fall right back down on the couch.

I cleared my throat. "Hi, Clay."

"It's good to see you." He smiled.

I chuckled, my mind instantly pulled back to that day. The day I left; the day he chose a job over me. I lifted my glass to my lips.

"Wish I could say the same, Clay." I took a sip of my wine, the bitterness hitting my tongue.

Clay shuffled his feet, lifting a hand to scratch his neck, a soft laugh leaving his throat. "I guess I deserved that."

I stood, taking a single step toward him, a sly grin on my lips.

"Okay, well, it looks like we will be seeing each other a lot, so. . ." He held out a hand for me, his eyes intense on mine. "For Milo and Madeline?"

I narrowed my eyes and looked at his hand and then back to him. Sighing, I took his hand in mine and shook. "Yeah. . ." I trailed off.

Clay grinned, letting go of my hand and giving me a quick nod before walking into the kitchen. But even though his hand was no longer in mine, all the warmth leaving with him, I could still feel the spark that trailed up my arm.

I rubbed my hand on my leg, doing my best to ignore that feeling that lingered, and turned to join them in the kitchen.

I got this.

Chapter Nine

-Clay-

I was screwed.

Royally screwed.

The instant her skin touched mine, I was screwed. Every memory, every touch, every kiss came flooding back into my brain the moment I saw her. I missed the feeling of her hand in mine. I didn't know how much I missed her. All the feelings I had forced out for so many years crept their way back up, and I had to sit and smile and pretend like everything was perfect.

"So, Clay." Ophelia's soft voice pulled me back to the dinner table. Madeline had made stuffed pasta shells, serving them with salad and breadsticks, our own personal Italian restaurant right in her dining room. "You're here for the entire summer?"

I nodded. "Yep, right until after the wedding," I replied, stating a very obvious lie.

"Clay's staying here while we go on our honeymoon. He's going to watch Niko," Madeline said, not even looking up from her plate.

Ophelia's face froze, and she slowly turned to look at Madeline. Madeline raised her eyebrows and clenched her teeth at Ophelia trying to show a smile. Ophelia's glare was one I had seen before when I had forgotten to tell her a detail or two, one that said *what. . . the. . . hell?* Ophelia had no idea I was watching Maddy's dog.

"Oh, really?" Ophelia looked at me, her wine glass gently hitting her bottom lip.

I inhaled and nodded, forcing my eyes to connect with hers and not focus on her lips. "Well, someone has to look after the big doofus. We'll have fun, won't we, Niko?" As if on command, Niko barked from his bed. He was a well-trained dog, no begging from him in the slightest, but the sound of his name got some reaction. I turned and reached out my hand. Niko came up and hit his nose to my palm before giving my wrist a small lick.

"Niko, place," Madeline said sternly, and the husky went back to his pad, sitting only to watch us intently.

"Will Niko be with you at Milo's place?" Ophelia asked, a stern tone lingering in the back of her throat.

"Nope," Milo answered for me. "School will be starting by then. Hannah agreed to stay there with Holly while Madeline and I are in Colorado."

"Oh my gosh, you guys. We haven't told you about Marble. . ." Madeline began, clapping her hands together in front of her.

Ophelia, however, didn't let her friend talk. She instantly looked at me and spoke. "And after the dog sitting, back to *Seattle?*" Ophelia asked.

I furrowed my brow and nodded. *What is she getting at?* "Back home," I answered. "What about you, Phe? Back to New York?" I shoved a stuffed shell in my mouth, biting off a little more than I could chew, with dinner and with Ophelia.

Her eyes hit me like a dagger at the use of her nickname, and I had to stop myself from choking. In college, I was the one who started calling her Phe in the first place, and when Madeline began to call her the same, it stuck. That was what I called her as we danced, when we kissed, and when we were curled up together in between the sheets. She was always Phe. *My* Phe.

"Don't call me Phe, and yes," she hit back, "seeing as my business is in New York, my apartment is in New York, and my entire life is in New York, yes, Clayton, I will be returning to New York. I'll get a hotel while you're staying here with Niko."

"When do you leave? I'm sure we can be adult enough to stay in the same house for a day or two." I stabbed another piece of pasta with my fork. "And I've always called you Phe."

The idea that Ophelia and I may be staying under the same roof brought excitement to my dull little life, but the glare and disdain on her face told me she would not be falling for that. I put two and two together. She had no idea I would be staying here for a week.

Ophelia rolled her shoulders and exhaled. "I leave the Monday after. I wanted to give myself time to organize and pack, but it looks like I'll be doing that from a hotel room now, and no, you are not allowed to call me *Phe*."

"Why not?" I demanded, my voice harsher than it really needed to be. *Stand down. . .*

"Because, Clay, that nickname is for people I love and consider family, which obviously isn't you."

"I'm just trying to be nice and friendly, to start a conversation and try to be normal." I dropped my fork with a clink on my plate.

"Nothing here is normal, Clay. The only reason I'm sitting at this table with you is for my best friend and her fiancé. You just happen to be a part of the deal too."

"This is all because I called you Phe?" I rested an elbow on the table, leaning in toward her just enough to feel her fire.

"*Do not call me. . . Phe.*" Her voice softened as she said her nickname. She took a deep breath and sat back in her chair with so much force that the chair slightly moved under her weight.

I pursed my lips and didn't respond. She was getting irritated, and the more I pushed, tried to make things as normal as possible, the more upside down they would get. I had to remind myself that

I was the one who messed up. I was the one who ruined what could have been.

"Ok, you two," Madeline stopped us. "I really wanna tell you about the honeymoon we have planned. . ."

"Now's not a good time, Maddy." Ophelia pushed back her chair, dropped her napkin on the table next to her plate, and walked out of the house, slamming the door behind her with a *bang*.

I sighed and looked at Milo and Madeline across the table, both giving me a death glare, one to kill you on the spot.

"What?" I asked, as if I didn't know.

"Come on, Clay. You had to call her Phe and suggest she stay here with you? And mention New York?" Madeline furrowed her brow.

"I always called her Phe," I mumbled.

"Before you broke up with her."

"It's been ten years," I started, only to have Madeline point a finger at me, her eyebrows raised and her eyes almost bugging from her head.

"Exactly, it's been ten years, Clayton. Meaning you have aged *ten years,* so maybe—just maybe—act like it. I get you don't want her to know what's going on in your life, but that doesn't mean you need to act like everything is peachy keen and perfect when it's not. Ophelia is a lot more understanding than you think, and she has a lot on her plate right now so stop being a jerk." Madeline never put down her finger.

I looked over at Milo. He simply raised his eyebrows, pursed his lips, and looked down at his plate.

After a few moments of silence, I looked over my shoulder, seeing Ophelia's dark hair in front of the window. Her glass of wine sat on the table next to her half-eaten meal. Following my gut, I stood, grabbed her wine glass, and walked toward the door.

"Just be nice," Madeline whispered as I placed my hand on the doorknob.

Ophelia turned her head to the sound of the door opening, but the second she saw it was me, she scoffed and turned away.

I approached with caution, holding her glass with my fingertips, extending it out to her. "I think we need to start over," I mumbled, waiting for her to respond before taking a seat next to her on the bench. Her dark eyes met mine again, and she gently took the glass from me, instantly taking a gulp. I sat down on the bench, as far from her as possible.

"I'm sorry," I said softly, not exactly sure what to say. *I'm sorry* was the only thing that came to mind.

She shook her head and lowered her glass. "For what? Being an asshole ten years ago or dinner just now?"

I raised my eyebrows. "Um, for dinner?"

Once again, she glared at me.

"What do you want me to say, Phe. . . Ophelia?" I corrected myself.

"I don't even know," she said, "I was hoping this would be easy."

I sighed. "What? Seeing your ex after over a decade isn't easy?" After the words slipped from my mouth, I knew adding sarcasm to the mix wasn't the most brilliant move.

"Clayton. . ." Her Southern drawl appeared as she said my full name, drawing it out with a sigh. I hadn't forgotten that accent, the way she said certain words, especially "Clayton." It always knew how to make my heart skip a beat.

"Okay, I'm sorry," I finally said.

"You keep saying that, but I'm pretty sure you have no idea why you're sorry." Ophelia glanced slightly toward me. My body was turned toward her, relaxed as possible, hoping it would help ease her tension.

I shrugged, reaching up to rub my neck, feeling that knot that still lingered there. "You're right. I don't know what to apologize for. Madeline told me to stop being a jerk."

She shook her head. "You weren't being a jerk. You were just trying." She set her wine glass on the bench next to her, shoving her free hands in between her legs, her shoulders slouched as she turned to look at me. "I'm sorry for getting mad and storming out. I just wasn't expecting this."

"You knew I would be here, right?" I asked.

She nodded.

"I knew you would be here, too. I'll admit I didn't think it would be for the entire summer so that was a shock, but maybe if we just started over?" I asked sheepishly.

Once again, her eyes met mine, and I felt chills. It was like I was back to that day in college, that first time meeting Ophelia and having that instant attraction. Her hair was wild back then, with curls that could not be contained, eyes that were adventurous. You could feel her sparky personality just being in the same room. But with all of that, it was her smile that made me fall in love with her. It would radiate through the room and take anyone's bad day and make it better. Her smile led to sweet touches and kisses and filled my heart with more joy and love than anything else. Seeing her now, her hair attempting to be straight, even though it was trying to be wild, her eyes full of doubt and her mind racing a million miles an hour, I wanted to know what was going through her mind.

I wanted to see her smile again.

She heaved a sigh and looked out toward the street. "You know we have to plan a party together?"

"I heard about that." I smiled.

"I already have a lot going on."

"I'm semi-aware. But I'm flexible. I can do most of the planning. I'm not doing anything anyway." I stopped myself from letting too much slip. "I mean, my team is aware I'm needed here. I've been working remotely, and I can pretty much set my hours." I lied through my teeth, and the way Ophelia's eyebrows furrowed and her eyes narrowed told me she knew something was different.

She raised one eyebrow, sat up straight, and looked me up and down before finally setting her gaze on my eyes. "Either way." She finally sighed. "We'll make it work. I'll need your phone number so we can communicate with each other, not through Milo and Madeline. It would be nice to just—"

"Start over?" I suggested again.

She gave me a slight nod. "Start over," she whispered.

"In that case." I inhaled and stood from the bench, removing my hand from my pocket and holding it out in front of her. "It's good to see you, Ophelia."

Ophelia looked at my hand, pursing her lips before she reluctantly took it in hers. The spark was still there, and lightning flew through my arm. I finally exhaled, letting the breath go, taking all the sparks with it.

"It's good to see you too, Clay."

Chapter Ten

-Ophelia-

Every piece of fabric was laid out in front of me. The scissors were gently placed on the lace, and the measuring tape hung around my neck. A pencil was stuck behind my ears, and a cushion of over a hundred pins was ready to go. I was in full work mode. I had Madeline's measurements, the design pinned up on the wall, and the relaxing voice of Ben Rector playing in the background. The only thing that was off? My outfit.

Normally, I wore comfy pants and a t-shirt, and my hair would be in a poofy bun on top of my head. But today, Carter had me in a white blouse with a black, loose-fitting vest and slacks. My hair was down and perfectly styled, attempting to be straighter than it normally was. Professional. I even had makeup on. All for show.

Having this much focus on me made it hard to concentrate. The lighting had to be perfect for Carter, and if a single strand of hair fell in my face, Carter would stop me and gently place it back to where it was.

I kept telling myself this was going to be my life now. At least for the next three months.

Carter had shown me one of the first posts, Madeline and I gushing over the drawings and her picking out the design. Thankfully, he had used my caption instead of writing one himself: *A magical moment helping the wonderful bride pick out her gown. Nothing beats that smile.* The post had over five hundred likes so far, and my new Instagram handle was climbing—new followers every day. This was happening. It was really happening.

Carter had taken more up-close photos of the fabrics and some of me, posing me just so, and once he took the SD card out of his camera, I knew I was free. I grabbed a hair tie and yanked my hair into a ponytail. It was longer when it was straightened, and the pony hit my shoulders, but finally, I could get into my work and start Madeline's gown.

Carter hung around back, and the light tapping on his keyboard was honestly very relaxing. The next thing I knew, I had every piece cut to the measurements and ready to hang on the mannequin. I had just pinned on the first layer of the skirt when I heard the studio door open. I wasn't expecting anyone. I stuck a pin in between my lips and looked up.

"Hey, Madeline told me I could find you here." Clay walked toward me with two paper coffee cups in his hands. "I hope you don't mind me dropping by. I thought we could talk about the party as you worked." He held out his arm, handing me a cup.

It had been a few days since the dinner, and I had tried to keep myself occupied enough that I wouldn't have to text him to begin the party planning, but in reality, he was right. The planning had to start soon. I kept the pin between my lips, which was helping me from dropping my jaw in shock. I looked at him and then down to the coffee.

"It's an Americano." He gave me a cheeky grin. He remembered my favorite coffee?

I removed the pin and licked my lips, taking the cup from him, our fingers gently touching. "Thanks," I said softly, taking my first sip of the coffee. "Oh. . .yeah, I needed this," I hummed, turning back to the table with the fabric.

"So, you're making a custom dress for Maddy?" Clay asked, coming up to my side, looking at the lace on the table. "Ivory?"

"She didn't want white, and yes, this will be one hundred percent custom made and her gown only." I instantly turned my head and shot him a glare. His eyes went from the lace to me, his eyebrows raised. "Milo thinks I'm helping her pick out a dress and doing alterations, not creating a dress from my own design, so don't you *dare* tell him anything."

He raised his hands in surrender. "My lips are sealed."

"They better be, or next, we will be planning your funeral," I muttered, taking another sip of my drink.

"Noted. Did she choose the design?" he asked, his eyes trailing to all the fabrics on the table.

"Of course, she did. I gave her a few options, and she picked the one she loved the most. Milo is going to faint when she walks down the aisle."

Clay chuckled, walking around the table to look at the drawing on the wall.

"Really, please don't tell Milo." I couldn't stress that enough.

Clay turned back to me. "You can trust me. I won't tell him anything. I get keeping the dress from him, but I'm curious as to why we're keeping the fact that you're the designer from him though. Shouldn't he know that?"

"Madeline wants to surprise him. She told him I was too busy with my next seasonal line, which isn't far off from the truth, but do you really think I'd let my best friend get married without me designing her dress?"

He let out a loud, single laugh. "Yeah, no. I'm pretty sure we talked about that when we set them up." Clay's eyes narrowed, and his gaze went behind me. He was holding his coffee, a single finger pointing toward Carter. He mouthed, *Who's that?*

I turned and looked at Carter, his eyes still focused on his computer screen, his mouse moving quickly.

"Oh, that's Carter. He's taking photos of the process for my Instagram." I shrugged him off and went back to the table of fabrics. I grabbed the second layer for the skirt and handed Clay the pin cushion. He took them without question. "He took a bunch of photos, and he's most likely editing them now."

"I'll need some more here in a moment, Miss Fuller," Carter's voice echoed.

"Can I leave my hair up?" I asked, turning back to look at Carter. He looked up at me and simply nodded before returning to his computer. "I have to look professional for the photos," I added, stepping toward the mannequin.

"Does Madeline know her dress is being plastered all over the internet?" he asked, following me with the pins.

"She does. I wouldn't have done this without her say so." I placed the satin fabric on the mannequin and grabbed a pin from Clay. "She won't be tagged, and Milo is being hidden from all posts." I bent down and carefully placed the pin.

"So, then, what's the point of posting it?"

"Well, it's for my boutique." I grabbed another pin.

"Your boutique?"

I nodded, placing the pin. "Yeah, I'm getting my own boutique." I looked up at him and smiled.

Clay's eyes were wide, and his jaw was slightly dropped, almost as if he were surprised. Why had that shocked him so much?

"Is that hard to believe?" I asked him, coming off sounding harder than I meant to.

He closed his mouth, blinked, and shook his head. "No, no. Not at all. I'm kind of shocked you don't already have a store."

I shrugged. "I have my own brand, but I go to markets and then store owners buy them to carry in their stores. One of my clients approached me about opening my own storefront with her. The contract is signed, and it's a done deal. We'll open after the wedding."

"That fast?"

I nodded. "Yup, she wants to open with a winter line and this"—I waved my hands around, gesturing toward the table and mannequin, even turning to Carter—"is supposed to help boost the opening."

Clay pinched his brow again. "That's amazing but—" He stopped and lifted his coffee to his lips, forcing his thought to stay in his mind.

I grabbed a pin and raised my eyebrows at him. "But what?"

He shrugged. "How are you supposed to design a wedding gown and a winter line at the same time?"

My arms dropped to my side, and I heaved a sigh. The one worry I had about opening the boutique, the one thing I hadn't shared with anyone else, Clay asked in a second. *How did he do that?* I looked over at him, tilting my entire body. His eyes were heavy on me, awaiting my answer.

"No one else has asked me that." I sighed. "And to be honest, I don't know. I can use some of my previous designs, but JoAnn will know them. She bought some last year. And honestly"—I groaned, stabbing the pin back into the cushion Clay was holding, —"I've thought about asking her if it can be a wedding gown boutique. I've really enjoyed coming up with these styles."

"Well, it's *your* boutique, right? It should be what you want it to be."

"Well, JoAnn will own the store. It will be *only* my designs that are sold there, so I have to appease her as well. Owning my own store isn't in the cards for me yet," I said begrudgingly.

"Wasn't that your dream?"

I lightly shook my head. "My dream was to move to New York and become a fashion designer, which happened. So, now I get to focus on new dreams, like having my name above a store on 5th Ave, even if I don't *own* it. In a way, it's better. I won't have to handle the financial end of it. My dresses can be in the store but I'm not required to be there. I can focus on the designing, and my fashion will be on 5th Ave." I smiled at the thought. "That's my new dream."

"But with wedding gowns?" he asked, his voice toneless as he took another long drink of his coffee, the pin cushion still sitting in his free hand.

"That would be the ultimate dream," I muttered.

"Miss Fuller," Carter interrupted, "Can I get some close-up shots of you and the mannequin? Placing the fabrics?"

I slapped my thighs, thankful that Carter was pulling us away from this conversation. "Sure." I started grabbing a few pins to put between my lips when Carter stopped me.

"I'd like it if your friend can hold the pins, that way the pins aren't in your mouth. Oh, and can you take your ponytail out?" Carter fumbled with his camera, replacing the SD card.

I glared at him, tilting my head. He didn't even notice the glare. I reached up and pulled my hair tie, allowing my hair to fall on my shoulders. I ran my fingers through it, feeling the curls already coming back.

"I'm pretty sure he said I could keep my hair up," I mumbled, slipping my hair tie on one of Clay's fingers.

He chuckled. "You're gorgeous either way, so I don't see why he's making you take your hair out."

Wait, what?

I took a deep breath, shoving any flutters that would be forming down, and went to pose for the camera. Clay hid behind the mannequin, making it easy for me to grab a pin when I needed it, but trying to stay out of the shot. The entire time Carter took pictures, with the faint clicking in the background, the only thing I thought of was Clay Nolan calling me gorgeous.

Chapter Eleven

-Clay-

I watched as Ophelia let the photographer get up close and personal as he clicked away on his camera. She would take a pin, pretend as if she were placing it, and then pause, waiting for a click to move again. I stayed out of the picture completely, holding the pin cushion as close to her as possible.

Once Carter was satisfied, he went back to his computer to begin to edit the photos. Ophelia followed, wanting to see what he had worked on so far. I almost followed but stopped. Instead, I went back to the table covered in all the fabrics she was using for Madeline's dress. I was baffled that all this fabric would be used on one dress, especially when the drawing looked so simple.

I felt my phone vibrate in my pocket, pulling my attention from the lace. I set my coffee and pin cushion down and dug for my phone.

Milo: How's it going?

Clay: I mean, she took the coffee.

Milo: That's a plus.

I shoved my phone back in my pocket, carefully picked up my coffee—having the instant vision of it spilling all over the lace—and turned to leave, making my way ever so slowly to the door.

"Hey, Clay. You're leaving?" Ophelia's voice rang through my ears. "We haven't talked about the party yet. I'm done here, so we can talk now if you want."

"Nah, it's okay," I waved a hand.

Ophelia furrowed her eyebrows. "You can stay. I just have to pack up. Madeline drove me on her way to work. Would you be able to take me back to her place? We can chat on the way."

I inhaled sharply. Normally, I would jump at the chance to take someone for a ride in my Tesla, except I didn't have my Tesla. I had Milo's truck.

"Uh, sure."

Ophelia gave me a slight grin as she began to fumble with everything on the table.

"Do you cart this everywhere?" I asked as she folded the lace and satin up and placed them neatly on the table, scooting the mannequin off to the side.

"Oh, hell no." She chuckled. "JoAnn is kindly renting this space for me. I leave everything here. Carter, would you mind locking up when you're done?"

Carter nodded from the computer. "I'll just use this caption we discussed?" He pointed to the screen.

Ophelia nodded and rolled her eyes slightly. "You bet. See you later."

I swallowed and waited for her to gather her things, pulling her hair back into another ponytail before flinging her bag over her shoulder and grabbing a portfolio. I raised my eyebrows and took a deep breath.

"Let's go." Ophelia smiled as she tilted her head toward the exit.

"Bye, Carter." I waved, following Ophelia out the door. "He's just going to edit photos and post them?"

Ophelia nodded, entering the busy street. "Yeah, he'll be fine." She turned her head from side to side. "Madeline mentioned you traded your Mazda for a Tesla. I've never ridden in one."

"Oh, well, sorry to disappoint but. . ." I dug through my pants pocket to pull out Milo's key fob. "I have Milo's truck." I clicked the button, and Milo's blue Chevy beeped, the lights flashing as it unlocked.

Ophelia furrowed her brow and looked at the truck. "Wait, where's your Tesla?"

"At Milo's place." I headed over to the truck, opening the back seat for Ophelia's belongings, then opened the passenger door for her. The entire time she climbed in, she looked at me, her eyebrows raised and her teeth slightly showing. "I mean, it's not charged."

Once she was in the cab, I shut the door and walked around the bed of the truck, grumbling under my breath the entire time. *Remember, Clay you're still a hot shot accountant.*

"Why haven't you charged it?" Ophelia's voice hit my ears the second I opened the door and climbed in the truck, tossing the fob in the cup holder before turning the engine.

How was I going to answer this without sounding like an idiot? It had some charge to it, it was just uninsured, and the Washington plates weren't registered. I couldn't drive it.

"Oh, well, there aren't many charging stations. . ."

"There are a lot of charging stations. They may not be *Tesla*, but there are charging stations," she interrupted.

"Yeah, well, I drove it from Washington on one charge and haven't been able to get to a station. Milo's been letting me use his truck." I pulled out onto the road, trying to keep myself from making eye contact. "Plus, I've been working from home, so no need to really go anywhere."

"Home?"

"Well." I sighed. "Milo's house."

"Doesn't Milo only have two bedrooms?"

"I've been staying on his couch," I added sheepishly.

She hummed. "Why not get a hotel?"

"Because I haven't seen Milo in a long time, and he's letting me stay for free, so there's that." I gripped the steering wheel, watching my knuckles turn white as I felt Ophelia's eyes on me. "It's only for three months, then I'm back home, but we have a party to talk about."

Ophelia sucked air in between her teeth. "Ah, yes. The party. Any ideas?"

"None whatsoever."

"Oh, good, so we're both at a loss."

"Well, at least we're on the same page, just like old times," I mumbled, tilting toward her, giving her a grin. My grin wasn't reciprocated. Instead, I got yet another glare.

"No, Clay. And for the record, I don't think we're on the same page," Ophelia responded.

I pursed my lips. Just like that, the friendly conversation ended, and the car went silent.

After we talked on the porch, a simple starting over, it made me think we could do this. That Ophelia and I could let go over what happened in the past and maybe. . . become friends again. I even made it a point to find out where she was today, take her a coffee, talk to her. I stood there and held that silly pin cushion, watching as she pursued her dream and told me about her future, what was coming her way, and the entire time I couldn't help but imagine myself in it. By her side as she cut that ribbon on her store, designed the wedding gowns, and brought each one to life.

But here we were, one simple mention of *old times,* and I was back to knowing I was a failure, not just in my life at the moment, but with Ophelia too.

I pulled up in front of Madeline's house, one part of me grateful the awkward silence was over, the other angry that she was, yet again, turning her back to me.

"I'll call you," Ophelia said, point blank as she opened the car door.

I nodded and gave a smug smirk. "Yeah, okay. The party will get planned."

She gave a light chuckle and then shut the door, only to open the back seat to grab her portfolio, not saying a single thing to me as she did.

"Bye, Phe—Ophelia," I called as she slammed the back door.

I watched as she walked in the house, Niko barking from the window. Madeline's car was sitting in the driveway, so I knew I'd either get a text or a lecture later from her about this. Rolling my eyes, I turned back to the steering wheel, placing my forehead on the leather.

"Clayton," I grumbled to myself. "Why do you have to be such an idiot?"

As if it were answering my question, my phone buzzed from the cup holder. Groaning, I answered.

"Yeah?" I mumbled.

"I hope you're up for a fun night." Milo's voice echoed through the Bluetooth.

"A fun night," I repeated, shifting the truck into drive, taking one last glance at Madeline's house. "You know I'm poor, right?"

"I got you covered. We're meeting up with Elliot." I could *hear* his eyebrows wiggle.

I heaved a sigh. I had met Elliot once in college while he worked with Milo as an EMT, but we obviously didn't make an effort to become friends. If it weren't for Milo, I would have never met the man. But now that we were both a part of Milo's wedding, we would be getting to know each other, and in all honesty, that was the last thing I wanted to do.

I rolled my eyes, giving in to him.

"Okay, what time?"

Not to anyone's surprise, Milo took me to a bar. A semi-nicer one, where a live band was playing mainly country covers. Though the band was decent, this definitely was not my kind of music. I didn't recognize anyone on stage, but Milo smiled as we found a table. I followed him, keeping my focus on the crowd and maneuvering to the small round table Milo had snagged.

"Did you know there was a live band tonight?" I asked once we sat down.

Milo waved to a waitress, who gave him a flirty smile and came over to us, a drink carrier in hand with no drinks on it. I rolled my eyes.

"Just remember, you're getting married," I commented.

Milo glared over at me. "Do you want a drink or not?" he snapped.

I raised my eyebrows and shut my mouth, leaning into my chair, folding my arms over my chest. As much as I was trying to be sarcastic, there were no two people who fit better together than Milo and Madeline. The glare from Milo stung. He didn't think my "joke" was very funny. He blinked, wiping the glare from his eyes as he turned to the waitress who was approaching.

"Three house drafts, please," Milo ordered, another smile came from the blonde waitress. "Stop being an idiot. Besides, you could talk to her."

I shrugged. "Not my type."

"Wasn't Rebecca a blonde?" Milo noted.

I glared at him. "No, she was a brunette," I grumbled. "Again, blondes aren't my type."

"Oh, right," Milo shouted as another country song picked up. "Only Ophelia is your type."

The waitress showed back up and placed three beers on the table. Milo grabbed his beer and wiggled his eyebrows.

"How was seeing her today?" he asked, setting his beer back down after a long swig.

"Fine, before I pissed her off."

"What did you say this time?"

I furrowed my brow and shook my head. "She's just not going to let go of what happened."

"Did you expect her to?" Milo pinched his brow and locked gazes with me.

I shook my head, letting that be my only answer to his question, and leaned on the table, grabbing my beer to take a pull. "So, where's Elliot?" I asked, changing the subject.

Milo let out a laugh and then pointed to the stage. On the stage the band started singing the Ed Sheeran song "Castle on a Hill." The more I paid attention to them, the more the lead singer began to look oddly familiar. His brown hair was sticking up in all different directions most likely from being pushed back more than a few times, and his acoustic guitar hung around his neck. He was really into the song, singing with his eyes closed, every now and then his scruff hitting the mic but he never took notice. I made a face and returned to Milo.

"That's Elliot?" I asked, pointing to the singer.

Milo nodded. "He's almost done with his set and then he'll join us."

"Was he always a singer?"

Milo nodded again, looking back at his friend. "Oh, yeah, he kept things interesting on overnight shifts."

"Does he only sing country?"

"Well, Madeline asked him to sing a lot of Thomas Rhett songs, so he's been learning those, and I guess he added them to his set." Milo leaned in as the song ended and the crowd began to clap. "He's not only in the wedding. He's providing the music."

My eyes went wide, and after sipping my beer, I turned to look at the stage when the Ed Sheeran song came to a close. "Like all the music?"

Milo nodded. "He's good." He smiled, dragging out the word longer than necessary.

"All Thomas Rhett? All country music?"

"Thank you!" I heard from the stage. "As always, it was fantastic playing for you tonight. It always gets me when you guys get up and dance!" The crowd cheered as Elliot waved to them.

"You didn't have to pay for us to get in here tonight, did you?" I asked Milo.

He shook his head. "Nah, it's just Elliot."

"He seems to be pretty big." I motioned to the people sitting closer to the stage, noticing how there was a small dance floor. A few couples were still hand-in-hand, lingering as Elliot spoke to them.

"He doesn't do this to get paying gigs. I mean, sure he'd eventually get paid, but for now, they're just having fun playing music. He owns his own business, so this is kinda his side gig." Milo shifted in his seat.

"He's not a paramedic?"

"Hell no, I'm not a paramedic." Elliot came up behind Milo and slapped his shoulder. I didn't even notice him leave the stage. "I only did that through college. How you doin', Clay?"

I glanced up at the now-dark stage, the rest of his band members packing up. Turning back to Elliot, I saw his guitar resting on his back. He took his seat next to me and grabbed his beer. Sweat dripped down his forehead, lightly staining the collar of his t-shirt. I furrowed my brow and tried to pull my attention away from his appearance.

"I'm doing fine, thanks. I didn't know you were in a band," I responded.

Elliot turned to the waitress, waving his hand at her. She gave him the same flirty smile and came over with a glass of water. He chugged it down the second it hit the table.

"It's hot up there." Elliot laughed.

"I can imagine," I mumbled, lifting my drink to my lips.

"Ignore Clay. He's kinda going through a hard time." Milo slapped my back, moving his hand so I rocked back and forth. I shot him a glare and set my beer down on the table.

"Yeah, man." Elliot turned his attention toward me. "Milo told me you were let go from that firm in Seattle."

I inhaled. "Yeah, well. . ."

"Oh, I wasn't talking about Jackson and Rye." Milo raised his eyebrows and looked over at me. "I was talking about—"

"Don't." My glare deepened. Milo pursed his lips, and his eyebrows raised. He was giving me a dumb little smirk.

Elliot's eyes went from Milo and then to me. "A girl?" he asked point blank.

I didn't answer. I didn't even acknowledge his question. I was completely avoiding the conversation.

"His ex."

"Anyway. . ." I shifted in my seat. "Are we going to order food or sit here and talk about how pathetic my life is?"

The two looked at each other and then at me, both giving the other the same look before they turned back to one another and started conversation. It went from Elliot's set to Holly being across the globe, and then back to the wedding. The whole time, I just listened, paying just enough attention that if they were to ask me a question, I could easily answer, but truth be told, my brain was somewhere else.

Today started out fine. I had woken up and had a decent breakfast. I showered and shaved, drank a few cups of coffee, and then saw Ophelia.

Ophelia.

That's when my day got better.

I had told myself a few times, now that I was going to fix my life, that I needed to get it in order. And today, it felt like Ophelia was part of the equation. For the first time in months, I felt warmth again, like I could pull it all together, as if my life wasn't entirely in shambles. Watching her do something she loved, the passion that filled the room, pulled me back to what I *could* be what I *wanted* to be again.

"Clay." Milo caught my attention. "I'm heading out. You coming, or are you walking home?"

"Yeah, yeah. . ." I stood, bringing myself back to the present, ignoring the luring thoughts that were in my brain. "Unless Elliot wants to give me a ride." I half chuckled.

"I live on the opposite side of Portland," Elliot replied, digging in his back pocket for his wallet, placing a hundred on the table. I raised my eyebrows, missing the days I could do that. "But why don't you go ahead, Milo? Clay will meet you at the truck. I need to talk to him about something."

Milo cocked his head and raised an eyebrow, giving me a look of concern.

Elliot waved him off. "It's groomsman stuff. Now go."

Once Milo was out of earshot, Elliot turned back to me, placing a hand on my shoulder.

"Don't be upset with Milo, but he filled me in on everything today. He thought I needed to know what was going on, so I know you lost more than you're letting on." He paused, looking over his shoulder at Milo, who was staring down at his phone with a stupid grin, no doubt texting Madeline. "I just wanted to let you know I'm here. If you ever need to get away from Milo or just talk, I'm here to listen. I don't do much, so I'm always around."

I chuckled. "I'm not one to talk, and you don't do much? Milo said you own a business."

"That's the great thing about owning it. I make my schedule. We don't have to talk. We can just hang out and play some videos games or—"

"Well, if you know more than *you're* letting on, then you know I had to sell my gaming systems."

Elliot narrowed his eyes and let out a small hum. "Good thing I have them then, huh?" He smiled and dropped his hand from my shoulder. "My door is always open. Okay, man?"

He gave me his phone number, and then we left, meeting up with Milo by his truck before we all said goodbye and went our separate ways. I grabbed my phone and opened a new text thread, pulling up Ophelia's number.

Something had to give, right? We already agreed to start over. I just had to stop opening my dumb mouth. I had to remember that we weren't in the past anymore. We were two different people. I had to make this work one way or another if I wanted the warmth again.

Clay: We're starting over, right? No more mentioning the past. You in?

I held onto my phone, waiting to see those three little dots. They weren't coming. The message switched to read, but she wasn't responding. I took a deep breath and looked out the windshield. I wasn't sure how much time had passed, but once my phone vibrated in my hand, I had never unlocked it so fast.

Ophelia: I'm in.

Chapter Twelve

-Ophelia-

Chord Overstreet crooned in the background as I bent over my desk, Carter taking pictures as I drew. The music helped get me in the winter mood, trying to find the right designs that I knew JoAnn would like in her store, and yet, the only things I wanted to concentrate on were gowns.

Clay got it in my head that I needed to speak up, tell her that I wanted more than just seasonal lines, that *I* could be more than seasonal lines. I wasn't feeling these drawings, and with Madeline's wedding gown pinned to the mannequin, ready to be sewn and staring me in the face, all I wanted to do was gowns. And yet, I had to pretend I was into this design for the purpose of Instagram.

I inhaled, throwing my pencil down in front of me, stretching my arms over my head. Carter lowered his camera and looked at the backscreen before flipping it over to take his SD card out.

"Got what you need?" I asked.

"For now, I think. You're very photogenic," he said bluntly, not even looking up from his camera.

Chuckling, I grabbed my phone and unlocked it, instantly opening Instagram. The boutique's account had almost over five thousand followers and only three posts. The first was an introduction of me, standing in front of Madeline's house, a giant smile on my face as I struck a pose, letting everyone know that a boutique was opening and that I was "so excited" to get started on everything. The next was Madeline and me going through the designs and picking her dress, and then just me and a mannequin, Clay's hand holding the pin cushion as I worked on the gown.

I focused in on that pin cushion, noticing how he was holding it so it seemed like it was floating, trying his hardest not to be in the photo. As my eyes tried to find his fingers, a notification popped on. One new follower. I tapped on the little heart, and my eyes went wide.

Clayton Nolan has started following you.

It took less than a second for me to tap on his name. He hadn't posted on his feed since last Christmas, a congratulatory post to Milo and Madeline, featuring an old photo from college, his arm right around Milo's neck with his tongue sticking out between his teeth. I chuckled at the photo and scrolled back up, the blue *follow back* button right under his profile picture.

I tapped it, locked my phone screen, and set it down.

I inhaled, unsure why that had me rattled.

I admitted to Madeline that I had a good time while Clay was over. It was easier to talk to him than I thought, and just having him there was comforting. I told her the stupid comment he made about the past and *being on the same page*. She raised her eyebrows at me and shook her head.

"You two have always been on the same page. You just won't admit it," she grumbled. And with that, the conversation ended.

We weren't on the same page. . . were we?

I tapped my fingers on the desk, making my pencil roll to the side.

I glared at my phone, as if it would have all the answers. I heard Carter clicking away in the background, his tiny mouse so loud, even over Chord Overstreet's "Hold On."

"Hey, Carter," I suddenly blurted out, standing up from my desk and making my way over to him. His eyes moved from the computer screen to me, his head staying firm in one place. "How long have you known JoAnn?"

He raised his eyebrows and went back to the computer. "I've been the photographer for all her boutiques and have helped with her models for the past five years. I was at that show where she purchased your line."

I narrowed my eyes and nodded. "Do you think she would go for gowns only in the boutique, or would she want the seasonal styles?"

Carter's eyebrows raised, and his eyes went wide. That was the best reaction I've ever seen out of that man before. "She doesn't own a wedding gown store. It may interest her. I do know that she loves all the designs you've done, so in all honesty, Miss Fuller, it wouldn't hurt to ask her."

"She loved my wedding gown designs?"

Carter nodded. "She even told me to focus more on that during the trip. She wants that to be the focus of your account."

"So, if I asked her—"

Carter interrupted me. "It wouldn't hurt." His eyes, for the first time since I'd met him, locked onto mine. Almost as if he were telling me something.

I heaved a sigh and straightened my back, folding my arms over my chest. "Are you telling me something, Carter?"

He shut his laptop and stood from his desk. "I think you already know the answer to that." He picked up his laptop and shoved it in his bag. "I'm going to head out and get some lunch. Are you done for the day or. . .?" Carter's question trailed off.

I looked back at my desk, my phone still sitting on the papers or doodles. "I'll be here for a bit longer, then I may be done. But, if you are done with pictures, tomorrow is the bigger day. I'll be piecing the dress together tomorrow."

Carter gave me a slight smile as he slung his bag over his shoulder. "Madeline will be here?"

"Well, of course. I need her here to make sure my measurements are accurate."

He wiggled his eyebrows. "Perfect, I'll be in touch tonight for a caption. Oh, and. . . email JoAnn."

I tightened my lips into a smile and nodded. Watching him leave the studio, I went directly to my phone and opened a text. I circled my thumb over JoAnn's name, but my mind shifted and clicked on another thread instead.

Ophelia: Hey, Clay. You wouldn't happen to be free for lunch today, would you?

Those three elusive dots appeared instantly.

Clay: Tell me when and where, and I'll be there.

Maybe meeting at the food trucks wasn't the best idea, but it was the more casual plan. I didn't want to end up in a fancy restaurant, sitting across from Clay with wine glasses and a candle in between us. We were starting over, just as friends, nothing else. Food trucks were the next best thing.

I stood in the center of the square, tables and people all around me, my eyes searching for Clay. There were hundreds of people here. As my gaze followed the crowd, Clay finally came into view. He was wearing gray slacks, a white button-down shirt with the sleeves rolled up, and aviators covered his eyes. His brown hair was neat, but the wind added just a bit of flair to it. As I watched him, I felt like I was in a movie, watching the love interest walk up in slow motion. Hundreds of people surrounded him, yet he was all I saw.

I took a sharp inhale and blinked my eyes a few times. *Pull yourself together, Phe.*

"Hey, sorry I'm late," he said as he approached, leaving his aviators on but flashing his smile. "Food trucks? Good choice. What do you want to grab?"

I exhaled finally and looked around at the trucks. You would think with me waiting here, I would have already known what to eat, but alas; I couldn't think of what sounded good. I took another look around, moving my entire body. My mind was spinning. I wasn't this girl who got flustered when a guy entered the room. I was Ophelia Fuller, New York Fashion Designer who was getting her own store front, advocate for women everywhere, organizer of events and fundraisers for BLM charities, proud of who I was and where I came from, especially seeing how far I'd come since college. I was *Ophelia Fuller,* and I was a force to be reckoned with. I did *not* get flutters because of a *man.*

And yet. . . here I was.

I cleared my throat. "Tacos?"

A corner of Clay's lips raised as he removed the aviators. "Sounds great." He wiggled his eyebrows and headed toward the taco truck.

Taking a deep breath in my nose and letting it out through my mouth, I followed. His entire demeanor shouted business. I knew I was seeing Seattle Clay, the Clay he wanted me to see. He didn't know I knew he was fired, and that he wasn't just staying with Milo. I needed to remember that. This was for show, and yet it felt so normal, so real.

He walked slightly ahead of me, something he always used to do in college, except my hand would always be in his. His arms stayed at his side, one hand sliding into his slacks pocket, and I had to resist the urge to reach out and grab the other. Clay turned to look at me over his shoulder, making sure I was still close, that same smirk on his face.

"What made you choose the trucks?" he asked, motioning toward the taco truck as we approached.

"They're close to the studio. I need to go back after lunch," I lied. I was planning on going straight to Madeline's house, feed the dog and write up an email to JoAnn. "I didn't pull you from a meeting or anything, did I?"

Clay scrunched his nose and shook his head. "Nah, just some data entry."

"Lead accountants do data entry?" I furrowed my brow, hoping to catch him in his play, but he smiled and shook his head.

"When your team is behind, you do what you have to do, and sadly, that is data entry." He pointed to the truck. "What do you want?"

"Oh, um." I began to dig in my purse, but Clay's hand on my arm stopped me. With my hand still deep in my bag, Clay's eyes met mine, and the smirk still sat on his lips.

"I got it. What do you want to eat?"

"Um, oh. . . uh." Flustered, I looked up at the menu as the guy in the truck waited for us to order, "Vegetarian taco, rice, and black beans. . ." I muttered.

Raising his eyebrows, he turned to the man, pulled his wallet from his back pocket, and ordered for us, adding a few Vitamin Waters. I watched in amazement as he handed the guy a credit card with confidence. I caught Milo's name on the back and pursed my lips. Once he had the card firmly back into his hand, he shoved it back into his wallet.

"When did you become a vegetarian?" he asked, pocketing the wallet.

"I'm not. I just like vegetarian tacos," I answered.

Clay gave a small chuckle, turning his back to me once more to get the drink. I rolled my eyes and mentally hit myself for giving such a stupid answer.

"You can't go wrong with this truck anyway," I added, "I'm going to grab a table. Will you get the food?"

Clay raised his eyebrows and nodded. I could feel his eyes on me as I turned my back and walked to the nearest table I could find. I had a sway in my step, one that I normally didn't have. I paused, forcing myself to slow down and just act normal. It was Clay. Just Clay. *What the hell is wrong with me!?*

"Vegetarian taco just like you requested." Clay came up behind me, setting the tin foil containers on the table. "And a Vitamin Water," he finished, placing the bottle down with a slight thump. He walked to the other side of the table and pulled out the metal chair, taking a seat, watching me mimic him.

"Thank you. You really didn't need to buy me lunch," I said softly.

"Don't mention it. I wanted to treat you." He smiled.

I gave a sly smile, looking down at the taco and beans in front of me. Clay had gathered everything needed to eat, he flipped his napkin out and put it on his leg. Grabbing his fork, he instantly picked up some beans.

"So," he started, "what brought you to ask me to lunch today?"

I saw you followed me on Instagram, and you've been lingering in my head for the entire day.

"Don't we have a party to plan?" I asked instead, ignoring the thought that flashed through my mind.

"Eventually, but we have time. Don't they want to do it the weekend before the wedding?"

"Yeah, but we should probably start to think about it, don't you think? I mean, didn't you come to talk about it the other day?" I gently picked up my fork, circling it around in the rice and beans, blending them together in the perfect combination of deliciousness.

"I have a few ideas."

"Like. . .?" I trailed.

"Well, we can rent out the Piano Bar. You know, their—"

"Blind date." I smiled. "Madeline was so nervous that night. She took forever getting ready to go. She must have changed her outfit five times before settling on the one she wore."

"Milo was the same way. Remember he told us he was getting off his shift, but he really wanted to take a fifty-minute shower and get ready in peace. I talked Madeline up so much he was nervous. He was expecting another Ophelia." Clay chuckled, picking up his taco and taking a bite, closing his eyes in pure bliss as he ate.

"Well, back in college that would have been an interesting combo. Another Ophelia." I laughed. Back in college I didn't know what I wanted with my life. All I knew was that I wanted to design clothes, and I wanted to be with Clay. I tightened my lips at the thought. At least one of my wants came true.

"Milo wouldn't know what to do."

"You could barely handle me in college. Having two Ophelias would have been a bad idea." I laughed, louder than I normally would. "Anyway, what's another idea? I like the Piano Bar idea but hit me with some more."

"We can go dancing downtown. We can go bungee jumping. We could go to Depoe Bay and—"

"I'm sorry, did you say we could go bungee jumping?" I stopped him.

He lifted his head, his eyes wide. "Yeah."

"Bungee jumping?"

Clay laughed. "Yeah. It would be fun."

"Have you ever been bungee jumping? Because I don't think Madeline has ever been or ever will go bungee jumping."

"All we have to do is ask." He wiggled his eyebrows. "Milo would be down. And they could go together. It would be kind of romantic."

I stared at him. "It would *not* be romantic. It would be traumatizing."

He laughed. "The Piano Bar then?"

I nodded, taking another bite of my rice and beans. "I think that may be the best bet. I can't believe you would suggest bungee jumping."

Clay laughed, his smile catching my eye. "I'll look into it, but don't say no to bungee jumping just yet," he said through his laugh. "Oh, and for the record. . ." he stopped and lowered his fork, catching my eyes, holding my gaze. "I loved '*handling*' you in college. You said it like it was a bad thing. It wasn't, and. . . I miss it."

As quick as the moment began, it was over, and he was back to talking about the Piano Bar, even pulling out his phone to check if they did private parties, giving a little victory cheer when they did. But as he moved the conversation forward, I was stuck on his comment.

Chapter Thirteen

-Clay-

In Seattle, I had a cleaner come to my apartment once a week. I would make coffee and have breakfast every morning, but I would mainly eat out for dinner, making the dishes the easiest chore in my apartment. My bathroom was always clean, nothing on the counter except my comb and toothbrush holder. I had a service for laundry, and the bed sheets were always cleaned. I lived the life of luxury.

Here, I didn't have that.

And I was starting to like it.

Normally, Milo was awake before me. In the past few months, he would tip toe around as I slept on the couch, always being nice enough to make coffee for both of us, even pouring some in a mug for me and setting it on the coffee table, hoping the pure scent would bring me to life. He would make breakfast, either cereal or eggs and toast, for Holly and me before starting his day. He left the dishes in the sink, towels on the ground in the bathroom, and a basket of unfolded clean laundry sat in the hallway.

I had to start somewhere if I wanted to continue to keep going. No more sleeping in, no more covering my head with the blanket. Instead, I set an alarm on my phone, the first one in months, and woke up when it rang, instantly hopping in the shower. I shaved and hung my towel on the hook, my dirty clothes in the basket. After I was dressed and semi-ready, I would make coffee and breakfast, throwing Milo for a loop the first time I handed him a coffee mug. It had been a few days of my new routine, and even though I wasn't back to my old self by any means, it felt better to be doing something. Felt almost normal.

This morning, Milo was wandering in from his night shift, his eyes half closed as he dropped his bags on the floor. His phone was pinched between his shoulder and his ear. He gave me a slight nod.

"I'm glad you're having a good time, Holly." He yawned. "Yeah, I'm tired. I just got home from my night shift."

"Tell Holly I say hi," I whispered.

"Uncle Clay says hi. Yeah, I know he's awake pretty early. He even made coffee." Milo laughed.

I shook my head, rolling my eyes. I couldn't really get mad at the guy for his comment. It was true, after all.

"I need to get some sleep, sweetie. Tell your mom I said hello, and I'll text you when I wake up, okay? Keep sending me photos." Milo smiled, his face showing more exhaustion than normal. "Love you too. See you soon." Taking his phone away from his cheek, he blinked and focused his eyes on me. "I'm tired."

"I can tell. I would offer you coffee, but—"

"Hell no," he mumbled. "I'm calling Madeline, eating some toast, and then climbing in bed. Thank God I don't work tonight."

"Bad night?" I asked, placing a bagel in the toaster.

He groaned. "Yeah, car accidents mainly. Almost lost a girl, but we got her to the hospital on time."

"I remember in college it would take you days to get over a night shift." The toaster popped, and I turned to grab the bagel, placing the plate in front of him.

He raised his eyebrows, taking a seat on the peninsula. "I just have to disassociate myself sometimes. It hasn't gotten any easier, but I do love my job."

I leaned against the stove and brought my coffee to my lips. "You always have." I grinned, taking a sip.

Milo rubbed his eyes, blinking a few times before reaching for the cream cheese on the counter. "Thanks for the bagel. I like this new Clay."

"Me too," I muttered.

He took a bite and closed his eyes. "What are you up to today?" he asked through a full mouth.

"I am going to find a job," I said with confidence. I pushed myself off the counter and turned to fill my coffee mug again. Once I looked back at Milo, his eyebrows were pinched, and his chewing slowed. "What?"

He swallowed. "A job?"

"Well, yeah. I have to look around online first, but it's about time I get one, don't you think? I can't keep wearing your clothes or using your credit card."

He laughed. "Baby steps. Start with a job. I need to call Madeline. See you in a few hours?" He stood, grabbing his bagel from the plate.

I heaved a sigh and nodded. "Sleep well," I responded, taking another gulp of my coffee.

Milo lifted the bagel in the air as he walked into his bedroom, shutting the door behind him.

I finished my coffee and cleaned up the kitchen, making sure the dishwasher was full and running before I sat at the counter with my laptop. *Baby steps.*

Baby steps were not as easy as they seemed. I had spent the last three hours in front of my laptop, finding jobs that I could possibly apply for with my record and emailing my lawyers from the Jackson and Rye lawsuit, asking them when I would have this dropped from any background check. I had an email back from him quickly enough but no luck with any jobs.

My lawyer's response was simple and sweet, but it did nothing to calm my nerves.

We're working on something with J&R, trying to help you out. Give us time. Be in touch.

I slumped my shoulders and slammed my laptop closed, causing a louder sound than intended. I glanced at Milo's door. He was still sound asleep, and I had no intention of waking him. It was barely noon. The man needed rest, and my eyes needed something else to look at besides job listing and emails.

I slipped my shoes on, grabbed my phone and wallet, and headed out the door, locking it behind me. Once I got behind the wheel of my Tesla, planning on driving as slow and safe as possible, I started it and listened to the soft purr of the electronics, a sound I had missed. I pulled up my texts and tapped on Ophelia's name, hoping she was thinking about me too.

Clay: I'm free the rest of the day. Are you at your studio? Would you like a coffee?

Thank goodness for Madeline's Starbucks app. She loaded it on my phone and told me to treat Ophelia from time to time. She was loving her ever-growing star count.

Those three dots bounced, and my stomach mimicked them.

Ophelia: I just left, actually. Heading back to Maddy's.

I looked at the words on the screen. I just missed her, yet I still wanted to see her.

Clay: I was going to head to the Piano Bar and ask about renting the upstairs. Care to join?

Ophelia: You won't give up, will you?

Clay: Not a chance. I'd love to see you today.

Ophelia: Okay, let's go tonight. I still have work to do. Pick me up around 5?

I glanced at the clock on the monitor. Four hours.

Clay: Pick you up at 5.

I gave my Tesla a little bit of juice. I took her through a car wash and vacuumed out in between the seats—not that they were dirty—and took a rag to remove any spot of water left on her paint job. *Man, I love this car.* It may not be getting *me* in the right direction, but hey, self-care happens differently for everyone, and for me, it was my car.

I went back to the apartment and made a small lunch, hoping Milo would still be there to keep me company until I went to pick up Ophelia. Instead, I found some cash and a note in his scratchy handwriting.

Don't lose your savings. I'll be at Madeline's. See you later. - Milo.

I chuckled and grabbed the cash, folding it up and placing it in my wallet. I needed to start keeping track of all Milo has given me. I knew the man wasn't made of money, but he was still helping as best he could. Free rent, free meals, letting me use his cards every now and then. Hell, the man even offered to put me on his phone plan. One day, I knew I would be able to pay him back for everything, and hopefully give him more in return.

A little after 5:00, I pulled up in front of Madeline's house. Milo's truck sat in the driveway, and they were on the porch when I walked up. Madeline had a huge smile on her face, and Milo had one single eyebrow raised.

"What?" I asked as I approached.

"She changed. She looked fabulous anyway. I mean she always does, but she *changed* for you," Madeline teased.

I shook my head. "I changed, too." I motioned to my body. Jeans and a t-shirt. Casual. Comfortable.

Madeline bit her bottom lip and swayed her body, bumping into Milo.

I furrowed my brow and looked at Milo. "Thanks for the cash. I promise—"

"I know, you'll pay me back. Where are you guys heading?"

"Now that I can't tell you. Wedding stuff."

"You're planning the party?" Madeline's voice raised as she sat forward on the bench, Milo's arm dropping from behind her.

The front door opened, and Ophelia stepped through. I suddenly forgot how to breathe, the air leaving my lungs simply refused to return. She was radiant. Simple and ready for the warmth the evening would offer, wearing a muted orange button-down blouse that fit loosely and jean shorts, a white belt standing out over the muted colors. Her hair, which had been straightened the last few times I'd seen her, was wild, falling over her ears and shoulders with large gold hoop earrings poking through the dark contrast of her. My stomach fell, and my lungs continued to fight for air.

"Do you really think we'd tell you if we were planning your party?" Ophelia looked at Madeline, sticking her tongue out through her teeth before turning to me. "Are you ready?"

I cleared my throat, reminding myself that I was still human and needed to function. I nodded, another cough coming through my throat. I looked at Milo, whose eyebrows were at the top of his forehead. "Yeah." I looked back to Ophelia. "Let's go."

She flipped her head back, her hair bouncing as she placed her sunglasses on her nose.

"Bye, Phe," Madeline teased.

"See ya, Clay," Milo mumbled.

I gave him yet another look, one that was a mix of *hell yeah* and *save me*. He pursed his lips and gave me a slight smile. I stuck my hands in my jean pockets and followed Ophelia to my Tesla, rushing to open the door for her. She deserved to be treated like a queen. I ran around the back of the car, avoiding the looks from Milo and Madeline as I climbed in the driver's seat.

"Got the Tesla charged?" Ophelia asked.

I started the car, once again loving the soft sound. "It was time. She needed to be driven."

"How long has it not been driven?"

I pulled into the street and shot Ophelia a look. "*She* hasn't been driven in—" I stopped myself. I was going to say months. "Well, since I got here."

I could see her eyebrows raise behind her sunglasses. "Well, I'm happy to be her first passenger. Now, the Piano Bar?"

I wiggled my eyebrows and focused back on the road. "The Piano Bar."

Chapter Fourteen

-Ophelia-

When we arrived at the Piano Bar, I was suddenly thrown back in the past. The last time I was here was just a few weeks before Clay and I broke up, and here we were again. The bar top may have been updated and there seemed to be a few less pianos, but it still felt the same. Despite being open for the last hour, the bar was slow. A few people sat at the bar top, and the bartenders readied everything behind them, but there was hardly any movement, and it was brighter than I'd ever seen it. The emptiness of the bar felt unreal. I had never seen this place stagnant. The stage was set, and a performer was already doing a sound check, motioning toward the back of the bar where another man sat with a sound table.

"No way." Clay chuckled. "That's Elliot." He pointed to the stage, a wide grin on his face.

"Elliot? Milo's groomsman, Elliot?" I asked, looking from Clay to the man on the stage.

Clay nodded. "I had no idea he was performing tonight."

Elliot was singing into the mic, no music to back him up, testing the sound. He sang a song I recognized from Madeline's house, his eyes focused on the lights in front of him, motioning his hands up and down and then finally giving a man a thumbs up. Clay placed a hand on my arm and began to lightly lead me forward. As we got closer to the stage, Elliot's focus went from the man to us, and a wide smile formed on his lips.

"Clay!" he shouted into the mic, a squeal following him. "Oh, man, sorry. Sorry, Connor," Elliot waved his hand to Connor and stepped back from the mic. "What are you doing here?" he asked as he jumped off the stage.

"We're here to talk to the owner actually." Clay grasped Elliot's hand and shook it. "This is Ophelia," he said, smiling, turning to me and placing the same hand on my back.

Elliot's eyebrows raised as he looked from me to Clay, and then his smile turned into a smirk. The all-knowing smirk. Elliot knew our story.

"I can get you in with Craig. What for?" Elliot tried hard to erase his smirk, but the way his eyes bounced from me to Clay told me he was having a hard time. He rolled up his shirt sleeves, revealing a tattoo on his forearm, and waited for Clay to answer.

His hand was still firm on my back when he said, "We've been put in charge of planning a bachelor party for Milo and Madeline, and this is where they first met."

Elliot let out a chuckle. "Oh, yeah, I remember! He was heartbroken for weeks after that infamous blind date. Are you thinking about reserving the upstairs?"

"That's the goal," I said before Clay could talk. "So, we need to talk to Craig?" I tilted my body to look up at Clay.

"I bet you I can get you in for free. I play here twice a month. Let me see what I can do." Elliot's smile grew.

"Are you playing tonight or just fooling around with the mic?" I asked, stepping slightly toward him, forcing the warmth from Clay's hand to leave my back.

Elliot turned back toward the stage. "Nope, I'm playing. Show starts at eight. Call Milo." He turned back to Clay. "Get him and his girl over here."

Clay raised his eyebrows and looked down on me, a grin tugging at the corner of his lips. "What do you say?"

"I say. . ." I reached in my purse and dug for my cell phone. "I'm calling Madeline now."

"Perfect." Clay smiled. "Elliot, can we meet Craig?"

"Sure thing." Elliot nodded in the direction of the bar and began to make his way there.

Clay looked at me, as if asking for permission to follow. I gave him a quick nod and waited for Madeline to answer the phone. She was most likely still on the porch with Milo. Those two could stay there forever, a book in her hands and his arm around her. Pure happiness.

"Hey, Phe. What's up?" Madeline's voice interrupted my train of thought.

"Are you down for a fun night?" I asked.

Milo, Madeline and Jamie arrived at the Piano Bar at 7:30, all ready and excited to hear Elliot play. Milo assured us he was fantastic, Clay backing him up. Madeline was gushing. She was beaming, telling everyone that even though he was playing at her reception, this would be her first time hearing him. To say she was excited would be an understatement. The five of us gathered around a small round table closer in the middle of the bar, closer to the bar top than the stage. Elliot came to greet us, but his company didn't last long. Before he left to set up his stage, he assured us drinks were on the house tonight.

The entire time he was there, I noticed his gaze on Jamie, giving her more smile than he did the others; however, Jamie didn't even take notice.

"I wonder if they have mango-ritas here." Jamie leaned into the middle of the table.

"A mango-rita?" Milo pinched his brow and looked over at Jamie.

"It's good!" Jamie defended.

I chuckled and turned to Madeline. Clay was across the table from me, sitting next to Jamie, and I was squished between her and Madeline. I wouldn't admit it, but Clay was too far away.

"I'll go to the bar, mango-rita's all around," I announced, twisting in my chair.

"Please no," I heard Milo grumble.

"Ooh, I'll come." Madeline jumped off her chair, leaving the other three at the table.

She grabbed my shoulder as we walked up to the bar top, a skip in her step. "So. . ." she hummed. "How was the afternoon with Clay?"

I shrugged. "I don't know why you're so interested. We came here, and that's it."

"You've literally been here for two-and-a-half hours? You got all dolled up to come to an empty bar for a lengthy amount of time?" She leaned an elbow on the bar top and gave me a glare. One that said she didn't believe me in the slightest.

"We were talking to Elliot and Craig. We got a lot accomplished actually." I waved my hand down to the bartender. He nodded and finished up the drink he was making before turning to us. "And I am not dolled up." I looked down at my burnt orange blouse and shorts. "If anything, I'm dolled down."

"Whatever you say, Phe."

"What can I make you ladies tonight?" The bartender came up to us, placing his palms face down on the counter.

"Five mango-ritas please." I smiled at him. He winked and then turned away to begin making our drinks. I turned to glance back at the table. Clay was talking to Jamie, a smile on his lips. He ran his hand through his hair and turned to smack Milo on his arm, getting him involved with the conversation. I heaved a sigh and turned back to Madeline. "So, you've never heard Elliot sing and you agreed for him to sing at the wedding?"

Madeline shrugged. "It was a deal breaker."

"You and Milo don't have deal breakers."

She smiled, her cheeks turning red. "You're right."

"Here you are, ladies. Mango-ritas." The bartender met my gaze again, raising one eyebrow, a flirty smirk filling the air between us. I grabbed my glass and brought the salted rim to my lips. "Craig tells me your table is covered tonight, so you let me know what else I can get you."

"Oh, she will." Madeline grabbed two glasses and turned her body. "I'll be right back for the third glass," she added, leaving the bar top. I watched her walk back to the table. Jamie cheered, and Milo gave her a look of disgust.

"You're going to love it!" Jamie shouted.

I grabbed the second glass and walked back to the table, sliding the drink toward Clay. He raised one eyebrow, and his gaze went from the orange liquid to me.

"Thank you," he stammered. "I think." His hand reached for the stem of the glass, his eyes intense on me.

I gave him a slight smirk and settled back into my chair. I took a sip. *Damn. Jamie was right. This is good.*

"Oh, hey, look—" Milo hit Clay's biceps with the back of hand trying to get his attention. "There's Elliot."

They both wasted no time in leaving the table, making their way to the third groomsman, leaving the bridesmaids at the table. Jamie picked up her drink and hummed after her sip.

"Ok, so," she began, catching both mine and Madeline's attention. "Clay is. . ." She hummed. "Maddy, why haven't you introduced us? How old is he?"

I raised my eyebrows at her rapid-fire questions. Trying to tune her out, I took a long sip of my margarita.

"Clay's in his mid-thirties. Milo's age." Jamie scrunched her nose but leaned in closer to Madeline as she spoke. "He's in between jobs, and he's been living with Milo, so I figured now wasn't the best time to introduce him to anyone."

"The man's driving around an unregistered Tesla," I grumbled softly.

Jamie coughed, her back straightening up once again. "He drives a *Tesla*! How rich is he?"

"From what I know, he used to be well off, but then he lost his job." Madeline looked at the boys still talking. Elliot glanced our way, giving us a slight wave.

"Do you think if I asked him to dance tonight, he would? I mean, he's a bit old for me, but do you think I should ask him to dance?" Jamie asked.

I tightened my lips and turned to look at her. She sure jumped the gun, didn't she? I blinked, ignoring the fact that I had no right to be jealous and turned to Madeline, whose eyes were heavy on me. "What?" I asked.

Jamie looked from me to Madeline and then back to me. Her eyes widened as she made the connection. *Clay used to be mine.*

"Oh, Phe. I'm so sorry. I didn't know."

"Jamie." I sighed. "Clay and I have been over for a very, *very* long time, and I think you should dance with him tonight."

Liar.

Jamie raised her eyebrows. "You think? Am I even his type?"

"Women are Clay's type," I said with a hint of sarcasm in my voice. "So, yes, Jamie. You are definitely Clay's type. Even if he's a little too old for you."

Okay, so that last comment came out a little harsher than I planned. Madeline raised an eyebrow and shot me a look.

Jamie thankfully didn't notice and turned to look at Clay as he and Milo talked to Elliot. He let out a loud laugh, one I hadn't heard in ten years. I sighed, closed my eyes, counted to ten, and took a drink. *I got this.*

Once Elliot took the stage, the bar was brought to life. He certainly had a following here in Portland, which made me wonder about the rest of the country. He announced his band and the playlist for the night, telling the crowd he was treating his best friend's bride to be a sneak peek into what he would be singing at their reception.

"I gotta warn you." Elliot chuckled. "It's a lot of country."

The crowd laughed, but that only made them love him more. Madeline was extremely giddy. Although she'd only had the one drink, she still giggled and swayed, holding onto Milo's hand the entire time. Milo and Clay had moved on to beers, and Jamie and I each enjoyed a second mango-rita.

And I sat, like a third wheel on a double date.

Milo and Madeline would lean in and talk to each other, resulting in small little kisses and giggles. Jamie had leaned in even closer to Clay, setting her hand on his arm, paying him a little too much attention. Needless to say, I was rolling my eyes a lot just watching them.

Every now and then, I looked at the bartender, who always winked back at me.

Maybe you could go home with him tonight. . .

Nope. No, no, no. That is NOT Ophelia Fuller.

Elliot's voice softened, and the music faded. I turned my attention to him as he went and got a drink of water and grabbed an acoustic guitar.

"Let's slow things down just a tad. Not too slow, but just enough. Madeline, here's *Grave.*" Elliot smiled as he looked at our table. Madeline sat up in her seat, her jaw dropping.

Elliot crooned the opening line to the song. No music accompanied him at first, just him and his voice. I sighed and watched. I'll admit, he was almost as good as Thomas Rhett himself. It was the same song he was singing when Clay and I first walked in, one that I knew Madeline loved. She sat upright in her chair, her eyes wide as she took in the song. Faster than he could react, Madeline grabbed Milo's arm and pulled him out onto the dance floor, where they instantly latched on to each other. Milo mouthed the words to the song to her, looking at her as if she was the only thing he ever needed.

"Clay, wanna dance?" Jamie asked as she ran her fingers over to his hand.

Clay sighed and looked at me for a fraction of a second, then back at Jamie. "I'd love to." He smiled back.

Hey, that's my smile.

Clay took her hand and led her out to the dance floor with the other couples, slipping his arm around her waist as she trailed her palm up his chest and laced her fingers in his hair. He pulled her close and with him being so tall, he gazed down as she looked up to meet his eyes.

I shook my head, took a deep breath, and downed the rest of my drink.

What the *hell* has gotten into me?

Elliot sang the lyrics, taking the love of his life with him when he dies, making every woman in the bar swoon, as he watched his friends dance and kiss in front of him.

"*I'm gonna take you to the grave with me. . .*" I said aloud, matching Elliot's tune. The music picked up, and Milo and Madeline kissed, while Jamie gave Clay a flirty smile. The smirk he returned only made the fire rumble in my stomach.

"Damnit," I grumbled, standing up from the table, leaving my drink behind. I didn't want to watch this. I couldn't watch this.

After making it to the street, not knowing I needed the air, I took in a deep breath, the warmth hitting my lungs, pulling me back to reality. I was the one who told Jamie to dance with him, the one who insisted Clay and I were nothing and who claimed I wasn't hurt from all those years ago. So why was I feeling this way? Nerves ran up my spine, and anger slipped into my heart. There was no other word for it.

Heartbreak. Jealousy.

No. I wasn't heartbroken, and I definitely wasn't jealous. I was stronger than that.

I stood up straight, took my millionth deep breath, and looked up at the night sky.

You are Ophelia Fuller, and you are worth more than that.

I opened my eyes, spun on the balls of my feet, and made my way back into the bar. More people had joined them on the dance floor, cheering and clapping. The song was over. And I was glad I missed it.

"That's not their first dance, but what do you think, Maddy? Do I need to sing that at your wedding?" Elliot asked, his voice booming over the crowd's cheers. Madeline skipped to the stage, waving her hand down for Elliot. Elliot left the mic and leaned down to let her whisper something in his ear. He laughed, lifting his chin in the air before giving Madeline a quick kiss on the cheek. "In case you want to know, she said yes."

I gave a slight smile. Of course, she said yes. I sat at the table, running my fingers over the stem of the glass, watching as Clay and Jamie made their way back. Jamie was holding onto Clay's arm, but when his eyes caught mine, I saw the same look Milo had given Madeline.

Chapter Fifteen

-Clay-

"What did you do?" Milo asked a few days later as I cracked the egg on the burner.

"What do you mean?" I played dumb. I knew exactly what he was talking about.

Two days ago, I picked up Ophelia. She looked amazing. We spent time and laughed together. . . then I was ignored for the rest of the night. She looked pissed when I got back to the table after a quick dance with Jamie, but as the night went on, she laughed and smiled with Madeline, all but leaving me in the dust. I clearly upset her, but my dumb ass didn't know how to make it better.

"You know exactly what I mean," Milo mumbled, reading my mind.

"Hey, can I borrow the truck tonight? Dinner with my parents, which, as always, you're welcome to come to." I quickly changed the subject, not wanting the third degree from him.

Could I have reached out to Ophelia and made things better? Sure. Did I want to? Yes. Was I mortified to? Also yes. What would I have said to make the situation better?

Hey, sorry to have danced with Jamie and totally thrown off your night. It didn't mean anything. It was just a dance.

Nothing I could have said would have turned this sucky situation better again. There was simply no going back. So, I chose the coward's way and just let it be.

I turned back to the eggs and flipped them, watching the yolk crack, swearing a bit under my breath.

"You know you can; actually, I may join you. Madeline is busy tonight with wedding stuff, and I haven't seen your parents in a while." Milo walked into the kitchen, grabbing a coffee mug and humming at my egg in the pan as he leaned against the counter. "Now seriously, what did you do?"

I shrugged. "I just really made her mad."

"This is what, the forth time?" he asked, bringing his mug to his lips.

"If we're counting the break-up, I think so."

"I'm counting it, aren't you?"

"I'd rather not," I grumbled. It would be better to strike it from the record completely. Act as if it never existed. "Do you think she is?" I asked sheepishly.

"You proposed and then a week later dumped her for a job. I'm no expert, but I'd say she still hangs on to it, especially after being forced to spend time with you. Madeline tells me she's fine, but. . ." Taking a sip of his coffee, he paused, cocking one shoulder. "She's always been good about moving on."

I nodded, turning off the burner and transferring my egg to the piece of toast.

"What time is dinner?" Milo shoved himself off the counter.

"Six. My mom is making shepherd's pie."

"Perfect."

Milo was instantly wrapped in a bear hug by my mother the moment we walked in the door. She had to be updated on all the wedding details, loving how he and Madeline had finally found their happily ever after. I gave Milo a small wave and headed into the kitchen, seeing my dad at the table, a book in hand with Grim already at his feet, waiting for his table scraps.

"No wonder that cat is so fat. Mom feeds him from the table, huh?" I asked, pulling a seat out to sit across from my dad.

He looked up at me from his large glasses, shifting just a little in his seat to place the bookmark back in his novel, gently setting it on the table.

"*Of Mice and Men* again?" I asked, motioning my chin toward the thin paperback in his hands. His favorite, no doubt. He reads it at least once a year.

"Are we going to be able to actually talk to you this time or are you going to storm off like you did in high school?" he asked, his solemn voice vibrating through my ears.

"I may have overreacted a bit last time, I'm sorry, Pops."

"Make sure you tell your mother that. You know we love Milo, but if you brought him just so we wouldn't bring up you getting back on your feet—"

"No, Dad," I interrupted. "I invited him because you always tell me to. I'm happy to report that I have sent out a few resumes this past week. I'm trying."

He gave me a single nod, his lips tugging at the corners. "No Home Depot?"

I chuckled. "No, Dad. A few law firms and startups, data entry. Gotta take baby steps, right?"

"Milo was just telling me Ophelia is back in town." My mom's voice rang through the room as she and Milo finally sauntered into the kitchen. "Have you been seeing her again? It's been so long, and we always loved her."

It was true, they did. When I first brought her home to meet them, it was love at first sight. She came to all the family functions and she and my mom would talk about anything and everything.

She fit right in, not only capturing my heart but theirs as well. I told my parents about my plan to propose before I popped the question. They wanted me to use my grandmother's ring, but I declined, not knowing what Ophelia would say or do. In hindsight, it was a good thing I didn't take it.

"Um. . ." I began.

"They have been planning the bachelor party together," Milo answered for me, taking his seat and reaching for the cup of water that already sat on the table. "But she's been busy, hard to get a hold of."

"I'm sure she wouldn't mind some company while she worked," my dad chimed in. "She's in fashion design, right?"

"Yes, sir." Milo nodded.

"I think I've seen her on Instagram." My mom sighed, bringing more food to the table. I instantly reached for a roll.

"You have an Instagram?" I asked, looking up at her as she sat down.

She tilted her head and smiled. "Your cousins are on there, and I like to see their families. Ophelia may have shown up a time or two. I'd always hoped you would get your head out of your ass long enough to figure out you messed up."

"Mom. . ." I grumbled.

"She was the best thing in your life, and then you let her go." She pursed her lips and shook her head, not having to finish the thought.

I gave a slight nod, agreeing with her.

"We've been keeping our distance," I finally admitted.

"He made her mad," Milo added, a mouth full of bread.

I tilted my body and glared at him.

"What did you do?" My mom asked, her head tilting in my direction.

Milo took the lead and answered. "We all went out one night while Elliot was performing. He sang this amazing romantic song, and Clay here decided to dance with the other bridesmaid."

"She asked," I added under my breath, defending myself.

"Clay left the house? Willingly? To go to out?" my dad asked, his fork floating in the air.

"I go out."

"More so lately than before." Milo turned to meet my gaze. "Baby steps."

"I want to know why you danced with the other bridesmaid and not your soul mate." My mom's eyes were heavy on me, giving me the full-on mom glare. I raised my eyebrows and had to fight the urge not to go to my bedroom in shame. I was over thirty years old, and she still had that effect.

"Jamie asked," I said sheepishly. "And then I told her I still. . ." I stopped, taking a sigh. Jamie was the only other person besides Milo and Madeline that I told I was still head over heels for Ophelia. I had a hard time getting it out as we danced, but thankfully she was understanding, telling me to take a risk and ask her to dance. But just one look at Ophelia told me she would have said no. "I told her I was still going through some things and needed to not add a girl in the mix," I lied.

My mom's eyes narrowed, and everyone suddenly looked at me. Milo, my dad, my mom. They all peered into my brain, picking apart the lie until they finally accepted it.

And then, at the same time, they all three said, "Baby steps."

The topic of Ophelia ended with that, the conversation turning back to the wedding and my resumes.

Later that night, after Milo and I had gotten back to his place and played a game, he and I went into our rooms for the night, and I stared at my phone. Ophelia's text thread was pulled up. The little conversation we'd had was meaningless; arrangements for the party or getting together for lunch. Simple, to the point nothing special about them other than they were all from her.

My thumbs moved like lightning.

I'm sorry for whatever I did to upset you. I think I know what it was, and it was uncalled for. I'd really like to get together with you soon, just to talk or plan the party. That's it. Give me one last chance.

Hours passed. I lay awake in my temporary room. Holly's toys were all packed away in boxes, and the glow of her fish tank gave me just enough light that it made my mind buzz. Hours passed with no answer from Ophelia.

Chapter Sixteen

-Ophelia-

*H*ell *no.* I thought for the eightieth time since reading Clay's text a week ago.

Under no circumstances would I give him one more chance. I purposefully kept my distance, avoiding his name on my phone completely. The night at the Piano Bar had caused too many emotions, ones that I wasn't ready to accept just yet. I had to force myself to shut those away, be *me* again. I immersed myself in work, getting Madeline's dress ready for a fitting, helping Carter with Instagram, and designing more and more clothes for JoAnn. People would see what I would want them to see. I had done it once; I could do it again.

Remember, I told myself over and over again these past weeks, *he proposed to you and left you the first chance he could. He's. Not. Worth. It.*

That's right. No man was worth it.

So why, even though I was mad and hurt, did I still catch those small flutters whenever I thought about him? Which, I'll admit was more than I liked.

I shook away the thoughts and focused on the ivory fabric in front of me. Madeline stood on the pedestal as I made a small detail to the dress per her request. I was concentrating, silent as I focused on the train, making it a little longer, adding more to the under layer to fill it out. I was in the zone—semi in the zone. Clay's name would appear in the lace, and every time I reached for my pin cushion, I wished he were there holding it. I would scoff and then return to the dress, emotions not relevant.

"You doing okay down there?" Madeline asked, breaking the silence.

"Yup." I popped the *P*.

"Doesn't seem like it. In fact, you've been off for a while now. Wanna talk?"

"Nope." I popped the *P* again.

"Oh, ok." Madeline moved slightly, bringing all the fabric with her.

"Maddy." I wrapped my hand around her leg and pulled her back. "I need you here."

"Oh, I'm here," she mumbled. "I'm here for whatever you need. Designing wise, book recommendations. . . I have a lot of second chance romances that will make you swoon."

"Madeline."

"Milo and I would be 'friends to lovers.' On Instagram they always talk about these tropes and what you would be if you were a book trope. People on there think my love story is fake. They say it's not true and that I made it all up," she rambled.

Pausing to let Carter take a photo, I raised my eyes at her. "You're comparing your love life to a book trope?"

She shrugged a shoulder. "I mean, why not?"

"And you're friends to lovers?" I stood and walked in front of her, folding my arms over my chest. I saw Carter behind her taking a look at his camera before looking back up at me, clearly annoyed I stepped out of frame.

"And you would be second chance."

"Madeline, life is not a book."

She gave me a smirk. "It could be if you wanted it to be. I even had a small grand gesture with mine. Going to him, even though I was right in the middle of something. . ."

"My show," I added.

"You told me to go," she added hastily, "but I went to him and told him everything. And look at us now. He even proposed in a bookstore."

"I remember. He told me he was going to do that."

Madeline blushed. "It was perfect."

I heaved a sigh and looked at my friend. "Clay proposed to me in bed. We were just lying next to each other, nose to nose. He just put his hand on my chin and said he couldn't see his life without me. And then he asked me to marry him."

"Phe. . ." Madeline sighed.

I blinked. "Well, a week later, he dumped me."

"But he's here now."

"Lying to me. He still hasn't told me anything about his job or how he's living. He's closed off and a jerk, quite frankly."

"He's not a jerk. he's just—"

"Just what?" I snapped. "I'm sorry, Maddy. But I am not his second chance. He's not mine. I'll text him, and we will plan the party, and I will be polite and cordial for the wedding, but afterwards, I'm going back to New York and he can just watch me flourish from here."

"Phe, that was a bit harsh, don't you think?" Madeline's voice lowered. "I get he upset you. I saw how excited you were to go out with him that night. Even though you claimed it was just for the wedding, I could tell there was something in your eyes. Then you left and came back a totally different person and have been 'closed off'"—she air quoted—"ever since. You told me you showed only what you wanted us to see, and I'm pretty sure that's what you're doing now."

I wiggled my foot on the floor, moving my body. Biting my lip, I took in her words. Madeline was never this blunt with me. It was always the other way around. I furrowed my brow and let the words sit, stew for a moment, before I answered her, and I could see in her expression that she was willing to give me all the time in the world. I had to be open and honest, even if I didn't want to be.

Dropping my arms to my side, I spoke. "He gave me a look after dancing with Jamie. One that said he was falling for me. One that scared me shitless. I don't have time for this 'second chance romance' you are saying we are. Party planning? Yes. Designing clothing for a store I'm about to open? Sure. Being open to the possibility of Clay and I being friends again? Fine. . . but no romance. I need to ignore these feelings, these stupid butterflies, and focus on what's really important."

"You're important, Phe, and those little feelings and flutters are there for a reason. Don't ignore them."

I exhaled, my shoulders slumping. "If I text him back, will you drop it?"

A smile grew on her lips. "Don't hide anymore. I want to know what's going on through that head of yours, and yes, I'll drop it if you text him back. Doesn't have to be right now." She raised her hands in surrender. "He needs you. I know he does. Even just as a friend."

I gave her a single nod and then walked back to the train, bending down to adjust the pins one more time.

"I know he does," I said softly. "I'll text him."

I stuck a pin in the train, connecting the two pieces of thin satin. Shifting my mind, I sat on my legs and placed my hands between my thighs.

"If you and Milo are 'friends to lovers,' and you're saying Clay and I are 'second chance,' what does that make Jamie?"

Madeline let out a long breath, "Ooh, I'm not sure on that one, but, man, that girl needs a good romance. There are so many tropes to choose from."

Chapter Seventeen

-Clay-

What's the worst that could happen? I took a deep breath, asking myself the simple question that had been ringing in my head since parking Milo's truck in the parking garage. *The worst that will happen is they will tell you no. Go up there, pretend like you are the most valuable person on the face of the planet, and land that damn job.*

I had sent out several resumes and job applications over the last couple of weeks, and a few called back. Only one set up an interview. I had pulled out my best suit, ironed and pressed it—by myself, thank you very much—and shined my shoes. I flipped down the visor to give myself a quick look over before I grabbed my phone and Milo's key fob, shoving them both in the inside pocket of my suit.

Stepping out of the truck, my hands went back to the familiar motion of buttoning up my suit, slipping a hand in my pants pocket. I took another deep breath, looked down to make sure my shoes were still shiny, and then took the first few steps to the building's entrance.

I'll admit, I looked good. I channeled Seattle Clay with all my willpower, pulling myself out of the trenches for the first time in months, ready to conquer the world. They'd be idiots not to hire me with how I looked. *Fake it till you make it, right?*

The only interview I had been able to secure was a low-entry accounting position at a law firm in Portland, a start-up that had a low budget and even lower expectations. They wanted employees, and I wanted—needed—a job. Hopefully, they would bypass the background check. I didn't need that mark hanging over me forever. I had my portfolio with my college degree, internship, and work at Jackson and Rye nestled inside of it. I had all the experience they would want.

The receptionist gave me a visitor's badge and told me to take the elevator to level five. Level five? My office was on the 33rd floor with Jackson and Rye, with glass walls and a view of the city. I always felt closer to the top, like my time was coming. In this world, the higher you worked in the building, the more important you were, right? And now, I was only worth a five. But I took the badge with a smile and pressed that five circle with so much confidence. Milo would be proud.

The waiting room was cushy, and two other men sat out there with me. Younger than myself. They looked fresh out of college and nervous. I inhaled, pulled my phone from my pocket, and opened Instagram.

Not that I had meant it to, but it was becoming a habit to check Ophelia's feed every day. Carter was working wonders with the photos, and Ophelia's captions and hashtags were gaining her followers by the minute. The latest post was Ophelia herself, posing with a large smile, one that could be seen across the room, holding fabrics up, showcasing them next to the design that they were for. She looked happy, but her eyes told a different story. It was in the photos of the wedding gown where she really shined. Madeline's face was hidden in most of the photos, close ups of the design on the loose lace.

Each photo was stunning, but when Ophelia was in them, it was even more so.

Locking my screen, I looked around the room. It had been two weeks since the night at the Piano Bar, and Ophelia had only texted me once. She didn't acknowledge my text I had sent her, a simple *we'll talk soon* was all I got in return. She still needed space. I had written a few drafts since then but had deleted them all, never to be seen again. I wasn't sure what I could say to make it better, if there was even anything at all that could make the last moments between us fade away into nothing.

Sighing, I dropped my hands between my legs.

That was going to be harder than it should be.

"Mr. Nolan?"

I turned at the sound of my name. A blonde stood at the doorway, her eyes on us three men sitting. I stood, tucking my phone back in my pocket and buttoning up my suit, giving her a slight smile. She smiled back.

"This way."

The office was small, cubicles lined the space with the employees staring at the computer screen. Phones rang off in the distance, and the clicking of the keyboard hit my ears. The sounds were all familiar, ones I had heard every single day until I got my own office. I exhaled through my lips. *You'll have that again.*

"Mr. Nolan, meet Mrs. Regina Karrs, she'll be conducting your interview today. Can I get you anything?" the blonde asked, keeping her body stiff as she introduced me.

I gave her a sly smile. *Remember, you're worth a million bucks.*

"No, thank you." She smiled back at me and turned to leave the room. I focused my attention on the older brunette on the other side of the conference room table. She wore an elegant suit, her hair falling from behind her ears, showing off massive pearl earrings.

"Mrs. Karrs, it's a pleasure to meet you." I stepped forward and held out my hand.

Mrs. Karrs stood, gripping my hand to shake it. It was firm, not what I was expecting, but strong, nonetheless. She was *business*.

"The pleasure is all mine, Mr. Nolan." —she waved to the chair opposite her, sitting once again. —"Please, have a seat."

Unbuttoning my suit, I sat. I hadn't been to an interview since right after college, and suddenly, I was scared. I had no idea if I should cross my legs or lean forward to make eye contact. So, much like the blonde that escorted me, I stayed stiff as a board.

"Tell me a little about you, Mr. Nolan. I see you've only worked for one firm since graduation?" she asked, holding up a piece of paper to read it. I assumed it was my resume.

"That's correct. I got the job with Jackson and Rye almost directly out of college and worked my way to the top of their accounting team." I smirked. I was always proud of my work ethics. I was never afraid to boast about it.

"And why did you leave them?" Mrs. Karrs asked, furrowing her brow.

"I relocated. My best friend is getting married, and I wanted to return home to Portland." *Fake it 'til you make it, Clayton. Fake it 'til you make it.*

"You've been unemployed for a long time it seems. Taking a bit of a sabbatical?" Mrs. Karrs set my resume down and laced her fingers together, resting her chin on top of her hands.

I heaved a sigh and smirked. "No, ma'am. I wanted to settle in Portland before securing a job."

She narrowed her eyes and nodded, giving me a slight hum. "Do you have family here?"

"My parents, yes. I grew up here." I smiled.

"Me too. We went to the same University, but that's not at all surprising." She chuckled and leaned back into her chair. "Portland is amazing."

I nodded back to her, giving her what I hoped was a sincere smile. "It really is. I'm glad to be back, honestly. Even though it's a large city, it's less hustle and bustle than Seattle was."

"Did you like Seattle? I've never been."

"Oh, it—" I paused, remembering Seattle in all its glory in my mind. If she wanted the honest answer, it was that I loved Seattle. I loved everything about it. The only thing it was missing was. . . in New York. "It was great for that season of my life, but now it's time to move and grow in other areas."

She hummed. "Tell me, Mr. Nolan. If you could redo anything in your career, what would it be?"

I raised my eyebrows. *Getting blamed for embezzlement and losing everything I had, only making the regret of not going to New York worse.*

"Honestly, ma'am." I sighed. "I loved my career with Jackson and Rye. I learned a lot and worked my way through the ranks. I don't think I would change a single thing about my career as an accountant so far. I love numbers and understanding them is what I do, and I'm good at it."

"Even this embezzlement charge?"

Shit.

"I can explain that." I leaned forward, feeling my soul leave my body.

"Mr. Nolan, we are a small practice. My partner and I just started the company three months ago, and we are still in the red. We are gaining clients every day, and we are focusing on us as a whole. During this time, we have found our finances somewhat harder to manage than we expected, so you could imagine our shock when Jackson and Rye's head accountant applied for a job." She placed her hands on her stomach and leaned back into her seat. I had no words, but thankfully she did. "You were all over the news, Mr. Nolan. You almost went to trial, if you hadn't paid them off. So please, I'd love to hear you explain it."

"It was a team member, right under my nose. Since I was in charge of him and his work, his actions fell on me, even though they could never find the exact person. I paid them a settlement so I could eventually find another career. I didn't want it to be on my record forever," I said honestly.

"You do realize that paying a settlement makes it look like you're guilty, right?"

"I do now. I never really thought of it that way before."

Mrs. Karrs hummed again, her eyes giving me a complete once over before she sat back up in her chair. "Mr. Nolan, I think you understand why I can't offer you this job right off the table."

I broke her eye contact, looking down at my shoes.

"But. . ."

I looked back up at her.

"I am interested in you. I did something I normally wouldn't do when I saw your name appear on my list. I contacted your lawyer."

"Excuse me? Isn't that illegal?"

"It's a morally gray area." She waved her palm over the table. "But I wanted to know what he thought of you. Let's call it a character reference."

"He's not listed on my resume," I argued.

"Mr. Nolan, your face was plastered all over CNN, MSN and FoxNews. Everyone knows who you are, and it wasn't hard to figure out who your lawyer was. So, I called him."

I heaved a sigh, suddenly wishing I had asked the blonde to bring me a bottle of water. "Okay. . . and?" I grumbled.

"He's impressed by you. And not just in the 'I'm the lawyer and he's my client, so I have to talk good about him' way. In the real sense. He told me he was trying to work a case with Jackson and Rye to clear your name."

My eyes hit hers like arrows. I was dumbfounded. Is this what he was talking about? "I didn't. . ."

"I know, he told me he hadn't shared specifics with you, but it's been almost a year since the settlement and he thinks he can strike this from your record, making you a free man again."

"I'm sorry, but how is my lawyer sharing this information with you legal?" I asked again, screwing my face in a way that I didn't even think was possible.

"Why don't you let me worry about what's legal, and what's not?" Mrs. Karrs laughed. "Do you want this job or not, Mr. Nolan?"

"Yes," I said quicker than I could think to answer.

"I'm interested in you, but I can't do anything unless this embezzlement charge is gone, do you understand?"

I nodded, ever so slightly.

"Good luck, Mr. Nolan. If and when this is ever erased, reach out to me and the job is yours." Mrs. Karrs crossed her legs and leaned back into her chair once again. For just being a start-up law firm, this woman was no joke. "Kelly can show you out." She nodded.

I cleared my throat and stood, noticing the blonde, Kelly, appear back in the doorway.

"We'll be in touch, Mr. Nolan," Mrs. Karrs called as I left the office.

What in the actual hell?

Never in a million years have I written an email as fast as I did when I got back to Milo's apartment.

I need you to explain to me what you're up to. Mrs. Karrs just informed me that she had a conversation with you. You really think you can clear this? I need to know what is going on.

I slammed the laptop closed as soon as it sent and stared at the kitchen in front of me. If this could be gone, if what she said was true, I could do anything. I could even. . .

My brain began to race at a million miles an hour. I jumped from working at their small law firm to opening my own accounting business. . .

In New York.

"Nope, don't go there, Clayton," I grumbled to myself.

"Don't go where?" Milo's voice came from the front door, as he walked through with Elliot.

I watched them both. With my mind going faster than the speed of sound, I hadn't heard the door open.

I sighed. "Nowhere."

"Oh, good, 'cause we are having a guys' night." Elliot smiled, placing a six pack on the counter.

"No offense but. . ." I began.

"Oh, total offense. This is my only night off this week, and there's a game to be played. I need to relive my teenage years by beating your asses at *Call of Duty*," Elliot said, grabbing his first beer from the case.

Milo shrugged a shoulder as his phone rang from his pocket.

"No," Elliot shouted. "No girls."

"It's Holly." Milo glared at him.

"Okay fine," Elliot mumbled. "Tell her we say hi."

Milo rolled his eyes, stepping into his bedroom to take the call from his daughter.

"How much have you had to drink already?" I asked Elliot.

"None. Truth be told, I'm not much of a drinker, but this seemed fitting."

"Getting drunk and playing *Call of Duty*?"

"Just being normal for once," he mumbled.

"Normal?" I leaned on the counter, crossing my arms, my tie folding up on the counter.

"When you own a company and try to be a rockstar at the same time, life can get a little overwhelming."

I shrugged. "So pick one."

Elliot pointed at me and hummed. "Wish I could, my friend. Wish. I. Could."

Elliot left the kitchen and fell onto the couch, grabbing the Xbox remote that had been sitting on the coffee table. The man looked stressed, not the same fun Elliot I saw performing on stage. He had a weight behind his eyes. How could he turn it off and on so easily? Was it the job that took it out of him or the performing?

It couldn't be the singing. He was so carefree and alive on the stage. It had to be the job.

"How's your job search going?" he asked, taking a drink of his beer before turning to me.

"Slow, I had an interview today, but I don't think anything will come of it."

"You know I may have—"

"Okay, sorry." Milo burst back in the room, placing his phone on the peninsula. "Holly had to tell me all about the coast today. She said she's building quite the magnet collection for Madeline. What are we playing?"

"*Black Ops,*" Elliot answered, his train of thought ending once Milo sat next to him. "Clay just told me I had to pick my job or my singing career."

"Singing, right? You've always wanted to be a performer." Milo started the game, relaxing into the conversation as if he had been there the entire time.

Elliot grumbled, "Yeah, but you know. . . family."

"It can't be too hard to choose, right? You are more alive on that stage than anything. Wouldn't your family see that?" I asked, never taking my eyes off the screen as we went through the beginning motions.

"Easier said than done, my friend. Have you ever had a knot in your shoulder, one that no matter what, you couldn't get rid of? I have one, always when I'm at the office. It's not that I hate being there. But it's become more stressful over the past couple of years, and being on stage takes that away for a moment." Elliot rolled his head from side to side. "But the family doesn't feel that knot. . ."

I reached my hand up to the spot on my neck, almost out of instinct. It always used to be there, its presence known, day in and day out, as I sat at my desk. I would twist my neck and roll my shoulders, but it would never ever fade. I had even made a note to get a massage, which never came, thanks to a lawsuit. But now, here in Portland, the knot had slowly faded, becoming less and less in the last few weeks. I had told Elliot to pick, yet, here I was, still terrified to pick for myself.

The small steps I was taking to better my life were working for sure, but there was one thing that made me feel as happy as I knew Elliot did when he was singing. One thing that I had been missing.

"Excuse me," I mumbled, putting the controller on the coffee table and standing.

"We just started the round," Elliot said loudly as I made my way to my bedroom.

"I'll be right back," I shouted before I pulled my phone from my pocket.

I needed to pick.

Clay: Hey, you busy?

That could have been better but. . . what was my new motto? Baby steps?

To my surprise, Ophelia responded. *Hi, no, just leaving the studio.*

Clay: Are you going to be at your studio tomorrow? I'd love to see you.

Baby steps also included leaps of faith sometimes.

I stared, not expecting an answer, knowing I came on too strong but as if it were fate, one came.

Ophelia: Yeah, I'll be there all day. Bring coffee.

I smiled, locking my phone and tossing it on the bed before going back to join the guys.

Chapter Eighteen

-Ophelia-

JoAnn,

Being here in Portland has put a lot in perspective for me and I needed to ask you a question regarding the boutique. I'm wanting to do gowns and only gowns, and I'm wondering if this would be something that would interest you. Evening gowns, wedding gowns, gowns you would see on the red carpet. I have attached a few scans of some drawings. These are mainly wedding gowns, but I do have multiple designs in mind for dresses, better than what you saw in Portland last year. Let me know what you think.

Ophelia.

I ran my fingers over the keyboard quickly glancing at the time on the bottom of the screen. Jamie would be here soon for me to work on her dress, and Clay was supposed to show up with coffee

in hand. He never set a time. He just told me he'd "love to see me."
And even though I knew nothing would come of it, I wanted to see
him too.

You're just being polite. No harm could come from a
friendship, I told myself, trying to refocus my mind. Remember,
he's not worth the heartache. He's not worth it. No man is.

But then. . . I'd love to see you.

I needed to calm these little flutters. Push them out. Ignore
them. Work.

First and foremost, this email needed to be sent. I couldn't get
into the headspace to design another seasonal line. I wanted to
design gowns, and I knew the only way to do that would be to pull
this email out of the drafts folder and send it on its way. What's the
worst that could happen? She would say no.

The studio door creaked open, and I said a quick prayer it was
Clay, before looking up only to be greeted by Jamie. She had a skip
in her steps and a smile beaming at me as she waved. I smiled back
and looked down the email one last time, hitting the save button
before leaving the computer open on the desk.

"Wanna know what the best part about working for the bride
is?" She chuckled. "You get the morning off to get started on the
dress for her wedding, and no one asks questions."

"Madeline has that authority?" I asked, a little shocked.

"Hygienist extraordinaire." Jamie put her hands on her hips
and cocked her body to the side, giving me the cheesiest grin.

I let out a chuckle and stood, pushing myself off the desk and
going to pull Jamie in next to me. She bumped my hip with hers,
and I led her over to the design table. I laid out so many drawings,
any kind of dress you could imagine for a bridesmaid. I knew that
whatever Jamie picked, I would simply make two. Even though
Madeline said we could choose our own dress style, I knew that
deep down, she would want us to match.

"You have a short sleeve, halter top and sleeveless. Knee
length, three quarter, and long skirts. . . there's even a wrap-around
design there. I'm thinking chiffon fabric for our dresses. It will

match Madeline's the best. So you, my dear, pick a design, and then we will go to colors." I waved my hand in front of the table as Jamie pulled away from me, leaning down into the drawings to study them.

"You drew all these?" She looked up, almost as if she was stunned.

I chuckled and nodded. "Well, yeah, it's my job. You knew that."

"I'm not sure what I was expecting when you said you designed clothes. All I know is teeth and dentures." Jamie shrugged. "These are beautiful."

I let out a soft breath and smiled. "Thank you. I really love it."

"Clay told me you were talented, but. . . these are next level, Phe." She put down the drawing to pick up another.

"Clay?" I asked. "You two hit it off then, I take it?" I forced a smile.

Jamie chuckled in her throat. "Oh no, he's still very much in love with you."

"Why does everyone say that?" I rolled my eyes. In the back of my mind, I knew he was. Hell, I was dealing with some emotions there, my mind still reeling with simple comments he had made and glances he had given me. But I was determined to force them out. *He's not worth it.*

"Because it's true. He told me when we danced. He was very polite." Jamie pointed to a drawing, "I love this one."

My attention span was glued on her though, not even paying attention to the design. "He told you?"

"Ophelia, are you that blind to it? He danced with me to be polite and then gracefully shot me down. His exact words were, 'Not to be rude, but I'm still madly in love with someone else. She may not know it or love me back, but she's all I can think about.'" Jamie tilted her head and raised her eyebrows at me, her lips curling slighting in the corners, a sly smile forming. "He loves you."

The door to the studio opened, breaking my trance as I looked up to see Clay, dressed casually in jeans and t-shirt with his hair slightly disheveled, a smile on his face and two coffees in his hands. Jamie turned, glancing back at me when she saw him walking toward us.

"Oh, hey, Jamie," Clay said as he approached. "Sorry, if I'd known you would have been here, I would have brought you a coffee. Your Americano." He smiled, handing me my paper cup.

I smiled slightly, taking the cup, purposefully touching his fingers.

Stop it. . .

"Oh, no worries. Thank you though. I won't be here long, just enough time to pick a dress and. . . and what, Phe?" Jamie turned to me.

I blinked and brought my cup to my lips, hoping it was hiding the smile that was trying to escape since Clay had entered the room.

Get. A. Grip.

"Well, you're my model, so I need to take some measurements as soon as you pick a design. Carter was here to help with Madeline's measurements, but since it's his day off and Clay's here, he can input them. Can you?" I turned back to Clay, who gave me a crooked smile and nodded, a piece of brown hair falling in his eyes.

"I'd be happy to," he said softly.

"Great." I spun back to Jamie, suddenly in my work mode. "You said you loved a style?"

She nodded and watched Clay behind me. "I really like this one." She lifted an A-line, scoop neck dress with a knee-length, multi-layered skirt. Simple and easy to make.

"Perfect. Color?"

"What's the worst color a bridesmaid could wear?"

"Teal." Clay spoke loud enough to get our attention. He had moved over to the desk, standing behind my computer with a post-it note and pen in his hand, ready to take the numbers.

Jamie let out a laugh. "I don't think Madeline's color is teal."

I laughed and shook my head. "She doesn't have a specific color, but I'll text her. Let's get your measurements so you can get back to work."

"Take. Your. Time." Jamie smiled.

The entire time Jamie was there, which wasn't any longer than an hour, Clay hung in the background, not once asking to repeat a number. But then again, he was a numbers guy. I remember in college when we would study together, his textbooks were full of equations that I couldn't understand, and mine was doodles on a pad of paper. He would be so focused on those numbers almost nothing could bother him, whereas one small distraction would take my attention from the art in front of me onto something else, and that something else was usually trying to distract Clay. I was normally ninety-five percent effective.

I would always take his pencil away from him, placing it behind my ear. That always made him bite his bottom lip. His eyes followed my every movement, his hands would always find my hips as I crawled on top of him, his books falling to the side. I would run my fingers through his hair, kiss his neck, his collar bone, his lips. Anywhere I could. It was magnetic the way we fit together, even back then. I could feel his skin pulse against my fingertips, even now as I tried my hardest to focus on that number on the measuring tape.

"Ophelia." Clay's deep voice rang across the room. I stopped, dropped the measuring tape, and looked at him. He had a sly smile, only one corner of his lips raised. "I don't think Jamie's arm span is ninety-five inches."

I blinked and looked at the measure tape. "Oh, no. . ."

Jamie laughed and shook her head, side eyeing me as I gave Clay the correct number.

"You good?" she whispered.

"Shh. . . I need to concentrate."

Jamie left with a quick hug and smile on her face, leaving me and Clay alone in my small studio. Running my hands along my hips, I made my way over to Clay. He peeled off the post-it note and stuck it to my computer.

"Well, that was fun." He smiled. "If you need help with my chicken scratch, just ask me. I can translate."

I scoffed. "Yeah, right. I think Carter was ready to murder me with Madeline's, and his handwriting was worse than yours," I said, peeling the sticky from the computer screen. He had acronyms for the type of measurement and then a small number next to it. It was chicken scratch, for sure.

"I'm assuming that Madeline's dress had a lot more measurements than that." Clay scooted out the chair at the desk and sat down, lifting his arms behind his head to lean back. "Being a wedding dress."

"True, but Madeline's dress is simple too. There were a lot more difficult designs, but the one she loved has simple lace, as you can see." I held out my hands to Madeline's dress on the mannequin. It had been pieced together and sewn, waiting for Madeline to come to a fitting.

"What happened to the rest of your designs?" he asked.

"I still have them. I keep all my designs, whether they get made or not. All my drawings and sketches are held there," —I pointed behind him—"in my portfolio."

"And this email?" he nodded toward the computer, where I had completely forgotten I had JoAnn's email still open.

I narrowed my eyes at him. "You read my email?" I asked, folding my arms.

"I didn't mean to." He lowered his arms and leaned forward, resting his elbows on his legs, his eyes still fixed on me. "But when I came to get the post-it note, it was blaring me in the face."

"You read my email." I should be angry over the invasion of my privacy, but for some reason, I wasn't. Perhaps, him seeing it would be the final push I would need to actually send it. It had been a draft in my inbox for days now. This could have been a good thing. "Do you think I should send it?"

He nodded, not even a hint of hesitation. "If it's what you really want, which I know it is, then you should hit send."

His eyes searched mine as he stood from the chair, taking just a few steps toward me, shoving his hands in his pockets.

"A lot has happened to me recently. . ." he began.

I inhaled. Was he about to tell me everything? No more pretending that he was a hot shot in Seattle still?

"And I've had to try to piece my life together. Last night, Elliot said something that gave me a little push, and once I texted you, things seemed to get clearer. I think as soon as you hit 'send,' things will get clearer for you too."

I bit my bottom lip. "What, um. . ." I coughed. "What do you mean, you tried to piece your life together?"

Open up to me, Clay. . .

"Stupid things—working remotely, breaking up with Rebecca. You know, things that seem huge at the time, but in the long run, don't matter. Things that would fog my brain, seemingly important, but not. I'm just now finding those really important things." He was closer to me now, his eyes heavy on mine. "So, are you going to hit send and be Ophelia Fuller, Wedding Gown Designer, next big hit on Say Yes to the Dress?"

I exhaled and narrowed my eyes at him. "I've read it about a million times. . ."

"Do you want me to hit send?" he asked, shrugging and tilting his head.

I looked behind him at my computer and then met his eyes once more and, ever so softly, nodded.

His smile grew as he turned his back to me, basically ran to my computer and leaned his palms on the desk. "Ready?"

I looked at him, a buzz in my body as I watched him there. Did he remember this is how my application got sent into Harold Martin all those years ago? I had it written and ready to go, and he was my final push to actually apply. Then when I got the job, he cheered and lifted me off the floor, kissed me and told me how proud he was of me.

With that memory clear in my mind, I nodded.

His smile grew, and then his fingers were on the mouse pad. I heard a faint click, and his arms went up in the air.

"Done."

I laughed, bending over before I ran toward him. He stepped to the side and welcomed my energy by lifting me off the ground. I wrapped my arms around him and laughed. He held onto me, the same feeling I remember from before. Nothing had changed. He was still Clay. *My Clay.*

I rested my hands on his shoulders, pulling myself up to look at him. His smile was still there, and his eyes were beaming. He was just as happy as I was, all over an email. I bit the inside of my lip and fought the urge to kiss him. I noticed his eyes look quickly at my lips before focusing once again on my eyes.

"You did it. Now we wait for the answer, and when you get the response you deserve," he said softly, "we'll celebrate."

"Celebrate," I repeated, whispering as my eyes searched his. I cleared my throat, suddenly remembering I was at least a foot off the ground. Clay was over six feet, and I was barely over five. With his arms firmly around my waist, I was basically flying.

"Phe," he said, a sweet hum escaping his lips. "I'm sorry, for that night. . . at the Piano Bar."

I swallowed, shaking my head quickly. "Nothing to be sorry about, nothing at all. I may have overreacted, and I'm sorry for pushing you away," I muttered back, stopping myself before I became even more of an open book.

His eyes kept mine, the brown haze all too familiar. I coughed, looking down to the ground, before muttering, "You can, uh, put me down now."

Clay grinned again, a sly grin this time, not his full smile. "Yeah." He gently lowered me to the ground, but kept me in his arms, a place, at the moment, I was happy to stay in.

Maybe he is worth it.

Chapter Nineteen

-Clay-

I sat quietly as Ophelia finished for the day. I was there if she needed a measurement read aloud and when she got a jam in her sewing machine, I was there to hold the lace as she gently pulled it through. I was there when she dropped the most important bead, and we both got on all fours trying to find it. I was there for every smile, for every laugh and nose scrunch she made as she carefully pieced the dress together. And at the end of the day, she gave me a hug.

I could still feel the tingles in my arms from holding her off the ground, not wanting to put her down, but to pull her closer instead, press my lips against hers and tell her every detail about the last ten years without her. That, even though I pretended to be happy, I never was, and now that she was in my life again, I was starting to see the brightness in each day. With her in my arms once more, that same urge came back. Thankfully, before I could word vomit everywhere, Ophelia spoke first.

"Madeline's coming tomorrow to do her first official fitting. If you promise to keep your phone away, you can join us." Ophelia smiled, pulling out of my arms. "Just remember. . ."

"I know, I know." I chuckled, keeping my fingers on her skin just a little longer than I meant to. "Milo can't know a thing. Madeline won't mind me being here?"

"I mean, do you have anything better to do?" She raised an eyebrow and slung her bag over her shoulder. "Besides data entry?" she added.

I narrowed my eyes. "I can push my meetings back." I smiled. "Carter will be here, I'm assuming."

She flung her head back and groaned. "Don't remind me."

"You enjoy it." I smiled, following her out of the studio. She pulled her keys from her bag and grabbed the handle.

"Maybe just a little bit." With a smile, she closed the door.

I made it back to Milo's apartment, opening the door and expecting him on the couch, but looking into a dark and empty apartment made me groan. I still wasn't used to being alone here. Even though he was home more since Ophelia was at Madeline's, he still spent his free time with her. I would say that seven out of ten times I would come home to a dark apartment, waiting for Milo to come keep me company. The other night with Elliot was interesting; it reminded me that maybe being alone wasn't as fantastic as I thought it was.

I pulled out my phone, thought about texting Milo, but decided against it. Reaching for my laptop instead, I opened my email to see a return from my lawyer, the subject line catching my attention. *Possible appeal J&R urgent.*

Clayton -

Does the name Brian Walker mean anything to you? It's come to our attention he may be behind the embezzlement, and if we can prove this, we can appeal your case. Please provide a character reference on Mr. Walker.

Brian Walker? Brian was one of my top team members. Give that man a task and he had it done with no questions asked. He was a great team lead and friend. It couldn't have been him, right?

I pulled out my phone and pulled up his contact. It had been months since I've spoken to him, would he even have my number still? I shook my head. At this point it didn't matter who did and who didn't have a part in it. Even though Mrs. Karrs said if my name got cleared I would have a job again, not just data entry, it just didn't matter.

I set my phone down and hit reply, typing out a quick email. . .

He was always driven and would do any task accurately. I never was worried about him or his work ethic. I'm not sure he would even be capable of embezzlement. I even considered him a friend while living in Seattle. Nice, settled, someone I trusted and could confide in if needed. What's the chance this could get appealed and when?

Just as I was about to hit send, my phone buzzed beside me. I flipped it over and saw Ophelia's name. I didn't even think twice.

"Phe?"

"Clay, 9-1-1." Her voice was frantic. I glanced at the clock on the microwave. It has only been forty minutes since we'd left the studio. What could have been so urgent? "I don't have the fabric for Jamie's dress."

"It's not at the studio?" I asked, a smile on my lips. My stomach fluttered, knowing that she called me to fret over fabrics. She was stressed, and I was the person that came to her mind.

"No, I knew I was going to do chiffon, but when Madeline gave us maroon as a color, I swear I had some! Madeline's out with Milo. Could you take me to the store? Please, I'm begging you."

I laughed. "No need to beg." I closed my laptop and stood, grabbing my Tesla fob and house key. "I'm on my way."

She sighed in relief. "I need to Google a fabric store and just pray they have chiffon."

"I'm praying. . ."

And with that, I was out the door, speeding my way—carefully—to Madeline's house. I parked on the street and almost jumped from the Tesla, stopping myself from skipping to the door when Ophelia opened the door and ran past me to the car.

"Come on!" she shouted, waving her hand toward me as she opened the passenger door. "They close at eight!"

I laughed and slowly walked back around the car. Her eyes were locked on me the entire time. I slid in the seat and looked over at her, giving her a grin. Her brown eyes were wide, and her jaw was slightly dropped.

"Go!"

"Where am I going?"

She waved her phone at me. "I have the address pulled up. Does your fancy Tesla hook up via Bluetooth?"

"She sure does. Show me the way." The Tesla started with a hum, and the tension in Ophelia's shoulders drained as we drove down the road.

The last time I was in a fabric store was during a final for Ophelia. She had to make a formal dress and needed to gather all her supplies. I was lost, but thankfully, Ophelia seemed to know exactly where she was going, heading straight to the bolts of thousands of fabrics that sat on the shelves. She ran her hands along all the different shades of maroon, as if she were studying them.

"How many different shades of maroon are there?" I asked, taking in everything in front of me,

"You'd be surprised. Jamie will pull it off, but this is not really my color." She sighed.

I wanted to say *you could pull off any color,* but I kept my mouth shut. I looked over at her from the corner of my eye, watching as her eyebrows moved with concentration as her fingers felt the fabrics between them. I smirked, loving each and every expression that her face provided.

"I like this one." She pulled a bolt out. "What do you think?" She held it up so the red hit the chestnut shade of her neck.

I raised my eyebrows and took a deep breath. This woman was beautiful in every way. Nothing could compare to her, and she was asking me what I thought. I exhaled.

"Phe, you can wear anything and still be beautiful."

She dropped the bolt and glared at me. "That's so cliché."

"It's true though. You say Jamie can pull off any color, but in reality, you can. Hell, wear that diarrhea green color down there, and you'd be prettier than Madeline." I pointed to a fabric near the end of the row. She turned to it and quickly turned her head back to me, her golden hoop earrings hitting her cheek.

"You mean *pickle?*"

"*That* color is called *pickle*?" I widened my eyes.

"Yes, colors are not named after disgusting things. They are named after foods or flowers or things you would find in nature. Asparagus, Jungle, Ruby, Rose—that kind of thing. Not *diarrhea green*." She twisted her lips, which made me smirk. "Back to the topic on hand. This color, on me. Yes. . . or no?"

Giving me a questioning look, her eyebrows higher than I had ever seen them, she raised the maroon to her skin again. I sighed and smiled. "Yes, absolutely, you would look stunning in that color."

Ophelia gave a small laugh and pulled the entire bolt off the shelf. "I hope they have more," she said as she passed me the roll.

I looked at the bolt. All I could see was a very large rectangle of fabric wrapped around a piece of cardboard. How did this become a dress? I pinched my brow as I looked back at Ophelia. She was hunched over, trying to find another bolt of the same shade.

"How do you make a dress out of this?" I muttered.

Ophelia looked up at me, craning her neck. "What?"

"How do you make a dress from this?" I asked again.

"Clayton." She stood and placed her hands on top of the ream in my arms. "You take measurements, and then you cut the fabric, and then you piece it together on a mannequin, and then you—"

"Okay, I get it." I stopped her.

She pursed her lips together, a corner lifting in a sly grin, before returning to the rows of fabric. "It's not that hard."

"To me it is. Just like how numbers aren't your thing."

"Numbers are terrible," she corrected.

"Nah, they're easy." I fumbled with the bolt in my hands. "This though."

"Is just math in a different way. I deal with more numbers than you think." She patted my shoulder and walked behind me. "I need to find someone to see if they have more of this color, and while I'm here, I should grab a few things."

I turned to follow her. She was determined, heading to the different aisles, grabbing more pins, another pin cushion, and some more scissors. "Don't you have a million scissors at the studio?"

"Back at your office, what's the one thing you seemed to have a massive amount of at your desk and even though you had a million of them you always seemed to need more?" she asked, not looking at me but at the scissors.

I thought. "Pencils and calculators. I always ended up using my phone."

"Scissors are my pens and calculators."

"Fair enough."

"Why are you using a calculator anyway? You never used one in college."

I shrugged. "Bigger numbers, important numbers, and if you mess up once, it messes the entire firm up. Clients are asking why their invoice is higher, and the big man upstairs is asking why their client owes less than they were quoted. Numbers can get jumbled sometimes when you're stressed too, so calculator."

She picked another pair of scissors and placed them on the ream. "Okay, now I need to find someone. . ." She turned her head up and down the aisles, finally spotting an attendant. "Oh, excuse me!" She waved her hand in the air and chased after them. I chuckled, picturing her in New York, waving after a taxi the same way.

New York hadn't changed her like I thought it may have. She was still the same girl that I fell in love with back in college. She still had her quirks, and her Southern accent came out during certain words. My heart always skipped a beat when she called me Clayton. The drawl that was there, the energy. She was still everything I ever wanted.

Ophelia came up to me and grabbed the bolt from my arms, instead giving my empty hands the scissors and pin cushion. She spoke to the attendant, and the girl nodded, narrowing her eyes as she reached for her scanner.

"We don't have any more, but our location in Gresham does," she said smugly as she looked at the scanner.

Ophelia gasped and looked at her watch. "How many, and when do they close?"

"They close at eight, and they have. . ." She looked at her scanner again. "Four bolts."

"Perfect." She spun her entire body to look at me. "Can we go to Gresham?"

I shrugged and smiled. "Why not? Let's go."

Chapter Twenty

-Ophelia-

Five bolts of ugly maroon fabric were shoved into Clay's Tesla. The dark red stood out against the white interior of his car, and my small bag of supplies grew more once we raced into the Gresham store. We made it with thirty minutes to spare, and yet again, Clay followed me around the aisles. This time, he was pushing the cart of fabric. The cart was so small he had to hunch over to push it, and I had to stop myself from watching for fear that I would giggle.

I never giggled.

Except when it came to Clay.

The moment I was up in his arms earlier, something clicked, and for some reason, I didn't want to hold those pesky giggles in anymore. I still had feelings for him. Sure, Madeline had told me this, and Jamie had told me he still loved me, but after years of heartbreak and moving on, I never wanted to admit it. Now here I was, with him following me around like a puppy in a fabric store, enjoying every second of his company.

I didn't want to be without him.

On our way out of Gresham, he was silent. He watched the road and made sure his speed was constant. I could tell this was his first time driving at night with expired plates, but he was trying. He avoided passing people and even put it in cruise control if he could, but then he started to slow down more, even flicking his hazards on. Was he that nervous to drive with expired plates?

"Well," he groaned as he pulled off to the side of the road, bringing the Tesla to a complete stop. "We are, uh. . . out of charge."

I widened my eyes and looked at the screen in front of us. I didn't notice the red blinking light before. "What?" I asked, with a shock in my voice.

Clay swallowed. "We're out of charge." He leaned back into his seat and grabbed his phone in the middle of the console. "And the nearest charging station is. . ." He pulled up Google, and I waited. "In Portland, twenty minutes away."

"Don't Teslas have a backup charger or something?"

"Some do. I don't."

"And we didn't charge it before we left. . . why?" I asked.

"I knew you needed to get to that store, and I was worried if we charged it, they would close."

I bit my bottom lip. I inhaled sharply. I blinked, ignoring how adorable that was. "Okay, this is not a problem. We will just call a tow truck and get towed to the nearest charging station."

"Um. . ." he muttered, hesitation in his voice. "No, we don't need a tow truck. I'll just call Milo. His truck can tow it." Clay thumbed through his phone again and landed on Milo's name, hitting the call icon before lifting his phone to his ear.

He was scared. I guarantee he was nervous that if we called a tow truck, they would impound his car. No insurance, expired tags. . . Lord knew how much he owed on it. I sat, my hands on my lap while he talked to Milo.

"Okay, yeah, no. . . we can wait. Thanks, man. . . see you soon."
He heaved a sigh as he ended the call. "Well, I have good news and
bad news."

"Bad news first."

"He's in a movie with Mads, but they will be done in about an
hour and half, but good news is, they're coming." Clay looked over
at me and smiled.

I forced a chuckle. "That's great. Mads can approve the color
then." I exhaled and looked from Clay to outside. "So, what do we
do for ninety minutes?"

"Are you hungry? I'm sure there's places to eat. I may have
enough juice to get us to a diner."

"You're willing to try?"

"She's got about five miles left in her. Let's find a diner."

I laughed, a real one this time. "Yeah, okay. At least let's get *her*
off the freeway." I side eyed him as he slowly got back on the
freeway, his hazards blinking the entire time. "Does *she* have a
name?" I asked sarcastically.

"Yes, it's Tessa, so you need to be nice to her."

"Tessa!?" I threw my head back and laughed.

"Don't listen to her, Tessa. . ." Clay hummed as he patted the
dashboard in front of him.

"Oh, please. . ." I grumbled.

Clay chuckled under his breath, a smile on his face that made
my stomach turn.

Tessa barely made it to the diner right off the exit. It wasn't that we
were in the middle of nowhere; Portland to Gresham wasn't a bad
drive, but when there was no way to charge the car, we slowly
putted up to the parking spot. I chuckled. Who'd have thought that
a Tesla would putt toward a building?

Clay turned the car off and plopped his hands on his thighs,
turning to give me the biggest grin.

"See? She made it."

I formed a tight line with my lips, holding back a smile and laugh. "Yeah," I choked. "She made it."

Keeping his eyes on me, a corner of his lips up and his eyes narrow—a cheeky look I had seen plenty of times—he opened his door. His hair flipped to the side, and he turned his torso and climbed out of the car. I followed, closing the door with a click and meeting him in front of the car. Almost as if on instinct, I reached for his hand, and as if his muscle memory took over, he grasped my palm in his. The movement was so smooth, so *normal* we both let it happen, we both accepted it.

The girl behind the counter waved to us, and Clay gave her a slight head nod before he led me over to an empty booth.

"So, I doubt they have vegetarian tacos. . ." Clay smiled, his hand slipping from mine. "But I bet their burger is the best."

"Order anything. Tonight's on me." I folded my arms on the table and leaned closer to him. "Thank you for taking me to two different stores to get fabric and running out of juice for me." I smiled, his eyes instantly locking with mine.

"Anytime." He smiled, a sparkle in his eye.

Man, his eyes. . . a dark hazel, almost brown, with just enough green to get lost in. I heaved a sigh and broke eye contact, just in time for the waitress to come up. Despite being after eight, Clay ordered a coffee and a burger. I stuck with water but opted to get a plate of fries.

"That's it? Fries?"

"Yes, but if I decide your burger looks good. . ."

"I'll cut it in half." He smiled. He blinked and cleared his throat. "So, now that we have the fabric, what's next?"

I rolled my shoulders and sat up a little straighter. "I cut it to the measurements and piece them together. If you keep coming by, you'll see the entire process, and I bet it will blow your mind."

He smirked. "I'll make sure my schedule is cleared."

I narrowed my eyes at him. Was he ever going to tell me? "How is Jackson and Rye? You still work there, right?"

He heaved a sigh and nodded. "Uh, yeah; still there. Still. . . chugging along."

"Is it everything you thought it was going to be?" I nudged. Maybe if I poked and prodded, he would give in.

What was he afraid of? That I would be mad? That I would tell him I told you so? That I would rub New York in his face? If that's what was going through his head, then he had me all wrong. Well, let me rephrase that. A few weeks ago, I would have done that but not today. Not after remembering why... I shook my head, pulling myself back to him.

"It's exactly what I thought it would be. I climbed the ranks so quickly. I loved going to work, I loved getting that office with my name on the glass door, I loved going out with my team after, and I loved my apartment. I loved Seattle." He stopped, as if noticing all the 'ed's he was adding after the word love. He *loved* it, not *loves* it. "But working from Portland isn't that bad. I get to set my own schedule basically, and since my team does all the heavy work—"

"Except those data entry days," I added.

He scoffed. "Yeah, except those. I'm able to take the time away. I never vacationed before, so I had a lot of time saved up."

"You never came to see your parents? How are they?"

He raised his eyebrows and sighed, his shoulders slumping. I could tell he wanted to talk about anything but himself, yet, that was all I wanted to talk about.

"They're great. My dad's recently retired. . ."

"Paul retired! I can't see that?"

He laughed. "Yeah, and he's working with his hands. Building things out of wood. Pens, chairs, tables, clocks. . . all kinds of things. He's pretty good actually. He's been begging me to take that job at Home Depot so he could get a discount on wood." His smile grew.

He slipped, and I raised my eyebrows. "Job at Home Depot?"

Clay's laughter stopped. "Oh, well, just a joke. He thinks I'm here for an extended amount of time so I must be unemployed." He chuckled through the lie, bringing his hands up to the table to play with the sugar packets. "I have to go see them next weekend. Family dinner time."

I smiled. I had always loved Clay's parents. They were accepting, kind, and always a joy to be around. I wondered if they missed me like I missed them sometimes. "I'd love to come," I said, surprising even myself.

"Really?" he asked, raising an eyebrow. "They may get the wrong idea." Clay smirked, a slight smile showing.

"Oh, come on, they're adults. I'd love to see them. They were always nice to me. When's dinner?"

"Next Friday at four."

"Well, perfect. A week and half to warn them I'll be coming."

His smile grew. "Alright, I'll let them know to set another plate."

I nodded with a smile right as the waitress set our drinks down. Clay reached for his coffee mug like his life depended on it. He took a long drink, almost downing the mug.

"Would you like a refill, sir?" the girl asked, watching as he set the cup down.

"Uh, just water, thanks." He smiled up at her.

I rubbed my lips together. He was nervous, and it was adorable.

He cleared his throat. "Okay, so. . . I told you all about Seattle. Tell me about New York."

I leaned in closer. "What do you want to know?"

"Is it everything *you* thought it'd be?" he whispered.

"And more," I said honestly. He raised his eyebrows. "Look at me. Look at where I am. You know how they say the grass is greener on the other side? The grass *is* greener in New York. Starting as a lowly designer for Harold Martin to having runway shows all over the United States and London to having my own storefront. None of this would have happened if I hadn't gone to New York. The grass is definitely greener, Clay."

"I'm proud of you, how far you've come. Never letting things stand in your way and never stopping. It's a feat, and you've done it." He grinned, avoiding looking at me. He played with his fingers and spun his empty coffee mug around on the table. Finally, after a few moments of silence, his eyes met mine. "Do you have any regrets?"

Only you. . .

"None whatsoever. My dreams have come true," I said bluntly. I didn't mean for it to be harsh or even if he took it that way, but he rolled his lips and nodded, letting his hands fall onto his lap. "What about you? Any regrets?"

He was silent. He wanted to say something, I could tell, but he chose not to. I so desperately wanted him to open up to me. I wanted to know why he was lying, why he thought I couldn't know. Taking a deep breath, he finally spoke, leaving my question unanswered. "Have you heard back from JoAnn yet?"

I slumped. "No, not yet. She's busy, and Carter hasn't really taken any photos of the dress as it is now. It's still on the mannequin, and once Madeline gets in and she sees the Instagram posts, I'm sure she will say yes."

"She'd be stupid not to."

I opened my lips to respond, but the waitress dropped a burger and a plate of fries in front of us. I eyed the burger, watching as Clay slid the plate toward him, taking the toothpick from the bun.

"How much do you want?" Clay asked, not even looking up from the plate, grabbing his knife from the napkin.

I smiled. I didn't even have to ask. He just knew I would want some. "Just a little bit," I mumbled, my smile forcing its way through. Was I blushing? I could feel the heat in my cheeks from one simple question, one simple gesture, but would he be able to tell that I was blushing.

Clay cut the burger in half and gently slid a part on my plate, taking a few fries while he was at it. I chuckled.

"I said a little bit."

"Yeah, but I know you. You're going to want more." He looked at me through his eyelashes, that same smirk on his lips.

"You're full of smirks tonight," I said softly, taking my half of the burger to take a bite. "Oh," I mumbled, "That's delicious."

Clay looked at me, the corners of his mouth up. "They don't make them like this in New York, do they?"

I shook my head. "I mean, yes. New York has some amazing burger joints, but this just hits the spot."

"Everything hits the spot." He took a bite and hummed in ecstasy.

"Told you."

Chapter Twenty-One

-Clay-

Hooking up a Tesla to a Chevy was a lot harder than I thought, but we got it done. Milo drove with hazards on, going well below the speed limit, but as soon as we pulled up to a charging station, the adventure was over, and Tessa was plugged in. I helped transfer all the fabric into Milo's truck and then leaned on the hood of the car, crossing my feet and sticking my hands in my pockets. To get a full charge, I'd be here awhile.

Milo approached, scratching the back of his neck. "Madeline is going to take the truck to the studio and drop off all the fabric. Mind if I hang out with you?"

"Not at all. It's going to be a bit." I shrugged as I turned back to the unit. "Looks like thirty minutes or so."

Milo cocked a shoulder. "I have all the time in the world."

I looked at my watch. "Doesn't Holly normally call soon?"

"She called on the way here. They are headed to Scotland next." Milo leaned up next to me on the car, crossing his arms.

"Scotland?" I parroted, looking over at Ophelia and Madeline as they talked by the truck. Milo started talking, but I couldn't pay attention to Holly's escapades around the world. I was stuck watching Ophelia. The way she lit up around Madeline. Ophelia leaned in close and whispered into Madeline's ear and then glanced my way. Were they talking about me?

She gave me a wave, screamed "Thank you" at the top of her lungs, and then climbed into the passenger seat. Madeline ran over to give Milo and kiss goodbye, patting me on the shoulder before running back to the truck.

"Are you having déjà vu from college too, or is it just me?" I asked as the truck pulled off onto the road, both girls leaving us guys behind.

"Just you. Madeline would have never kissed me in college." Milo laughed, shifting himself back on the hood. "How was the day with Ophelia?"

"Great." I sighed. "I'm going back to the studio tomorrow."

"Still using my Starbucks card, I hope. Racking up those points?"

"Is it yours or Madeline's?" I countered, pinching my brow to look toward him.

Milo clenched his teeth. "Madeline's, but hey, she's not complaining. She likes the stars and wants to get the new cup coming out for pumpkin spice season." He chuckled. "Seriously, it's going okay between you two? Nothing for weeks and now planned days at the studio?"

I met his gaze and nodded slowly. "She let me call her Phe."

His eyes widened, and he tilted his body away, shock radiating from him. "That's huge, especially since she made a big to-do about it at dinner."

"She wants to go have dinner with my parents. She said she misses them."

"Dare I say things are looking up for you, Clay? You're even acting differently."

"Differently how?"

"Like the old you, the one from college. Not Seattle Clay, but the Clay I met back in OU. Almost like you're. . ." He trailed off, turning to look at the car we were sitting on. "Happy."

Happy.

A smile spread across my lips as the single word floated through my brain. I wasn't one hundred percent, that's for damn sure. . . but I was getting there. I was finding my way back to. . . her.

Two coffees in hand, I entered the studio with my guard up. Madeline was there, most likely with her dress on, and I had no idea if she knew I was coming. I knocked and twisted the knob, raising my arm to cover my eyes.

"I have the Americano as requested, and my eyes are closed until told otherwise," I announced.

I heard Madeline's laugh. "It's okay, Clay. I'm changing behind a screen. As long as *you don't have your cell phone,* you are welcome to come in."

"Phone is in my pocket, and it's off. I will give it to Carter for reassurance," I stated, lowering my arm to see a large black screen—when that appeared, I had no idea—and Carter sitting alone at the desk. His camera was ready to be used, and several pieces of fabrics and jewels were laid out on the table near him. I set down Ophelia's coffee and pulled my phone out, handing it to Carter. "Here you are."

Without looking up from the computer, he took my phone and set it face down.

"Hello to you too, Carter. I hope you had a good few days off."

Carter begrudgingly looked up from his computer. "Good morning, Clayton. Good to see you again. Try to keep your hand lower when taking photos this time, okay?"

I gave him a thumbs up and turned back to the table.

My entire mood today was, for lack of a better word, giddy. I woke up earlier than normal and showered, checked my email for news from my lawyer (none yet) and ate some toast before gallivanting off to Starbucks to grab Ophelia a coffee I knew she would want. I wanted so badly to be around her, just in the same room because with her everything made sense. Today was a big day for her and her new store, finally getting the bride in the dress she had been working on for weeks, and I was going to be there to witness it.

Ophelia popped out from behind the screen and gave me a bright smile. Her hair was poofy, just the way I loved it, being held out of the way by a gold headband. Her signature gold hoop earrings swayed as she moved. She wore a tank top that flowed around her waist and white shorts. On her feet, instead of heels, she'd donned a pair of flats. She looked comfortable. Breathtakingly comfortable. It took everything I had not to scoop her up and curl up with her on a couch.

"Thank you for the coffee," she sang as she picked up the paper cup. She hummed. "Whatever Starbucks you go to, they make this perfectly and need to teach the gal in New York." She took another drink.

"Okay, I'm coming out," Madeline called.

Carter jumped to attention, his camera ready to go. He came right to my side, aimed his camera toward the screen and waited.

I heard Madeline take a deep breath before stepping around the screen, and she did so gracefully. She kept her head down, her red hair in a messy bun on top of her head with pieces falling down and her free hand holding on to the skirt with her fingertips. The moment she looked up, both Ophelia and I dropped our jaws.

"Oh, wow," I whispered. Madeline was absolutely stunning. I had seen the dress on the mannequin but seeing it on her was something extremely different. It fit her perfectly, insinuating her every curve. The ivory color made it look more modest, not as bright, and the floral design on the lace matched her personality. I was simply in awe, and if I was, I couldn't imagine what Milo would be like.

She gave a slight chuckle at my comment, and Ophelia raised her hands to cover her lips with her fingers.

"Maddy," she whispered, taking a step toward her friend. "This is unbelievable."

Carter hunched his back and followed Ophelia.

"You're acting like you didn't just help me put it on." Madeline laughed.

"Yeah, but that entrance," I defended. "It's a good thing I'll be standing next to Milo because he may faint."

"Well, that entrance was highly staged, thanks to Carter's direction." Madeline looked over at the man behind the camera.

"We may have to do it again, this time with you stopping for a photo," Carter said, raising his head just slightly from the view finder.

"Well," Ophelia grabbed Madeline's hand and pulled her over to the sunlight. The dress flowed behind her, the train a shorter length than I had seen. "I see some adjustments I need to make, Clay. . . pin cushion?"

I chuckled under my breath, set my coffee down and grabbed the brand-new purple pin cushion. "I liked my gray one," I said, giving this new one a squeeze.

"I still have that one. This one is just new and shiny."

"A pin cushion cannot be shiny," I protested with a hint of sarcasm.

"Technically, no, but this one is brand new as of last night and it is shiny."

"But it's fabric. . ."

"If I have to call your Tesla *Tessa,* then you have to accept the fact that my pin cushion is shiny." Ophelia's eyes met mine. They were bright and warm and dare I say excited? Was she enjoying this silly little banter about a pin cushion?

"Okay, you two." Madeline stopped us. "Dress first, flirtatious banter later."

"We're not. . ." Ophelia trailed off, shaking her head. "Okay, anyway, pin cushion."

I held it up.

I stood in silence as Ophelia took pins and made adjustments to the dress, which weren't a lot. Madeline stood still and just watched in the mirror as Ophelia circled her, Carter following her around like a puppy.

"Psst," Madeline whispered my way. "How's the party planning going?"

"We just have a few details to hash out, but we have the location. We need the guest list when you have it. The sooner the better for invites, right?"

She shrugged, getting a "don't move" from Ophelia. "Makes sense, I guess. I'll get it together as soon as I can."

Keeping her face straight, she looked over at me, giving me a crooked smirk. She inhaled and looked down at Ophelia and Carter.

"I don't think I like having my photo taken," Madeline whispered to me while Ophelia and Carter were down by her feet. "It's nerve wracking. What if Milo sees it?"

"He won't," I whispered back. "He doesn't even know I'm here today. He thinks I went to a job-" I stopped myself and looked down at Ophelia. I almost said interview. "A meeting," I added quickly.

Madeline nodded. "Do you really think he'll like it?"

"Maddy, I almost fainted, so yeah. . . I think it's safe to say he will like it." I looked at my friend. The way she blushed just thinking about Milo made me wonder if Ophelia blushed thinking about me. "He would faint if you walked down the aisle in a garbage bag," I added, stepping away from Madeline.

"There is no way on God's green earth that she is walking down the aisle in a garbage bag with me as her best friend." Ophelia stood and shot me a glare, pulling another pin from the cushion with force.

Both Madeline and I raised our eyebrows at her. I pressed my lips to a tight line and simply nodded. "No, ma'am, never," I agreed.

Lowering herself down, she placed the pin and then stood with a jolt. "Okay, I think that will do it."

"Miss Madeline," Carter said, pulling Madeline away from the mirror. "Could I get a few shots of just you, please, and a pose for your entrance?"

Madeline heaved a sigh and looked at me. I gave her a reassuring nod, and she turned back to Carter. "If we must."

Ophelia rubbed her neck and sighed. "I'll leave you to pose the bride. I need to make some notes." She gave Madeline a gentle pat on her shoulder and carefully walked to her desk. Grabbing both our coffees, I followed her.

"Now what?" I asked as she sat down in Carter's chair, rubbing her finger on the mouse pad on her laptop, bringing it to life.

"Now I fix those little pins, and we try the dress on again." She grabbed her drink and took a long pull. "Hmm. . . seriously? What Starbucks have you been going to?"

I chuckled and leaned my palms on the desk. "Any word from JoAnn yet?"

"I haven't checked. I'm too nervous."

"Check right now." I jerked my head toward the computer, wiggling my eyebrows.

She narrowed her eyes and breathed in. "Alright, but you stay right there." She gave me a stern glare before turning to her computer. Moving her fingers gracefully on the pad, she clicked a few times before pausing to, hopefully, read an email. Her eyes darted from side to side holding me at suspense the entire time.

"Well?" I trailed, wanting to know the answer more than she did at this point.

She rubbed her lips together and closed the laptop down. I used to be a pro at reading her expressions. I could tell you exactly what was going through her mind with one glance, but she had gotten better at her poker face, and it was killing me. She placed her palms on the table and pushed herself up. Making eye contact with me, she finally broke.

She let out a long, shaky sigh and covered her smile with her hands, her shoulders hunching in.

"What!?"

"She loves the idea." Ophelia dropped her hands and smiled. "She loves the idea!" she called again. "She wants to see some of the designs pinned on the mannequin, told me to send over some that her team can get to work on soon. She's absolutely in love with Madeline's dress, and she can't wait until she can see the photos from today. And Clay! She basically said yes!" Ophelia screamed.

It took all my strength not to jump over the table and scoop her up in my arms and share this excitement with her. It didn't even matter to me that Madeline and Carter were in the room. I had to fight the urge all the same. I desperately wanted her in my arms again.

"Said yes to what?" Madeline came bustling over, trying to walk gently but as fast as possible to us. I turned to watch her and glanced at Carter, who looked like he had just been defeated as she left him alone by the screen.

"JoAnn likes the idea of only gowns being sold at my boutique." Ophelia clapped her hands together, trying to contain her excitement in her small body. I had a feeling one way or the other she was going to let it all out somehow.

I smiled. I wanted to be there when she released that energy, out in the open. I imagined her dancing at a club—no. . . that was college Ophelia. This Ophelia would go to a classy restaurant with her friends, have a glass of wine and celebrate in a more adult way. I wanted her to scream at the top of her lungs, enjoying the moment and letting the world know what she accomplished.

Madeline squealed. "Phe!" She stopped herself from jumping to give Ophelia a hug. "Okay, Okay. What's his name?" she whispered.

"Carter," I answered.

"Carter." Madeline spun quickly. "Are we done? Please tell me we're done because I need to get out of this dress so I can give my friend a hug."

Carter looked down at his camera and back to Madeline. "Yes, I suppose. Miss Fuller, I'll need a caption."

"Yeah, I'll get you one." Ophelia was still smiling, her voice shaky with excitement as she carefully led Madeline over to the screen. Once the two girls were behind the screen, I went over to Carter, listening to them talk all about the gowns Ophelia saw in her head.

"Can I see?" I asked Carter, pointing to his camera.

"They're rough. . ."

"That's okay. I'd like to see them."

He shrugged and showed me the small screen. He began to click through them, all focused on Ophelia's hands and the dress, Madeline's entrance, every photo perfect in every way.

"I knew JoAnn would say yes," Carter said softly. "She's in her element with the dresses, and JoAnn can see that. When she was working on the winter line, she wasn't. . . she wasn't. . ."

I looked from the camera to him. "She wasn't glowing?"

He shook his head. "Nah, she needs to do gowns. I knew JoAnn would see what I did." Carter turned off his camera and flipped it to get the SD Card.

I looked back at the screen where Madeline and Ophelia were still chatting about everything, their voices higher pitched and excitement bursting through the room. Even from behind a screen, I could see her glow.

Chapter Twenty-Two

-Ophelia-

Clay: I have a brilliant idea. It's a celebration of sorts, and you just need to trust me. Are you free Monday?

Ophelia: I can be. Not so sure I trust you though.

Clay: An Americano is involved.

Ophelia: Exactly how much money have you spent on coffee for me these past weeks?

Clay: Pay no attention to the dollar sign. Do. You. Trust. Me?

Ophelia: . . . Yeeesss. . .

Clay: Great! Monday at 10am. I'll pick you up. Wear something comfortable and tennis shoes! Tennis shoes are required.

I furrowed my brow at my phone, glancing up at Madeline, who stood with her mug of coffee to her lips, wearing her bright blue scrubs as she finished getting ready for the last workday of the week.

"I'm pretty sure I didn't pack any tennis shoes," I said, looking back down at the phone and then to her, my brows still pinched.

"That's all he said? That you need to trust him and wear tennis shoes?" she asked, setting her mug on the island.

I looked back at my phone and read the thread once more. "Yup, he wouldn't even answer my coffee question. If the man has no money, why would he be bringing me coffee every day?"

Madeline took a deep breath. I knew she had been keeping some things quiet about Clay since he didn't want me to know details, but I could tell by her expression she knew exactly how he'd been buying me those coffees. I tilted my head and narrowed my eyes at her.

"He may have been using my app. I load the card labeled 'Ophelia' and he racks up the stars."

"Madeline. . ." I groaned, holding back a smile. "Don't load that card anymore." I set my phone down and pointed at her.

Madeline dropped her jaw and raised her brow. "He wants to impress you. He wants to be friends again, and coffee was the peace offering. He even remembered your order from college and everything. It's sweet. Plus, I'm getting the points. Pretty soon I'll be able to get that mug I've had my eye on." She smirked.

I shook my head. "Okay, fine, whatever. Indulge him. Back to the tennis shoes."

"We're the same size, I have a pair you can wear."

"You're sure? I have no details other than to wear something comfortable and tennis shoes. He could be taking me on a hike." I stood, walked around the island to fill my mug with my second cup of the day.

"I have hiking boots too. Milo and I took Holly this past spring. They murdered my feet."

"He said comfortable."

"Okay, then." Madeline basically ran out of the kitchen, Niko right at her feet. The big floof seemed to know exactly where she was going. He bounded down the hall in front of her and rounded the corner before she even got there. "Well, come on," Madeline called.

I followed, finding her bent over in her closet, Niko's tail wagging beside her. I leaned against the doorframe and chuckled.

"Here, these are what you want." Madeline held up a pair of tan shoes, Niko's eyes following them the entire time. "These are Niko's favorites, but no matter how hard he chews, they look brand new, and they're waterproof." She held out the sneakers.

I looked at the shoes and back at the dog. "He's eaten these?"

"Well, not these, but my last pair he tried to demolish. Trust me, wear these with your white shorts and shirt with some color that will pop, and you will be adorable and comfortable for your date with Clay."

Date.

I coughed. "It's not a date, Maddy." I took the shoes and turned my back. Niko gave a whine and then was at my side in minutes, his blue eyes looking up at the shoes.

"Pretty sure it is." Madeline chuckled, following me down the stairs. "You'll be here all day, right? No studio today?"

"I wasn't planning on it. I have to work on these wedding dress designs, and Carter said he is uploading more to my Instagram today, so I need to proof the photos and come up with captions." Just listing off my to-do list made my head spin. This was my world, fashion designing and blogging, working for designer companies, but with the word date looming over my head, it made it all seem more hectic. "On second thought, maybe I need to go to the studio and tell Clay Monday won't work."

"Don't you dare." Madeline grabbed her bag and slung it over her shoulder, reaching in her for keys. "Studio maybe, Monday? Hell no. You're going wherever he's taking you. Got it?"

I rolled my eyes. "Yes, Mom."

Madeline nodded. "Gotta get my practice in before I become an official stepmom. I'll see you tonight?" She smiled.

I nodded and waved as she walked out the door to her car, leaving me alone in the doorway, still holding a pair of tennis shoes.

I closed the door and turned to see Niko still looking at the shoes as if they were his favorite toy.

"No, sir." I leaned over and scratched behind his ear. "You aren't eating these shoes. Even if it's not a date, I still need to look my best."

He let out a loud groan before yawning, a howl closing off the yawn.

"Very nice." I chuckled, setting the shoes on the floor and standing. "Come on, bud. Let's go to the studio."

"I'm very allergic to dogs," Carter mumbled as Niko and I made our way into the studio a few hours later. I had never brought Niko here before, but I may have been trying to save the shoes. I knew he wasn't one to destroy the house while we were away, but those eyes he had made me nervous.

"I'll keep him over here. I'm just designing today. Plus, if you take any photos, people on Instagram really love dogs." I chuckled. "Maybe we can make it a story. I guarantee people will love it." I set my portfolio next to the desk and pulled my chair out.

"I didn't think you were coming in today." Carter reached into his camera bag. "But if it's okay with you, I'll take some photos of what you're working on. Do you have those captions for me?"

"I don't mind at all, and I wasn't going to, but then as I thought about all I had to do, I thought it would be best for me to work here. I'll answer a few messages on Instagram and then start to design. Oh." I shot my eyes at him as he got closer to me, walking in a huge arch to keep away from Niko. "I'll be taking Monday off, so feel free to relax that day."

"I won't be here next week actually." Carter raised his camera and leaned on his knees, snapping a photo of Niko. "I'm flying out Sunday to be with my family. My son is testing for a green belt in karate, and I need to be there."

"Of course you do. That's a huge accomplishment. Tell him congrats for me." I gave him a large smile, shocked that he was finally talking to me. After weeks of silence and nothing but photos, Carter was actually talking.

"That's why I need to get all these photos taken now, so I'm glad you came in today. What are your plans for Monday?"

"Just seeing a friend. I have that party to plan still, and since you won't be around, I may take the week too. Friday, I have a dinner planned, and maybe I can post to my Instagram. I haven't in a while." I watched as he snapped more photos of Niko, and he seemed to pose. "Maybe we can put the dog in a dress?"

Carter didn't laugh. He looked up toward me and pinched his brow.

"It was a joke."

"I'm aware," he responded.

I shook my head and turned my back to him, reaching out to get my phone to check the new feed. Carter had been diligent about uploading photos at least every other day, but lately, since the wedding gowns had been approved, it's been every day. Madeline's gorgeous photos had the most hearts so far. People were even asking for the dress to be for sale. I already had interest in the gown, and my heart sang whenever I saw someone comment or send me a message. I even had a few brides wondering if I did custom dresses for other clients. It broke my heart to have to tell them no, but that if they waited a few more months, I'd have plenty to show off.

This was going to be phenomenal.

This was going to be a dream come true.

A notification pulled down over my Instagram feed, JoAnn's name appearing.

JoAnn: We need to talk about the change. I noticed the wedding gowns are taking off on your feed. Zoom meeting? Monday?

I took a deep breath and responded, trying to sound as professional as possible. This was the woman making it all possible.

Ophelia: I can't on Monday. Carter is flying out Sunday for a week, so I made plans with a friend. Does Tuesday work?

Those small little dots danced, then stopped, and started dancing again.

JoAnn: Tuesday works better for me, actually! Noon?

I caught my breath. Phew.

Ophelia: Works great. Talk to you then.

With a smile on my face, I closed the screen and set my phone down on the table. I could hear the faint click of Carter's camera, the sound no longer filling me with anxiety but hope and excitement. I couldn't believe this was all happening.

This is happening.

On Monday, at exactly 10:00 a.m., Clay pulled up in Milo's truck. I grabbed my bag and ran outside, not even giving him a chance to come to the door. Not that he didn't try. He was dressed in simple jeans and a gray t-shirt with black laced boots that hung out of his jeans as he walked toward me, coffee in hand.

"Okay, so by the way you are dressed, I take it we aren't going on a hike?" I asked, taking the coffee from his hand.

"A hike? Phe, I know you would hate me if I took you on a long hike," he said, placing his hand on my back to lead me toward the car. He opened the car door and held it open for me, catching my eye as I stepped through. "Just trust me, okay? This is going to be great." He shut the car door gently and wiggled his eyebrows before walking around the hood of the truck and climbing into the driver's side. "Here, I'll even let you pick the music," he added, handing me his phone.

"Oh, you'll regret that," I mumbled with a smile, instantly opening up his Spotify to Chord Overstreet.

"I highly doubt that." He smiled as he started the truck, shifting the engine in drive and hitting the gas, pulling us off onto the street and on our way.

Almost an hour later, filled with calming music and no more explanation from Clay, we pulled up on a side road, and Clay killed the engine. He pulled out a piece of paper from the middle console and began to look around the truck. I followed suit, taking in the beautiful green scenery around me, but my mind began to wander. Madeline told me about when Milo blindfolded her for their first official date and how she made the comment that he was going to kill her. My mind went exactly there, but instead of saying anything, I inhaled sharply, held my breath, and turned to look at Clay.

"We have to walk now, about fifteen minutes west," he mumbled, leaning on his side to shove the now-folded paper in his pocket.

"Ah," I sighed. "Hence the tennis shoes."

"I'm glad to see you followed my request." Opening the truck door, he literally hopped out of the seat. His hair flopped once he hit the ground, which let's face it, for him wasn't far at all, and then he walked over to me, offering his hand as I climbed from the truck.

"You can thank Madeline, now—" I gripped his hand tighter, loving the feel of his palm in mine. What was it about holding someone's hand that gave you all the jitters and shocks that trailed up your arm? "Are you going to tell me what we are doing? Because I gotta admit. . ."

"It seems like I'm gonna kill you? Madeline told you the blindfold story, huh? Milo told me that too, but trust me, this is so much better than driving around in circles to get your date lost before going to Powell's."

"That was sweet. He gave her the perfect day."

"And..." He took one step and turned his body to face me. Walking backward, he still held onto my hand. "If you stop wondering what's going on, you're going to have a blast. Trust—"

"Trust you. I got it. Just wish I had more information, is all."

Clay squeezed my hand and chuckled. "We're almost there."

I watched him as he moved forward, a look of excitement on his face. His strides were getting quicker as our feet crunched the dirt road below, the sun beating down on him through the trees. Clay wasn't focused on the surrounding scenery. He was focused on what was directly in front of him. He was a man on a mission, every now and then he would glance over at me from the corner of his eyes, his soft smile growing larger every time our eyes met. My brain started to float through the motions, simply enjoying my hand in his, my body inching a little closer with each step. I pushed back some curls with my free hand and looked at the sneakers on my feet.

"I think we're here."

Clay's voice pulled me from the ground and to the scene in front of us. A group of people were standing around a bridge with an open side, a large truck with a trailer on the other side of the bridge. And on the side of the truck in large, red letters were two words I never thought I'd see.

Portland Bungee.

"Um. . . Clay?" I stopped, my hand still in his, forcing him to yank to a stop as well. "That's. . . that's. . ." I muttered, pointing toward the group of people.

He chuckled and pulled my arm forward. "That's a way to celebrate."

"Celebrate!?" I shouted. "By bungee jumping!?"

"Yeah, it will be freeing. . . trust me."

"You've said that way too many times for me to actually trust you." I pulled on his hand, but still found myself following him. I wasn't actually going to jump off this bridge, was I? Just as the thought entered my head, I heard stomping and a loud scream from the bridge. A woman had just jumped off on her own and was now screaming—a thrilling scream—as she plummeted to the ground.

"Hey there!" A man stopped Clay as we approached the truck. "You here to jump with us?"

"Yes, sir, we are. I booked a tandem on Friday." Clay smiled, way more excitement in his voice than there should be.

He booked a what?!

"Ah perfect, you two are just in time. It looks like your waiver has already been signed online and it says cash payment upon arrival." The guy tapped away on his iPad while Clay ruffled through his back pocket, letting go of my hand to grab his wallet to pull out a few hundred-dollar bills. What the. . .

I could run. I could run back to the truck right now and not do this. Instead, I found myself hugging my arms close to my body, watching as others got attached to the bungee, and then they ran off the side of the bridge. Once Clay had finished with the man, he wrapped his arm around my shoulder and gently pulled me to the crowd.

"Don't hate me," he whispered in my ear, his voice a deep rhythm that vibrated through me.

"I don't hate you," I said softly, sharply turning my head toward him. "I loathe you."

He laughed. "Good to know things haven't changed."

"You signed a waiver for me?" I grumbled.

"Had to. I had to sign the waiver before even booking an event."

"Event?" I parroted. "This isn't an event. We are planning an event. A party is an event. This is downright insane," I grumbled, watching as they helped the man up back on the ledge. His hair was ruffled, and his body was shaking, perhaps out of fear, but the smile on his face said otherwise. "You said tandem?"

"I knew you wouldn't want to jump alone, so I paid for us to jump together."

"Together?"

"Hey, are you my tandem jumpers!?" another man asked, holding the bungee line up. "You're up next, so if you could stand over here while I gather everything."

"We're jumping together?" I asked again, simply for clarification.

Clay turned down to look at me, his smile saying more words than he knew he was. *You're safe with me. You can do this. This will be life changing. We're in this together.* "Yeah, they basically hook us—"

"I-don't-need-to-know-details," I said faster than my brain could form the words. It's amazing how he understood me.

He trailed his fingers down my arm, my skin lighting up as his fingertips landed on my hand. "You'll jump?"

I looked up at him, his chin down and his eyebrows raised, the biggest puppy eyes I had ever seen. He was too damn cute.

I let out a loud groan. "Yes, I'll do it, but know I am NOT happy about it, and you have some major making up to do after this."

"One condition." He raised a single finger in between us. "I want you to scream at the top of your lungs, 'I'm Ophelia Fuller, wedding gown designer.'"

"You can't be serious?"

"Oh, I am. We"—he pulled on my arm, taking a step back toward the man with all the equipment, —"are celebrating."

The employee, who introduced himself as Jeremy, began setting us to jump, letting us know that the large band he wrapped around our waists would hold us together and the hooks around our ankles would keep us tied to the bungee cord. He repeated over and over that everything was completely safe. He suggested Clay wrap his arms around me and hold me tightly to his body, but that it would be okay if he let go.

"Don't you dare let go," I growled up at him.

"I won't," he promised.

Jeremy kept telling us all the ins and outs of what was going to happen, but my mind wasn't listening. I was one hundred percent focused on the drop I was about to take. The bridge was over a running river—a slow-moving river—but a river, nonetheless. My mind was buzzing. *There are rocks down there. The cord can snap. You won't get to design wedding dresses if you're dead!*

"Um, Clay," I muttered as he wrapped his arms tight around me. I snaked my arms around his waist and buried my face in his chest.

"I'm going to start to rock you, and then when I say three, you'll fall. You'll feel a pull with the cord. . ."

"Clay," I said again.

". . . and you'll fly back up. That's the best part. Then you'll go back down. That will happen a few times until the cord relaxes. . ."

"Clay," I said a little louder.

". . . and we will guide you back up."

Jeremy, shut up!

"Sounds like a blast." Clay smiled.

No, it does not.

"Clay." I pulled my head up to look at him.

"Okay, here we go," Jeremy shouted, putting one hand on my back and one on Clay's, slowly starting to rock us back and forth. "One. . ."

"Clay, I'm not doing this," I said, catching his attention.

". . . two. . ."

"Oh, yes, we are." Clay smiled, placing a small kiss on my forehead. His lips left my skin faster than they touched, but the feeling was still there. And for a second, half a second, I forgot what I was about to do.

"Three."

And just like that, I was falling.

Clay was shouting "whoo" as we soared through the air, my head buried in his chest, his arms never once losing their grip on me. I felt the tug and jerk as my body flung upward again. I began to shake.

"Phe," Clay screamed. "Phe, open your eyes! Shout it out at the top of your lungs!"

I let my breath loose. Finally, being brave, I opened my eyes just as we began to fall back down. The world around me moved like a blur, and the air whooshed past my ears. My hair was flying uncontrollably, and Clay's eyes, somehow, were focused on me. I looked up—or down—at the water as it came closer, a blue blur of motion. I was flying.

"Shout it, Phe," Clay said again, the wind blocking his voice.

I took a deep breath as our bodies jerked once more, and I shouted at the top of my lungs for the entire world to hear. . .

"I AM OPHELIA FULLER!!!"

Clay's arms tightened as the words fell from my tongue, and he buried his face in my neck. I could hear as he laughed, letting out the most contagious sound I had heard all day. Our bodies blended together as we slowed down, the world coming into focus, my brain putting all the pieces together. Every nerve in my body was on fire. I could feel everything as the world came back into focus, but all I could see was Clay.

We were gently pulled back up onto the landing, Clay letting go of me so I could grab Jeremy's hand. Once my feet were firmly planted on the ground, Clay standing tall next to me, the adrenaline surging through my every cell, I took one last look at the river below.

I did it. I flew.

Jeremy bent over at my feet to begin to unhook all the straps, but if I were honest with myself, I was tempted to jump again. Run off the board with my arms spread wide, eyes open, just to fly again. I looked up at Clay, his hair completely out of sorts, his face flushed but the same smile, the same look of thrill and adventure in his eyes that I knew I had.

I could fly again. . .

Ignoring Jeremy at my knees, I stepped forward and closed the gap between Clay and me, wanting to take that fall again.

Chapter Twenty-Three

-Clay-

Before I had any time to react, Ophelia's lips were on mine. Her fingers were gripping my t-shirt and my entire weight was falling toward her. Her lips were exactly how I remembered them, soft and full of passion. Every part of me was already shaking with adrenaline, and this kiss added to it, the perfect kindling to the already blazing fire. I parted my lips ever so slightly, telling myself to stay calm the moment she accepted the deeper kiss. I slid my arm around her waist, wanting her body against mine completely, but it was then she pulled away, breaking the kiss and quickly turning away from me once again before I had any time to react.

She kept her back to me and her face down. Her shoulders were going up and down with every breath she took, and once Jeremy had her free, she bolted. Taking off down the road off the bridge and passing the bungee truck.

"I take it you weren't expecting that," Jeremy laughed as he worked with the straps and hooks around me.

I shook my head. "No. . . no, I wasn't."

"Well, are you going to follow her?" he asked, nodding his head in her general direction. "She's walking pretty fast."

"Yeah, um. . ." I stammered. "Thanks."

I took off in a jog, catching up to Ophelia faster than she expected.

"Phe, wait," I shouted, coming up to her side.

"Do *not*"— she turned her body, a finger pointed at me—"call me Phe."

I stopped jogging and took a deep breath. Her eyes were wide, and the finger that was aimed at me was shaking ever so slightly. She was still on a rush, and I could tell she wasn't sure how to act. Something was going through her mind, something she needed to get out.

I took a deep breath. "I've been calling you Phe for—"

"Nope, not right now. I'll allow it after we're done here. Do you understand?" Her eyes were wide, and they pierced into me. I nodded. "You have a lot of explaining to do, Clayton."

"What?" I asked, my voice shaking. I wasn't sure if it was from the jump, from the kiss, from her calling me Clayton or a mixture of all three.

"You have explaining to do. A lot of it. First of all"—she spread her arms out and lifted her chin toward the sky—"what made you think that I'd ever, *ever* want to go bungee jumping!? You brought it up weeks ago as a joke! A *joke*! Not to be taken literally! Yet here we are!"

Her voice rose with every word. I wasn't sure it could get any higher. And as it rose, my smile grew.

"But you had fun, right?"

"That's beside the point."

"That *was* the point! I knew you and Maddy went to some bar to get some drinks to celebrate, but you need to unleash another way. By telling the world that you are Ophelia Fuller, and you did! Look at you, screaming to the heavens, Phe . ."

"Don't."

"Ophelia," I corrected. "I am so incredibly proud of you. You deserve the world, and I wanted to give it to you in some way."

"By bungee jumping?'

"You were flying," I said softly.

She let out a loud groan and leaned forward, resting her hands on her knees, taking in a few deep breaths. "Okay fine," she finally shouted. "That was thrilling, and I was tempted to jump again but"—she flung herself up again—"I still can't believe you did that."

I chuckled and took a few steps toward her, wanting so badly to reach out and touch her, pull her close again, and kiss her. "I knew if I told you, you would've said no."

"How much did this even cost?"

I shrugged. "That doesn't matter."

"Yes, it does, Clay." She took a step back. "When are you going to tell me?"

Well, shit.

"Tell you what?" I asked, my voice breaking.

"Clay, I already know. I just need to hear it from you." Tilting her body, she sighed, her shoulders relaxing. "Why are you so scared to tell me?"

I shuffled, not exactly sure how to form the words. If she knew I had been lying, why push the matter? I bit the insides of my lips, moving my feet back and forth and kicking the rocks on the ground. I placed one hand on my neck and the other I shoved into my jeans pocket. Just by looking at me, you could tell I was a nervous wreck. My body language screamed it, and yet I couldn't bring myself to relax.

"Clay. . ." Ophelia said softly.

I broke.

"I was embarrassed. I didn't know how to tell the woman I broke up with that I failed miserably. I wanted you to think I still had my shit together. I didn't know how to form the words to say that you were right, and I was wrong. Fuck, Phe. . ." I took a deep breath, avoiding her eyes. "I didn't want to give you another reason to hate me because after all these years, you're my biggest regret."

I let out my breath and finally made eye contact with her. I could feel tears welling in my eyes, but I didn't cry. I refused to cry, so I held them back. I stiffened my jaw and clenched my teeth, completely unsure with how to follow that. I word-vomited everywhere and maybe said too much. Ophelia's stance had relaxed. Her eyebrows were raised, and her eyes were full of uncertainty. We were both stone.

What seemed like hours after, Ophelia took a deep breath, raising her shoulders before exhaling and dropping them back down. She took a step toward me and reached her arm out, offering her hand to me.

"Come on." She motioned down the road, where Milo's truck sat waiting for us. "We need to talk."

We sat in the truck, having yet to turn it on, both of us just staring at the front window. I wasn't sure where to begin, but thankfully, Ophelia made sure I didn't have to.

"When did you lose your job?" she asked softly, almost sounding as if she were afraid to ask.

"How long have you known?" I asked instead of answering.

She turned toward me and sighed. "Since I got in. Madeline told me about the party planning and then mentioned you were going through a hard time. Then I was told to act as if I knew nothing." Ophelia tucked her hair behind her ear. "I think I was doing a pretty good job at that."

I chuckled. "Yeah, you were." I shook my head and pinched my brow. "I should have known Maddy would have told you."

"Clay." She reached over the middle console and placed her hand on my arm. "When did you lose your job?" she asked again.

I counted back in my head. "About nine months ago, maybe. I've honestly lost count." I finally met her gaze. "You had to have seen the news on it?"

"I don't watch the news, Clay. I avoid it like the plague. Honestly, all I see is what Google gives me and fashion bloggers. I think if I had seen your name, I would have. . ." She paused, taking a deep breath before turning back to me. "But you've been living with Milo for nine months?"

I shook my head. "No, only for the last couple of months. I kept my apartment until the last second. A part of me was hoping it would blow over, like they would come asking for me back." I laughed. "We see how that turned out."

"No, tell me, Clay. If I trusted you enough to jump off a flippin' bridge, you can trust me to tell me everything." Her hand lightly squeezed my arm.

I rolled my neck and licked my lips, heaving a sigh. "There's not much to tell. A member of my team was embezzling right under my nose. I was in charge of them and their accounts, and it slipped right past me. Four million dollars fell through the cracks, and I didn't notice it. How could I miss four million? Since they couldn't pin who exactly it was, they terminated the entire team, including me. Then they sued me for the four million and instead of going to multiple court battles and jail, I settled. Admitted guilt and paid them off."

"You just *had* four million dollars to give them?"

"Pretty damn close." I rolled my eyes at myself. I was starting to really hate Seattle Clay. Who had I become? "In stocks and in savings. The first thing I did when I got home was paid off my Tesla. That's how I at least have that. Then I found a lawyer, one who I thought was damn good, and started to figure out how I could get through it. When we agreed to settle, I paid them the four million, plus interest, and then their lawyers' fees, my lawyer fees, and by the time everyone was paid. . . I had enough to make it a few months. I had to sell my condo, making only enough to pay off the remaining loan, I couldn't even take the equity that was in it; and then I came here."

Ophelia was hanging on my every word. She had shifted her body to face me, both hands now resting on my forearm. I reached over and took one of her hands in mine, our fingers lacing together. A simple comfort I didn't know I needed.

"Milo's been letting me sleep on the couch and use his truck since I couldn't afford to register the Tesla, and have been without car insurance for a while now. Holly was welcoming, very accepting that 'Uncle Clay' just needed to crash for a bit. He's been leaving me little amounts of cash some morning, not a lot, but I've kept track and I intend to pay everything back once I get another job." I scoffed. "*If* I get another job."

"Home Depot," she muttered, remembering my comment from the other night.

"The only place who would hire a felon." I shrugged. "I had a job interview at a small law firm, a data entry accountant, but I should have known they knew about everything. Yet, they still brought me in for an interview. She said she had been in touch with my lawyer, and that he's trying to clear my name. They think they know who was actually embezzling. She said she'd hire me if I got my name cleared."

"Can that happen?" Ophelia asked softly.

"I'm not sure," I admitted. "My lawyer seems to be working on it without giving me too much detail, which I think is wrong, but it's happening. So, until then, I'm keeping track of things, even down to when Milo came to tow my Tesla to the charging station."

"I would have paid for a tow truck, you know." She smiled.

"I wouldn't have let you. I already owe Milo so much. I didn't want to have to ask you for anything."

"And the coffees?" She smirked, telling me she already knew the answer to that. "What about this? Bungee jumping can't be cheap?" She motioned her head out the window, toward the bridge.

"No, I paid for this. I had enough to splurge here. I needed you to fly." I gave her a crooked smirk. It had taken up most of my savings, but it didn't matter. Ophelia soared this afternoon. "Besides, you seemed to enjoy yourself, and that's all that matters."

She narrowed her eyes, but her lips formed a tight smile. Would she let me kiss those lips again?

"Give me your phone." She sighed as she removed a hand from my arm.

"Why?" I asked, leaning over to pull my phone from my pocket.

"Because Madeline can't keep buying my coffee. I know she's enjoying the points, but I could use those stars too."

I watched her open the Starbucks app and log out of Madeline's account, typing in her own. I chuckled, watching her, and all tension went out the window. I didn't know why I had kept everything from her; she used to be the one I would tell everything to. The one person who I saw myself with every day, and here she was years later, after everything we had been through, adding money to a Starbucks card so I could still bring her a coffee every morning.

Our eyes met as she handed me my phone back. "Now you can buy me coffee guilt free, and I'll make sure to keep that card loaded."

"Phe," I whispered.

She held up a finger to silence me and shook her head. "Nope, you don't even have to pay me back. Just come to the studio every day with a coffee and hold my pin cushion."

I placed my phone in the cup holder and shifted my body, facing her.

"You don't hate me?"

Narrowing her eyes again, she inhaled. "Believe it or not, Clay, I've never *hated* you. Just. . ." She paused, licking her lips.

"We can be friends, right? I don't need to tiptoe anymore, and you can tell me when I'm being an ass. Things friends do."

Ophelia let out a long, low breath. Her eyes met mine before she shook her head. "I don't think there is such a thing as being *friends* with you, Clay. I think jumping off that bridge proved that. Just. . . stop lying to me. . . okay?"

I gently reached up and placed my hand on her neck, my fingers sliding into her curls. I acted on muscle memory as my thumb traced her jaw. I leaned forward and gently touched my lips to hers, feeling the warmth enter my body, my heart racing as she accepted my kiss. I pulled away and looked at her, her eyes heavy. "No more lies. I promise."

Chapter Twenty-Four

-Ophelia-

Jamie held her arms straight out as I pinned a few more places on the dress. All three girls were in the studio today, taking turns taking photos with our phones, actually enjoying the Carter-free spur-of-the-moment photo shoot. It was almost noon, and Clay hadn't shown up yet, not that I was watching the clock or anything, but I kept sneaking glances at the door, hoping he would arrive with a coffee as he always did. I had a lunch meeting with JoAnn in a few hours, and a part of me wanted him there for that. As if he was the confidence booster of the century.

Madeline was patiently waiting her turn to get in her dress, using my phone to snap some photos of Jamie in her bridesmaid dress.

"I still can't believe you kissed him," Jamie said, a hint of swoon in her voice.

"I can," Madeline said matter-of-factly. "I can't believe you actually jumped off a bridge."

I gave a small laugh. "It was a spur of the moment, adrenaline-induced kiss, and. . . well. . . the one in the truck was just as unexpected." I turned, thankful that my face was away from Madeline so she wouldn't see my reaction. I could feel the heat rise to my cheeks, and even if my darker skin hid the red undertone, Madeline could always tell when I was blushing. I dipped my chin and tightened my lips, narrowing my eyes to try to pull the heat away. With a quick glance at Madeline, I could tell she saw it. Her expression said it all.

"It's romantic." Jamie sighed.

It was.

I pursed my lips, focusing yet again on the dress.

"Hold still," I muttered, hoping they would change the subject.

I had told Madeline everything the night before, literally watching her melt on the couch as I recounted our kisses. I didn't expect her to tell Jamie, but here we were, and I honestly loved hearing the story for the second time as I tried to focus.

Jamie stiffened her stance and looked forward, her face void of expression.

"Well, you don't have to be a statue." I chuckled.

"You get either or, Phe," Jamie twisted her torso, moving the entire dress with her. "Statue or free moving. There is no in between."

"Being her coworker, I can confirm that is true." Madeline smiled, raising the phone once again to snap another picture. "I think it's adorable he finally told you everything. He's been trying to impress you since he walked in that door the first night."

"He didn't need to lie to impress me, but I understand. He didn't want me to hate him." I stood up and pushed Jamie's arms down gently, backing away to see how the dress looked. "What do you think, Maddy?"

"I love it. You're a genius, Phe."

Jamie smiled and moved her hips back and forth. "It's perfect."

"Well, almost. I have to finish the alterations, but it will be." I put one hand on my hip as Madeline handed me back my phone. I brought it back to life to look at the time.

Madeline patted my back. "He hasn't texted yet."

My eyes widened. "Oh, I was just checking the time. I have a meeting with JoAnn," I said, only halfway lying.

"Mmm hmm," Madeline hummed.

"Is Clay coming?" Jamie smiled as she spun in a circle, watching the dress flow around her.

"I'm not sure. We didn't agree to anything."

"Only that he would bring you coffees," Madeline smiled.

As if he knew we were talking about him, my phone dinged. I instantly lifted it and focused on the screen. Madeline smiled.

"Speak of the devil." She gently touched my shoulder and walked over to her dress on the mannequin. "Can I change before he comes?"

"Oh, yeah, of course," I answered, not exactly aware of what she asked.

Clay: I took the bus today. I'm on my way, I promise.

Ophelia: The bus, huh?

Clay: Milo needed his truck and Elliot was a tad hungover. I have your coffee, and I'm on my way. I'll be there in ten minutes. By then, your coffee will be at the perfect drinking temperature.

"Is he coming?" I heard Madeline shout from the screen.

"Yes, he took the bus." I locked down my phone and set it on the table. I knew if I responded, we'd start flirting and yes, we'd kissed, but I wasn't sure I was ready to flirt with my ex.

Jamie came up from behind me and smiled. "Maybe he can take photos of all of us? Is your dress done yet?"

I laughed, louder than I expected to. "Oh, hell no. I have gowns to design, an Instagram to manage this week without Carter, and a party to finish planning."

"Clay told me it was almost done," Madeline shouted.

"If 'almost' means we still need food and a guest list, then yes, it's almost done."

"I have it! I have the guest list!" Madeline came around from the screen, her dress fitting her like a glove, a dream, and she dashed to her tote bag on the chair.

"Maddy, not so fast." I moved toward her, envisioning the lace train being stepped on and ripping to shreds. "The train. . ."

"Here." She bent over, ignoring me and pulling a piece of paper from her bag, jolting up as if she was learning the bend-and-snap from Elle Woods. "We invited a few of his coworkers, and some people from the office—"

Jamie let out an audible groan. Madeline turned and gave her a glare.

"Just the other hygienist and Dr. Brenner, oh and Elliot's band. They're going to play for us that night."

"Maddy, you have about thirty people on this list. You said small." I looked up at her, my eyebrows lifting to my hairline. "We haven't even talked to Elliot about the music yet."

"Elliot slipped the location and said that he's covering most of the amenities there, so why not take advantage?" she asked, cocking a shoulder to her ear.

I folded the paper up and tucked it in the waist of my pants, making a mental note to give it to Clay when he arrived. I blinked at her and glanced once more at the door. *Has it been ten minutes yet?*

"Okay, yes, that's doable. But here I thought we were almost done. Jamie, please remind me to text Elliot later. Madeline"—I pointed to the pedestal Jamie was on a few moments ago—"please get on the pedestal and walk gracefully."

Madeline gave a curtsey and gingerly stepped up on the pedestal.

"Now," I said as I approached. "I need to perfect that skirt today. What shoes are you wearing? Did you bring them?"

Madeline nodded. "They're in my bag."

The studio door opened, making us all turn. Clay entered, only one cup in hand, but looking extremely casual. No gray slacks, no button-up shirt, no shiny belt or shoes. He was simple, almost the exact same outfit as yesterday, except he was missing the black boots. I ignored the flutter from my stomach as he came up with a grin, his eyes hyper-focused on me.

"Wait," Madeline shouted, making all of us turn back to her. "Clay, please bring me the heels by my bag. I'm afraid to move for fear of death."

"Don't be dramatic." Clay chuckled as he grabbed the shoes off the chair.

"No, Ophelia will kill me," Madeline muttered, giving me the side eyes as Clay held out the shoes. "I *walked* over there a second ago, and she yelled at me."

"You were going to step on the train," I defended myself. "Just put on your shoes. I'll be right back."

I turned my back to her and rolled my eyes. Clay gave me a slight smirk from the corner of his lips. "Drink this," he said, handing me the cup. "You'll feel better."

"Thanks." *Wait, do I kiss him hello? Do I give him a hug? A handshake? What do I do?*

"Dress fittings today?" he said, motioning his chin to Madeline, who was holding up her skirt while Jamie helped her put on her shoes.

"You got it. Will you be my pin cushion holder again?" I asked, looking up at him, hiding a smile with the coffee cup.

His smile widened, and damn, his eyes sparked. "That's why I'm here, isn't it?"

There I go again, blushing.

"Oh, here." I pulled the guest list from my pants and handed it to Clay.

"What's this?" he asked, taking it to open it.

"Guest list. We have some more planning to do." I smiled up at him.

"Shoes are on!" Jamie exclaimed, coming up to us and circling her arms around Clay's waist, giving him a side hug. He wrapped his arm around her shoulder and gave her a slight squeeze.

"Where's my coffee?" she asked, pulling away from him. He had a foot on Jamie, and the fact that she had to lift her chin to the sky to even talk to him was hilarious.

"Sorry, Jamie. I only cater to Ophelia."

Madeline's dress was back on the mannequin. Jamie's was laid out neatly on the chair next to it, and Clay sat on the opposite side of my computer as I waited for JoAnn to join the call. The last time I had seen JoAnn was right before I left for Portland, and my body was full of nerves. I wasn't *nervous* nervous, I was *excited* nervous. We were talking about the shop, the Instagram, the designs, everything, and Clay was here to hear it all.

My computer dinged, and after a few moments of the internet being glitchy as always, JoAnn's smiling face was there on my screen. I smiled in return, only to see Clay grin as he watched. Maybe having him here would be too distracting.

"Ophelia Fuller!" JoAnn shouted. "I cannot believe how much the Instagram for the store has blown up!"

"I know." I held back a chuckle. The more the wedding gowns showed up, the more followers I gained. The store's feed officially had more followers than my own. "People are loving the gowns, and I simply can't believe it. I can't wait to show you what else I have."

"I have things to show you too, and I hope you'll be pleasantly surprised." JoAnn spun the computer around and showed me a cash register set up still in the works, but nonetheless there. My eyes widened. She kept moving the computer, allowing me to take in all the surrounding elements.

"JoAnn," I said, keeping my excitement in, "you have some designs made already!"

There were three mannequins with my wedding gown designs draped over them. I could tell they were mockups and not finished by any means, but they were there. They were real.

"We have the five designs you sent, mocked up for you to see. Everyone here is in love, and we can't believe we didn't think of this." JoAnn's face came into view as the computer went back to her. "Carter has been talking about the gowns nonstop, even your bridesmaids' dresses."

"I can't see Carter talking non-stop. He's so quiet here. He just follows and takes photos."

"Oh, honey. Carter and I have known each other for so long. Between emails and phone calls, I know more than you. The gowns are phenomenal, so here's what I'm thinking." JoAnn shifted herself in her seat. "If we are going to do this, we really need to focus on that November opening. New Year's weddings and into spring, peak wedding season. How many designs do you have?"

"How many do you need?"

"I'm thinking," She wiggled her fingers around, tilting her head from time to time. While she concentrated, I pointed to my portfolio; silently asking Clay to grab it for me. I had brought every design with me. I knew I had something in there. Clay stood as quietly as he could and brought over my portfolio. All of this happened before JoAnn said, "Between twenty and thirty wedding gowns and maybe ten to fifteen bridesmaids and gown designs."

I opened my portfolio and thumbed through. Each design had preferred fabrics, and I had close-up sketches on the details. "I have about twenty here. I can whip up a few more. My brain is always buzzing with ideas. As for bridesmaids, I'll need to come up with a few more. I only had the few designs, and then, of course, I already have an evening gown line."

"Oh, yes. That dress in Portland." JoAnn lit up.

I pointed a finger. "My friend Madeline is actually going to be wearing that to a party I've been planning for her. I'll make sure Carter is there to get plenty of photos of it while she's acting like a million dollars."

"Fantastic, I love it." JoAnn clapped her hands once, keeping them close to her body. "Send me over those designs as fast as you can so we can begin to manufacture them. We will run everything by you. I'll send over some photos of the store and what we've got going on here and a new contract—"

"A new contract?"

JoAnn nodded. "To reflect the change in the line. I bet you can imagine a store with thousands of dollars of wedding dresses in it is going to cost a lot more than a seasonal line."

I nodded. "Oh, yeah, no. I'm sorry, I didn't think about that part of it. I was never into numbers."

Clay let out a small "ha" at my comment. He was my numbers guy. I never worried about my finances when he helped me manage them. He raised an eyebrow and looked over at me.

"Oh, no worries, Ophelia. That's why we have accountants."

Clay nodded, agreeing with her, both eyebrows raised.

"It goes without saying that your portion will be larger. Worth it, I promise you. I have a feeling you are going to be the next Vera Wang."

Clay's jaw dropped, forcing me to look up at him, completely unsure as to how to react to her comment.

I cleared my throat and shook my head. "That's definitely a dream, and I will try my hardest to take us there."

"I have no doubts. I'll send that new contract with Carter for you to sign, and then he will fax it over to me. As soon as we get those designs, we will get to work."

"Sounds perfect."

We said our goodbyes, JoAnn lingering a little longer than I would have thought she would have wanted, asking all kinds of questions about Portland and Madeline, about how the wedding planning was going. JoAnn, I could tell, was going to be more than an investor and collaborator. It seemed like she genuinely cared. Once the screen went black, I closed the computer and looked at Clay.

His feet were up on the table, leaning back into the uncomfortable chair. His hair was disheveled from running his hands through it a few times, and his arm resting on the desk, his fingers drawing circles on the table.

"What?" I asked him, forcing my smile to stay simple and the heat from rising to my cheeks.

He nodded, gave me a sly smile and said, "The next Vera Wang. Now that's the shit."

Chapter Twenty-Five

-Clay-

You're coming on too strong, Clay. 'I only cater to Ophelia. That's the shit?'

I needed to redirect my mind, to get those kisses out of my head.

Impossible.

She gave me a taste, and now I wanted—needed—more, but I had to be calm. I had to chill out.

Opening Pandora's Box with Ophelia was easier than I thought it would be, and hell, did it release a lot of tension. Tension that I didn't know I was holding in by trying to be who I was in Seattle. Now that she knew every detail, it didn't matter, and the best part— she didn't hate me.

She didn't hate me.

We stayed at the studio until well after the sun had set. It was late, and we had eaten nothing but junk food and drank more coffee than I care to admit, but she had more work cut out for her now. She quickly sent her completed designs to JoAnn, and then I watched as she sketched a few new ones, the ideas flowing from her mind like a waterfall.

While she sketched, we talked about anything we could think of. She told me all about New York and her life there, finally buying her apartment in the heart of Manhattan.

"Do you remember when you told me we should live in Brooklyn?" she muttered.

I smiled at the memory. Us trying to figure out our life together as she became the person she is today. I chuckled but didn't respond. Would I have ended up where I am now if I had moved with her to New York? Would I have found a place like Jackson and Rye to work? Would we still be together? I bit my lip and furrowed my brow, my eyes on her as she leaned down closer to the paper.

"You're thinking too hard," Ophelia muttered, not even lifting her head to look at me. "I know that look, that concentrated overthinking look you always get. You get it with numbers too."

"What look?"

She lifted her head and pointed at me, her pencil stuck between her fingers. "That one. Stop overthinking."

"I'm not overthinking."

"I bet I know exactly what is going through your head." Ophelia twirled the pencil in her fingers and began to sketch again. "I think about that too, but it's not what would have happened."

"What would have happened?" I asked, keeping my voice lower, my eyes centered on her.

She frowned and shrugged her shoulders. "Doesn't matter, does it?"

I narrowed my eyes and tilted my head, letting out a long sigh. "I guess not."

Ophelia dropped me off at Milo's apartment after her sketches were done. She smiled at me as I said goodbye and opened the car door, half of my body already out of the car. I was tempted to lean over and give her another kiss but decided against it. The other two were welcome. I wasn't sure what this one would bring. So instead, I promised coffee in the morning.

Milo and Elliot were both in the apartment when I walked in, two beers on the coffee table in front of them, a Marvel movie on the screen.

"*Endgame* again?" I chuckled, locking the door behind me and opening the fridge to get a can of beer for myself.

"Elliot's only seen it once, so it was the obvious choice," Milo said, not taking his eyes from the screen. The Hulk was about to put on the makeshift infinity gauntlet, and Milo was going to be glued to that screen until the end.

"Yeah, but I don't need to see it again," Elliot groaned as he stood from the couch, grabbing his beer to meet me in the kitchen. "You're the one I needed to talk to, anyway."

I took a pull from my can and pinched my brow. "Me?"

"Yup." He sighed as he reached down and brought up a large binder. He slammed it on the counter and placed his hand on top. "These are my books, and they are kinda a mess."

"Finances?" I grinned. Numbers. My second favorite thing.

Elliot shook his head. "I don't do numbers, and when I took over this company for my dad last year, I didn't realize how much of a mess he left the finances in. His mind started to go downhill, and he was determined to still work, but"—he flung open the binder—"he began to lose track of the vendors and contractors we dealt with, and everything became a mess. I didn't know it was this bad."

I grabbed ahold of one of the rings and pulled the binder toward me. Instantly, I saw contracts and purchasing forms everywhere, no rhyme or reason for the mess in front of me.

"I take it you want me to take a look?" I asked, looking at some of the papers in the binder. "I'm going to need more than this to go off of. I'll need account histories and—"

"I know," he interrupted, taking a seat at one of the bar stools. "I'm in the office tomorrow, and I was wondering if you could swing by?"

"Don't you have an accountant?"

He held out his hand, palm up, toward the binder, as if showing the pure fact that the accountant was no longer taking responsibilities. "The guy is like eighty, and he refuses to retire, so I"—he drug out his words—"may have fired him this morning with the hopes that you would help out."

"You fired an eighty-year-old?"

"I may have exaggerated his age."

I rubbed the back of my neck, trying to keep my excitement at bay. This is what I loved about my job at Jackson and Rye. I managed accounts left and right. I knew their every move when it came to their money. I loved being the one in charge of it. Numbers and I meshed, and we meshed well.

I chuckled. "You want an embezzling accountant going through your books?"

Tilting his head and pointing a finger at me, Elliot began, "First of all, you're not an embezzling accountant. You just got stuck in a sticky situation, and second"—he dropped his hand—"yes. I'd rather trust you than some hot shot out of college."

"He used to be that hot shot out of college," Milo shouted from the living room, the battle between the heroes and big bad guy just starting to happen.

"I did," I agreed.

"Weren't we all?" Elliot shrugged. "So, will you take a look?"

I raked my teeth across my bottom lip and nodded. "Yeah, I'd love to, actually. Can I keep this, try to make heads or tails of it?"

"Please." He pushed the binder closer to me. "Tomorrow? Say eleven?"

I closed the binder and took another drink from my beer. "Sounds like a plan."

I was taught to dress the part. Even though it was just Elliot, and it was just to take a quick look, I dressed as if I was going to meet a new client for the first time. My nice shoes, gray slacks, belt, and white button-down shirt, complete with a tie. I took a photo from the bathroom mirror and sent it to Ophelia.

Clay: Channeling my J and R days. How do I look?

Ophelia: Pretty damn amazing. Good luck.

I gave myself one more look over before heading out to the bus stop, gliding my fingers along Tessa as I walked past her. One day, maybe. Until then, the bus would do. Thankfully, it was a nice day outside, and the ride to Elliot's office wasn't that long. It helped that I had Ophelia's constant texting in my pocket. I would smile with each new joke, each new draft of a sketch that she would send, and when she finally sent me a photo of her and a cup of coffee, I knew I was a goner.

There had to be a way to keep her in my life this time around.

I didn't want to lose her again.

Locking my phone, I slipped it into my pocket and made sure I had Elliot's large binder under my arm. I closed my eyes and tried to focus on my task at hand: numbers. Specifically, Elliot's numbers. I was able to piece together some of the papers he had given me, some invoices that still needed to be paid and vendor information, but it was still no good without his accounts.

Elliot's company took up an entire three-story building. Glass walls and white trim made the building stand out against the stone walls that lined the street. Walking in, I saw two large conference rooms, both with large TVs but empty. The receptionist was sitting patiently at her computer and behind her was the open floor plan of multiple desks scattered around. A few of the desks were empty. Others had what I assumed was an employee and client sitting with them.

"Hello, I'm Clay Nolan." I walked up to the receptionist, standing as tall as I could. "I'm here to meet with—"

"Elliot, right? He's been waiting for you. I'll go grab him," she said with a smile.

I narrowed my eyes and took another look. I thought Elliot was a contractor, but this is not what I was picturing. Before I could find any kind of sign, Elliot's voice appeared.

"Hey, man. This way." Elliot led me past the desks and into his office, which had glass walls and was ridiculously clean.

"I didn't know you were an architect."

Elliot sat behind his desk, dressed similarly to me. It was as if he had two personalities. Stage and business. Even though he was dressed for business, I could see the stage wanting to burst free. He loosened his tie and grumbled. "My dad was an architect, and this was his firm. I went into business, per his request, and we've grown. Bottom floor is me and my team of architects. My dad loved the open floor plan. Second floor is design. They all tend to spend most of their time up there. It's more 'homey.' Third floor is where we present to our clients. We have multiple meeting rooms and display cases up there. We get a lot of foot traffic, believe it or not. We deal with contractors and vendors from"—he waved his hand around—"everywhere, and he left it all to me."

"He passed?" I asked, trying to sound remorseful, take the seat across from him and placing the binder on the desk.

"No, but he was diagnosed with Alzheimer's three years ago, and he went downhill fast. I worked with him for the first two years, but a year ago, he left everything to me." He gave me a cheesy smile and spread his arms.

"And apparently, he left you a mess?"

He groaned and bent over, his forehead hitting the desk. "Unfortunately," he grumbled, rising his head from the desk.

"How bad are we talking? I went through these." I tapped the binder. "You have some open invoices."

"Oh, I'm not worried about those getting paid. We are making good money, but I need it organized. That's where you come in."

"I can definitely help you get it in line, and then when you're ready to hire an accountant I can show him what we've done and —"

"No, Clay." Elliot held onto the edge of the desk and leaned forward. This man had no professionalism in him at all. "I want you to be my accountant."

I narrowed my eyes at him. Was I hoping that this was going to happen? Sure, but I wasn't expecting it. I didn't want to assume anything. "You know I don't work with a firm, right? I have no business license or anything."

"We'll make it work, even if I have to pay you under the table."

"Yeah, that's not happening." I stopped him.

"Well then, we will figure something out."

I chuckled. "Okay, how about this, I'll help you until you can find a properly employed accountant?"

Elliot smirked. "No deal. I really would like you to be my accountant."

"Let's just get these numbers not such a mess at first, and then we'll talk about it, okay?"

"I could hire you. At least while you're here, that would be a way to make it legal." Elliot leaned back in his chair and began to run his thumb nail over his lip, his head lightly nodding.

"You won't be letting this go, will you?"

Elliot shook his head. "Nope. So, first things first. Let's get you a W2 and set you up a profile here. Let's count today as your first official day." He leaned forward and grabbed his computer mouse, already clicking away.

"You're willingly hiring me?"

Elliot spun just as a piece of paper came out of his printer. He grabbed it and placed it on the desk, a pen on top of it. "That was always kinda the plan. Welcome aboard."

Forty minutes later, I had papers signed and a salary agreed on; I was given a quick tour of the office. Elliot promised me my own office, but I simply asked to work from home most of the time, still visit the office of course, but my priorities shifted. I wanted the time with Ophelia. I was upfront with him. I expected him to turn into a "boss" instantly when his eyes narrowed and he gave me a side eye, but then his face formed a huge smile and patted my back.

"I don't care where you work, as long as my finances get organized." He laughed.

Then, with a document being sent to my computer with all the information I would need to get started, I sat on the bus, a smile on my face as I came to the fact that I finally had a job. A paying job. I was no longer a bum just crashing on Milo's couch.

I dug my phone out of my pocket and opened Ophelia's thread.

Clay: Elliot offered me a job.

The little bubble appeared quickly. I bit my bottom lip, waiting for her response to come.

Ophelia: That's amazing! Now you get to tell your parents you don't have to work at Home Depot.

Clay: Speaking of, dinner this Friday with them. You in?

Ophelia: I told you I was. I wouldn't miss it for the world.

I sent back a time I would pick her up and then locked my phone. I couldn't help but think that everything was coming together because of Ophelia. She was the reason I pulled my head out of my ass. She was simply becoming my everything again, and I knew. . .

I was in love with her.

Chapter Twenty-Six

-Ophelia-

Even though I wouldn't admit it aloud, the week went very slowly without Clay with me in the studio. I was ready to see him again, ready to have his hand in mine. The perfect way to end the busy week I had.

I pursed my lips, tilting my head to make sure my signature golden hoop earrings were in place, then I added a second layer of gloss to my lips. It was just dinner with Clay's parents, something I had done *plenty* of times in the past, but this time simply felt different.

Paul and Elizabeth Nolan were two of the nicest people I had ever met. They were always willing to have us over for dinner, willing to listen to our dreams, *my* dreams. Seeing as my parents, who were supportive in their own way, kept to the warmth of Georgia, Paul and Elizabeth were like my second set of parents.

My own parents stayed in their bubble, choosing the humidity over the rainy days Portland had to offer. They had come out for my graduation, meeting Clay then and actually said he was a great choice for me, excited as to what would happen for us, only to curse his name a few years later. I chuckled to myself, shaking my head. I couldn't help but wonder what they would think of us now.

Us.

I glanced at my phone, noticing I only had a few more minutes until Clay came to pick me up. I slipped on my heels and gave myself one final glance in the mirror. A simple black dress flowed down my body, hitting all my curves while still being modest. I wasn't sure how to dress, but I knew I wanted to look and feel good.

Giving Niko a pat on the head goodbye, I stepped onto the porch right as Clay pulled up in Milo's truck. As always, he climbed out and ran up to meet me, grabbing my hand as if it were just as natural as it was in college.

"Now just a warning," Clay started.

"That's not the way to begin a conversation. Hello, Clay." I smiled at him as he opened the passenger door for me. "How was your day?"

He narrowed his eyes and smirked. "It was good, filled with numbers. Elliot's books are coming together, albeit slowly."

"It's good he has you then." I smiled.

He gave a soft sigh and licked his lips. He cleared his throat. I could just tell he wanted to kiss me, but he was resisting. "How was your day?"

"Fantastic," I said, catching his smile as he shut the car door. "Madeline's dress is ninety-six percent done, just in time for her final fitting and bridal photos with Carter. Okay, now." I tilted my head to look at him. "What do you need to warn me about?"

"My parents are over the moon thrilled that you are coming." He slipped his hand in mine, lifting it to his lips to place a gentle kiss on the back of it. "You look beautiful."

"Why are you warning me? I'm excited to see them, too." I tightened my fingers around his, feeling those light flutters hit my stomach after the simple kiss and him calling me beautiful.

"They may talk your ear off. My mom squealed on the phone when I told her you were coming. I haven't heard her squeal in years so. . . just a warning."

"I'm sure I'll have an amazing time. I'm not worried."

And I wasn't. Even when Clay opened the door, and we were greeted instantly by Elizabeth, who pushed her son aside to give me the biggest hug I've received in a long time. She hadn't changed. Her brown hair was still in curls, and her eyes were still full of life and promise. She held me at arm's length and smiled, shaking her head in disbelief that I was standing in front of her.

"Oh, Ophelia." She pulled me in for another hug. "It's been way too long!"

"Mom, let the woman breathe," Clay said from behind her. When I opened my eyes to find him, he was crouched on the floor, petting an outrageously huge black cat. "Grim, bud. You need one of those wheels I've seen."

"Oh, he does not." Elizabeth spun. "He gets plenty of exercise."

"Running up the stairs to our bed does not count as exercise, Liz." The booming voice came from the kitchen, becoming clearer as Paul made his way into the living room with us.

Paul looked exactly like Clay—just as tall, with brown hair that had been taken over by gray over the years. He had gained some weight around his middle, but his welcoming demeanor hadn't faded. If anything, it was amplified.

"Hi, Mr. Nolan." I smiled at him, giving him a small wave.

"Now, Ophelia, how long have you known me?"

"Too long," I responded.

"Long enough to drop the 'mister' and call me Paul." He walked over and wrapped me in his arms.

These two were so welcoming to me, even after what had happened between Clay and me. They let bygones be bygones–, never held grudges. My parents would probably warn me he would leave me again. I shook the thought away. That wasn't going to happen again. . . at least I hoped it wasn't.

"Okay, Paul. How are you? Clay told me you've retired?" I asked as he pulled me in his arm, leading me into the kitchen.

"Oh, yeah, a few months ago. Right before Clayton moved home, really."

"And you're building things? With wood?" I asked.

He furrowed his brow at me, his glasses moving up the bridge of his nose a touch. "Just dabbling. Except Clay refuses to go work for Home Depot so I can't make as much as I want because the wood costs so damn much."

Clay stood in the kitchen, helping his mom grab plates and even from a distance, I could see his eye roll. "You agreed you wouldn't talk about that, Dad," he grumbled.

I gave a small laugh and gave Paul one more squeeze before letting him go to join Clay and Elizabeth in the kitchen. She was still working on dinner, which was, by the looks of it, pointing back to her Irish roots. Irish Pasta, with all the comfort food to go with it. Garlic bread had just come out of the oven, making the entire kitchen smell fabulous, and the mashed potatoes were still steaming in the serving tray.

"Oh, Elizabeth." I came up behind her, placing my hand on her shoulder. "This all looks amazing."

"Well, I was going to cook a Shepherd's Pie, but Clay suggested I keep it simple and not scare you with too much meat."

"I would have loved anything here." I reached for a towel. "Let me help. I can take the pasta and potatoes to the table."

"Thank you, dear," she said sweetly.

I made two trips, first placing the potatoes in the middle of the table, and then coming back with the pasta. Clay stood at the table, close to me, as I set the dish down. When I stood and arched slightly to look at him, he gave me a sly smile.

"Thank you," he whispered.

"It's just pasta," I whispered back, holding back the urge to kiss him. His five o'clock shadow proved that he was comfortable.

Normally he was clean shaven around me, but this was who he was now. I wanted to trace my finger along his jawline. Instead, I formed a fist to keep my fingers from doing things they shouldn't.

"Not just that."

I raked my teeth on my bottom lip. "I know."

He held my gaze at first, wanting to break the space between us, but instead, he just looked at me. His eyes began to roam my face, my hair, my collarbone, and finally my lips. His gaze was heavy on me as the heat began to build in my own body. I didn't know how much longer I could pretend I didn't want him, because it was obvious now, to me and to everyone in the world, that I did. The kisses we had shared were only the beginning of what we could be, what I still wasn't sure I wanted. But his eyes still wandered. I watched him, breathing in the moment, wanting to breathe him in, as his knuckles gently glided along my cheek. I inhaled, holding my breath as he slowly leaned toward me.

"Okay, dinner is served!" Elizabeth shouted, breaking our moment. Clay blinked and inhaled, turning toward his mother. Just that five seconds gave him the exact same reaction it had given me, except he was going to give me more, and I wished Elizabeth hadn't broken his trance.

Clay pulled out the chair and waited for me to sit before taking his own seat next to me. Paul and Elizabeth sat across from us, and the fat cat made his way into the kitchen and under the table.

"The cat begs?" I asked, watching as his tail disappeared.

"He's fat for a reason." Clay leaned in toward me, placing his fabric napkin on his lap. "Mom gives him table scraps."

"I do not." Elizabeth got defensive, looking at her son. "But yes, Ophelia, he thinks he's a dog."

"Because you give him table scraps," Clay mumbled.

I shook my head and picked up my fork, reaching over to grab a piece of garlic bread. "So, Paul is doing woodworking. Elizabeth, what have you been up to these days, besides cooking amazing food?"

"Just staying at home. I read. I crochet. I cook—"

"She watches way too much television," Paul joked. "She quotes shows more than books. She's also on a pickleball team."

I raised my eyebrows and smiled at Elizabeth. "Pickleball?"

"Since when?" Clay asked, his mouth full of bread.

"I joined last month, just a few games here and there." Elizabeth sat up a little straighter. "I have a match coming up. You should come!" She brightened up as her gaze drifted toward me.

"When?" I asked with just as much enthusiasm.

"Wednesdays. Not this coming Wednesday, but in a few weeks."

"Oh, well, I'll be back in New York soon after the wedding," I muttered, genuinely sad that I couldn't see Elizabeth kick some ass at Pickleball. No doubt she was amazing.

"I'd love to see you play, Mom. I'm sure I can figure something out once all this ends. We're still planning Milo's party, and Ophelia is knee deep in wedding gowns now." Clay turned to me as he mentioned wedding gowns.

Elizabeth smiled. "Wedding *gowns*, as in more than Madeline's dress?"

I blushed and nodded. "Yes, actually. I'm getting my own boutique. I had a client who was impressed with my line last year and wanted to invest in a boutique. We went from being seasonal lines to gowns." I beamed. I was still so excited about it, almost so that I would jump off a bridge again.

"She's being modest," Clay said, his eyes focused on mine. "Thirty designs and a shop on 5th Avenue. This investor already has some mock designs up, and her Instagram has blown up." He looked back to his parents. "She opens up in November."

"And I'll have Clay to help me keep my finances in line."

"Well, Ophelia. That is amazing news. We knew you had it in you. We saw your line in Portland last year, that last dress." Elizabeth made a "whoo" sound as she turned to look at her husband.

I swallowed. "That's actually for Madeline, too. She's going to wear it before the wedding, either at the party or the rehearsal dinner." I turned to Clay. "I'm assuming you'll be there as my pin cushion holder, right? I've made adjustments, but you never know."

"I'll ask Elliot if I can work remotely that day. I'm sure he wouldn't have a problem with it. He told me he didn't care where I worked, just as long as I got everything in order. This week I was at the office, but I'm sure I can lug my laptop into your studio," Clay said, not even dropping a beat.

"The office?" Paul asked, taking his attention off his plate for the first time since pickleball. "What office?"

It was Clay's turn to sit up a little straighter, and damn, he deserved to boast about it. "I was hired by an architecture firm to help organize their accounts. Elliot took over for his dad, and unfortunately, his dad wasn't the best at numbers in his later years."

"Clayton," Elizabeth whispered.

"Don't get too excited. It may just be temporary, but hey, it's something."

"I don't think it's temporary." I placed my hand on Clay's forearm. "I really think Elliot is going to keep you around. He'd be stupid not to. And when I have a question, I can always call, and you can handle it from here."

Clay furrowed his brow, and his eyes twitched. He didn't like the idea of handling my finance questions from across the country, I could tell. A part of me hated it too.

"Have you thought about taking on more clients?" Paul said, pointing his fork at Clay.

"I work for Elliot. I'm his employee. I don't think he'd appreciate me bringing on more accounting clients when I need to focus on his books."

"Maybe you could start your own business. Jackson and Rye and that ugly black mark you always mention won't stop you from starting something of your own. I bet that news has died off, and people have forgotten who Clayton Nolan is, anyway," Elizabeth suggested.

I dropped my jaw and angled my body toward him. "You could do that."

"I just need to focus on paying Milo back. I don't have too much longer before he moves in with Maddy, and then I'm most likely moving in here, that is until I can get enough saved up for my own place. Elliot gave me a pretty decent salary." Clay looked down, poking at his pasta. "But that's something I can think of in the future."

"Well, I am glad you're finally getting it all together. Maybe Ophelia had something to do with it," Paul mumbled, turning his attention back to his food.

Clay looked at me, that smile he gave me before returning to his lips. "It was all because of her. I had to impress her somehow."

Elizabeth chuckled and the topic returned to her Wednesday match with details of pickleball. I blushed and reached over under the table, gently placing my hand on Clay's knee. If only he knew how much had happened for me because of him. I don't think I would have ever sent that email to JoAnn if he hadn't clicked that send button, and I never, ever would have had gone bungee jumping if I wasn't in his arms.

Maybe we still meant more to each other than we realized.

Chapter Twenty-Seven

-Clay-

My phone buzzed in my pocket as I made my way up the stairs to Ophelia's studio. I had my laptop in my bag and folders of Elliot's accounts that still needed to be gone through, but since I had made a major dent in the office, I knew working off site would be fine. Even Elliot basically kicked me out of the office. But the buzzing in my pocket made me think that maybe he had forgotten to give me something, or that I was needed back there.

Before I grabbed the door handle, I answered my phone, not even paying attention to who it was.

"Clay Nolan," I said, lifting the strap of my bag higher on my shoulder to grab the handle without spilling the coffee in my hand.

"Clay." The voice of my lawyer, Justin, rang in my ears. It had been weeks since I had heard from him, yet here he was. "I have some news for you."

"Oh, hey, Justin. If you could give me just one moment to get settled here." I placed my bag on the ground, setting Ophelia's coffee next to it. Justin, however, kept going without letting me get another word in.

"Brain Walker. I sent you an email about him. We haven't heard back from you."

I closed my eyes and tried to remember the email. It had seemed so long ago that I had completely shifted my focus from it. "Yes, sorry. I've been busy. I sent a response. Did that not cover it?"

"We never received a response. Are you sure you sent it?"

I thought, well maybe I never did send that email.

"Oh, maybe not. . ." I mumbled, rubbing my hand against my forehead. "If you give me just once second, I can check—"

"No need. I can just get all of this on the record." I heard him fumble around.

"On the record? Kind of like talking to a potential employer?"

Justin let out a chuckle. "Regina." His voice raised. "She called me as a reference, and I just told her the truth. I gave you an outstanding recommendation."

I rolled my eyes. "In a morally gray character reference." I remembered her words during the interview.

"Never mind that. Brian Walker?" Justin changed the subject. "Can you add a quick character profile on him?"

"Can you tell me why?" I asked, leaning against the wall, my free hand rubbing the nape of my neck as I waited for his response.

He heaved a sigh. "He started working for another firm about five months ago—"

"How come Brian can land another job, but I can't?" I interrupted.

"Because it was your name on the lawsuit, not his."

Okay, he had a point. I sighed, which apparently told Justin to keep talking.

"And that firm is now missing two million, and their lead accountant is being pinned. However, he has proof none of it came from him. We think Brian is framing him—and framed you. The other firm has filed a suit, and he's the common factor. We are 99.8% sure that he's the cause of all the jobs lost from Jackson and Rye, and if he's charged, we could appeal and get your charges reversed." Justin said, all toneless, matter-of-factly.

"Reversed?"

"All I need is a character profile."

Suddenly, the door to the studio opened, making me jump. Ophelia stopped, hunched her shoulders and covered her mouth, whispering a quick apology before she started to slink back in her studio. I reached out and gently touched her elbow, giving her the okay to stay. She slipped the door open and came out into the hallway, leaning her shoulder next to me, trying to stay silent as I spoke with Justin.

"I can't really say anything bad about him. He always did his work, quickly and accurately. He was able to stay when we had a bigger case to work on, and he was always willing to take on new caseloads. I can't see him as the embezzling type, to be honest." I kept my hand on Ophelia's elbow, lightly brushing my fingers against the back of her arm. Just having her in the hallway with me brought comfort. "Hell, I even considered him a friend while I lived in Seattle. I wish I could tell you something that would pin everything on him, but all I recall was a good employee. Why would he pin everything on me? How?"

Justin gave a long hum and then finally spoke. "He's the common factor. We'll have to keep digging, but like I said—"

"99.8% sure he's the one, huh?" I asked, finishing the sentence for him, looking up at Ophelia. "You'll keep me posted?"

"Of course. This involves you, even if it doesn't feel like it. I just want the charges against you to be dropped and the real guy behind bars. Do you know if he paid anything during the settlement?"

"No one did, just me."

"Well, again, it's because it was all pinned on you. They wanted you out."

"Yeah, yeah, yeah. . ." I grumbled, remembering the feeling of stress that was placed on me during the lawsuit. They definitely wanted me out. Rubbing the nape of my neck again, I felt that place where all my stress would sit. These past couple of months, I hadn't had any tension there, and I wasn't interested in bringing it back.

"I'll be in touch, all right, Clay?"

"Sounds great. Thanks for the call." We said our goodbyes, and once the line was dead, I dropped my phone to my side, Ophelia's body still close to mine. "I wasn't expecting a phone call from him today." I pushed myself off the wall, dropping my hand from Ophelia's arm. I bent down to grab my bag, carefully picking up her coffee.

She took it from me. "Is this regarding your case?"

I nodded. "I think so, but not really?" I swung my bag over my shoulder and grabbed the door handle, opening the door for Ophelia to step in. Once inside her studio, I saw Carter already taking photos of the two bridesmaids' dresses that were on the mannequins. One was already sewn and completed, the other still held together with pins. "Is this your dress?" I asked, smiling over at her as I walked toward it, paying no mind to Carter.

"Yeah. . . I had to make it sooner than planned. JoAnn wants to post them on Instagram." Ophelia came up behind me and reached out to touch the fabric that we had searched for. "So, here it is."

I looked at the dress, back to the table where all her designs sat neatly in a pile, her computer open with digital designs for adding color. "How do you do all of this?"

She let out a deep breath. "Let's just say some of the wedding planning has fallen on Jamie's shoulders. I really didn't expect it to be this much work. We've even fumbled on the party planning, so much so that Elliot has taken over."

"Nah, don't worry about the party. We still have time to plan it. I've got the invitations, and I can even work on decorations. Do we need decorations?"

"Maybe centerpieces?" She clenched her teeth, forcing me to smile.

"Centerpieces?" I laughed. "Music? Lighting? Food?"

"Elliot said he'd perform some songs, but I'm sure he doesn't want to sing the entire night, seeing as he's the one who has to be on stage during the reception. So. . . maybe we need to form a playlist?"

"I'll ask Elliot what he's performing."

"And then tell me, and I'll create the playlist. And the Piano Bar is providing the food?"

"That. . ." I pointed at her. "I don't know."

"We should see if that waffle truck can cater. Milo and Maddy *love* that waffle truck." She narrowed her eyes and tilted her head, her hair falling to the side. She had straightened it today, having half of it pinned back, but what I assumed was a million bobby pins.

"I'm sure it will all fall into place. We have time."

She let out a deep sigh. "And you said not to worry about the party," she repeated, folding her arms.

I mimicked her stance. "Exactly, there is nothing to worry about. We got it handled."

Dropping her arms, Ophelia heaved another sigh and turned back to the dress on the mannequin. "We're both busy," she said softly, her fingers touching the shoulder of one of the dresses, fixing a wrinkle in the fabric. "Even when you were pretending to work, we didn't put our focus on this," she mumbled. "But now you're actually working and have your lawyer contacting you."

I shrugged, leaving her by the mannequins. "No overthinking and no stress. We have plenty of time to get this party put together, and when we do, we'll go bungee jumping again to celebrate."

She let out a laugh and looked at me over her shoulder. "I am never going bungee jumping again."

"We'll see," I sighed, taking a seat at the desk, placing my laptop next to her with the files from the office.

"Nope." Ophelia popped her *P* and turned back to the dress.

"I love it when you do that," I mumbled, opening my laptop to try to at least get some work done.

"Do what?" She turned quickly, her hand finding her hip.

"When you pop the *P* at the end of words."

"I don't do that." She rolled her eyes and turned back to the mannequin, Carter instantly showing up at her side.

"Of course you don't." I chuckled under my breath.

I knew her Instagram had reached new heights. People were following her left and right, and the designs of the wedding gowns she had posted were being shared over and over again. She was accomplishing so much in such a short amount of time. It simply amazed me. And even through all this, she was worried about a party. She somehow was managing to put others first, even me.

This woman. No matter how hard I tried in the past, I couldn't shake her. Through all the women, all the promotions and material things I had gained, she was always in the back of my mind. Even when those things were directly in front of me, all in arm's reach, I never realized how much I missed this feeling Ophelia gave me. And now here she was in front of me again, with a dream that was coming to life even with the exhaustion hiding behind her sweet eyes. Ten years of trying to forget her only landed me here: in love with her again, determined to find a way to make whatever we were work.

"Ophelia," I muttered, unable to stop the words that were falling off my lips. She turned, placing her hands on her hips once more. She smiled and tilted her head, almost making me lose the words at the tip of my tongue. "Let me take you out."

She pursed her lips and narrowed her eyes, moving her hands from her hips to cross her arms over her chest. Her gaze was heavy on mine, and I desperately needed to say something.

Ophelia exhaled and simply said, "No," before turning back to the dress.

My heart dropped. I inhaled, holding my breath as I forced my brain back to my computer, booting it up and reaching to grab the file. I asked. And she said no. Don't know what compelled me to, but I asked. It didn't change anything. I would still come here and hold that pin cushion when she needed me to, and we would plan the party.

Ophelia's hand appeared over mine. The warmth of her touch compelled me to look up to her. I tried to show no emotion that her no hit me harder than I expected, so instead, I gave her a smirk and raised an eyebrow.

"Clay," she said sweetly. "You can't take me out because *I* would like to take you out."

Have I mentioned that I was royally screwed?

Chapter Twenty-Eight

-Ophelia-

Clay looked dumbfounded, as if he couldn't believe I asked him out. That I would want to spend more time with him. The weeks that were filled with tension, I'll be honest, mainly on my part, seemed to slip away the more he opened up. He let me into his life again, and everything felt so natural. Falling into the same place we were felt as if it was the right next step.

His jaw dropped slightly, right before a small smile grew. "That's backwards," he mumbled, turning his hand to lace his fingers with mine.

"Are you saying a girl can't take a guy out on a date?" I protested, confidence radiating through me.

"No," he stuttered. "I just, I mean. . ." *Gosh he was adorable when he was nervous.* "I would love to go out with you."

I nodded, raising one corner of my lips before releasing his hand and returning to my dress on the mannequin. Carter stood, his camera pointing toward the floor, a look of annoyance that I took the time out of the photo shoot to ask Clay out on a date. I gave him a smile and then positioned myself in the same pose as before. How people weren't getting tired of seeing me with pins between my lips and hunched over was beyond me, but those photos were the ones that made the page.

After a few moments of silence, I heard the faint clicking of Clay's computer, his fingers moving at the speed of light, and what made me smile was knowing that he most likely wasn't touching the letters. It was only the numbers that he was hitting.

After dinner with his parents, the moment at the dining room table, I had been battling with myself to ask him out on a proper date. One that I could treat him with, give him the perfect day, just like Milo had given Madeline. The only problem was, Clay had changed a lot since college, and I had no idea how to create the perfect date for him.

Dinner was out of the question, and anything adventurous wouldn't be able to top bungee jumping, not by a long shot. It had to be something memorable, something to redefine who we were as a couple. If that's what we even were. It was just a date. One date. But it had to be the *perfect* date. Where was that confidence from before? Did it just fly out the window as soon as he agreed, as soon as he said he'd *love* to go out with me?

"Hey." Clay's voice broke my concentration. The camera sounds paused, and I heard Carter grumble. I stood up straight, reached up to place my hair behind my ear and looked over at Clay. His face was angled toward his laptop, a piece of paper in his hand floating in the air, but his eyes were firm on me. "You're overthinking it."

I scuffed and dropped my hands. "I am not." How dare he use that against me? I was the one who told him not to overthink, not the other way around.

He gave me a slow smirk and licked his teeth, wiggling his eyebrows before returning to the computer. Was that a tint of red to his cheeks? "All right," he responded simply.

"You're not in your element this time, Miss Fuller. I suggest a break?" Carter groaned. "I'll see what I can salvage from these. Perhaps you can respond to messages from Instagram?"

I hummed at Carter, trying my hardest not to glare at him as he turned his back and walked to his tiny desk.

"Your computer has been making a lot of noises over here." Clay motioned his head toward my laptop, that same tint of pink on his cheeks still lingering as his smirk got bigger.

I narrowed my eyes at him, walked to the desk, and spun my laptop around, wheeling my chair over to sit and face him. I could look up date ideas while pretending to be on Instagram. He would never know. I got this.

I am Ophelia Fuller, wedding gown designer, fashion extraordinaire. I can plan a date.

If we were in New York, I knew just what I would do. I would take him to the best pizza place in the city, then we would stroll Central Park. We would hold hands and maybe steal a few kisses, nothing too serious, but we would end the night back at my place, playing board or card games while drinking his favorite bottle of wine. The night would end with the perfect goodnight kiss, and then I would curl up falling asleep thinking of him. I would maybe even get a text goodnight when he got to his destination. Just the thought made me swoon.

I could feel myself swooning.

Literally.

I bit my bottom lip and used my computer to pull up Madeline's texting thread.

Ophelia: I have a strange request, but you gotta go with it.

Since she was at work, the three little dancing dots took a few moments to appear, but once they did, my heart rate picked up.

Madeline: Explain.

Ophelia: Can I. . . borrow. . . your house next Saturday?

Madeline's response was three question marks followed by the questioning look emoji. When I quickly typed out my idea for a date with Clay, those little dots didn't dance for long.

Madeline: YES, YES, YES! I'll stay at Milo's. He'll be thrilled.

I let out a small chuckle, which made Clay's eyes turn to me, his fingers still planted on his ten-key.

"Just a wonderful message from a potential bride," I lied.

He raised his eyebrows and returned to the computer.

Ophelia: It will NOT be an overnight thing, so maybe head back when Clay gets back to Milo's?

Madeline: I have a feeling it will turn into an overnight thing. You two have a lot of time to make up.

I rolled my eyes, responding: *That's not going to happen anytime soon. I just want to take him on a date and enjoy some alone time with him. Next Saturday? Just plan on a late night with Milo?*

Madeline: 100%. I'll need all the details when I get back.
Ophelia: Of course.

Satisfied and less a nervous wreck than I was fifteen minutes ago, I slammed my laptop closed and looked up at Clay, lacing my fingers together to rest my chin on them. He stopped what he was doing and mimicked my pose.

"Wanna go grab some lunch?"

"Let me finish this email to my lawyer, and I'd love to."

I was tempted, so very tempted, to lean over the table to give him a kiss. But I refrained. I pushed myself off the desk and went to gather my things. A few Instagram messages answered, an annoyed Carter, and a date in my future. I felt good, almost on top of the world good. I could probably jump off another bridge good.

Hours after Clay had left, I stood in my empty studio. Just me, my glass of wine, and music serenading me in the background. The blinds on the floor-to-ceiling windows were open, the Portland city lights flickering in the background. I raised the desk as much as I could and angled it so I could stand and sketch, bringing more wedding gowns to life.

For a brief moment, it felt like home.

I gripped my pencil, the blank sheet of cream paper in front of me, but suddenly, something else called me.

I turned to the trunk that held all my fabrics. Every piece of cream, ivory, and white was gently placed in the trunk that came all the way from home, and underneath the pieces, was the dress. *The dress* that landed me JoAnn as a client. The showstopper that earned audible gasps from the audience last summer here in Portland. The dress that Madeline was going to wear during this party.

I pulled it from the garment bag and pulled it over the mannequin. I had Madeleine's exact measurements, and all I needed to do was take off a bit to get it to fit her perfectly. The deep purple seemed darker in the mood lighting in the studio, but the soft light that surrounded me made the crystals sparkle. This dress was simple, this dress was stunning, this dress defined who I was as a designer, and I was proud to call it mine.

The tighter bust would accentuate her every curve dipping down to the lower neckline, giving Milo enough room for imagination. The crystals that circled her waist would give it enough flare, but not enough to take the eye away from the woman wearing it, and the knee-length slit up the floor-length skirt made it just sexy enough. This dress was going to make Madeline shine brighter than her wedding gown, and I could not wait to get her in it.

Once it was in place, and a few pins were ready to go, I lifted my camera and took a photo, the soft light hitting it just right. My first thought was to send it to Maddy, let her know what she would be trying on, but instead, my fingers found Clay's name. I sent the photo with no captain.

Clay: That's beautiful. Your design?

Ophelia: For Madeline to wear at the party. Do you think she'll like it?

Clay: I think she'll love it. It's amazing. You're amazing.

I locked my phone, not returning his message, and held it close to my chest. I didn't plan on this. I came to Portland with the hopes of staying locked in a room, getting dresses ready and creating designs for my next line. Instead, I was here, in an amazing studio being rented out by an investor, mannequins surrounding me with gowns and a view to die for. With every design having been accepted and the manufacturing of the gowns in various sizes beginning, everything I wasn't expecting was coming to life.

A store front, wedding gowns, and a little flutter in my heart.

I knew something amazing was going to happen when I signed that contract with JoAnn months ago, but I never expected this.

And I didn't plan on Clay.

I didn't plan on having these feelings return for a man I thought I wanted nothing to do with ever again.

Chapter Twenty-Nine

-Clay-

"Okay, I have a question for you," Elliot said as he and I walked around the Piano Bar's venue. Ophelia was mapping out where tables would go, and Elliot was standing right where he said the makeshift stage would go. I shoved my hands in my jeans pocket and looked up at him, ready for his question. "What do you think of Jamie?"

My face instantly warped into confusion. I raised an eyebrow and stared at him. "I'm sorry, what?"

"Jamie, that girl from the Piano Bar, the one you danced with?" he asked.

"I, um. . ." I mumbled, "that was *weeks* ago."

"I think Elliot wants to know if she's single and if you would be okay if he asked her out," Ophelia called from the other end of the room.

I looked back over to Elliot, who had a stupid grin on his face. His teeth clenched as he waited for my answer.

"I'm not. . . I'm not dating her," I stammered.

Elliot heaved a sigh. "I just saw you guys dancing and—"

"You know everything that's been happening in my life these past few months, and you still thought—" I shouted, a bit louder than I intended. Ophelia laughed as she came up to me and kissed me on the cheek.

Elliot shrugged. "You danced with her that night and seemed pretty cozy."

I glared at him, Ophelia's giggle still lingering in the background. "I literally have a date this Saturday"—I pointed at Ophelia—"with this one, and you thought you had to ask me about Jamie?"

"Clay." Ophelia groaned. "Jamie is a wonderful girl, Elliot, and I'm sure she would love to be asked out."

Elliot looked at Ophelia, giving her a sweet smile before turning his head sharply back to me. "See? Was that so hard?"

I shook my head at him. "I'll just stick to your accounts and not your dating life."

Elliot scoffed. "Well, thank you, Phe, for the insight. And for the record"—Elliot pointed at me—"I didn't know you asked *her* out."

"I did, and she said no."

"But you just said—"

"Then *I* asked *him* out, and we have plans on Saturday, hence why we are here now." Ophelia came up and poked me in the shoulder. "We need to finalize these details, and since you know this place better than anyone. . ." Ophelia gave him a cheesy grin, one that made me smile and want to pull her close. I loved all her facial expressions, but the ones that made her *her* were my absolute favorite.

Elliot folded his arms and narrowed his eyes at me. "Well, the party is what, in three weeks? So, we need to plan on who's attending. We need a headcount so I can tell Craig so he can tell the staff. I'm assuming they are providing drinks?"

I nodded, turning back to the bar top behind me. "We have their favorite waffle truck catering, and invitations have been sent out. There is about thirty people on the list, and we have a few RSVPs, nothing too crazy."

"Thirty is a good-sized crowd. Is uh. . ." Elliot walked past Ophelia and me, heading toward the empty bar. "Is Jamie coming?"

Ophelia laughed, rubbing her hands through her wild hair. "Yes, Elliot yes. . . Jamie will be there."

"Oh, well, that's great news." Elliot cleared his throat and began to talk about how Craig would set up and staff the event.

Every detail had flawlessly come together, and the stress of the party was dwindling. I could even see the load come off Ophelia's shoulders. Her week had been nonstop. Fitting Madeline for the final time into her dress, setting up more and more posts and having more and more meetings with JoAnn as her store came together. Even though it was, to quote Phe, "all coming together," there was still a lot of work that had to be done, and checking this off the list was going to make everything easier.

And then there was our date. The only detail I had was to be at Madeline's house at 6:00 on Saturday, and she would take care of the rest. The days just weren't moving fast enough, but at the same time they were moving too fast.

"Wanna know what would be a blast as centerpieces?" Ophelia spun, catching both mine and Elliot's attention. "Trivia cards. All about Madeline and Milo's relationship. We have *years* worth of trivia. That would be perfect."

I chuckled. "Yeah, it really would."

She gave me her brightest smile, slowing time down just a bit. "I'll get right on them. I bet I know more than you."

"Oh, that's a challenge."

I parked in Madeline's driveway, surprised that no barking husky greeted me as I walked up the steps and knocked on the door. I dressed casually, yet nice enough if a fancy restaurant was involved I would fit in. Dark jeans with a white button-up shirt, a blue tee underneath that poked out at my collarbone. I combed back my hair, which was getting unruly and needed a trim, and shaved, nearly nicking myself a thousand times thanks to my shaky hand.

The last date I'd had been on was with Ophelia ten years ago. I never dated in Seattle. I always met the girl at a bar or work meeting and we ended up back at my place. Clay Nolan didn't date, and that was known around Seattle. But that wasn't who Clay Nolan was supposed to be. And the fact that it was Ophelia who answered the door, her smile greeting me and lighting up the entire world, made every nerve fade away.

She was stunning. Her hair pulled back into a tight bun on the top of her head, a green ribbon tied around her head like a headband. The green dress she wore hit every curve and stopped just at her knees, showing off her perfect legs. Her nails were painted white, standing out as she reached her hand to me, palm down. I gently took it in mine and brought it to my lips, giving it a sweet, soft kiss.

"Hi," she whispered.

"You look beautiful," I whispered back. "I am very underdressed."

She twisted her hand in mine and wrapped her fingers around my palm, pulling me into the house. "No, you're handsome and dressed just right. We are staying in tonight."

I pinched my brow and closed the door behind me. "Staying in?"

She gave me a single nod. "Yep. We've already done so much in the city. I mean, how do you top bungee jumping?"

I laughed and let her lead me into the dining room. She had dinner set out on the kitchen island and the kitchen table was set for two, candles included. Ophelia had made pizza from scratch and paired it with garlic knots and wine. Everything looked amazing and smelled even better.

"Now," she began, pulling her hand from mine and walking around the kitchen island to present the pizza to me. "I remembered you were a fan of all things spicy on your pizza, so I made two. One with all the peppers under the sun and one with pineapple for me. The crust is New York Style with parmesan baked right on the bottom. Trust me, it's to die for. And the garlic knots —"

"Phe." I stopped her, making my way toward her, I gently took her waist in my hands and turned her to face me. She brought her arms up and rested them on my shoulders, her chin high in the air as she looked up at me. Even with heels, she was still shorter. "This looks amazing. I can't believe you did this."

"It was nothing." She closed her eyes, tilted her head and grinned. "Madeline helped a little bit."

I returned her smile, leaning down to kiss her, unsure if she would let me, but when she raised to her tippy toes—yes, even in her heels—to meet me halfway, I couldn't resist. I touched my lips to hers, breathing her in as she moved a hand to the nape of my neck. Her fingers laced in with my hair, and I inhaled, remembering how her kisses used to be versus how they are now. And I melted.

Breaking the kiss, she took a single step back, licking her lips as she ran her hands down my arms and led me to the table. We each grabbed our plates and took them back to choose our slices, and as soon as we sat, she filled our glasses with my favorite red wine.

"Not only did you remember the toppings I liked on my pizza, but you remembered my preference on wine?" I chuckled.

Ophelia sat down next to me, her chair angled toward mine. "There's a lot I remember about you, Clay."

I took a sip before placing my glass down. "Oh, yeah? Remind me."

She gave a small chuckle. She shifted her hips, crossing her legs. Biting a corner of her lip, she gave a small cough. *She's so damn cute. . .*

"I remember how you'd rather work on Microsoft Excel than read an actual book. The way you would drink coffee with two creams and one sugar, but I think you drink straight black now." I nodded that she was indeed correct. She met my eyes and took a deep breath. "I remember that you would relax by playing *Call of Duty,* and that it bothered you that Milo would always sneak in and play a few rounds with you. You would get mad at your professors for assigning too little, always complaining that your classmates had no idea how to do the work because they were always coming to you. I remember the way you would get excited about a new notebook, or that you loved to lay out in the grass to watch a meteor shower. I remember the way you would laugh at the stupidest things but get emotional over those dog commercials, even though you never had a dog."

"Hey," I stopped her. Every little detail she remembered pulled at my heartstrings. I had remembered everything about her during our decade apart, but I was certain she had blocked everything about me out. She never had—ever. I swallowed and tried to think of words. "Those commercials are heartbreaking, and you always cried." I took a bite of pizza and it exploded on my tongue. "Holy hell, this is amazing."

"I remember how you love to eat thin crust pizza, and you would always let me order pineapple on it, even though you hated it," she added, her voice soft and smooth.

I swallowed and leaned over, gently landing a kiss on her lips. A soft hum vibrated through her throat as the simple kiss lingered.

"Pineapple can go on pizza," I admitted, "but you're right. I don't like it, but it always made you do a giddy dance when you took a bite. I liked the little dance," I whispered against her lips. She leaned her forehead on mine for a split second before pulling away, returning to her wine and pizza, the look of joy never once leaving her eyes.

Once dinner was over, I helped clean the table, ready for the next step in this date of ours. I was torn between wanting to skip to kissing her, holding her in my arms until Madeline came and kicked me out, maybe even after then, and taking our time, making it last forever. I glared at the clock, trying to will it to slow down. That way, I could get the best of both worlds.

I watched her move, the green dress swaying with each turn, captivating my entire attention. Why did I let her walk away all those years ago? I could have had her always. I could've been calling her mine this entire time. All the things that I thought replaced her never gave me the kind of happiness that she did and just thinking of all the moments I missed killed me.

She spun and faced me, the glow radiating from her. Without thinking, I instantly slipped my hand on her waist, feeling the warmth of her body under my palms, pulling her close to me. I kissed her again, breathing her in as her body pressed against mine. I didn't know what else was in store for us, but I did know I just needed this to last a little longer.

"Are you ready for a game?" she asked in a sly voice, tilting her head, raising a single eyebrow.

"What kind of game?" I asked, not loosening my grip on her.

She took a step back, forcing my arms to fall. "It's fun, trust me."

"I'm not sure I can trust you."

"Clayton." She stretched her arms and arched her back. "If I can trust you enough to jump off a bridge. . ."

My chin dropped, silent laugher making my shoulders bump. Her hands trailed down my chest. Her back relaxed as she melted against me. I raised my chin and gave her a fleeting kiss. "Let's play your game."

An hour later, I sat on the sofa, cards laid out in front of us as she tried to guess the two words from my single code word. I had never played a card game on a date before, but we had never laughed more than we had right now, and we hadn't even drunk that much wine. When she chose the code word "evil" to have me guess "plot" and "lair," and I failed miserably, I almost leaped across the coffee table, but now it was my turn, and she was struggling just as much to guess the final word on her board.

The code word was "cushion," and she had guessed the wild card (cat), but the obvious one (pin) she was struggling to find.

"Come on." I laughed. "This is the easiest thing."

"No, it's not." She leaned forward on her knees, sending me a death glare, keeping her laugh at bay. "No other word goes with cushion. It's not 'cold' because, well, that wouldn't make any sense at all, and it's not 'Africa.' I mean, it could be because there *are* cushions in Africa, and it's not 'novel' well. . ." she trailed off again, sitting up straighter, keeping her hands firmly on her knees. "Maddy has tons of cushions that she lays with while she reads. . ."

"Phe." I laughed.

"Give me another clue."

I shook my head.

"Come on Clay, please. *Cushion* literally only went with 'cat.'"

"Think, really hard. You of all people should know this. It's become a thing with us, and it's hurting my soul that you haven't guessed it yet." I slouched, resting my elbow on my knee, placing the key card face down on the sofa next to me so she couldn't see it. She had to guess it. It was clear as day.

"Can I phone a friend?" she asked, hope in her eye.

I shook my head. "Absolutely not."

"Clayton," she snapped. "If you don't tell me, you can kiss your goodnight kiss goodbye."

"Seriously?" *Now that's not happening.* She leaned back on the couch and folded her arms, crossing her legs, her gaze purposefully avoiding me as she tilted her chin. *God, she was gorgeous when she pouted.*

"Oh, yeah. No, that's not happening." I stood, and took the three steps around the coffee table, loving the small squeal she gave as I towered over her, my hands on either side of her on the back of the couch, looking down on her as heat traveled through my body.

"I will be getting that kiss, and if you deny it when I leave, then I'm taking it now."

I leaned down, closing the inches between us when she placed her fingers on my lips, stopping me from moving any farther.

"Just tell me the word, and I'll kiss you for the rest of the night," she whispered.

I exhaled. "Pins," I whispered.

"Shit, really?" Ophelia's eyes widened, and she moved me to the side, leaning forward again to look at the words. She scoffed and laughed at herself. "Would you believe me if I had told you I didn't even see that word?" she asked, her voice light from the laughter as she leaned back into the couch, facing me.

"No." I smiled. "I'm your designated pin cushion holder, so when I saw that word, I knew you would get it like that." I snapped. "But I guess this game is just a little too much for you."

"You failed at 'evil,' may I remind you." Her eyes widened.

My smile only grew. "I'm better with numbers."

Narrowing her eyes, she shook her head at my stupidity. "What else are you better at?"

"Depends," I whispered. "Do I get that goodnight kiss?"

To answer me, she placed her palm on my chest, her fingers kneading their way up to my collar. She laced her fingers around the fabric and pulled me to her. This kiss was the one I wanted since I saw her the first night at dinner, the one I dreamed about, the one I remembered from so long ago. This kiss was meant for me, and me alone. Shivers ran up my spine as I scooted closer to her, my hands finding her body even with my eyes closed. They knew just where to go, where she wanted to be touched.

I caressed her jaw, slowly moving to her neck and shoulders. I ran my fingers down her arms, feeling her goosebumps rise as our lips never broke contact. The tips of my fingers grazed her thigh as she broke the kiss, moving swiftly in one fluid motion so she was on my lap, leaning back down to my lips in a second. Her hands began to roam my body, her fingers playing and tugging with the buttons of my shirt, and once her fingers grazed my skin, I had a sharp inhale of breath, Ophelia awarding me with a smile.

Our lips moved together. Our tongues found each other and teased. Our breathing and heartbeats synced as we moved the way we used to. I moved, my lips finding her neck and collarbone, Ophelia raising her head as gasping, sending more heat through my body. She moved against me, and I was a goner.

"Oh, Clay. I can feel you," she moaned into my ear, her fingers running through my hair as I kissed her skin. "I *feel* you."

"I've missed you." I raised my chin to look at her. She was even more beautiful in the moment, if that was possible. Her dark skin glistened as the fire rose in her. I kissed her chin and ran my thumb along her jawline. "I can't tell you how much I've missed you." I kissed her lips, her breath stopping as it deepened.

Ophelia was the one thing that made sense to me. Everything else fell into place because of her, and I wasn't going to let everything shatter again. *No more regrets.*

Chapter Thirty

-Ophelia-

My mind swam as Clay kissed me, his hands finding every part of me that used to bring me to life, and I was happy to report they still did. I had been touched like this plenty of times before, but with Clay it was different. His hands belonged to my body. Even fully dressed, his hands were meant for me.

I sat on his lap, feeling him grow with each kiss and every touch, knowing that as much as I wanted this, wanted him, I needed to stop. I needed to control myself, and I needed to get a grip on what was happening.

But I didn't want to break this moment. I didn't want it to end.

I began to unbutton the rest of his shirt, pulling it free of his pants, completely wrapping his body around my hands. I wanted all of him. Memories began flooding back as the heat built between us. Our first date, our first kiss, our first time, every single moment that we had that I had forced myself to forget was back, and no matter how hard I would try to stop them, they were there. Every piece of Clay was back in my heart, and I wanted more.

But that small piece of reality kept talking in the back of my head. We needed to take things slow. We had time for this.

"Clay." I stopped, giving my head a small shake to bring me back to reality. "As much as I want this—"

"Phe, you have no idea how much I want you," he mumbled, his voice deep as he kissed me.

I moaned and trailed my fingers to his chest, feeling his abs flex with my touch. At this rate, Madeline was going to have to stay over at Milo's because he wasn't about to stop this. His hands raced up my back, finding the zipper to my dress and slowly he pulled it down, his other hand slipping past the fabric onto my skin. His fingers were cold, cold enough to make me arch my back. His touch was everything I didn't know I needed.

"Clay." I sighed again as he dipped his head, his mouth finding that right spot as the shoulder to my dress slumped. I ran my fingers through his hair, trying to be gentle with the right amount of force. "I want this, I want you, but I think. . ." I gasped as he kissed my neck, his hands roaming over my bare back.

Heaving a heavy, lustful sigh, he fell back onto the couch. His lips were plump from my kisses, and his eyes were glazed over. His hair was a mess, thanks to me, and his breathing was slow. He looked sexy as hell, and I had to close my eyes to say what I was about to say.

"We need to take things slow," I muttered.

"I really wish we didn't have to." He sighed, his hands falling from my back to cup my face. "I've missed this, missed you, so much. I can't believe you are letting me kiss you, letting me touch you again."

I wrapped my fingers around his wrists. "You can keep kissing me," I whispered, which instantly sparked him to sit up again, his lips finding mine, "but not as hot and heavy as we were getting."

Dropping his head on my shoulder, he sighed in defeat.

"Think about it." I locked eyes with him as I lifted his face to me, kissing him gently. "We don't need to make up for lost time. We just get to start over, and most people don't sleep together on their first date."

He opened his mouth to say something but closed it, his teeth tapping as he held his jaw tight.

"You did, huh?" I asked, thinking of all the years in Seattle he could have slept with numerous women. "Didn't you?"

He took a deep breath and shrugged. "I didn't really date in Seattle. I wasn't focused on that."

"But you had girlfriends?"

"Can't I kiss you again? I liked that a lot better." He gave me a slow, sexy smile, almost making me break, but instead, I arched my back away from him, still firmly planting on his lap his hands now on my legs holding me in place, his fingers slipping beneath my dress.

I shook my head. "I don't want to rush this. I don't want to ruin anything."

"Nothing is going to get ruined. I'm not going to let it. Sure, okay, yes. I had girlfriends in Seattle, a few of them, but none of them amounted to what you were, what you *are*," he said, running his hands up my arms, a small burst of electricity following. "I promise I won't ruin this. I want this. I want you, and I'm willing to do whatever you need to make it work."

I wiggled my body against him. He dropped head on the back of the couch, a small moan leaving his lips. I grinned, knowing I still had that power to cause him to lose himself. "Does that include holding my pin cushion?"

"If anyone else ever holds a pin cushion for you, I'm out," he said heavily.

I broke out in laughter, falling back against him. He wrapped his arms around me and held me close, taking his fingers to zip my dress up for me. I snuggled into him, feeling his heartbeat against my chest and the rise and fall of his breaths.

As if a switch flipped, Clay and I fell into a rhythm over the next few days. He would greet me each morning with an Americano and a kiss, some lingering more than others, and then he would sit at my desk with his laptop and papers from his new fancy job and type away. His clicking became just as needed in my studio as my music. He packed up when I did and made sure I was safe at Madeline's before giving me a kiss goodnight, almost trying to get me to let him stay.

It was hard not to.

But we were going slow. And that was okay with me.

I wanted to savor these moments with him, knowing full well that in a few short weeks I'd be back in New York, and he'd be here. We'd make the long-distance work, though. It was a given. It was a conversation that we would have before I left, but we both knew that we were stuck with each other now, and we wouldn't have it any other way.

The day came for Madeline's bridals soon enough, and we were packed and ready to crawl into her car and take her to a park. Carter insisted they all be outside. The store's Instagram page was still growing, reaching close to fifty thousand followers. I had been teasing these bridals for weeks now. I would show off the dress from multiple angles, showing that it was the first official Ophelia Fuller wedding gown (not to be sold elsewhere, of course), and it was creating so much hype.

None of this bothered Madeline as she played with the lace on the skirt and tried to adjust the bust one last time.

"I assure you." I reached over and lowered her hand from the seam. "It's going to stay in place. You look stunning, and I'm kind of upset that Milo can't see these photos before the wedding day."

Jamie's eyes met mine from the rear-view mirror. She had offered to drive in case I needed to make any adjustments from the backseat. The dress was perfect, but Madeline's hair, on the other hand, was going to need some touch up. Carter sat in the passenger seat, loading his camera bag and reading his first SD card.

Madeline's eyes widened. "Please tell me he's still blocked from the page."

I gave a single nod. "He's blocked. Can't even look me up."

She exhaled, taking a long, slow breath from her lips as she turned and looked out the window. "I can't believe I'm marrying Milo in three weeks."

I smiled at her, a flood of happiness rushing through me for my best friend. I remembered the day they met so vividly, the way those two completely shut off from the rest of the bar. They didn't even notice when Clay and I snuck out. Back then, we couldn't keep our hands off each other, and now, all I wanted was to have him near me.

I shifted in my seat and pulled my phone from my bag. Clay was at the office with Elliot, the first time since our date that we had spent the day apart, and I missed him. Maybe he could meet at the park? Maybe I could take him to dinner after? Maybe. . .

"Are you going to text him?" Madeline whispered, leaning over to me.

I smiled, felt the heat rise to my cheeks and shook my head. "Yes," I said, matter-of-factly.

"I love it." Madeline's voice was soft as she turned back to her dress, her palms flat on her thighs as she ran her hands over the lace. "Almost as much as this dress."

My phone pinged in my hand, and when Clay's name appeared before I could even text him, my heart turned just a little bit.

Clay: Good luck today with the bridals. Maybe sneak a picture for me?

Ophelia: No sir, these photos will be hidden from your Instagram feed as well.

Even though Clay had promised a million times he wouldn't show any of this to Milo, I still told Carter to hide his name when he posted the photos. I was taking no chance. The bubble danced as he typed, but then it stopped, and a FaceTime call came bursting through.

I answered it quickly, shifting my body from Madeline so she would be completely hidden. Before I could say hello, his voice rang through my ears.

"What do you mean I'm hidden from the feed? I see your posts every day. I like them. I save them. I've showed my parents."

His ranting made me laugh, which made Madeline turn to look at me, biting the tip of her tongue.

"You can't see because I am taking no chances that Milo will see," I said, a grin tugging at the corners of my mouth. This man always made me smile. I simply couldn't help it.

He furrowed his brow and dropped his jaw, a small piece of brown hair falling into his face. Behind him was a busy office. A few people passed by his desk, taking a peek at who was on his phone. Elliot even appeared and waved at me.

"That's not fair at all," he grumbled.

"Uh, yes, it is," Madeline retorted. "Under no circumstances can Milo see this dress. There will be a bloodbath."

"He's asked me a few times when you and Phe are going to go shopping. He knows it hasn't happened yet, and he's getting a tad bit nervous," Clay said, his expression completely changing since he knew he was addressing Madeline.

"He's not nervous. I know he's not nervous," Madeline said. I pursed my lips and watched her face twist.

"Okay, maybe he's not *that* nervous. We have all been fitted for our tuxes. He looks good, by the way."

"I know. I helped him pick it." Madeline leaned over in the seat, trying her hardest to tilt her body toward the phone screen. I pinched my brow at her and moved the phone to my shoulder, completely blocking Clay from any view.

"Phe, maybe you should just give the phone to Maddy. That way I can talk to her—"

"Oh, no," I interrupted. As cute as their little conversation was, he was not going to trick me that easily. "You, sir, are forbidden from seeing Madeline right now. Her hair is perfect, and her makeup is spot on and you"—I pointed at the screen and pinched my brow—"are forbidden."

He laughed, which sent a chill down my spine.

"Okay, okay." He waved a hand up. "I get it. Forbidden." He paused for a moment, his lips turning into the smile that made me want to kiss him. "See you tonight?"

I nodded.

"My place this time. I'm making you dinner."

"You don't cook," I grumbled.

"Well, when you're unemployed, you tend to learn a few things."

In the background I heard a shout. "You aren't unemployed. Now, get back to work!"

I laughed at Elliot's reaction, knowing full well it was a joke. Those two had gotten closer in the past few months than Clay would like to admit. He may have lost a job, but he gained a new friend.

"Boss man is after me." He winked at me, that smile never once fading. "See you tonight."

"Bye."

He wiggled his eyebrows and ended the call. My screen going blank.

"Okay, you two are adorable," Jamie said from the front seat.

"It's almost like no time has passed between you two. You just fit right back together," Madeline added.

At first the statement made me smile, running my thumbs against my phone, wishing he would call me again, only to pull back. No time had passed, nothing had changed. In reality, everything had changed.

Chapter Thirty-One

-Clay-

I was a man in love, and no one could convince me otherwise. The days flowed easier, knowing that Ophelia had my heart safely with her. Nothing could stand in my way; nothing could bring me down.

Not even an email with the subject line *Urgent, J&R Appeal* that came seconds after I hung up with Ophelia.

I hovered the cursor over the email a few times, circling the word *urgent* before I finally opened the email. I leaned forward with my chin resting on my thumb as I quickly read.

Mr. Nolan,

This morning, Brian Walker has been charged with embezzlement from Hunter Wallace Law Firm. After being brought in, he confessed to the four million embezzlement from Jackson and Rye last year. He is pleading guilty on all accounts.

Jackson and Rye have been notified and will drop the charges on you and the remaining members of your team. Mr. Walker's case is still being processed, and we will have a firm timeline for you soon. Please be aware that you may be brought in for questioning and as a witness in any trial that may arise.

I highly suggest we motion toward appeal against Jackson and Rye. Yes, the charges will be dropped completely, but in order to receive your settlement back, an appeal would guarantee your money be returned to you.

I look forward to hearing from you in the near future. I'll be in touch.

Justin Gardner; Attorney

Leaning back in my chair, I ran my hand through my hair, planting them firmly on the top of my head.

"Fuck." I mumbled under my breath.

"Hey now." Elliot's voice materialized behind me. "Watch your language."

I lowered my hands and spun in my chair, the smile on his face turning to concern when he saw my face. For sure, I was stunned, my eyes wide, my jaw dropped and my hands still on my head. I let out a deep breath and pointed to my laptop. Elliot furrowed his brow and leaned in over my shoulder to read the email. After a few moments, realizing that he had to read it twice, he backed away, his face mimicking mine.

"Fuck," he mumbled.

"Right."

"I'm not one to swear, really, but that warrants one."

I exhaled through my nose, staring at the computer screen, reading it one last time.

. . . motion toward appeal. . .

I laughed, a chuckle that radiated through the room loud enough to get some looks from those around me. I clenched my teeth and mouthed a quick sorry to them before turning back to Elliot.

"Does this mean I'm in the clear now?" I asked quietly, pointing to the computer.

Elliot shrugged. "I'm a business owner, not a lawyer. I have no idea what this means, but it seems pretty black and white there on the screen that you, my friend"—he slapped my shoulder—"are no longer the embezzling accountant everyone took you for. Are you going to email them back?"

I blinked a few times before reading the email for the millionth time. "I don't know. Should I appeal?" I twist my body, craning my head to look at him.

Once again, he shrugged. "I would if I were you. How much did you pay them again? You could get all of that back."

Get it all back...

Milo left that evening for his night shift, after making sure I wouldn't burn the apartment down. ("Milo, I've been making breakfasts and dinner for weeks now"), and then just a few moments later, there was a light knock on the front door.

I was straining the pasta, a towel over my shoulder when I heard it, and I almost dropped the pan. She was here. My breath was shaking, my heart rate picked up, and my palms started to sweat. I set the pot back on the stove and ran toward the door, opening it with a smile. Ophelia tilted her head, cocking a hip and giving me a smile that paused the world around me.

Ophelia Fuller was the most beautiful, the most daring, the most compassionate, talented, strong woman in the entire world, and I couldn't believe I got to call her mine.

I blinked, snapping myself out of my trance. I returned her smile, taking a step forward to wrap her in my arms. I lifted her off the ground, spinning around to walk back into the apartment. Ophelia's hands rested on my shoulders, sliding together on the back of my neck, her fingers lacing in my hair. I kicked the door shut and walked to the kitchen. My eyes not once leaving hers, I set her down on the counter, my hands trailing her back and to her legs.

It was second nature to kiss her, as if I had never stopped kissing her. All those years vanished when my lips touched hers, and everything just made sense.

Ophelia hummed against my mouth as she broke the kiss, gently kissing my chin as I backed my head away, giving her a crooked grin.

"Well, hello." She sighed.

"Hi," I whispered back, wanting to kiss her again. The oven beeped, forcing both of us to look behind me.

"What's for dinner?"

"Baked chicken and alfredo pasta. Nothing too fancy." I stepped back, leaving her sitting on the counter as I turned to pull the chicken from the oven.

"I thought you said you could cook," she chuckled.

"And this is cooking." I turned, presenting the glass of chicken to her. She raised her chin, tilting her small frame forward to look at the chicken sizzling in the glass dish. "You can thank Betty Crocker for this. However, I decided to add the alfredo pasta."

"Well." Ophelia leaned back onto the peninsula and crossed her legs. Her small white heels dangled as she bobbed her knee up and down. "It smells wonderful."

After finishing preparing the meal, Ophelia helped me set the table, taking over all the plates and silverware while I handled the food. We would pass each other in the kitchen, and her hands would find my arms, my stomach, my shoulder, any part of me that she could touch just in passing. And once we were sitting at the table, we sat right next to each other, our knees touching as we ate. It was comfortable, and it was perfect. Everything I envisioned it would be.

"How did Maddy's bridals go?" I asked before taking a bite of the chicken, which turned out fantastic, if I do say so myself.

She hummed as she finished her bite. "It was perfect. She was stunning. Carter took her to the mountain, and we climbed and climbed, but it was worth it. Every shot was brilliant, and Madeline glowed like I'd never seen her before. Just you wait. We'll have some framed at the wedding."

"I'm still offended you wouldn't let me see. I've seen her in the dress," I joked, hoping she would catch onto my sarcasm.

She narrowed her eyes at me, twisting her lips before saying, "It's different this time. She was one hundred percent bride here, not just Madeline in a fancy dress."

"Made by the best wedding gown designer in the United States," I mumbled.

"And I really didn't want to risk anything, so yes"—she dropped her fork—"the photos are on Instagram and no"—she stabbed a piece of chicken and raised it to her lips—"you cannot see them until the wedding day."

I raised a single eyebrow. "Fair."

Ophelia chuckled, placing her hand on my thigh. "How was the office today? I'm sure Elliot keeps you on your toes."

I shrugged a shoulder. "He's actually pretty fun to work for. He's laid back and easy."

"Are we talking Michael Scott laid back? Do you have conference room meetings every day? Do you have award ceremonies?" she asked, her voice raising with each question.

I rolled my eyes. "First of all, I've worked there three weeks, and they've had one conference room meeting, and I wasn't invited. Second, you know I haven't seen *The Office*."

"But you knew who Michael Scott was."

I leaned in and gave her a quick kiss, getting the reaction I hoped it would. A soft smile on her face, and her eyes starting to get glossy. "Only because of you and Madeline. All the memes."

She laughed. "I'll make a note to send you more, but really, how is it? Do you love it? Is it helping?"

"Of course it's helping. I've already been able to pay Milo something in rent, and I was able to buy the food tonight, no credit card from Milo needed. And yes, I love working with numbers again. I know numbers. They make sense and have a definite answer."

Ophelia's small voice filled the air. "Compared to what?" she asked, a smidge of hesitation lingering.

"Well, for instance." I put my fork down and leaned forward. "I got an email today. . ." I grabbed my wine glass, lifting it to my lips before finishing. "From my lawyer."

Instantly, her eyes went wide. "What did it say?"

"An old co-worker, Brian Walker"—she nodded along, following my words—"he was charged today, confessed to everything, and I may have shot for an appeal and a clear record. Everything could just be. . ." I waved my hand in front of the table. "Erased."

Ophelia's jaw dropped, and her shoulders hunched. Her eyes, if possible, went wider. "Erased," she said, shooting herself back upright. "Just like that?"

"Just like that." I pinched my brow. "I think."

"Clay. . ." she stumbled. "Clay, that's amazing. That's something you lead with. That deserves more than a chicken dinner and a glass of wine. We need to celebrate."

I chuckled. "You didn't like the last time I picked our celebration tactic, so I thought this would be better. Plus, we had already planned this before I got the email."

"Okay, that's true. I wasn't totally on board for bungee jumping, but next time we go, it's on me, and it will be a way to celebrate."

"Next time? You said there wouldn't be a next time," I said, a hopeful sound to my voice that Ophelia didn't even acknowledge. She just kept talking, which made me smile.

"But, Clay, this is huge. Imagine getting all that money back, being able to get your apartment back in Seattle. Registering the Tesla and being able to keep Tessa insured and charged. Imagine all the things you lost just coming back to you."

"Well, yeah." I shifted in my seat. My mind had been buzzing all afternoon. Did I even want to appeal? Did it even really matter?

At this point, I had gone through so many downs, feeling as if I was at rock bottom. But now I just felt as if I was moving forward in the right direction. There was that small possibility that going for an appeal would cause all of *this* to go away. "But what if I don't want that anymore?" I asked, my voice raspy from the wine.

Ophelia furrowed her brow for a second and looked around the kitchen, as if the answer to my question would be dangling on the surrounding walls.

"Why wouldn't you?" she finally asked.

"What if I like what I have now." I grabbed her hand and laced my fingers through hers. "What if I don't want to lose what I had gained from losing it all?"

Ophelia's eyes were focused on our hands, her thumb rubbing my knuckles. She rubbed her lips together, and I could see she had no idea as to how to respond. The only thing I truly gained was her. I never wanted to lose her again.

"I think I need to sit on it, really decide if I want to go through that or just take the clear name, not worrying about the hefty price tag that came with it. I really like where I'm going, and I don't need to go in reverse. I have a great job, one that can lead to more, possibly my own company someday. And I have my family and friends, people I would only see once or twice a year before going back to my empty apartment. And I have you."

Her dark eyes fluttered up, meeting mine.

"I really, *really* like where I am headed."

"It seems to me," she muttered, her forehead resting against mine. "That you may have already made up your mind. That you don't need to think about it anymore."

I cupped her face and kissed her. She was absolutely, without doubt, right. I didn't need to think. I already had my answer right in front of me.

Chapter Thirty-Two

-Ophelia-

When Clay walked me to the rental car, giving me a lingering kiss before closing the door, waving goodbye as I drove out of sight, everything seemed perfect. So why, when I was close to Madeline's house, did I pull off on the side of the road and start to cry?

The only other time I can vividly remember feeling this way was on my way to the airport, moving to New York for the first time. Madeline drove me, and I was tough on the outside, giving her the smile I knew she needed to see that I was going to be okay. But once I got in that terminal, I hid in the bathroom and cried over my heartache. I allowed every emotion to come pouring out into that stall, and then I locked them up, never letting anyone see them ever again. It's what helped me become who I am now, the strong and independent fashion designer who just landed her dream. If I had cried my way through those first few years in New York, when my heart hurt the most, I never would have made it here.

And now, a decade later, I attempted to do the same thing.

I didn't break under pressure. I didn't get jealous. I was focused, and I definitely knew what I wanted.

I knew I wanted Clay.

So why? *Why.* . . was I crying!? Why was I scared? Why did hearing him say he had everything he wanted and needed scare the shit out of me?

Thoughts whizzed through my brain. My time in Portland was coming to an end. I'd go back to New York, and what then? What would happen as soon as this wedding was over? Would he come with me? Would he leave me again?

Without having an answer to my own question, I lowered the visor and wiped away my tears. Pinching the skin below my cheeks, I took several deep breaths, telling myself to focus. I put the car back in gear and drove the rest of the way to Madeline's, making sure my eyes were calm and a smile was on my face before walking in the door.

She would only see what I wanted her to see.

Before I knew it, it was the night of the party, only seven days until Milo and Madeline's big day. Madeline had come to the studio to try on the dress, and I had to talk her out of taking it off, that it was hers to keep no matter what, and that Milo was going to drop when he saw her. There were absolutely no adjustments to be made as she slipped it on so the fact that Clay wasn't there didn't hit as hard as it would have. He was a full-blown accountant now, trying to work his way through Elliot's accounts, proud to say he was almost at ground zero.

But even though he was busy, as was I, we still made time to finalize everything for the party, spending some nights together getting everything just right. We had gotten most of the guest list to respond—a bigger shindig than we originally thought—but with the little details being ironed out with Clay and Elliot, I knew it was going to be an amazing night.

My phone buzzed on the dresser, dancing in circles as I zipped up my own dress. JoAnn's name lit up the screen. I furrowed my brow and answered. All of my designs had been accepted, and from the photos she had sent me, we were ready to move forward with the store.

"Hello, this is Ophelia," I said in my most professional, modest voice.

"Ah, hello, Ophelia!" JoAnn's voice rang through the other line, sharp and intense. "How was your day?"

"It was great, thank you." I smiled. "Madeline came and tried on the dress for her party tonight. Seven more days until the wedding! I know Carter has some amazing photos of her dress."

"Oh, he does. I've seen them! That's actually why I'm calling. Carter and I have been talking, and we'd love to get some photos of you here. In the store, with the people making your designs, that way we can post the store opening. We're so close.. . . I really think you need to come out here for a few days."

"Oh, but," I interrupted her, "I have to be here for the dress rehearsal and the wedding," I stammered.

"Oh, yes, and I am in no way taking you from that, just a few days. When's the rehearsal?"

I placed my hand on my forehead, trying to envision the calendar in my head. Could I really leave and go to New York before the wedding? I'm sure Madeline would understand, but I had promised her my attention here. And. . . Clay. . .

"Um, it's. . . uh. . ." I lowered my hand. "rehearsal is on Friday, wedding is Saturday."

"I can have you back Thursday night. Fly out tomorrow and be here for four days. That would give us plenty of time, and you can see the gowns—"

I interrupted her again. "Can't this wait until I get back? I fly home the Monday after—"

"Ophelia, I am closer to opening this store than you think. We have worked so hard, and I really feel like you being here would help us get further so we can complete the project. If you're here, that's just the cherry on top."

I inhaled a deep breath of air. "Let me talk to Madeline," I mumbled.

"Let me know ASAP, and I can book this flight for you. The one I have my eye on leaves tomorrow afternoon."

"Tomorrow, right. I'll talk to Madeline now and let you know —"

"ASAP," she reiterated.

"Right." I nodded, and JoAnn quickly said goodbye. Staring at myself in the mirror, I finally let out a breath I didn't realize I'd been holding. Nerves shot through me. I knew Madeline would tell me to go. She'd be supportive. She would basically pushed me out the door. My mind and heart went to Clay.

Rolling my shoulders, my strong demeanor back on, I left the room ready to tackle the night, but first, I had to talk to Madeline.

Madeline and Jamie were already in the living room, dressed and waiting for me. Jamie was wearing a tight dress that matched the purple of Madeline's custom, gorgeous, gown (*the gown,* the one that stopped the show, the one that Madeline treated just as delicate as her wedding gown), and then there was me. I dressed to fit into my New York life. The gold shimmered against my skin, and my curls sat on my shoulders, my gold hoops lighting touching my neck as I moved. Together, the three of us were a sight to be seen, and we were going to be the best dressed at the party.

"Oh, Phe!" Madeline said, taking my hands as I approached them. "You look stunning! You need to wear it at your store's grand opening."

I popped my hip and placed my hand side. "Not a chance in the middle of fall but thank you," I smiled, only to break the smile when I remembered the reason why I had to talk to her. "Oh, about that. I just got off the phone with JoAnn—"

"She's the one who bought the store, right?" Jamie asked, grabbing her small handbag from the couch, her strawberry blonde curls falling in her face. In the times I had seen Jamie, her hair was normally up, tighter—thanks to her job—but tonight, she let herself loose, and she was stunning. It was no wonder why Elliot was hoping to ask her out.

"She is. She's my biggest client." I reached out to Madeline and fixed her bustline. The small seam could be hidden, and even though I was the only one who noticed, I couldn't help but fix it. "Thanks to this dress. She wants me to fly out tomorrow so I can see the progress and take some photos with the store. She is closer to opening it than we thought she said next month. . ."

"*Phe!*" Madeline's arms wrapped around my neck, her face getting full of hair.

"Maddy, the dress." I pulled her back.

"Phe, this is amazing. I can't believe it."

I smiled at my friend. She had seen me through so much and, as I knew she would be—was always—my biggest support. Tears welled in my eyes, but I blinked them away.

"I'll be back for the wedding and the rehearsal. . ." I muttered, keeping those emotions locked down.

"Oh, I have no doubt. You wouldn't miss that even if it was the end of the world." Madeline rubbed my bare arms. "Have you told Clay yet? What does he think? I bet he's excited. Oh!" She gasped. "Take him with you."

I chuckled. "I don't think JoAnn will go for that, plus we are still taking things slow. We haven't talked about what's going to happen when I leave yet. And I *just* hung up with JoAnn. I'll tell Clay at the party. It's no big deal, just a couple of days in New York and then back home."

Madeline's phone buzzed, pulling her attention from me. "Oh, it's Milo. He and Clay are meeting Elliot at the Piano Bar now. Are you guys ready?"

"Extremely." Jamie smiled, linking her arm with Madeline. "I'm driving!"

I laughed as they made their way out of the house, each giving Niko a rub behind the ears. I followed, pulling my phone out to text JoAnn.

Ophelia: Book me that flight! Can't wait to see the store.

Her response was instant, as if she'd been waiting for my response since the second we'd hung up.

JoAnn: Paying now. See you and Carter tomorrow!

Just as I finished reading her text, another popped up, making my heart turn.

Clay: I can't wait to see you tonight. Counting the minutes.

Chapter Thirty-Three

-Clay-

"What was Milo and Madeline's first date?" I read aloud from the card as Milo and Elliot walked the tables, making sure every place was set and ready. Milo was insistent that we arrive before everyone else to give the girls a stress-free party. "A: a football game." I furrowed my brow at him. "B: being set up on a blind date, here at the Piano Bar. C: Powell's bookstore with a trip to Madeline's favorite waffle truck and, D: Seeing *The Avengers* in IMAX." I lowered the card and glared at my friend. "Ophelia wrote this card for sure."

After an amazing night that consisted of Ophelia and me trying to figure out who knew more about Milo and Madeline's relationship, we had twenty-seven questions. Each table had a trivia card with a photo of them in different stages in their relationship, including a photo that was taken at the proposal. They looked great on the tables.

"You hate football." Elliot came up behind me, his hands firmly in his pants pockets. All three of us were dressed semi-formal, each wearing a suit with no tie, slacks, and my favorite shiny shoes. Elliot's brown hair was a mess on top of his head, the sides freshly shaven, and his five o'clock shadow was showing heavier than I had seen at the office. The man definitely knew how to separate himself from his business.

"That technically has two answers," Milo answered, fixing the button on his jacket. "We were set up on a date, *and* I took her to Powell's and the waffle truck, so that's a trick question."

I flipped the card over. "The correct answer is B being set up on a blind date, here at the Piano Bar."

Milo shrugged his shoulders and nodded. "Okay, so you and Ophelia went way back."

"We had twelve years to go off of." I raised the card again. "What is Madeline's favorite book that Milo has bought her?"

"Oh, come on, how will the guests know the answer to that one?" Elliot grumbled.

I walked over to the display table, which held pieces of them for others to see. This was yet again one of Ophelia's ideas that she came up with while we were making the trivia cards. She knew exactly what items to display, including one single book. I picked up the paperback with the painted edges. It was in pristine condition, the spine not cracked and the pages still having that new book smell. I handed it to Elliot.

"*The House in the Cerulean Sea. . .*"

Milo smiled. "Oh yeah. . ." Taking the book from Elliot, he used his thumb to fly through the pages. "She's read this so many times, when I saw this copy in an email, I preordered it and got it as a random gift. I may have scored that night."

"Over a book?" Elliot raised a single eyebrow. "I wonder if Jamie likes to read."

Both Milo and I rolled our eyes. Elliot had asked about Jamie a few times and was even given her number, but never did anything with it. His brain was elsewhere, even if he was interested in Jamie.

Stepping back to the table, I placed the book down next to a photo of Thomas Rhett.

"Another question," Elliot shouted, turning toward a table to grab a card.

"You can play like everyone else." A deep Southern accent filled the room, and my heart skipped not just one, but a few beats. "Stop touching things."

Ophelia walked into the venue, her gold dress shimmering in the lighting of the bar. Her hair bounced, and her heels clicked on the ground. She radiated confidence and grace, and her eyes were focused on me. Sweet, sexy, bold—Ophelia Fuller was going to steal the show. She was a sight to be seen.

I watched as she walked toward me, flicking the trivia card out of my hand and placing it back on the table where it came from. She turned, gave me a sly, sexy smile and then gently slid a hand across my waist all the way around my back, until she was nestled into my body.

"You are exquisite," I whispered into her ear, kissing her temple.

"I know." She leaned into my kiss, placing her hand on my chest. "You don't look too bad yourself."

"Well, aren't you two adorable?" I heard Madeline's voice, and it pulled me from the trance Ophelia had put me in.

I furrowed my brow at her and watched as she wrapped her arms or tried to around Milo's waist. He, however, pulled her at arm's length and looked her up and down, taking in every inch of her.

"Was this," he stammered, "was this the dress we missed at the show?"

"The one and only," Ophelia said, her posture straightening as she smiled at the two of them. "Doesn't she look stunning?"

Milo didn't answer. He just pulled Madeline close and kissed her. A little hum came from Madeline as she sunk into him.

I looked over at Elliot, thinking he would be talking with Jamie, but he had made his way to the stage, picking up his guitar and starting to tune it. Jamie stood by the display table. Either he had yet to even talk to her, or she shot him down. I tapped my fingers along Ophelia's skin, making her turn toward me.

"This place looks great," I whispered.

"Can you believe we actually threw it all together? I mean, we did basically nothing." She smiled, taking in the room around her. "The guests should be coming soon. Elliot's going to play for us, right?"

I hummed, tilting my chin down slightly. "Just a few songs, he said, to 'Give Madeline a taste of the reception.'"

She laughed. "I'm sure she will enjoy every second of it." She ran her hands along my waist and stepped in front of me, her hands clasping behind my back. "I have something I need to talk to you about. Do you think we can try to sneak away before all the guests arrive?"

I furrowed my brow and opened my mouth to respond, but just as the words were about to come out, a loud cheer could be heard from the stairs. It seemed that every guest we invited all decided to show up at the same time, cheering and whooping as they approached Milo and Madeline. I smiled and looked back down at Ophelia.

"Sneak away later?" I asked.

She sighed and gave me a small smile, one I couldn't quite read. She nodded, her gaze traveling down to our feet. "Yeah, later," she whispered back.

I lifted her chin with my thumb and forefinger, bringing her lips to mine, giving her a fleeting kiss. "We should probably mingle."

She gave a small chuckle. "Let's go win that trivia game."

"Oh, that's an option?" I smiled at her as she ran her hands down my forearms, her fingers trailing goosebumps down my arms. "I don't remember getting a prize for a winner."

"Bragging rights." Ophelia winked.

Even though she showed a bright smile and fun outer shell, I could see something stirring in her eyes. She wasn't at ease. She was holding something in, and I had a feeling that something included me.

Turns out the trivia cards and display table were big hits, just like Ophelia had predicted. Even Madeline and Milo played along, trying to win the elusive bragging rights.

"I'm sorry, Milo, but I honestly don't know your favorite Marvel movie." Madeline sighed, putting her face in her hands.

Milo glared at her, dropping his arm on the table. I watched from across the table, taking a final bite of my waffle. It felt so strange to be dressed in a nice suit, eating a waffle covered in Nutella and whipped cream, but the moment Madeline saw those waffles, she lit up. As strange as it was, it made her night.

"I know your favorite book," Milo retorted.

"I don't really have a favorite book." Madeline lifted her head, keeping her hands ready to hide in again.

Ophelia leaned forward, pointing at Madeline across the table. "I even know your favorite book."

"And oddly enough," Jamie smiled. "I know Milo's favorite Marvel movie."

Madeline's eyes widened as she turned to look at Jamie, her hands raising up to block her face from Milo and she mouthed "What is it?" toward Jamie. Thankfully, Jamie just gave her a sly smile and shook her head.

"You learn a lot from taking x-rays every six months." Jamie laughed.

Elliot, who was sitting next to Milo, read the card as he shoveled a piece of waffle in his mouth. "What's the answer to this question?" He swallowed. "What do Milo and Madeline do when the power goes out?" He lowered the card. "The power doesn't go out that often."

Madeline lowered her chin, her cheeks turning pink.

"The real answer isn't on the back." Milo grabbed the card. "But for the sake of the game, we light candles and play board games, *Yahtzee, Codenames. . .*other games." He grinned.

Ophelia chuckled. "The real answer wasn't appropriate for dinner table talk."

Madeline's face went from a blush pink to red. She cleared her throat and stood. "I'm going to go see how my parents are faring. Elliot, when does the dancing start?"

Elliot raised his eyebrows. "Soon. The band will be here any minute, and I'll turn the playlist off."

Madeline ran her hand across Milo's shoulders. "Jamie, Phe, wanna mingle with me? Say hi to my parents and see if anyone else knows Milo's favorite Marvel movie."

Jamie instantly stood, completely oblivious to Elliot's eyes on her. Ophelia kissed my cheek and rose, her hand on my shoulder up until she had to let go. I watched as she walked away, her gold dress swaying as her hips moved. She was captivating. Even from a distance, I couldn't force myself to look away.

"What *is* your favorite Marvel movie?" Elliot asked, my gaze still locked on Ophelia as she gave Madeline's mom a hug.

"Depends on the phase—" Milo began.

"You have to choose one," Elliot interrupted.

I listened to them talk about which Spiderman was better while my mind drifted to Ophelia. She was still stiff, still uneasy as she flawlessly flowed through the night. There was something there she wanted to get off her chest. She mentioned she wanted to talk, but once the party began and the waffles were served, everyone got sucked into the game, seeming to shift her mind completely. I didn't foresee a time for us to sneak away to talk. Maybe while we danced, I could ask her what's wrong, what's on her mind.

She laughed at something Jamie said, but then her attention went to her small handbag, her smile vanishing as he pulled out her phone. She turned to Madeline and showed her the screen. Madeline nodded and gently touched her arm as she stepped to the side, taking a phone call.

I tugged my lips into a grin as she smiled and nodded along to the phone call. When her gaze met mine, she gave me a quick wave and smile, locking eyes as she finished the phone call. Once she ended her call, she tilted her head, cocked her hip, and winked.

God, I love this woman.

I need to know what is going on in her head.

"Hey, Elliot!"

Three men appeared behind us, all of them dressed as nicely as all the guests, except their ties were loose and their shirts were untucked. They gave us a smile and then turned their attention back to Elliot. He spun in the chair and smiled.

"Hey, guys. Just in time." Elliot stood. "Gotta set up. Are there any songs that I can't play?" he asked, turning to Milo.

"Just not *the* song," Milo replied.

Elliot winked. "Got it."

I turned to Milo. "*The* song?"

"Question number nine." Milo smiled.

I picked up the card and read off the answers, smiling when I knew the right one. Ophelia had played it for me the night we came up with all these questions, and we both agreed it was them to a T.

"I know it, I know it!" Madeline came up behind Milo, tossing her arms around his shoulders. "*Civil War.*"

Milo laughed and turned his head to give her a small kiss. "For the sake of the game, yes."

She smiled against his lips. "I love you. I can't wait to marry you."

"I love you more," he whispered, kissing her again.

I wanted—needed—to tell Ophelia those words. I had never stopped loving her. It didn't matter what was blocking her tonight. Whatever it was, I would push through it and make it work. Make us work. I just had to tell her those three little words.

Chapter Thirty-Four

-Ophelia-

Once Madeline had convinced Milo's co-worker to tell her what his favorite Marvel movie was, she vanished, and Jamie and I floated over to the bar. More people had come than we thought, but thankfully, the waffle truck had brought plenty of extras, and the Piano Bar was staffed with bartenders, making getting drinks even more possible. Tonight was turning into a blast, even if I still had to talk to Clay.

JoAnn's phone call made my heart rate pick up, sending over final flight details for Carter and me. I peeked over at Clay during the call, noticing his eyes heavy on me. He gave me a smirk, making me give him a wave and a smile. Just having his eyes on me gave me confidence. But now that the phone call was over and the news still had to be told, nerves began to set in.

He wouldn't be mad, would he?

Jamie ordered two mango-ritas for us and we both sat down at the bar, Jamie instantly bringing her drink to her lips.

"Mmm," she hummed. "I love this drink."

I giggled at her and took a sip. "Looks like Elliot's starting to set up." I twisted my body and eyed the stage. Elliot had taken off his suit jacket and was helping his band members plug in the numerous guitars and microphones they had.

Jamie gave me an eye, a stink eye possibly, and then turned to look at Elliot. "You're the second one to mention Elliot tonight."

"What?" I raised a single eyebrow at her, setting my margarita down. "I just said he was setting up."

"Apparently, people think we would make a good match."

I pursed my lips into a smile. "You don't think so?"

She looked at Elliot, her eyes following her every move. "No, no, I really don't. I don't want to date someone who wants to be famous."

I lifted my glass, took another sip, and bounced my eyebrows. "Don't table anything yet, my dear friend. I have it on good authority he's interested."

"He doesn't act interested."

"He's just nervous. I remember when Clay first asked me out. He was shaking and stumbling over his words. He was worried he was too nerdy to date me, but look at us now." I glanced over at Clay, who laughed as he and Milo held a conversation.

"Too nerdy to date you? That man is not nerdy at all."

"In college he was, still kinda is, but I love it."

It? Or *him.*

I sighed, taking a longer pull of my drink.

"Hey, everyone," Elliot's voice rang through the room, the music coming to a stop. "I hope everyone is enjoying their night, celebrating Milo and Madeline. If anyone doesn't know, I'm Elliot Whittaker, and I'm their wedding singer." He laughed at himself and rubbed the back of his neck, situating his guitar strap on his shoulder. "Does anyone else instantly think of Adam Sandler when they hear those words? Just me? Awesome." He laughed again, turning away from the mic, seeming to hate his own joke.

I rubbed Jamie on the shoulder and stood. "After he sings, you should ask him to dance. I'm sure he'd love it." I wiggled my eyebrows at her. "Now if you'll excuse me, I'm going to drag Clay on that dance floor."

Jamie laughed. "It's not dragging if he wants to dance with you. Have you seen the way he's been looking at you all night?"

"Oh, I have." I grinned. I walked over to the table where Clay was still talking to Milo, which seemed longer than it was moments before.

"I've been given permission to sing a few of the songs that are going to be played at the reception, except one." Elliot held up a single finger and looked over at Milo. "So, we've got five or six songs lined up. Oh, and I really love it when people dance."

He did a few chords of his guitar, his band followed and then Josh Turner's *Would You Go With Me* began to shape. I made it to the table just as Elliot's voice filled the air.

"This isn't Thomas Rhett." I looked at Madeline as I grabbed Clay's hand, making him stand from his chair.

Madeline stood and did the same with Milo. "He'll sing more than *just* Thomas Rhett. I snuck some Josh Turner and Jordan Davis in there too."

"How about some Ben Rector and Chord Overstreet? Maybe some Lumineers?" I looked at her with a wide smile on my face as Clay slinked his arm around my waist.

Her eyes narrowed. "I'll see what I can do."

More and more people joined us on the dance floor, including Jamie and someone she knew from work, and Elliot looked to be in his element on the stage. His eyes would focus on Milo and Madeline every now and then, and sometimes he would find Jamie.

Now could be a good time to talk to Clay, I thought.

Elliot was choosing slow and simple songs to play, ones to keep the couples close, and Clay's hands slid up my back, touching my bare skin, making everything come to life. I knew things were different. I knew *he* was different. This time, I knew we could make long distance work, something we didn't even try all those years ago. Would we have worked then? Would we be where we are now? There was a lingering thought that we would, but did I want us to? I didn't want him in another state. I wanted him there with me. I rested my head on his chest, and he kissed the top of my head, raising a hand to trace my jawline, his fingers sliding into my hair.

"Hey, Phe," he rasped, his voice barely a whisper.

I lifted my head to look up at him, and his lips instantly found mine. His kiss was perfect. Salty and sweet, the perfect amount of passion of want, desire. . . of need. Clay's kisses always had a hint of familiarity to them, but this one was new. This was one I would be craving. I've heard people describe kissing as fireworks, electricity shooting through them, but with Clay it was everything under the sun and then some. Every feeling rushed through my veins when his tongue gently danced with mine, our breathing in sync as we stopped dancing, just focusing on each other. My body tingled, running from my fingertips to my toes. As his kiss deepened, our heartbeats slowed as if we were the only ones that mattered in the entire room.

His forehead leaned against mine as he began to sway once again to the music. His eyes closed as I kissed him again and again, my mind became fuzzy.

"I wish," he muttered.

"Now," Elliot's voice stopped him, somehow sounding louder than when he sang. "This next one is kinda sad, but Maddy loves it so Maddy, I give you. . . 'The Hill.'"

Slowly, his acoustic guitar began, and Clay's hands cupped my face. His eyes, full of heat and passion and. . . worry?

"Phe, whatever is going through your mind, it doesn't matter. Only us, only this, matters," he began, his thumb brushing up against my lip. "I wish we could take back everything. I wish we could start from where we were ten years ago, pretend that these past ten years never happened. Can't we just begin again right before you turned and walked away? Can't we just—"

"What?" I asked, my mind focused on his words. *Right before you turned and walked away.*

I took a single step back, not entirely sure how to respond to that. I didn't want to erase the past ten years. Those ten years meant a lot to me. Erase the heart ache; yes. Erase the time spent wishing he was with me in that tiny apartment; yes. But those moments could be erased by *new* moments. The ones that were coming next, the ones we have yet to have.

Those ten years *meant* something in our relationship, and to have them all vanish, to just pretend like it never happened? I couldn't even begin to think what that would do. My brain rushed through the past few months. Clay arriving at the studio, coffee in hand. The food trucks, the trip to the stores, flying through the air with him. Would those moments where I began to fall fade too?

Maybe this is all happening too fast.

"Clay, that's not—"

"We could. I want to make this work," he interrupted.

I blinked, traced my fingers down his arms, feeling the way he shivered under my touch. "I do too, more than you probably realize, but—"

"Phe, we have to try," he whispered.

I furrowed my brow at him. He wasn't letting me talk. He wasn't accepting anything but the magic eraser.

I blinked and laced his fingers in mine. "We need to talk."

"Fighting for you, love That's the hill I'm gonna die on. . ." Elliot finished the song, and a round of applause erupted from the dancers, some shouts from the tables, and once again, just like the night I felt the sting of jealousy; Madeline ran up to the stage, and Elliot bent over to give her a quick hug.

I pulled Clay through the crowd, finding a side room where no one was sitting. He held on to my hand even though I could feel it shaking. Was that him or me shaking? Or both?

"Okay," I sighed, letting go of his hand to face him. I folded my arms around my chest and looked at the floor. My gold dress shimmered around my feet, pulling me back to the task at hand. I needed to go to New York, just for a few days, and that I did want to try. "JoAnn called me this evening."

"That's good. She always calls with amazing news." He took a single step toward me, his hands finding my arms.

"She wants me to go to New York to see the store before the wedding, take some photos with Carter there and help with production."

"Before the wedding?" Clay asked, his eyebrows pinched and he dropped his chin. "What about the rehearsal dinner?"

"I'll be back for that for sure. I'm leaving tomorrow, and I fly back Thursday night, just enough time to attend the rehearsal and fix anything with the dress before she walks down the aisle."

"You're leaving tomorrow?" Clay dropped his arms.

I nodded. "I'll be back—"

"You're walking away?" he stammered.

"No. No, no, no, not at all. I'm not walking away. Clay—" I reached for his hands, grabbing both of them and pulling them to my chin, kissing his knuckles gently. "I don't *want* to walk away, but you said you wanted to erase everything."

"Because that makes sense." Clay stopped me, his voice beginning to shake. "Phe, I'm so in love with you. I can't lose you again. I don't want to remember the time without you. Ten years of regret, ten years of wishing I had never let you go—"

"Clay." It was my turn to interrupt him. I let go of his hands and cupped his face. His eyes formed tears as he let out a breath. "Ten years ago, I thought I had everything, but the one thing I needed told me to leave. Ten years ago, you shattered my heart. As easy as it would be to pretend that never happened, it's going to take more than three months to mend it. I'm not giving up on you or on this, but we need those years to determine who we are now. What happens when I go back to New York? Would you even consider going with me?" My hands fell to his shoulders. "I think. . ." I inhaled, trying to form the words that I hoped wouldn't break him. "I think we took things too fast."

He shook his head and filled the small space between us. "We didn't though. I've been waiting for you for ten years. The moment I saw you again, I knew I loved you. I knew I made a mistake."

"I wish I could say the same, but that feeling had to come back. I'll admit I'm feeling something, but I need to know if it's real or not."

"It's real," Clay whispered, those two little words hitting my heart, nestling their way into it to stay and live forever. I closed my eyes and leaned my forehead against his. He was strong, solid, and warm, and for a split second, I considered telling him everything he wanted to hear.

"I'm leaving tomorrow for New York. I'll be gone for three days, and when I get back, we can decide what *we* are." I rolled my lips, looking at the details of him. His hair had slightly fallen in his face, his eyes were wet with tears that had yet to fall. His suit jacket was crisp, every edge in place. I ran my fingers through his collar, feeling the familiar fabric between my fingers. "Just give me some time."

He exhaled, finally letting the tears fall to his cheek. "I know how I feel, Ophelia, and that's not going to change. I'll wait for you for as long as it takes." He kissed me then, the same kiss on the dance floor. One that I wouldn't forget. "I'll wait, as long as it takes."

With one final kiss, he let me go, stepping away and leaving the room, filling the empty air with heartbreak and tension, which was the last thing I wanted. I took a few deep breaths, straightened my posture, and left the room, hoping to see Clay back at the table with Milo and Madeline, maybe joking about the trivia cards, but the closer I got, the more obvious it was that he had left.

Chapter Thirty-Five

-Clay-

I was tempted to stay hidden all day, but I managed to crawl out of bed, dragging my feet getting ready. I showered, running my hands through my hair as the water hit my scalp. Ophelia had texted early this morning, one that flashed through my mind over and over. I read it again as I poured my coffee. I read it again as I ate my toast and I read it out loud when Milo finally asked me what was wrong.

Ophelia: I'm not done with us. I'll be back on Thursday, and we'll talk then, maybe after the wedding?

Milo grabbed my phone from my hands and read the text himself a few times over, until he looked at me, dropping my phone to the counter.

"This is why you left early last night?"

I nodded, my elbows on the counter, my hands on the back of my head. I kept my head down, my eyes closed, still trying to wrap my head around the conversation we had last night. I've seen and been in plenty of fights with girlfriends. Rebecca was my last fight, right after I lost my job. Her worry was the money. The credit card she had in her name, the dinners we would go to every night, the life of luxury she had grown accustomed to. When we fought over *that,* a bread knife would cut the tension.

With Ophelia, there was zero tension. Not once did we raise our voices, not once did I grow angry with her, and I'm pretty sure she wasn't angry with me.

What I did feel was fear. From both of us.

I was terrified of losing her for a second time. Terrified that she would go to New York and decide that I wasn't worth fitting into her life there. My brain wrapped around the idea of going to New York, trying to start my own company there. I could do it. I *would* do it. If it meant I could be with her.

Her fear, she even said, was focused on us moving too fast. Me being an idiot again. Choosing something over her. . . again. History repeating itself. That was her fear. And it was a very, very valid fear.

"We. . ." I heaved a sigh. "Talked yesterday at the party. Right before I left."

I lifted my head to look at Milo. His eyebrows were raised, his palms leaning on the counter. "And?"

"Well, she left this morning for New York -"

"But she said she's not done."

"And will be back on Thursday. You get married Saturday, so it looks like we will talk on Saturday. Until then?"

"You wait."

I inhaled and dropped my arms to the counter. "I wait."

"Are you going to respond?"

I furrowed my brow and shifted in the seat, an uneasiness coming over me. I wanted to. I desperately wanted to, but a little nag in my brain told me to leave it be. Let her focus on her store, on her future, and I would be waiting for her.

I shook my head. "I don't think so," I mumbled.

"You know." Milo moved, pushing himself off the counter and twisting his body toward the coffee maker. He grabbed two mugs and filled them, turning back and handing me a drink. "Those three days where I thought I was going to have to move to Seattle, I didn't talk to Madeline at all. I didn't even text her, even when I wanted to."

"This is a bit different, don't you think?" I asked, grabbing the handle and scooting the black liquid to me.

Milo frowned and shook his head. "Not really. Not talking to her was the hardest thing for me at that time. You remember how down I was." I nodded. "She was mad at me, but even if I had gotten a text from her, it would have eased my mind a little bit. Maybe just one text, saying you'll talk to her soon, maybe throw in a 'show me the store when you get there.' It may help *her* mind calm down."

He left his kitchen, his mug in hand as he walked around the peninsula, slapping my shoulder as he passed and went into his room.

"Do you want to come with Maddy and me to Depoe Bay today? Map out the wedding site?"

I gave a small chuckle. "Sure. I still can't believe you're getting married on a cliff."

"That's where I knew I loved her for sure, so. . . a cliff it is." He disappeared into his bedroom, leaving the door open as he meandered into his ensuite bathroom.

I turned and looked around the apartment. The last couple of weeks, things had changed without me even realizing. Boxes began to pile up as he prepared for his move into Madeline's, essential items still left out for when Hannah was here with Holly. Time was moving too fast.

And yet, still not fast enough.

I slid my phone to me, using my thumb to bring it to life, still seeing Ophelia's text thread open. She sent it early this morning, most likely right before Madeline had dropped her off at the airport. I closed my eyes and breathed, taking in a few deep breaths before listening to Milo.

Maybe just one text would help her mind calm down.

Clay: I'll be waiting. Always. Enjoy your time, take it all in. You did it.

It was windy and cold on the coast of Depoe Bay. Madeline's hair was whipping all around as she and Milo walked with the owner, mapping out exactly where everything was going to go. Milo would turn and laugh as her hair hit her in the face, finally reaching into his pocket for a hair tie.

I kept back, giving them the space they needed while trying to see what was around. The wedding party would get ready at the hotel and then travel to the site. The chairs and archway would be just off to the side of the tent where the reception would be and once everything was over, the bride and groom would go back to the hotel whereas the wedding party would help take down the chairs and tables and travel to our own homes.

Or in my case, Madeline's home.

I had dog babysitting duty.

I remember that Ophelia said she would get a hotel, not wanting to stay in the same house as me. But now I wondered if that had changed.

My phone buzzed in my pocket, breaking my short walk away from Milo and Madeline. I shoved my hand in my back pocket, pulling out my phone only to see an unknown number. Curiosity got the best of me, and I answered.

"Clay Nolan," I said loudly, the wind picking up.

"Mr. Nolan, this is Regina Krass."

I could barely hear her, the wind making it near impossible for her to hear me.

"Mrs. Krass, yes, hello. I do apologize, I'm at the coast, and it's windy. Can you give me a moment to head into a shop so you can hear me?"

"Oh yes, of course I'll wait. I can hear the wind better than I can hear—"

I lowered the phone and ran. Milo called my name, but I was already on the boardwalk. I flung open the door to the first shop I reached, and as soon as I was inside, I hid in a small corner, surrounded by tourist shot glasses.

"Mrs. Krass, I'm so sorry about that," I mumbled, barely out of breath.

She chuckled. "No worries at all. What coast are you at? I thought a storm was rolling in this afternoon."

I leaned down to look out the window. "I'm at Depoe Bay with my friend mapping out his wedding site. What's the pleasure of this phone call, Mrs. Krass?"

"Well." Even through the phone I could hear a smile. "I've heard some amazing news, and I had to make this phone call myself."

"Some news?"

"Jackson and Rye dropped all charges. Your name is clear again, and so is your reputation."

"Right, I heard that they arrested the right man, but I haven't filed for appeal, not sure if I was going to move forward with that." I spoke softly, making sure no one else was around me.

"Appeal or no appeal, the charges against you have been dropped so," her voice trailed off as she took a deep breath before she spoke again. "I'd like to formally offer you the position of head of our accounting department. I'd like to see you back in the office soon so we can work through a contract and paperwork. What do you say, Mr. Nolan? We'd love to have you on board."

And with that, my mind went blank.

With my hands in my jeans pockets, I made my way back to Milo and Madeline, who now stood alone on the coast. The hotel owner had left, leaving Milo with a paper showing the setup.

"Hey look." He waved the paper in my face, the wind blowing it around more than he attended. "We have a plan."

"I don't know why she gave us this." Madeline took the paper from him and folded it up. "She assured us her staff would set everything up, and the only thing we had to worry about was take down."

"Where did you take off to?" Milo asked, watching while Madeline folded the paper up as tiny as she could.

"I just got the craziest phone call. . ." I smiled.

Chapter Thirty-Six

-Ophelia-

I was home.

I had been gone for months, and New York was still the same. My apartment had been waiting, taken care of by my neighbor, and thankfully, she had managed to keep all my plants alive. It felt warm and perfect, as if I'd never left. There was even an empty wine glass by my desk. Picking up the dirty glass, I glanced at the view. The afternoon sun was hitting the glass windows of the skyscrapers, lighting up the city.

I loved this view.

I loved this city.

A slight sound came from my bag as I passed into the kitchen. Reaching in to grab my phone, my heart lit up when I saw Clay's name. I was worried he wouldn't respond. I was terrified that he had decided I wasn't worth the chance, and that when I got back in a few days, it would be ten years all over again. But when I read the message, my heart fluttered, and my anxiety on the subject slowly faded.

I'll be waiting. Always.

Always.

I locked my phone, setting it down so the clear case hit the sun. The fact he'd be waiting calmed a nerve but sparked so many others.

Trying to occupy my mind, I rinsed the glass, filling it with soap to watch the bubbles form. Swirling the water before dumping it out, I let out a long, tired breath.

The entire five-hour flight, my mind was hyper-focused on what I'd just left in Portland. Madeline drove me to the airport, her lips shut tightly the entire time. I could tell she wanted to know what was going through my mind, but how could I tell her when I didn't even know what was going on? Then she dropped me off, got out of the car, and gave me a hug, whispering that she would be ready to listen when I was ready to talk. She squeezed me one more time and then climbed back in.

The moment I got through security, I texted Clay and then waited. . . and waited. . . and waited for a response for anything that would come through, but—nothing.

Until now.

I wish we could erase the past ten years—right before you turned and walked away.

Always.

I looked straight out the window to the building next to mine, then looked at the view from my desk, trying to find another distraction, any kind of distraction.

Three months couldn't heal ten years.

"Oh, Ophelia," I said aloud to no one, "you're overreacting."

I ran my hands through my wild hair and groaned as I traced the back of my head, settling on the nape of my neck.

My phone once again broke the silence in the kitchen. I turned to glare at it. Whoever it was could wait, I thought as I turned, ignoring the phone all together, walking into my bedroom to take a long, hot shower.

A few hours later, I walked up to one of my favorite restaurants in the city to meet JoAnn. The phone call I ignored was, in fact, JoAnn giving a few details on a meeting we *had to have* tonight. Carter had to be there as well in what she called an all-hands-on deck situation. I, for one, was grateful and willing to take the business meeting. Anything to keep my mind off a certain someone back in Portland.

Carter met me outside and held the door open as I walked past. It amazed me that just a few months ago, I thought he was a micromanaging businessman, but in reality, he was passionate about photography, and he seemed to enjoy working with me and JoAnn. Something told me this wasn't going to be the last time I saw or worked with Carter. There was still Madeline's wedding, after all.

JoAnn was already at the table, three waters set out and an iPad propped up off to the side. Carter and I gave each a glance, a small smile on each of our lips, as he approached the table. I stood up straighter, making sure my confidence was radiating through the room.

"Ophelia!" JoAnn opened her arms and stood to give me a hug. "It's so good to see you!"

"You too, JoAnn. You've been busy." I took the seat next to her, setting my bag on the floor next to me. I could see my phone peeking out from my bag. I reached for it but forced my hand to form a fist. I didn't need that right now. I needed this. I needed to focus. I blinked and unfolded the napkin on my plate to lay it on my lap. "So, do I get to see the store today?"

"Tomorrow, for sure. Today, we need to go to the factory. I'd like you to see the dresses so I can get your approval. There's one design in particular you ought to see." JoAnn mimicked my motions with her napkin and then reached for her laptop. "Here, let me show you."

She began to thumb through the iPad, showing off photos she had taken of the gowns being made. Some were completely ready, in plastic bags and hung with care. Others were still being processed. A lot of these photos were blurry, making it hard for me to see the details in the dress. I glanced at Carter, who had been his normal silent self while JoAnn talked our ears off, and I suddenly wished there were two of him so the photos I was looking at were higher quality.

The waiter had come and taken our orders and refilled our waters. All the while, JoAnn kept going on and on about the gown, as I looked at every photo, just trying to see if I could tell what the issue was.

"And then there's the logo of the store and the Instagram," JoAnn said, switching off the photos of the gowns and turning to another app instead. "I want your opinion on the sign."

"What are we calling the store?" I asked, taking a sip of my water. All her other stores were simply *JoAnn Harmon's*. Her name was well known. Even having my name next to hers was an honor.

She widened her eyes, and the corner of her mouth lifted. "Well, I have a few ideas." She tapped a few things on her iPad and pulled up a few mock logos. My jaw dropped.

Ophelia Fuller: Wedding Gowns.

Gowns by Ophelia.

Ophelia Gowns.

Ophelia's Bridal Shoppe.

I brought my hand to my chest, reminding myself to breathe. "My name?" I asked, my voice barely a whisper.

JoAnn gave a small laugh, then her smile grew. "Yes, dear. Your name. This is all you. I only invested in you. And it was the best investment I've ever made, if I do say so myself. First wedding gowns, then seasonal stores. All with your name."

I pursed my lips and forced myself to swallow. I knew I was designing gowns for her store, but I never thought the store would have my name on it. I felt the tears welling in my eyes, and I couldn't stop them. One tear hit my cheek, and I looked at JoAnn. I had no words, nothing at all to describe what I was feeling at this moment.

Click.

The sound of Carter's camera pulled me back, making me chuckle and turn to him.

"Oh, yeah. My crying is the perfect thing for Instagram." I laughed, wiping away the single tear from my cheek.

JoAnn reached forward and touched my forearm. "These are the mock logos, and I'd like you to pick. Whichever you choose will go above the door."

I swallowed again, giving JoAnn one last smile before turning to look at my name on her iPad. They all were perfect, but one, only one stood out above the rest.

"I love this one." I tapped on it, and it blew up on the screen. The swoops and rose color of my name. The embellished half circle coming from 'Fuller' pulled it all together, giving it flare. My heart exploded looking at it.

"I do too." JoAnn smiled.

I arrived back at my place later than normal. JoAnn showed me every inch of the warehouse and Carter followed, taking photos of me with all the completed gowns and helping the producers. My drawings were scattered on boards through the workshop and people would go and refer to them all the time. My small little 'OF' was in the corner in all the designs. The small issue they were having was just that—small. A simple change in the stitch fixed everything, and getting to step in behind that machine, watching my creation come to life was everything.

My mind was reeling, happiness bursting through every vein. This was real. This was happening. I was one hundred percent in my element.

I fell back onto my bed, *my* bed. I didn't realize how much I missed my bed. I sighed and gave the ceiling a soft smile before pulling myself up, sitting on the edge. I had ignored my phone all afternoon, dinner and the workshop giving the perfect distraction, but I needed to text Madeline. She needed to know everything.

Unlocking my phone brought all sorts of notifications. Hundreds of them. I didn't even know a phone could get that many notifications. A few texts from Madeline, showing me Depoe Bay and the hotel we would be getting ready at and a photo of the coast, a small Clay off in the distance but from her, that was it. The rest were from social media. The boutique Instagram feed had exploded, gaining new followers, and all the photos from today had already been posted. Starting with me at the restaurant, relieving the new logo and name of the boutique. That post had been pinned to the top, being followed by photos of me at the workshop, walking the rows and rows of gowns. Everything was just. . .

I sighed.

Magical.

And. . .

At the top of the list of likes. . .

Clayton Nolan liked your photo.

Every single one.

I closed the app, locked my screen, and hugged my phone to my chest. Closing my eyes, I felt yet again more tears form. I wished he was here with me.

Chapter Thirty-Seven

-Clay-

My dad can't sit near the stage. He may like Elliot, but if he sits there, he will moan and groan the entire time," Milo said from the kitchen, pointing at the large piece of paper he and Madeline were hunched over. "He'll want to sit with Holly."

"The other option is at the table with Hannah and Donald. Does he get along with them enough to sit there?" Madeline asked, a hint of irritation in her voice.

I knew from Ophelia that Jamie had done the seating chart, which, let's be honest, once all the guests arrived and people began to mingle, that seating chart would be completely forgotten about. The summer weather coming to an end created the perfect setting for their outdoor reception, that is, if the coastal wind didn't pick up. The open tent would cause even more chaos to the seating chart that they were currently bickering over.

"He gets along with Hannah. It's Donald that's the issue."

"Well, they responded, and they are eating chicken." Madeline argued. "Holly is sitting with them, so if Wallace wants to be near Holly, then he has to be at that table." Madeline's finger hit the table with a thud.

"I'll text him, but he won't be happy about it."

"He can hate me for it."

"Impossible," Milo mumbled, standing straight and pulling his phone from his pocket. "He loves you more than he loves me."

Madeline chuckled, a slight blush forming on her cheeks. I shook my head, rolled my eyes at them, and returned to my phone. I was comfy on Madeline's couch, facing them, my elbows on my knees and an uncompleted email on my phone screen.

I have decided not to move forward with an appeal against Jackson and Rye. Thank you for your advice. If I ever need legal help in the future. . .

I hopefully wouldn't need legal help, but isn't that the way you broke up with your lawyer? After the call from Mrs. Krass offering me a very cushy job, every piece of my future came together, and I had the best support system to get me there. All I needed to do was close this chapter of my life to move forward.

"He doesn't like that idea." Milo's voice broke my concentration.

"Does it really matter?" I asked loud enough for them to look up.

Milo furrowed his brow, and Madeline's jaw was slightly open.

"Would you want to sit next to your son's ex?" Madeline folded her arms.

"If I had a son, and that son had an ex, I probably wouldn't care," I admitted. "Plus, you guys all get along with Hannah and Donald. I bet your dad would have respect for that."

Milo pinched his brow, and Madeline raised a corner of her lip.

My phone dinged at the right time, allowing me to remove myself from their little tussle. Milo and Madeline didn't fight. They bickered. Over the stupidest things. And it never lasted long. My bet was they would be high-fiving the victory over the seating chart in five minutes, and then it would be forgotten about.

Swiping down the notifications, I saw the text from Elliot. I let out a small sigh. A part of me, a very large part of me, always wished that with every chime it was Ophelia. She hadn't responded to me, and I hadn't heard from her since she left the other day. Two long days of not talking to her, not seeing her. Two long days of missing her. How did I ever go ten years without her?

Elliot: I have some more paperwork for you to fill out. Honestly, I'm probably more excited about this than you are. Can you come by tonight?

I chuckled and responded: *Yeah, I can come by around 4, does that work? What kind of paperwork?*

Elliot: New contract and final paycheck. Nothing too big.

The words *final paycheck* stung. I had only worked with Elliot for a little over a month and all the money I had earned, which I'll be honest, was a decent chunk, went straight to Milo. Milo insisted it wasn't needed, but I was adamant about paying him back every penny. This paycheck was no different.

I had a plan coming in motion, and I only needed one final piece to complete it. I just needed to talk to that piece first.

A horn from outside grabbed my attention. I draped my arm around the back of the couch and glanced out the window just in time to see a very excited Holly jump—literally jump—from the back seat and bound up to the front door. A seemingly very tired Hannah climbed from the front seat and shook her head, heading toward the trunk to retrieve Holly's suitcase.

"Hey," I called, standing up from the couch. "Milo, you have a guest."

Milo stopped mid-sentence and furrowed his brow. His quizzical look only lasted seconds when he saw Hannah out front. He dropped his phone on the counter and bolted toward the front door. Swinging it open, he greeted Holly with open arms, lifting her as she shouted "Daddy" over and over. Madeline quickly joined them at the door and gave Holly a sweet side hug, kissing her temple.

"Holly, I've missed you! I need to hear everything; you were never detailed enough on the phone calls, and you didn't send enough pictures." Milo said into her hair.

I smiled, taking a few steps away to give them a reunion.

"Daddy, it was so cool! Scotland was amazing, my favorite place ever. We have to move there one day." Holly shouted.

"Holly, honey." Hannah's breathless voice came into the room. "I told you. . ."

"We'll definitely move to Scotland one day." Milo finished. "Hey Hannah," he chuckled as he pulled her into a side hug. She accepted his embrace and rolled her eyes.

"Please don't give her any ideas," she mumbled. "Hey, Clay." she smiled at me. "You're looking good."

"Uncle Clay is here!? Mommy!!" Holly shouted, leaping from Milo's arms. "Did you bring in my bag? I need to give Uncle Clay my present."

"Yes, honey. It's on top of your suitcase." Hannah shut the front door and nodded toward the living room. Madeline followed her, a look of pure happiness on her face. "I'm sorry Maddy, but she insisted on magnets. I tried to have her get other things but—"

"It's okay." Madeline smiled. "I keep all the ones from Holly at work. They make me smile."

I leaned against the kitchen island, enjoying the three of them settling as Hannah began to tell them about Holly's adventure around the globe. Milo draped his arm around Madeline, and the three of them talked like old friends. Their co-parenting from different states had worked out wonderfully, and I couldn't believe I had ever questioned it.

"Uncle Clay." Holly appeared in front of me.

I smiled down at her. "Hey Holly-Wood." I rubbed my hand on the top of her head, her brushed brown hair now a mess. "How was your trip?"

"It was great, Uncle Clay. I wish you could have seen it." She smiled, then she raised her arms and in her hands was a small item wrapped in tissue paper. "I tried to find you something while we were gone, but this was the only thing I wanted to give you. Mommy says it's kinda weird because it's from the airport, but I knew you'd love it."

She extended her arms and handed me the tissue paper. I raised a single brow at her and took the gift, unwrapping it carefully. Inside was a simple shot glass with the New York City skyline etched around it. My heart jerked. How did this little girl know exactly what I needed to see?

I finally looked up at her with a smile. "I do love this, thank you Holly, really."

"She wanted to buy that thing the day we left when we landed at JFK." Hannah came up behind her. Holly gave me a quick hug and then turned back to Milo and Madeline. "I told her there would be so many other shot glasses around, and how did we even know you used shot glasses, but she refused. Bought thirty-seven magnets for her dad and Maddy, but she only wanted you to get that shot glass." She leaned against the island and looked up at me.

Hannah and I got along fine when she was with Milo, but to her, I was just the friend that came with the husband. She was a different person than what I remembered. Mom of four beautiful kids, a kind and loving personality. Even after seeing the worst side of her, I could still see the genuine person she truly was.

"I love it, really." I held it up, twisting it with my fingers to see the skyline, before setting it down on the counter.

"You look good, Clay," she said softly.

"Sorry I never really got to say goodbye. I'm glad you had a great trip."

"It's okay. I knew you weren't asleep but. . . I didn't want to add more pressure." She exhaled. "But really." She pushed herself from the counter and patted my shoulder. "You look *good.*"

We smiled at one another before she turned to look at the seating chart that still lay unsolved on the counter.

"Milo," she said loud enough for them to overhear over the magnet excitement, "why is your dad sitting by the stage? He's going to want to sit with Holly."

Milo slapped his knees and stood, Madeline close behind him. "That's what I said!"

I laughed at the group, grabbed my shot glass and phone, and headed out onto the porch, letting them bicker some more over something that didn't matter.

"You're 100% sure about this?" Elliot asked, waving my final paycheck in front of me.

I didn't even attempt to grab it. "You said you were excited."

"I was. I *am*. Just going to miss having you around the office." He finally stopped waving the check, allowing me to take it.

"I won't be going anywhere soon. I just won't be in this office."

"Are you going to rent a space or. . ." he trailed off, stuffing his hands in his pockets.

"Honestly, I don't know. I think I'll just work remotely. I have my laptop and internet, and that's all I need for now, and then well. . . we'll see where I go from there."

He smirked. "Did you send that email?"

Pursing my lips, I shook my head and sat down. "Not yet."

"Have you texted her?" Elliot sat on the edge of his desk, crossing his feet and folding his arms over his chest.

Meeting his gaze for half a second, I shook my head again. "She said we'd talk after the wedding."

"Not even an *I miss you?*"

I didn't move. I just stared at his perfectly polished shoes. Though Elliot was fun to work with and knew how to handle business, I much preferred the worn-out jeans and t-shirts to the shiny shoes and suits that I normally saw him in. To my surprise, Elliot had become a friend.

"Do you think I should?" I asked, my voice low, hoping he didn't hear me.

He heaved a sigh and uncrossed his feet, wiggling just a tad to shove his hands in his pockets again. "I think you'd be an idiot not to. Oh, and while you're at it. Send that email."

Milo's apartment was now 94% packed in boxes. Everything that Holly and Hannah would need was in the front room, ready to be used and then packed away when they were done. Tomorrow, Elliot and I were going to be the movers from the apartment to the house and then, after the wedding, all Milo had to do was unpack and settle into his new home and life. I was in the apartment for a few more days, then with Niko, then. . . on to my future.

I leaned against the kitchen peninsula, looking out at the bare living room, boxes towering high against the wall, my computer and phone in front of me. A text thread and email ready to be sent. I had no issue completing the email, telling Justin that I valued the work he put in for me, and that I would be able to arrive for any court as needed, but no appeal. I had made my decision there. I didn't want my old life back. Hitting that send button was the easiest thing I had ever done. I remembered hitting it for Ophelia when she sent in her application to Harold Martin in New York, and then again to JoAnn when she wanted to pursue wedding gowns. If only I had her here to cheer me on for something so simple as denying an appeal.

Man, did I miss her. I didn't want to bother Ophelia, but I wanted her to know I loved her; that I was thinking about her this entire time. I wanted to know what was going through her mind. If she even remotely missed me. If she loved me.

As if my thoughts were being read, my phone buzzed, and Ophelia's name lit up the screen. I took a deep breath and answered.

"Hey," I said softly, trying to calm the frog that was in my throat.

"Hi," she responded. "How are you?"

"I'm good. I miss you," I said suddenly, no chance to stop myself.

"I miss you too."

I exhaled, letting out the breath I had been holding.

"I just uh. . ." she fumbled, coughing a little to clear her thoughts. "I just wanted to hear your voice."

"I'm glad you called." I whispered.

"I fly in Thursday afternoon. Madeline's picking me up but. . ." she took a deep breath, the air coming from her shaking. "I'll see you at the rehearsal, and we can talk after the wedding still. . . right?"

"Right."

"Ok um. . . I hope you have a good night."

"Phe," I said, stopping her from saying goodbye.

She hummed.

"I really do. . . miss you."

"I really miss you too, Clay."

Chapter Thirty-Eight

-Ophelia-

JoAnn slowly unlocked the door to the store. Paper still covered the windows, not giving me even a single glimpse as to what was inside. My heart did backflips in my chest. The warehouse was beautiful enough just watching the gowns being put together. What was going to happen when I saw the store? Would I even be able to contain myself?

"Ophelia Fuller, are you ready to see your very own wedding gown boutique?" JoAnn slid the key into the lock and turned to look at me, a smile from ear to ear.

I nodded, balling my hands into fists. The glass door opened, and Carter and JoAnn slunk in first, and they both started tearing off the paper that covered the windows. I stepped in, trying to see everything in the light from the windows, but as soon as JoAnn turned on the lights, it came to life.

Cream walls with white beams and accents, allowing the sections from dresses to be separated. The walls dipped into small arches where the dresses would be displayed, and empty photo frames sat in between each arch. Small accent chairs and sofas were scattered, still covered in plastic to protect them, and on the opposite wall, there was a pedestal with a gallery of mirrors, allowing the bride to see every angle. Toward the back was the counter, simple and plain with the same cream walls.

It was beautiful in every way. It fit with what I saw in my head, and even though JoAnn and I only spoke about it briefly, she was able to capture my vision. The pure fact it was here, it was real. . .

Tears began to well up in my eyes as I spun around the room, my palms flat against my stomach, a reminder to breathe.

"Well," JoAnn said softly, "what do you think?"

I opened my mouth to speak, but JoAnn started to talk again.

"The logo you chose will be made into a sign to go behind the counter, and I was thinking about metal floral accidents around. The frames that are empty. Well, Carter is going to pick his favorites from your trip to frame. We will have models and a photoshoot, and the chairs and sofas will go in front of each pedestal area for the brides. It's coming together very nicely. It's 80% done. . . but, what do you think?" Her thoughts were everywhere, filling in the gaps as she walked around, using her hands to bring the rest of it to life.

I swallowed, taking a deep breath before blinking, allowing tears to fall.

"JoAnn," I croaked, my voice coming out deeper and shaker than I intended. "This is. . ."

"I told you she'd love it," Carter mumbled, a smile on his lips as he raised his camera.

"I do," I finally mustered. "I really, really do. I can't believe it."

JoAnn clapped her hands together. "Wonderful! The back is the warehouse, and there's a studio upstairs. We got the perfect location, and I am just counting down until opening day." She stepped forward, grabbing my hand to pull me through the rest of the boutique. "Let me show you the back, and the mannequins and artwork to hang. I think you'll love it."

I knew I would. I loved everything I had been shown so far.

The only thing that was missing. . .

. . . was Clay.

Ophelia: Shooting you over flight details. You're still okay to pick me up, right?

I sent the text to Madeline, thinking she would be at work and unable to answer me, so when my phone instantly dinged back before I could put my phone down, I gave a small chuckle.

Madeline: Yes! And then you, me, and Jamie are going to be making the centerpieces!

I smiled, loving that something was being saved until the last minute. It wouldn't be a wedding without the late-night bridal party putting something together.

That sounds perfect. I can't wait. Pizza and wine will be involved, I hope, I responded.

Madeline: You know it. See you in eight hours!

Eight hours, not soon enough. My suitcase was packed and by the door, lighter than in June. I had brought everything back with me. There was no need to pack several suitcases and my portfolio. All I needed was right there in the one suitcase. Easy and simple, small enough to carry on the plane. The wedding was Saturday. I was leaving Monday, and a small sting hit my memory when I recalled that Clay would be dog watching Niko. I remembered saying I would book a hotel those nights.

But a softer memory entered my mind right after I thought about the hotel—Clay's hands around my waist, his kisses at my temple, his voice in my ear, telling me he loved me.

After the wedding. . .

Another small ding from my phone caught my attention. I instantly reached for it. Clay's name appeared on the screen with a thumbnail of a photo, and when I opened it to full size, I saw him,

Milo, and Holly all sticking their tongues out at the camera. Clay's eyes were squinting, his five o'clock shadow more prominent than Milo's, definitely telling me he hadn't been to Elliot's office this week. I missed this goofy side of him, and I was so in love with knowing he was letting it out more and more.

Clay: One last daddy-daughter day in the apartment watching Marvel movies. Holly graciously allowed me to join in the fun. See you tomorrow!

I saved the image to my phone and responded. *Tomorrow.*

I simply couldn't wait for tomorrow.

In the Uber to the airport and all the way through until I was boarded on my flight, I had one thing on my mind. Clay. And how I desperately wanted to be with him more than anything. I wanted him with me as I toured the boutique and when I made suggestions for changes. I wanted him next to me in my bed, his arms around me comforting my insecurities that I tried to hide so well.

There was absolutely no denying that I was in love with him, and I couldn't wait to tell him.

I couldn't do the distance; this trip taught me that. It opened my eyes to it. I made a plan in my mind, forming it all out perfect. I would ask him to move in with me, help him find a job here in the city, and watch as his life unfolded here like it should have all those years ago. We'd be together, in love, for the rest of our lives. Just thinking about it made my heart sing.

Madeline pulled up to the curb, and just like she did in June, she jumped from her car and ran to give me a hug. I laughed into her shoulder, happy to have my friend close again, even if I was only gone for three days, I still loved coming home to her.

"Please tell me you got pictures." Madeline pulled me at arm's length. "Carter hasn't posted anything since the warehouse, and I'm dying to see the inside. That logo!" She bent her knees and had the biggest grin on her face. Her support couldn't compare to anyone. She was always so excited, which made me excited.

"I have a few, but Carter will be posting after the wedding. I promise you'll see everything. And"—I tossed my suitcase in the back and climbed in the passenger seat—"we have an opening day. It's set."

Madeline dropped her jaw and turned. "Seriously, when?"

"November 17th." I smiled. "And you better be there. JoAnn said she's going to make a show of it, a ribbon cutting and everything. I'll need you there."

"Hell, yes!" she shouted. "I wouldn't miss it for the world."

I reached over and kissed her cheek, causing her to scrunch her nose.

Popping the car into drive, she gave a small cough. "Clay's good," she said, giving me a side eye as I settled back into the seat. "He's really good."

I smiled. "I missed him, Maddy," I admitted, my feelings finally coming out to someone. "I can't wait to see him. We have a lot to talk about. We said after the wedding, but I don't think I can wait."

"He'll be at the rehearsal tomorrow, and I know he has some news for you. He got a really exciting phone call while you were gone."

I turned to look at her. "Oh, yeah?" I swallowed. "About what?"

"He got offered a job, a big one. . ."

I furrowed my brow. "He's been working with Elliot, hasn't he? I mean, I figured that was just temporary but, he seemed to like working with Elliot."

"Elliot gave him his last paycheck already. Trust me, Elliot is excited about this too." She had a smile on her face, and her eyes had a sparkle to them that I couldn't understand. She was excited about his big new job offer. Where did I factor into this?

I blinked a few times and focused my eyes out the window. We talked on the phone; we texted a few times. Why didn't he tell me anything? My mind went straight back to that night. Thinking we were it, we were meant to be, and then the *stupid* job offer. . .

He's choosing the job again.

"Oh," I stumbled. "That's great."

"Phe." Madeline smiled over at me. "It really is great."

"Maybe I *will* wait until after the wedding to talk to him. We have a lot to do, right?" I shifted my focus, yet again hiding those emotions. "Centerpieces tonight and then the rehearsal. I know there's gotta be something on your dress to mend, and then there's Jamie's dress."

"No, Phe. Listen." Madeline tried to stop me, but my mind decided to focus on one thing, and that thing was being the best damn maid of honor I could be.

"Nope, you're the more important thing here. Clay and I said we would talk after the wedding, so I'll learn about this job and his plans after the wedding."

"Oh, Phe, come on. You were just so excited to see him, and now you won't listen to the entire story."

"Nope. This weekend is about you, Maddy. Not about me pining after some guy."

"Hmm," Madeline hummed. "I seem to remember you telling me something about how *it's not just a guy.*"

"But it is." I stopped her. "This weekend is about you, and then Clay and I will figure out whatever it is we are doing." I rolled my eyes, the elated feeling I had moments ago vanishing at the thought of Clay's path completely changing. I was being ridiculous. I knew I was. Long distance crossed my mind days ago, how it would work no matter what, but just being in New York without him made me never want to *be* without him. I knew it in my gut. Long distance wouldn't work. It was New York. . . or nothing.

At the red light, Madeline turned her entire body toward me, her eyes stinging as she stared at me.

I shrugged. "Come on, we have centerpieces to make."

"You're being ridiculous. At least let me finish." She read my mind. She always could.

"No," I snapped, turning my head toward the street. "It's green."

Madeline sighed, shaking her head at me before telling me what needed to be done for the wedding still. As she rattled off details, my mind wandered back. I had all my thoughts and emotions laid out, rehearsed in my mind during the five-hour flight. And now I had a wild card I had to fit in.

But first, I had a wedding to attend.

Chapter Thirty-Nine

-Clay-

Elliot honked his Jeep's horn as we arrived at the coast. The tent was already set up, and Milo and Madeline were talking with their officiant. Holly was circling the two of them, kicking the ground with her feet, a look of pure boredom on her face. All four faces turned to us as we parked, and Holly's dull expression turned to excitement.

I was in charge of her during this adventure. Milo and Madeline were going to be busy with the officiant. Elliot had to find the perfect place for the stage. Ophelia and Jamie were going to be setting up chairs and helping the event staff with the tables. Originally, Jamie had agreed to keep Holly entertained, but she asked for Uncle Clay, and I would be lying if I said that hadn't pulled at my heartstrings a bit.

I hunched my body and began to run up toward Holly, who instantly grabbed Milo's arm as she screamed and hid behind him.

Milo's body jerked to the side as she hid. And then again, I picked her up and threw her over my shoulder. She may be nine, but her squeal was that of a four-year-old—happy and full of life. I spun in a circle before setting her back on the ground.

Her body swayed as she pretended to be dizzy.

"Wanna go help Elliot?" I asked, placing a hand on the top of her head.

"Sure, but I don't think I can walk."

"Oh well, that's not a problem." I picked her up in one fell swoop, flinging her over my shoulder.

"Bye, Dad!" she shouted, her weight shifting as she raised her torso.

"We're not going far." I laughed. "Just to Elliot."

"Can we go see the whales too? Oh! Look!" Holly's voice rang behind me. "Jamie and Ophelia are here!"

I stopped, twisting my torso so Holly now faced Elliot, and there she was. Ophelia walked up with Jamie, wearing white shorts and that same burnt orange shirt she wore when we went to The Piano Bar for the first time. Sunglasses and her golden earrings—effortlessly beautiful in every way.

"Hey, Holly-wood. Give me just a moment, okay? I need to go say hi to Ophelia." I sat her on the ground and rubbed her head.

"Then can we go see the whales?"

"Definitely."

My eyes were glued on Ophelia as I walked out of the tent, my strides longer than they had ever been. I walked toward the woman I loved with a purpose. She was the only thing I wanted in my arms.

"Hey, Clay." Jamie smiled as I got closer and closer. I gave her a slight wave.

"Oh, hey." Ophelia turned toward her, my reflection in her sunglasses. "Please tell me the staff brought the chairs because Madeline said—"

I brought my hands to her face, cupping her chin in my palms, and before she could say anything else, I kissed her. With a moan of surprise, Ophelia raised her hands to my wrists and puddled into me. She hummed into my mouth, her tongue finding mine with ease, and when she broke the kiss, her eyes fluttered open behind the tint of the sunglasses.

"I have so much I want to tell you," I whispered.

"Me too." She kissed me again, lightly this time, feathers on my lips, only making me crave her more. "But. . ."

"I know, after the wedding. I think Milo is losing his mind over there." Keeping my hands on her face, I turned toward Milo, who in all honestly looked as cool as a cucumber. "Or maybe only Holly was. It was hard to tell."

"Oh, look." Jamie's voice made me blink, standing up a bit straighter, lowering my hands to Ophelia's arms. "Chairs!" She smiled at us and then ran up to the tent where all the tables and chairs sat folded up against the beams.

"Hey, chairs," I repeated, turning back to Ophelia. "I'm on Holly duty, but if you need help, I'm sure she is stronger than she looks."

Licking her lips, she smiled. "I think Jamie and I got it. Elliot, though, looks as if he's going to kill that event planner." Her head tilted, and her gaze trailed behind me.

Slipping my arms around her waist, I looked at Elliot, standing with his arms wide at the front of the tent, a look of frustration on his face as he said something to the woman in front of him.

"Nah, that's just his everyday look. I've seen it a lot at the office while he's talking to someone."

"That gal he's talking to looks like she can handle her own."

We began to take small steps together toward the group, the weight of her arm hitting my back as she pulled me closer.

"I got a phone call," I started, not wanting to wait until after the wedding to let her know my entire world was clearer now, that I had every step laid out and that everything made sense.

"Nope." She shook her head, mumbling. She stepped in front of me and removed her sunglasses, the deep color of her eyes locking with mine. She inhaled. "Okay, I know you have some news, but I'm already half-convinced that news is going to break my heart, so right now, we need to focus on our best friends getting married tomorrow. We have a lot on our plate as best man and maid of honor. They are our top priorities. They deserve it, don't they?"

I heaved a sigh and nodded. "Right."

"The moment they are married, we'll talk. I promise." She raised up on her tippy toes and kissed me, her hands trailing up my chest.

I breathed her in, wanting more of this, but I would wait.

For her, I'd wait another ten years.

"I've missed you," I said breathlessly as she lowered herself back down.

"I missed you too."

The look she gave me would send any man to his knees. Full of fire and passion with a calming effect, a look that was only for me. She ran her thumb along my stubble on my cheek before giving me one final kiss. Leaving me there with my hands frozen at my side, she walked up to Jamie and Elliot, began unfolding tables and chairs, and set up Madeline's seating chart to a T.

"Uncle Clay." Holly appeared in front of me, snapping me back to reality. A talent of hers, it seemed. "Can we go see if there are whales now?"

She reached out for my hand, her small palm vanishing in mine. I smiled at her.

"Sure thing, Holly-wood. Let's go."

The alarm clock went off way too early. Either that or the couch was more comfortable than I remember it being. I barely had time to turn over and grab my phone, silencing the evil buzz that came from the speakers.

"It's today!" I heard Holly scream, then she was a blur as she ran past me into Milo's room. "We're getting married today! It's today!"

I chuckled and sat up on the couch, watching as Milo was forced from his room.

"You need to shower and get ready, Dad." She tugged and pulled him into the bathroom. "You just know that Madeline is going to be a princess. She needs to marry a prince, not a smelly dad."

"Hey," Milo grumbled. "I am not a smelly dad."

"I'll make coffee." I stood to make my way to the kitchen as Milo craned his neck to me, mouthing "thank you," and Holly shoved him in the bathroom.

"You know, Holly," I said as I prepped the coffee maker, deciding extra bold coffee was called for today. "The wedding isn't until four. We have plenty of time to get ready and make sure your dad's not stinky."

Holly shrugged her shoulders and climbed up on one of the bar stools. "I know, but he takes forever getting dressed, longer than Mommy does."

"Speaking of your mother, when is she coming to get you?"

"Soon, then I'm meeting Madeline at the salon to get our hair and nails done."

I puffed out my bottom lip and nodded. "So, you get a spa day, and I get the stinky dad?"

"I am *not* stinky." Milo appeared from the bathroom.

"Dad!" Holly scolded him, pointing toward the bathroom. "Get in the shower!"

Milo slumped his shoulders and looked at his daughter. "I think Maddy would marry me no matter what I smelled like."

"Shower!" Holly and I bellowed together, followed by a chuckle from Holly.

Once Milo was in the bathroom and we could hear the shower running, Holly seemed happy with herself. "I need to call my mama." She jumped off the chair.

I poured my mug of coffee and then raised it to her as she began to head back into her room.

"Oh, and Uncle Clay?" She spun and smiled at me. "When you get married, I'll make sure you shower, too."

I raised my mug to her again, a small chuckle leaving my throat. "Sounds like a plan."

Giving me a smile, she left, leaving me to sip my coffee in semi-silence. I had a small bag packed by the edge of the couch, my suitcase filled and ready to go once the wedding was over. This was my last day here with Milo. After the wedding, it was a week at Madeline's and then. . . my parents. Steps were happening to ensure the future I wanted would form. I just needed that final piece to want it too, and I wouldn't know if she did until *after the wedding.*

Chapter Forty

-Ophelia-

Click, click, click.

Carter circled Madeline one last time before he slunk out of the room to give her some privacy, promising a peek before we left the hotel. Madeline took a deep breath once he was gone and went to stand in front of the full-length mirror. Her dress fit like a glove as she studied herself in the full-body mirror for the millionth time. She ran her hands down her stomach and rested them at her hips, her nails freshly done with the French tip manicure we had all gotten. Holly enjoyed her spa day more than anyone, relishing in the fact she was in the wedding, and that her daddy was marrying his best friend. With every mention of Milo, Madeline's cheeks would blush and a small lustful smile would spread across her face, but now, as she looked at herself, all those memories came flooding back.

"Thinking about your first date?" I asked, coming up to add some more flowers to her hair. "I remember you took forever getting ready. You tried on so many dresses, settling with that plain boring one."

"Hey." Madeline turned her head to look at me, a small strand of her auburn hair falling in her face. I reached up and tucked it behind her ear. "He remembered that dress, you know. If it wasn't for that date, we wouldn't be here now, would we?"

I tilted my chin to my shoulder, a sense of pride flowing through. "I'll take credit for that, thank you very much."

"You and Jamie. She's the one that put that bug in my ear."

"Damn straight, I did. Proud of it too. I dare say, Maddy, you have amazing friends." Jamie rested her elbow on my shoulder.

Madeline gave a soft laugh as she turned back to the mirror. She rubbed her lips together and let out a sigh. "I'm marrying my best friend today." She smiled, biting her bottom lip.

"Don't mess up your lipstick." Jamie lightly tapped her shoulder, smiling when Madeline let her lip flop back down.

Jamie shook her head and reached for the basket carrying all the flowers. "We're heading out soon, right? Wedding's at four?"

Madeline nodded. "What time is it?"

I glanced at the clock on the nightstand. "3:30."

She inhaled, turning away from the mirror. "Okay."

"I'll take these down. Meet you at the car?" Jamie said, holding the flowers to her stomach.

Madeline and I nodded as Jamie left the room, and as soon as we were alone, I wrapped her in my arms.

"Hey, Phe," she whispered.

I pulled her at arm's length and tilted my face. "Yeah?" I was half expecting her to tell me something about the dress, about the store, anything but what she actually said.

"I saw you and Clay yesterday. I need you to just—"

I shook my head, drawing her out. "Clay and I will be fine. We said we would talk—"

"After the wedding," she said in unison with me. She shook her head and gave a breathy laugh. "I'm really sick of hearing that from you. He's there now, you should go find him and tell him everything and listen to what he has to say because I know it's not what—"

"Madeline." I stopped her. "Today, right now, is about you. I'm focusing on you and only you."

"If you decided to pull him away and talk to him now, I wouldn't mind, even if you missed the wedding."

I smiled and pulled her in for another hug. "I promise you, I'll talk to him, and everything will be laid out. Everything is going to work out because. . . it has too." I pulled away and looked down at my feet. The maroon skirt flowed against my legs, and the gold shoes matched perfectly with my earrings. "It has to because. . ."

"You love him," Madeline whispered.

I raked my teeth on my bottom lip, not answering or finishing my thought. Madeline already knew the truth.

"Come on," I whispered, "let's go get you married to your best friend."

All three men stood at the cliff, the archway behind them. The lace that was draped around the wood moved with the light wind, and Milo stood, his eyes focused on us girls walking up. When his gaze found Madeline, I could see the shaky breaths and the movement in his feet. I turned to look at her, noticing as she only saw Milo. I smiled, knowing that I had created some of that emotion, that he still had no idea that that dress was created specifically for this moment.

And he loved it.

Holly walked down the small aisle of chairs first, scattering their pink flowers all over the grass. Jamie followed, and when it was my turn, all I saw was Clay.

He stood next to Milo, his hands clasped in front of him. His tux fit perfectly with the small rose poking out of the pocket. His hair was combed back, and he had shaved. He was focused on me, his eyebrows raised, and nothing but love shone through his eyes. I took my place next to Jamie and gave him a sweet smile, my mind imagining all kinds of situations where this was our wedding, and that he would be mine forever.

I blinked, a few tears hitting my cheek as I turned to watch Madeline come closer and closer to Milo. When did I start crying? Where did these tears come from?

Madeline gave me a soft smile as she handed me her bouquet and finally took Milo's hands. Her dress fluttered in the breeze, the sun hitting the ivory flower detail just right. I bent over and adjusted the train, and when I stood, I met Clay's eyes. He gave me a quick wink and a sweet smile. I pursed my lips and held on to him.

It's you. It's you. . .

"Hi, Milo," Maddy whispered. I let out a soft chuckle, which only let a few more tears fall.

"Hi, Maddy," Milo responded.

I took a quick breath and used the tips of my fingers to wipe the stray tear away, rolling my neck to refocus on the ceremony. The officiant started to talk, giving a small introduction of how Milo and Madeline became Milo and Madeline. The crowd laughed a few times when the infamous kiss was mentioned when Milo flung his head back, releasing a loud groan. He pulled his attention back to Madeline and mouthed "Why?" which only caused Madeline to place her hand on her stomach and laugh.

It was them, in every sense of the word—this was perfect for them.

And all I could do was watch Clay. He would laugh at his friend and turn to whisper something to Elliot. Holly, at one point, had floated over to him and he held her hand as Milo and Madeline exchanged their vows. But even though he looked immersed in the wedding, his eyes would find mine and shine. There was no fear in his eyes. Only love.

Why the hell did you have to wait until after the wedding?

I scolded myself. If I had just let him talk yesterday, I wouldn't be sitting here wishing the wedding would end. I wouldn't have watched his every move as he handed Milo Madeline's ring. I wouldn't be crying, just thinking that maybe he didn't want me anymore. That he would choose a career again, that he would say no to New York again.

I let out the breath I didn't know I was holding when the world came into focus, Milo dipping Madeline in their first kiss as man and wife. Clay was clapping, a smile spread across his face as the entire crowd stood and clapped. I shook my head, my eyes following Madeline as she laughed in Milo's arms. I glanced down at Holly, who danced around her dad and new stepmother.

My mind was reeling, and I couldn't stop the tears once they started. Madeline turned and gave me a hug, then reached for Jamie, pulling us into her arms, her laughter contagious. I laughed through my tears and watched as Milo took Madeline by the hand and walked with her over to the coast, where their photographer and Carter were waiting for them. The crowd began to talk and leave their seats, Jamie leaving toward the coast, Elliot close behind her, but I stayed at the archway, my feet frozen in place.

"It's after the wedding." Clay approached, his hands in his slacks pockets, tears in his eyes as well.

I felt my bottom lip shake. I simply nodded.

"I got a phone call—" he began. "One that kind of changed everything, and I almost called you in New York, but I didn't want to ruin your time there, plus this really needs to be said in person."

"I love you." I stopped him, the words falling from my mouth with ease. No strings holding them back anymore. "And Madeline started to tell me everything, but I just want you to know that. . . I love you. I'm happy you got another job, and that your name is cleared and that everything you lost is coming back to you and. . . I just. . . love you."

Clay's lips were parted slightly, his eyebrows pinched as he listened to me word vomit everywhere. This wasn't me. I was calm and cool and collected. I didn't word vomit. He took one single step toward me.

"What did Madeline tell you?"

I inhaled. "That you got a job offer, a good one."

"Yes, I did." He nodded. "But I didn't take it."

My heart stopped as my eyes met his. "What?"

"I didn't take it. I didn't want it." Clay's words were soft as he closed the gap between us even more. I could feel his body heat, and it took all my strength not to wrap my arms around him. "There was only one thing I really wanted, but I had to wait to tell her."

I let him reach out to me first, his hands finding my cheeks, his thumb brushing past the tears that had fallen.

"I have a plan in mind, and it's all coming together. I'm starting my own company. I have meetings lined up with potential clients, and hell, Elliot's my first one. Regina Krass, the woman who offered me the job, is going to be my next client as soon as everything is put together. This crazy plan, it's working, but it's missing a pretty important factor. You." He pressed his forehead to mine. "I love you, Ophelia Fuller. I have for my entire life, and this time. . ." He raised his chin, placing his lips to the spot where his forehead was. ". . . nothing, not even the best job the world has to offer, can keep me from you."

He chose me.

I melted; my entire body gave into him. I wrapped my arms around his neck, kissing him with everything I had. He felt so good, the way love should feel, the way we were meant to feel. Everything about this moment and the next and the next was us. Nothing would stop it. My body tingled as his arms wrapped around me, his lips warm and moving in sync with mine.

He pressed his forehead to mine once again, gently kissing the tip of my nose. I wanted to stay here forever.

"Excuse me, Miss Fuller. . ."

But there was Carter. . .

I gave a small groan.

"I believe, as a part of the wedding party," Clay whispered. "We are obligated to take some photos."

"As long as you're next to me in all of them."

"First of all." Milo leaned over the table. "I can't believe you made this dress."

The reception was in full swing. Elliot was singing, performing every song with his signature flair. Guests would come by the table and give Milo and Madeline hugs and congratulations, but all Milo was focused on was his phone. Once I unblocked him from my Instagram and everything came to his feed, he was hooked.

"What's hard to believe about that?" Clay asked, glaring at his friend, defending my honor.

"Oh, that's not what's hard to believe. What I want to know is how you kept it from me for so long. Especially after seeing this Instagram feed. It's in every picture. Maddy, look at these photos!" Milo lifted his phone to her, my store's Instagram pulled up. Now that he had access to it, I'm sure my notifications were through the roof. He had double tapped almost every photo, even shared a few of Madeline as her dress was being made.

Madeline chuckled. "I've seen them, Hubby."

I scrunched my nose. Hubby.

"I'm just in awe. I mean, look at all of these. I can't believe I hadn't seen them before."

"It was easy. All I had to do was block you from everything," I admitted.

"And you knew about this and didn't tell me?" He pointed at Clay.

"I was sworn to secrecy." Clay leaned back in his chair, draping his arm around the back of mine. "We all were. Thankfully, you didn't have to get your teeth cleaned. Jamie may have spilled some kind of beans."

Jamie laughed and nodded. "Oh, I definitely would have. Why do you think I avoided your house all summer?"

Milo furrowed his brow. "I just thought you hated me."

"She's the one who told me to date you." Madeline slapped her husband's bicep.

I loved this. This entire table, full of friends and family when Holly appeared. Hannah and Donald had kept her occupied most of the time, but she tended to wander traveling from her mom to Milo and then to her grandpa. She was full of energy, and nothing would stop her now.

"Alright, alright." Elliot's voice boomed over the crowd. "I believe it is time for the couple's first dance. Mr. and Mrs. Harris, would you please come to the dance floor?"

Elliot had sung all sorts of songs tonight, mainly country and mostly Thomas Rhett, but I was still holding out for one. Madeline smiled and stood, pulling Milo up by his arm as Elliot's band started to play the opening notes of "Us, Someday," the song that would always remind me of these two.

I leaned back into Clay and looked up to him. "Dance with me soon?"

"Wouldn't miss it for the world," he said, his lips brushing against my temple.

Flutters rose in my stomach as I rested my head on his shoulder, his fingers finding my bare arm and tracing little circles around my shoulder.

Across the table, Jamie had her chin resting on her fist, her eyes doey as she looked at us. I narrowed my eyes at her, gave her a small grin and then settled back into Clay's warmth, loving this moment where our best friends danced, and where I was his.

Milo and Madeline's dance ended and small claps and "whoops" came from the guests. Elliot made a funny comment about how there may or may not be cans on the back of Milo's Chevy, using the lyrics he just sang as inspiration. When I looked over at Clay, he narrowed his eyes, gave me a smirk, and shook his head.

"We're a terrible wedding party. We didn't decorate the car," he grumbled.

"They're just going to the hotel across the road." I pointed to the blue building. "If anything, we need the cans on the back of the car," I joked.

Clay's eyebrows raised, and he tilted his head at me, only one corner of his lips twitching up. "You're not. . . getting a hotel?"

I shook my head. "I don't think I ever was going to." I leaned in and kissed him, lingering just long enough for the world to fade, until I heard the song I was waiting for.

The one I heard as we first walked into The Piano Bar, the one he danced with Jamie with, the one I wanted to be ours.

"*You're my forever,*" Elliot sang, just like in The Piano Bar. Only his voice. Nothing else was needed. The man was an artist.

"This one," I whispered up to Clay.

He sat up a bit straighter, forcing me to lift my body off his. He stood and extended his hand to me. I felt the heat rush to my face.

"May I have this dance, Miss Fuller?"

I slipped my hand into his and followed him out to the dance floor, loving the way his arm slid around my waist, the way he felt against me as he led the way and as we danced. The lyrics meant more now that everything was certain with him.

I sighed, looking up at him. I lightly touched his cheek.

"I love you," I whispered.

"I love you so much," he whispered back, pressing his lips to mine as I melted, and the world vanished.

Chapter Forty-One

-Clay-

There were no cans on Milo's Chevy, which I instantly regretted the minute Elliot had said the comment. I was tempted to run around the reception to take all the cans I could find and tie them to his bumper, but Ophelia kept me grounded. She kept me there and present, and when we danced, the entire world came together.

Before the night ended, Holly had snuck in between Ophelia and me, asking if she could "step in" and dance with me. Ophelia humbly agreed and stood off with Jamie, giggling as the four-foot Holly stood on my feet as we danced to another country song. The way her eyes lit up, and she held back her laughter put knots into my stomach, and I couldn't wait to take her home.

With congratulatory handshakes, hugs and a shit ton of bubbles, everyone watched as Milo (giving Holly a huge hug goodbye, of course) escorted Madeline to his Chevy, and they drove the short distance to the hotel. The crowd started to head to their cars, leaving the event staff and the wedding party to clean up the tables and chairs, which, since I had motivation, happened very, very fast.

"Amazing set," Ophelia said once we were done, giving Elliot a hug as he finished taking down the stage. "You'll have to sing at my wedding, but I like a different kind of music."

"Not a fan of Thomas Rhett?" he asked with a laugh.

"Oh, no. I've grown quite fond of Thomas Rhett, especially that one song." She winked at me.

"Well." Elliot stretched. "I will only sing at your wedding if you marry this guy." He nodded toward me.

I shivered. That was definitely a possibility.

Ophelia and I piled into Madeline's car. The moment I was behind the wheel, our hands found each other, and they stayed together until we had to open the doors again, Niko barking and whining as we approached the house. I had brought my suitcase and bag over before we headed to the wedding, and Hannah was safe with Holly at Milo's apartment. I had the weekend with Ophelia before she went home to New York, and I planned to spend every second showing her how much I loved her.

I unlocked the door, allowing Ophelia to step in first.

"Niko, bud," she shouted. "Let's get you outside."

He jumped and whined with excitement as she led him through the living room into the kitchen and out into the backyard. Once the door was closed, I made my way to her, placing my hands on her waist and pulling her toward me. The chiffon fabric of her dress slipped through my fingers as my hands trailed up her back. Then I was kissing her, breathing her in until my head swam, and she wrapped her arms around my neck.

Giving me a sweet hum as she pulled away, she licked her lips, her eyes still closed, tempting me.

"When do you leave?"

She heaved a sigh as her palms trailed down my chest, removing my suit jacket. "Monday. Too soon."

"Well." I lifted her, her small giggle filling the dark kitchen. "Then we don't have any time to waste." I kissed her neck, teasing her skin with my tongue, trailing down to her collarbone.

She took a deep breath and arched her back. "We should let Niko in." She turned to the back door. "He barks a lot."

"Damnit," I grumbled into her neck. "I really hate that you're right because if it were up to me. . ."

"I know." She kissed me lightly. "Trust me, I know. It may seem like a short time, but it's not. We have all night long, Clay, and all day tomorrow." Her voice was full of lust. She wanted me as much as I wanted her.

I set her back down, kissed her forehead, and let her trail her fingers over my chest and arms as she left the kitchen. I let Niko back in, gave him a scoop of food per Madeline's instructions, and then watched as he made his way down the hall and into Madeline's room, skipping the guest bedroom all together. He jumped on her bed and groaned, his blue eyes looking up at me.

I walked into the room and scratched behind his ears. "We'll go on a walk tomorrow, bud. I promise. And before you know it, your mom will be home, and I'll be out of your hair."

I looked out to the hallway, the light from the guest bedroom shining out, a small shadow moving around the room. I smirked.

"Can you do me a solid and stay in here tonight?"

Niko heaved a sigh in response.

"Thanks, bud."

Ophelia was still in her dress, removing her golden earrings with her heels kicked off at the end of the bed. Her breathing was soft, her chest rising and falling with grace. I leaned against the doorway, slipping my hands in my pants pockets and just. . . watched. In awe. Her beauty exceeded any of the women I had met in Seattle. Her personality and her charm, the way she could take charge of any situation and how she was independent, her passion and her fire, the reasons why I loved this woman never stopped. The list would always be growing until the day I died, even then.

"Are you going to keep watching me, or are you going to come and kiss me?" she asked, her Southern drawl coming out more than I had heard it this summer. She dropped her hands to her hips, tilting her body as her smile grew, drawing me into her.

"If I kiss you," I whispered, "I'm not going to stop."

"I never want you to."

With that, I took her all in. My hands found her neck, her curls slipping through my fingers as our tongues danced together. She tasted sweet, the way I remember, with more spark. The way she hummed into me, moaning as I moved my lips back to her neck, my fingers finding the small of her back, tracing the edge of the dress until they found her skin.

She removed my vest, and her fingers fumbled with my tie, trying frantically to loosen it. I reached up and grabbed her wrists, pulling them down gently.

"You said it yourself, Phe. We have all night—and all day tomorrow."

"I know, I know. I just would rather you not be fully clothed during that time."

I laughed and pulled my tie, letting it fall to the ground as she unbuttoned my shirt, her fingers pulling the t-shirt out of my slacks.

"How many layers are you wearing?" she shouted, taking a step back to lift my shirt over my head. Her fingers instantly found my skin, the charge of electricity pulsing through.

"Too many," I responded, my lips barely touching hers, grinning, my hands beginning to work on the dress, playfully trying to make this last, even though I knew I wouldn't make it if I tried. Placing my palm on her back, I took a step, pushing her back onto the bed just in time for her dress to hit the floor. She laid out in front of me, almost bare, heat rushing through her body as I allowed my eyes to roam over her. My heart stopped. "Fuck, Phe. You're gorgeous, the most perfect woman—"

She grabbed my neck, pulling me down closer to her. Her breath was heavy as her eyes met mine, full of want. "Do you remember our date?" she asked as kissed my neck. I let out a soft moan as she nipped at my skin. "I could feel you." Her hushed voice sent chills down my spine. Her breath caused my body to react in just the right way.

My hands acted on instinct, finding the spots I would touch all those years ago. I felt the goosebumps rise as I caressed her stomach, my lips kissing every inch of her as her fingers glided through my hair, guiding me along the way. I could feel her heartbeat when I kissed right on her breast, my fingers hooking onto her panties, slowly pulling them down her legs, my fingers sliding to where they desperately wanted to be. She arched her back, my free hand finding the clasp to her bra, her shoulder wiggling to allow the fabric to leave, my hand instantly cupping her breast, my thumb finding the right spot to make her gasp.

Touching her was second nature, something I didn't know I needed to survive. How I had lasted this long without, I had no idea. The feeling of how soft her skin was, the way that everything was so new, yet exactly the same. I wanted to memorize her, to know every curve of her body, every place that made her gasp or moan—call out my name.

As if she read my mind, she spoke breathlessly, a soft whisper that jolted me in the best way, "Oh Clay. . . I need. . ."

"You feel the same—soft, warm, perfect. Like you belong here with me," I said, my voice shaky and deep as I began to kiss my way down her body.

"Clay," she moaned. I looked up at her, a smile on my lips as I watched her move. My fingers found her and slowly, I began to tease. She tensed, her entire body begging for more. "I *need* to feel you."

Crawling my way back over her, I kissed her once again, gently this time, leaving her wanting more. I felt her hands as they found my belt working to undress me. Shivers, tingles, heat, passion. Our bodies fit together. They always had. And the moment I found her, the moment we became one, everything bonded together.

I woke up the next morning buried in Ophelia's hair, my arm draped around her waist as we sprawled on the bed. The sun shone through the white curtains, the room quickly warming up. Ophelia had managed to put her underwear back on, and I had stumbled into my shirt and boxers, even though I knew they most likely wouldn't stay on for long.

I gently rolled away from her, making sure to keep the sheet on her skin as I left the bed, all her warmth staying right there. Niko watched from the doorframe, knowing very well he wasn't allowed in the guest bedroom. He sat with his tongue out, panting.

"Thanks for keeping to your mama's room," I whispered. I scratched his scruff and left the room, Niko close at my feet.

Once Niko was outside, I started the coffee, my entire being still in bliss from the night with Ophelia. I crossed my arms and leaned against the island, watching the coffee as it dripped into the pot, the smell filling the kitchen.

"Morning." Ophelia's voice came from behind me, her arms finding my waist faster than I could react. "You made coffee." She yawned, her cheek resting against my chest.

She had dressed in a tank top and lounge shorts. She was comfortable, she was sweet, and damn, she was sexy.

"I am the master at coffee." I kissed the top of her head, her hair still wild and free.

"Will you promise to always make me coffee? Or bring me Americanos?"

"I promise."

Raising her head, she looked up at me. "Come to New York with me," she said softly.

"Yes," I whispered back, the only answer that mattered—but...

She gently kissed my lips, a soft hum as she pulled me closer.

"But," I continued, "not now."

She furrowed her brow and leaned back, her hold on my waist loosening. "What?"

"I can't now. I may not have taken that job, but I need to get my company going. I can work from anywhere once it's started. Elliot and Regina have already agreed to work with me from New York, but I need to do a few things first. I need to save the money. I need to pay back Milo, and I need to register my damn car. I can't mooch off you while I start this." I tucked her hair behind her ear, watching as her face relaxed. "I told you, no job, no matter how perfect it is, will keep me from you. Just give me time."

"But you'll come?" Her shoulders relaxed, and her hands clasped behind my back. I could feel them as they formed a ball, the pressure on my spine, reminding me that she was still very much there.

I lightly kissed her. "That was my plan. I belong there—with you."

She let out a small hum, rolling her lips together, running her hands down my chest. Her mind was turning, maybe a little too hard, but when her eyes met mine again, she gave me a sly grin. "You're allowed to mooch off me, you know. I know you're good for it."

I laughed and shook my head. "No, I will not be *mooching* off you. I want to be able to *support* you." She opened her mouth to speak, but I stopped her. "I know, you don't *need* my support, but I want to be able to in more ways than just holding your pin cushion. I want to be there for you—always. It's not going to be easy. I need to prove to these potential clients that *I'm* worth it. No doubt, they will have all heard about Jackson and Rye, but even the news declared my innocence. I shouldn't be too nervous about it, but that feeling is always going to be there. I just need to prove myself." I locked eyes with her, her eyebrows pinched. "Give me six months. My parents are expecting me when Milo and Madeline get back. I'm moving in with them and then New York. Six months is all I need."

She shook her head. "No. No way. I can't do long distance for that long. Two months." She countered. She pointed at me, her features relaxing as she fell back into our rhythm.

I pushed myself off the counter and lifted her up, taking a few steps to the island, setting her down gently. She wrapped her legs around my waist, her arms around my neck, and she leaned on my shoulder. Even with the lack of sleep, she looked rested and stunning. I couldn't wait to wake up to her every morning, to have coffee and breakfast with her, knowing that it was going to be my life forever.

"Five months," I countered back.

Narrowing her eyes at me, she tilted her head back. "Three."

"Four. Give me four months, Phe, and then I'll be in New York with you."

She heaved a sigh. "You'll come for the opening of the store?"

"I wouldn't miss that for the world."

She smiled, brightening up the room more than the sun. *I love this woman.*

"Okay, deal. November trip and four months. I'll even buy a new coffee maker because mine is dreadful."

I raised my hand and cradled her cheek. "November, four months, and a new coffee maker. Deal."

We sealed the deal with a kiss. *November, four months, coffee maker. . . Ophelia. . .*

Chapter Forty-Two

-Ophelia-

All day, Clay and I laid in bed, getting up only to let Niko out and feed ourselves. The promise of having him in my near future made leaving somewhat easier, but it didn't help in the long run. I hated it when he left the bed to grab us a drink, or when I left to simply shower and use the bathroom. I wanted to be wrapped in him forever. Monday came too soon.

Clay insisted he drive me to the airport, saying, "Over my dead body is Ophelia Fuller taking an Uber. She needs a limo, but since I can't get a limo, Madeline's Toyota will have to do."

I kissed him for that—a sweet lingering kiss, getting a satisfied smile in return from him.

He climbed out of the car and got my bag from the trunk, wrapping his arms around my waist, lifting me slightly off the ground, giving me our last kiss until November. I closed my eyes and focused on him and only him. The weight of his arms around me, his chest pressed against mine, the way his lips felt as he kissed me. His taste. His scent.

He let go a sweet "I love you" in my ear, asking me to call him the moment I landed and then stood and watched as I turned and walked into the airport.

From there, it was a haze. I checked in and found my gate; I read as I waited to board the plane. I asked for water and a bag of peanuts. I tried my hardest to relax. The five-hour flight seemed to last forever, and when the New York skyline came into view, I felt empty and lost.

I turned my phone on the second we could and pulled up Clay's text thread. He had sent me a few texts as I was in the air. A few photos, ones that were supposed to make me smile. Him and Niko on a walk and the bed, still unmade from our night together. I so badly wanted to be back in that bed with him.

I left the plane.

I walked out onto the street, and I hailed a cab.

When I opened the door, my heart stopped.

What the hell was I doing?

As much as I loved this city, it didn't have that same feeling. The feeling I left back in Portland was stronger than what I felt here on the sidewalk.

Could I really do this without him for four months?

Chapter Forty-Three

-Clay-

Niko bounced up as soon as I got back from dropping Ophelia off. I smiled at him and scratched behind his ear, but the house felt empty. Sure, it wasn't *our* house, but the last couple nights it sure felt like it. A glimpse as to what was coming.

I leashed him up on his harness and took him for a long walk around the neighborhood, snapping a photo to send to Ophelia. She would get it when she landed, and hopefully, it would bring a smile to her face.

I opened my laptop and sent an email to Regina, going over the terms of a contract, and that I would be working from New York as soon as I possibly could. Her return email was instant. She was excited to start and would be setting up a meeting with her lawyer and partner to get the contract finalized, and then I would have her as an official client.

Elliot was just as easy to handle. His contract was simple and straightforward. We were already set up, and he was ready to pay in advance for the year, which I wouldn't let him. As eager as he was to be my first client in the new adventure, as he called it, we had to follow steps.

I left the house to meet with the bank, a small business loan in the clear, and then applied for a business license. *Nolan Accounting* was coming to life. Slow and steady wins the race. I had time to grow, but I was eager to see where it was going to take me.

But when the morning turned into the afternoon and I still hadn't heard from Ophelia, knots grew in my stomach. My instant reaction was something happened to the plane, so when I googled her flight number to see that she had landed safely, the knots slowly began to release. She was there, and she was safe. Her flight had landed thirty minutes ago, but when I dialed her number, it went straight to voicemail.

I texted Elliot. Maybe he could calm my nerves. Distractions.

Ophelia's landed, was all I typed.

Elliot: You miss her yet?

Clay: More than anything.

Elliot: You could move now, you know. You don't need to wait.

Clay: I just need to tie up these loose ends. I could use a distraction though. Are you free for lunch?

Elliot: I am. You're done with your checklist already?

Clay: Yes, and now I need a distraction. Lunch? Please? Maybe a few hours at the office?

Elliot: See you in thirty.

Hours passed, lunch with Elliot and working at his office, and no word from Ophelia. She was busy; I knew that. She was going to head straight to the boutique to meet with JoAnn. Maybe she had just forgotten to turn her phone back on. I knew she was excited to get going. Even her Instagram had blown up since Carter had posted a few teasers of Madeline getting ready.

I opened my app, scrolling through but finding no activity since the wedding.

It had been almost twelve hours since I last saw her, since I last kissed her and told her I loved her.

Pulling into Madeline's driveway, waiting to hear Niko's bark, I sent a quick text to Ophelia.

I hope your flight was good. I miss you already. Counting down the days. I love you.

Closing my phone and leaving the car, I trudged up to the house. Niko wasn't barking. Maybe he hadn't heard me. He wasn't the best guard dog, but when I touched the door handle to discover it wasn't locked, my anxiety peaked. I knew I had locked it before I left.

Slowly I opened the door, finally hearing Niko's tags jingle as I tried to be quiet. He came up to me, jumped up for a hug and, still being as silent as I could, I turned to the living room, and I was finally able to breathe.

"Phe. . ." I said, my voice shaking, my heart thumping through my chest.

"Hi." Ophelia was standing there, her suitcase next to the couch, her hands in front of her as she fiddled with her fingers. "So. . . funny story," she began.

I pushed Niko off, giving him a reassuring pat before I walked toward her, letting her speak even though my body wanted to lunge forward.

"I got to New York, and I opened my phone to text you. I saw all your photos, and I realized it was so dumb of me to go to New York without you. I reached the curb before I figured it out, but I turned right back around and got on the first flight back to Portland. I barely made it but here I am." She smiled.

I slid my hands in my jeans pockets, taking a few steps toward her.

"I can't wait four months, Clay. We've waited ten years, so why extend it? Ten years ago, you shattered my heart and kicked the pieces to the curb, but in these past three months, you have managed to pick up every single piece and place it back together. Now I feel empty without you. New York isn't home without you. I'm not whole without you next to me." She took a deep breath, and slowly got down on one knee. "Clay Nolan, I need you in my life. I want you to be the one who's holding my pin cushions. I want to go bungee jumping with you again. I want to fly with you. Let me help support you while you start this new adventure. Clay. . . will you marry me?"

I closed the gap between us, cradling her face in my hands. Her eyes were building with tears, a sweet smile on her lips as I leaned down. "I've been a mess without you, and it's only been twelve hours. I can't imagine my life any other way Phe. . . Ophelia. . . the woman of my dreams and the love of my life. Of course, I'll marry you."

The world fell into place when she kissed me, her hands finding my wrists as I melted into her.

"I love you," she whispered against my lips with a sweet smile.

"I love you."

Chapter Forty-Four

-Ophelia-

Nothing would compare to that night with Clay, not even our wedding night. The way we blended together, tender and passionate. The way we focused on each other, what we wanted and needed, it was unlike anything I had ever experienced. Clay was soft, gentle yet forceful and in control at the same time. The way he whispered that he loved me in my ear, the way his fingers created a shock in my body no matter where he touched me. It was perfect in every way, and I was so happy and so in love with the idea that it wouldn't have to end.

The week went by faster than either of us wanted, but we were busy getting everything in order. Clay met with Elliot and Regina, signing the final contracts and settling everything before he took his new company to the other side of the country. Elliot was more excited he would get to sing at our wedding. I told him the only condition was he had to learn my songs and sing "Grave" eighty times that night.

We met his parents for dinner one last time, telling them everything and getting nothing but pure joy from them. His mother screamed when I showed her the small temporary ring we had picked out, pulling me close and telling me she knew I was always the one who was going to break through to him. Clay had to rescue me from her grasp so I could breathe, but I was thankful, nonetheless. I was gaining a family, one that already held my heart. I was even grateful that we were able to sneak in a pickleball match before we made the trek across the country.

Clay registered his Tesla, found new insurance, and mapped out the drive to New York, complete with charging stops and the best hotels to stay at. He was excited, ready to leave as soon as Milo and Madeline returned. Hell, if it were up to him, we'd drop Niko off with Elliot and leave now, but I was insistent that we stay and talk to Milo and Madeline.

"I never really got to say goodbye to her. She just took off for Colorado," I defended.

"We will call them," he stated bluntly.

"Clayton." I glared at him.

"God, I love it when you say my full name. That accent." He stood from the island and kissed me. "Okay, we'll stay. One more night with you in Portland," he said.

As if they planned their drive, Milo and Madeline pulled in right as Clay had placed the last box of his things in the back of his Tesla. Madeline came running up to me as soon as she saw me on her porch, basically jumping that I was still there, and during dinner when we told them everything. They both shouted "We knew it!" at the same time.

"I will take full credit for this." Madeline smiled, wrapping her arm around my shoulders. "If I hadn't asked you to be maid of honor, and if Clay hadn't been the best man, none of this would have happened. I take full credit for your engagement."

"No, that was purely Phe's doing." Clay chuckled, leaning his elbows on the table closer to me.

"Nope, I take credit." Madeline smiled.

"Either way, I'm happy for you." Milo put his hand on Madeline's shoulder. "What's next? The company, the move? Marriage and kids, huh?"

"Marriage first, but we haven't talked about that at all. We've just been so focused on getting to New York," Clay admitted, a small white lie. We had mentioned a date once, but then went into full planning mode for the trip to New York. If it were up to us, we'd get married tomorrow.

"And November." I turned to Madeline. "You'll come to the grand opening?"

"Of course! Oh, Carter can post any photos he wants to now. Our photographer sent us the proofs, and to be honest. . . Carter's were better."

"He's a persistent little shit, but we're stuck with him. JoAnn made him the media manager for the boutique. He'll be there to take a photo of every bride that says yes, no tagging and blocking the groom of course." I winked at her. "Look, you have officially made the wall in the boutique." I showed Madeline the latest photo and her cheeks during the blush.

"Can I get that framed?"

"Of course, Carter is going to send you all the photos."

"When do you leave?" Milo asked, leaning back in his chair, looking over at Clay.

"Tomorrow morning, bright and early. It takes forty-four hours to get there, and we plan on stopping twice, not including the charging time for the Tesla." Clay raised his eyebrows. "When do you get Holly?"

"Tomorrow morning, bright and early," Milo parroted. "Hannah has to head home as soon as possible, and I have to turn in my key to the apartment, now that you won't be living there."

"That was never a plan." Clay chuckled.

"It never was. He was meant to move to New York." I stood and wrapped my arms around Clay's waist, feeling his firm body against mine as I kissed his chin.

"Again, I'm taking credit for this," Madeline sweetly said.

The next morning, before the sun was up, Clay and I made sure everything was in the Tesla, ready to go. The battery was fully charged, and Clay was excited to get behind the wheel again. Milo and Madeline woke up with us to say goodbye, making sure to tell Holly we would miss her. Clay hugged the fluff that was Niko and gave Milo a longer hug than normal.

"I'll miss ya, man," Milo said, a hint of grogginess in his voice. The man was still in his pajamas. I didn't blame him. "I'm happy for you two. I'm glad you're not that bum that arrived at my house five months ago."

"Me too." Clay laughed. "I just needed my sunshine again. I'll see you in November?"

Milo raised his eyebrows and gave us a slight nod.

"Keep me updated on the trip and be safe. We'll see you in November, okay?" Madeline gave me a hug, holding on a little longer than normal.

"I will. Thank you for a wonderful summer, and congratulations on being Mrs. Milo Harris."

"I love you, Phe."

"Love you more, Maddy."

Clay held open the car door for me and waved one last time before he climbed into the driver's side.

"You ready?" he asked as soon as he buckled.

"Let's go home."

Epilogue

-Clay-

The crowd was bigger than I anticipated. I was pushed back farther than I wanted, but I was still able to see everything happening in front of the store. The new sign above the door was stunning. *Ophelia Fuller, Wedding Gowns* stood out over the other signs on 5th Ave, and by the looks of the store inside, it was going to exceed everyone's expectations.

The crowd was mainly women, all wanting to get their own wedding gown created by Ophelia. Some tried to press closer to the door, others claimed they had had their appointment for months. I rolled my eyes, knowing what was happening behind the scenes as Ophelia worked her ass off these last two-and -a-half months.

There was a light pink ribbon in front of the door, taped on each side of the glass, and on a small glass table was a pair of golden scissors. Ophelia and JoAnn were inside, prepping the staff on all the people who were about to barge in the doors.

My heart was racing. I knew Ophelia was going to give a small speech before cutting the ribbon and opening the door, but she had refused to share it with me, telling me it would make a bigger impact if I heard it for the first time with everyone else.

"This is a shit ton of people." Milo appeared beside me, Madeline and Holly at his side. "I didn't think there would be this many people."

"Neither did I. Apparently, I'm not important enough to stand in front. All the women pushed me back," I responded, waving my hand to the crowd.

"My question is, why aren't you in there with her?" Madeline asked, pulling Holly in front of her and placing her hands on her shoulders.

"How you doin,' Holly-wood?" I asked, rubbing her hair with my hand.

"Excited for Aunt Phe." She smiled.

"Me too."

The last two-and-a-half months had been mushed together. The moment we arrived in New York it had been nonstop. Ophelia was busy every day at the warehouse and boutique, sometimes taking me along with her, making sure to give me a pin cushion every time I walked in the warehouse. I had meeting after meeting with potential new clients, happy to report that more than half of them had signed contracts.

I was able to pay back Milo, even though he would only accept half of what I knew I owed him, and Elliot and I had built a friendship even through the business aspect. He was still impatiently waiting for a wedding date for me and Ophelia.

But what he didn't know, what only a few people knew, was that Ophelia and I had gotten married yesterday. With Milo and Madeline by our side, we got married in Central Park. A small, simple ceremony where we pledged our love for each other, even taking it to the grave. I played with the wedding band on my finger, enjoying the smooth feel of it against my thumb, a constant reminder I was hers.

The crowd gave a small cheer as the glass doors opened and JoAnn and Ophelia stepped out, both looking stunning in their black dresses with pink belts to match the design of the store. Ophelia caught my gaze and scrunched her nose, giving me a cute grin. I mimicked her and then focused my eyes on JoAnn.

"This is amazing. Thank you everyone for coming to this big event, this grand opening. This is the biggest project I've put together in such a short time. It was hard and tough, but it was worth it in every way. I found this designer last year in Portland, Oregon and knew I had to stock her in my stores, and then, when I saw what she could do, it became so much more. I present to you, Ophelia Fuller." JoAnn stepped aside and motioned toward Ophelia.

The woman cheered and clapped as Ophelia went and stood next to JoAnn.

"Thank you." She smiled. "Seriously, thank you, from the bottom of my heart. It's so hard to believe that what seems like so many years ago, I was a fashion major in Portland, all these ideas in my head that I was slowly getting on paper. Drawing little sketches and using my little sewing machine to piece everything together. This would have never been possible if it wasn't for a few people, so before I cut the ribbon and show off my designs, I need to acknowledge them. First, to JoAnn for believing in me so much to offer to put this all together. To see my potential even before I could. Thank you, JoAnn," She turned to JoAnn, who gave her a slight nod, raising her hands over her heart. "And to Madeline, my best friend, who always pushed me in college, supporting me everywhere. If she hadn't asked me to design a custom wedding gown, I would have never gotten those ideas down, and they wouldn't be hanging in there now, waiting for their bride. I love you, Maddy. Thank you."

"Oh," Madeline said through tears. Milo rubbed her back and pulled her close to him, kissing her temple.

I grinned at them, thankful in my own ways for them, and turned back to my wife, who still took my breath away.

"And finally," she continued, "my husband. Without him—I'll be real open and honest here—absolutely none of this would be possible. When we met in college, he accepted me for who I was, inside and out, and then when I needed to apply to the big wig fashion guy in New York, he hit the send button. And when I was hesitant about asking JoAnn for this, he was the one to cheer me on, hitting that send button once again, and he was the one who listened and allowed me to fly. Clay, I love you so very much. I'm so happy we found our way back to each other. Thank you for helping me spread my wings." She took a deep breath, holding back the tears I knew were forming in her eyes. "Okay." She clapped her hands and turned to the table, grabbing the scissors. "Are we ready?"

The ladies cheered, and Ophelia, with the largest smile I had ever seen, cut the small pink ribbon in front of the doors. They fell to the sides, and the clapping and cheers grew louder. Even Holly shouted as Milo raised her up on his shoulders.

"Ophelia Fuller's is open!" JoAnn shouted as she and Ophelia opened the double glass doors together, letting the crowd into the store.

I finally approached Ophelia at the door, instantly taking her in my arms to kiss her.

"Are we flying today?" she asked against my lips.

"It's how we celebrate. Of course, we're flying."

Hours later, we stood at the edge of the bridge, the crew setting us up to jump. Unlike the first time we had jumped off a bridge together, Ophelia's face was full of excitement, as if she couldn't wait to take the leap. This time, we would jump at the same time, on opposite sides of the bridge. Ophelia wanted to spread her arms, and then we could jump together in tandem.

"Are you ready?" I asked her.

"Born ready." She smiled back, narrowing her eyes. "Are *you* ready?"

I nodded. "Let's fly."

We were led to our separate pedestals, each with a guide giving us instructions, and then they counted down. Ophelia's eyes met mine as we ran off at the same time. Flying.

The End

Milo and Madeline's Wedding Playlist

Want it Again – Thomas Rhett
Die a Happy Man – Thomas Rhett
Buy Dirt – Jordan Davis
Would You Go With Me – Josh Turner
Grave – Thomas Rhett
Love You Like I Used To – Russel Dickerson
Don't Threaten Me With a Good Time – Thomas Rhett
Notice – Thomas Rhett
Chasin' You – Morgan Wallen
Us, Someday – Thomas Rhett
The Hill – Thomas Rhett
Slow Down Summer – Thomas Rhett
Lay Low – Josh Turner
Castle on the Hill – Ed Sheeran
Remember you Young – Thomas Rhett
Like It's the Last Time – Thomas Rhett
Need to Not – Jordan Davis

Acknowledgements

That Next Moment was by far the hardest book I've ever written. I doubted myself through the entire process. I cried numerous times, and I can't even begin to tell you how many times I almost hit that delete button. But, I'm glad I didn't. Once Clay stopped being a complete grump, and Ophelia stopped being so stubborn, their story unfolded, and I am truly happy with where those two ended up. They got the second chance they deserved and I love where they are today. Just a sneak into their lives—I can confirm that Clay hyphenated his name. Clayton Nolan-Fuller just has a ring to it. Plus, after all he put Phe through, he would never ask her to take his name. Since this one was harder to write, it took more people to get me through it. Those who listened to me groan and those who pulled me out of desperation...

My husband, Spencer. He has never read my books, and I honestly don't think he ever will, but he listened to me the entire time. He listened and nodded as I complained about what I was doing to these characters and then he was there to hit "like" on every single one of my posts. He's my biggest supporter without reading a word, and I love him!

My amazing betas. Allie Samberts—for taking me on her first ever beta read, cheering me on and squishing almost every fear I had for this book, helping me polish it and make it what it is today. You're absolutely amazing Allie, and I'm so lucky to call you a friend! Chelly and Vee—you two are a ray of sunshine for Clay, helping me see that he can be loved even through his grumpiness. You two are fantastic, and I am so thankful for you! Your constant support means the world—truly!

My wonderful editor Cindy and proofreader Ashley—thank you both for turning a choppy draft into a novel! Thank you for catching all those drama dots and all those em dashes! You two know how much I love a good em dash! You both are fantastic! Thank you!!!

And as always, thank you to the readers for helping my crazy dream come true! I am so grateful for each and every one of you! Thank you!!

I'm pretty sure I say in each book it takes a village, and I'm pretty sure I have the best village there is to write a book.

Love - Stefanie K Steck

Also by Stefanie K. Steck

Standalones

All Because of Elowin
Under the Marble Sky

Moments of Us Series

That Right Moment
That Next Moment

Coming Soon in the Moments of Us Series

Book 3: Early 2024

About the Author

Stefanie K. Steck is a romance writer, full-time dental assistant, army wife and mom of three small humans and four fur babies (five if you count the hamster). In the little spare time she has, you can find her writing, reading, cuddling with her dogs, or watching the entire Marvel Cinematic Universe in one sitting. She is the author of *All Because of Elowin, Under the Marble Sky* and *That Right Moment.* The Moments of Us series is her new novels releasing in 2023 and 2024 – following a group of friends finding their moments for love.